FOUR DEGREES
of HEAT

FOUR DEGREES of HEAT

BRENDA L. THOMAS
CRYSTAL LACEY WINSLOW
ROCHELLE ALERS
ReShONDA TATE BILLINGSLEY

Pocket Books
New York   London   Toronto   Sydney

POCKET BOOKS, a division of Simon & Schuster, Inc.
1230 Avenue of the Americas, New York, NY 10020

Library of Congress Cataloging-in-Publication Data

Four degrees of heat.—1st Pocket Books trade pbk. ed.
    p. cm.
  Contents: Maxed out / Brenda L. Thomas—Sex, sin & Brooklyn / Crystal Lacey Winslow—Summer madness / Rochelle Alers—Rebound / ReShonda Tate Billingsley.
    ISBN 0-7434-9145-9 (pbk.)
    1. Love stories, American. 2. Summer—Fiction.

PS648.L6F75 2004
813'.08508—dc22

                                        2004040070

First Pocket Books trade paperback edition July 2004

10 9 8 7 6 5 4 3 2 1

For information regarding special discounts for bulk purchases, please contact Simon & Schuster Special Sales at 1-800-456-6798 or business@simonandschuster.com.

contents

MAXED OUT
Brenda L. Thomas

1

SEX, SIN & BROOKLYN
Crystal Lacey Winslow

67

SUMMER MADNESS
Rochelle Alers

185

REBOUND
ReShonda Tate Billingsley

251

maxed out

Brenda L. Thomas

Prologue

July

What the hell was I doing in this place? Bad enough they'd screwed up and chosen the right club on the wrong night. Or so they said. It was clearly not ladies' night. Now here I was in a back-roads country club taking shots of Crown Royal whisky. I looked around at the club full of women. They were expecting to be entertained by a stage full of dancing men, but unfortunately there were only about ten men in the club, including the ones that worked there. I hadn't wanted to come in the first place; exotic dancers played out years ago. But this was the South, and I suppose everything came late down here.

This was certainly not how I'd planned to spend the first month of my summer vacation. My mother had summoned me from Philly to Charlotte, where she'd been taking care of my grandfather for the last three weeks while he recovered from hip replacement surgery.

Mom kept reassuring me that Charlotte had changed since the early eighties, which was the last time I'd been there. After being cooped up in a Philly classroom with teenagers all winter, I didn't think the trip to Charlotte would be so bad. To add to my southern social life, Mom dredged up a few of the old girlfriends I used to play with as a teenager during my summer visits. This would be great. I could bond with a bunch of fat, ill-dressed, gold-teeth sisters.

As I sat across the table from them, I had to admit they weren't all that bad. Rita, Darla, and my favorite, Country Girl, were far from what I expected. Country Girl was probably even better off than me. At twenty-six, she was married to a physician and the mother of three children.

When the strip club went dark and the stage lit up with red and green flashing lights, I turned my attention to the runway. For an hour we watched as women strutted up and down the catwalk, wrapping themselves around a slippery pole, supposedly dancing. We were sitting near the front of the stage, so they could hear us cackling about how bad they were. They especially heard me when I said, after seeing one of the men put a twenty in a dancer's G-string, "Oh, hell no. I can dance better than that. Shit, I'll make him give me fifty."

The big-butt dancer flared back, "You think so, huh? I dare you to bring your high yella ass up here."

Embarrassed, I was just about to apologize when Country Girl spoke up.

"You damn right she'll come up there. And I got twenty dollars to say she'll outdance your fat ass."

Wide-eyed, I looked at Country Girl and whispered, "What the hell are you talking about? I'm not going up there."

The stripper stopped dancing, posted her hands on both hips, and shouted over the loud music, "Well, then, she needs to shut the hell up."

I was willing to do so, but the others chimed in. "Yeah, go 'head Maxie, strut your stuff—show them how you do it in the city."

I still wasn't about to go up on that dirty stage and dance for anybody. But then the other women in the club started betting the women at my table, and before I knew it there was almost five hundred dollars waiting for me if I went up onstage and danced. Since I'm a math teacher, it was easy for me to calculate the per-hour rate of five hundred dollars for five minutes of dancing.

I downed another shot of Crown and told myself, What the hell—I'm down South, and I can do whatever I want.

Week One

I so wanted to leave my head on the pillow. How could a person's head hurt so badly? What the hell had I drunk? And better yet, where was I? I opened my eyes, peeking from under heavy lids. I wasn't in my apartment, that's for sure.

"Maxine, when are you going to get up? The phone has been ringing for you all morning."

Hiding from my mother's screeching voice, I closed my eyes and pulled the covers over my pounding head.

"You look like you could use some coffee."

I put my hand outside the sheet to reach for it.

"What time did you get in last night?"

My mouth was dry, and my voice cracked when I asked, "What time is it?"

"You must've had fun last night, you little hussy, 'cause look at you. You slept in your clothes."

Sure enough, I was still in my skirt, which had shifted up to my waist, and my tank top had twisted itself under my breasts.

I couldn't do coffee this morning. I needed something cold to put out the fire in my belly.

"Look, sleepyhead, it's almost noon, and I have to take your grandfather to the doctor, so we're heading out. I'll see you later this afternoon. But do me a favor and pluck those string beans in the sink for dinner tonight."

With Mother gone, I stripped off my clothes and went in search of something cold. In the refrigerator I found a can of Pepsi. I pressed it against my forehead and my temples, then downed the entire can. I needed one more thing. I searched through my suitcase. Buried under my toiletries was my pack of Newports.

By the time I'd showered and had some coffee, my head had begun to clear up. I'd just sat down at the table to pluck my mother's string beans when my cell phone rang.

"Hey, Maxie baby, I'm on my way. I should be there in about three hours. Did you get the room?"

It was Lynn, my boyfriend of eight months, who lived in the apartment above mine but was rarely there because he was a tractor-trailer driver. I'd met him about a month after he'd moved in. His mailbox had begun to overflow, and when he'd come home later that week, I'd introduced myself and given him his mail. That night, after we'd ordered Chinese, we wound up in bed together, and we'd been there ever since.

Lynn had planned to stop and see me in Charlotte while he was en route to drop a load in Nashville. We hadn't seen each other in two weeks, and after last night I'd totally forgotten about his visit.

"Sure, it's all taken care of, but Mom wants us to have dinner with her. So can you come here first? You can park the truck on our lot."

"No problem, baby, as long as I can have you afterward."

I phoned the Westin in downtown Charlotte and reserved a room. Then I tried to reach Country Girl, but she wasn't around. I was desperate to find out what had happened at the club. All I could remember was getting up on that stage, closing my eyes, and dancing. I prayed that I hadn't taken off my clothes. Then I remembered the money. I found my skirt. Sure enough, stuffed in the back pocket was five hundred dollars.

Dinner came early in the South, so by four-thirty the food was done and we were waiting for Lynn to finish washing up so we could eat. I don't know what it was, but my mother's cooking changed when she was down South. It had a different taste—a southern flavor. Maybe because everything was fresher. There were fluffy turnips, tender string beans, and the chicken was so fresh I was afraid there was a coop in the backyard.

"Ms. Tate, you really outdid yourself."

"Thanks, Lynn. You know Max can cook just as well if she puts her mind to it."

I knew what she was doing. Mother had a fear that I'd be single forever, so she was always dropping hints when Lynn was around.

"Lynn has tasted my cooking plenty of times, Mother."

By the time Mom had fed Lynn two servings of her peach cobbler and I'd packed him a bag of food to take on the road, I was ready to leave. That's when Country Girl came barreling through the screen door. But this certainly wasn't the time for her to recount last night's activities.

"Good evening, everybody."

I jumped right in. "Country Girl, this is my boyfriend, Lynn."

"Hey, Lynn. Welcome to Charlotte. Maxine, you look a little tired this evening."

"Just trying to get adjusted to the southern way of doing things," I said, ushering her out the door ahead of me and Lynn.

"Well, I just wanted to stop by and say hello. Max and Lynn, enjoy your visit."

I knew what kind of night Lynn and I would have. Sex with him was usually the same. About ten minutes of foreplay, and then he'd take me from the back before falling off into a deep sleep. I didn't complain because I knew he was usually tired from driving. But for once I'd like to see his face when he came.

In the eight months we'd been seeing each other, he'd only made me reach an orgasm twice. I wasn't even sure what he'd done, because everything was so new at the time.

I'd never told him because I didn't want to hurt his feelings or change the way he made love to me—even without the orgasm he was able to satisfy me. I enjoyed being with Lynn, and all signs pointed to us having a future together. So there was plenty of time to discuss my sexual needs.

"Lynn, guess what I did last night."

"What, baby? Don't tell me. You been milking cows," he shouted from the hotel bathroom.

"It's not that bad. But seriously, we went to see some exotic dancers."

"I didn't know you were into that shit," he said, drying off as he came into the room. Lynn wasn't a tall guy, barely six foot. He was stocky and weighed well over two hundred pounds.

"I'm not, but I felt like I had to go out with them. But let me tell you the fun part." I wasn't even sure he was listening because he was busy cleaning his nails. "They were having a dance contest, and I won."

"C'mon, baby, stop playing. I know you can dance, but you didn't do no shit like that."

"Watch, let me show you."

Lynn sat on the side of the bed while I attempted to dance to whatever music was playing on the radio. I dropped my robe to the floor, and with my arms above my head, I shimmied around the room, rolling my hips to the beat. When he wouldn't stop laughing, I jumped on the bed and squeezed my breasts in his face.

"Maxine, you are a crazy woman. Looks like you're doing a bad imitation of Beyoncé to me," he said. In one swift move his strong arms lifted me onto his lap.

"Lynn, seriously, you don't think I could do it?"

"You can do whatever you want," he said, burying his face in the thick hair between my legs. His blanket, as he liked to call it.

I was enjoying the feel of his tongue, but he was ready, so he turned me over and mounted me doggy style. He rode me hard, pounding away, slapping me on the cheeks of my ass with one hand while holding onto my waist with the other. I backed myself into him, and that's when he released himself. He fell back on the bed, and after catching his breath, he pulled me under him. Within minutes he was snoring.

In the morning I headed back to my grandfather's house. The rising Charlotte temperature made me glad my mother had finally been able to convince my grandfather to get central air. But it didn't matter to me because my body sought out the sun. My pale skin needed some sun in the worst way. My legs had been covered all winter with either stockings or pants, anything to keep the cold out. So I changed into a pair of shorts and a tank top and lay out in the sun for as long as my body could stand it.

Later in the week I headed over to Country Girl's house for her July Fourth cookout. She lived in a four-bedroom colonial spread over five acres. She had well over a hundred people there, everyone talking over loud music, playing cards, and chowing down on a pig that had just finished roasting. Had I not just had a visit from Lynn, I might've been tempted to hang out with one of those fine sexy country men who kept hanging on to me.

I'd already learned that the South was no place for a woman to act shy, so once they pulled out the corn liquor, it wasn't long before I found myself dancing in the soul train line along with everybody else. It was good old-fashioned fun.

"Max, you are something else," Country Girl said, shaking her head at me.

Out of breath, I answered, "What you talking about?"

"The way you was coming down that line, I can't believe you don't wanna go to the club again."

"That's not funny. You know you never told me what happened anyway."

"And I'm not, but I will tell you that we're going to Belinda's party tomorrow night."

"I don't remember anybody named Belinda."

"Of course you don't. She spent her summers in New York while you were down here. Y'all both were trying to escape from your environment," she said, mocking my family tradition of sending young children south in the summer to escape the city.

"I don't know. I didn't bring any party clothes."

"Then you better go buy some, because Belinda's parties only happen once a year. So look for me to pick yo ass up around nine-thirty."

Charlotte's SouthPark Mall made it all the more easy to pass time finding clothes for the party. I'd been teaching school for three years, but I was far from your usual boring schoolmarm. Shopping was my weakness and was probably what separated me from the other teachers at school, who usually wore jeans or, at the other extreme, clothes that too closely resembled pajamas. The advantage of teaching in the inner city is that the children keep me abreast of the current fashions.

We arrived at Belinda's around ten that night, and I'm glad I hadn't had any preconceived notions about her, because I would've been dead wrong. Her house was located at River Run Country Club, on the ninth hole of the golf course. I assumed she'd been lucky enough to marry a lawyer or doctor, or maybe her family had money.

There were cars parked along the street leading to her property, everything from customized Cadillacs to Benzes. When we walked through the front door into the brightly lit foyer, Country Girl pointed out Belinda. She stood in the lavishly furnished living room with her back to us. Belinda looked to be all of five foot five, as she stood on a pair of three-inch spiked heels. She was wearing a short, tight-fitting fuchsia dress and had bone-straight auburn hair that landed at her perfectly rounded ass.

When Belinda turned around, I immediately took notice of her satiny black blemish-free skin. As I watched her petite body walk toward us, I couldn't help but notice her full breasts swelling out of her dress. I had to admit, Belinda was hot.

"Hey, Belinda. What's up, girl?" Country Girl asked, hugging Belinda around her waist that wasn't.

"This party is what's up. Who's this, your citified girlfriend? The one you was telling me about?" she asked, her eyes roving over my body.

"Yes, this here is Maxine."

When she talked I noticed she had one shiny gold tooth on the side of her mouth.

"It's nice to meet you, Belinda. Thanks for—"

Rather than let me finish, she tossed her hair around and said, "All I'm saying is, I heard you had skills to handle a crowd. You should hang out with me sometime."

I knew she was referring to my dancing at the club. Damn, I wished Country Girl didn't have such a big mouth.

"I was just having fun. You know, on my summer break." This sounded like a sufficient excuse.

"Like I said, you should hang out with me. Now, I gotta run. You know I'm the princess around here."

Belinda excused herself to visit with other guests. Everyone was clamoring to speak with her.

I turned to Country Girl, "I know you told everybody I went up on that damn stage."

"Maxine, chill out. Belinda's cool."

"She must be real cool, with a house like this. How old is she?" I asked, looking around Country Girl to try to see what was going on out back.

"She's twenty-two, and if you want to know, she's a professional dancer."

"Professional how? Alvin Ailey professional?"

Country Girl's rolling eyes told me she wasn't. "Now, you don't really think she could afford all this dancing around in a tutu."

"She's a stripper?" I asked, a little too loud.

"I wouldn't know what else she does, but a professional dancer is what she lists on her taxes."

"How would you know about her taxes?"

"Because I do them every year. Now, c'mon. Let's go outside."

When we reached the crowded pool area, I could hear a man over the sound system announcing that the fashion show was about to begin. On the deck of the pool stood what Country Girl confirmed was an actual pimp. Pretty Boy, as he was so inappropriately named, was dressed in a cobalt blue smoking jacket, matching silk pants, and slip-on alligator shoes. I must say, I was in a bit of a shock.

According to Country Girl, he lived in Vegas but was in town for a pimp convention, and Belinda's party culminated the event. I tried to question her further on whether Belinda was a prostitute, but she bypassed the issue by introducing me to her friends. Even though I'd sworn off drinking after the corn liquor, I stopped one of the barely dressed waitresses and ordered a glass of Chardonnay. I'd keep it light.

I stood at the bar and took in my surroundings. It was like something out of a Snoop Dogg video. Damn near all the men looked like pimps, with suits in every shade of the rainbow and accessories that were just as loud. Their jewelry consisted of heavy gold rings and diamond pinkies, and their necks were weighed down with chunky gold chains. I had no idea that pimping really was back in style.

I listened as Pretty Boy began introducing the scantily clad models as his hos. These women, some of them girls who looked to be as young as nineteen, were from all parts of the country.

On the veranda opposite the pool were three tables spread with food, everything from barbeque ribs to lobster tails. The DJ, who boasted of being from the dirty South, kept the dance floor jumping. Needless to say, by two o'clock I was drinking spiced ice teas and had allowed somebody's pimp to pull me onto the dance floor. I couldn't help notice, as did everyone else, when Belinda moved into the middle of the crowd. She'd changed into a body-hugging bright yellow catsuit that barely covered the cheeks of her ass. She danced with everybody, but I could see that dancing for her was an act of seduction. The way her body moved stirred something inside of even me.

By the end of the night I was curious to learn more about Belinda, and I had agreed to be a guest at one of her shows.

Week Two

Around midnight Belinda picked me up in her red S-Type Jaguar. I made sure my seat belt was intact because she was a fast and reckless driver. She talked to me at the same time as working her cell phone throughout the entire ride.

"Between the Carolina Panthers and the new Charlotte Bobcats, a girl can make a lot of money in this town."

"Doing what you do?"

"I don't do anything illegal."

"Just dancing, huh?"

"I'm just like you, Maxie. I'm an entertainer, or should I say, an independent contractor."

"Uh, I think you're mistaken. I don't know what Country Girl told you, but I'm a high school math teacher."

"Really, Max, being a teacher makes you an entertainer. You gotta entertain all them bad-ass kids to make 'em listen."

"I guess you have a point. But what's different is that you entertain for a lot more money."

"And if you add a little dancing to what you do, you could make some real money too."

"Sleeping with strange men?" I wanted to take back what I said, but it was too late.

"Some I do, some I don't, but none of them are strangers. Listen, Maxie, I've worked very hard to achieve my status. I'm no two-dollar ho. I'm the Princess, so don't look to see no dollar bills at my feet."

"I understand, but there's still a big difference in what I do and what you do."

"If you say so, Maxie, but you here with me tonight, so that's saying something in itself."

We stopped at a few clubs, including the one where I'd made a fool of myself. Belinda was warmly greeted and well known. Men were anxious to talk to her, and women were obviously jealous. She let none of it faze her.

By two o'clock we'd ended up at the smoke-filled Fox Trap club, where, she informed me, she was a silent partner, but tonight she was scheduled to perform for some people who'd specifically requested her.

I followed her into a dressing room crowded with women dressing and undressing for their dances. It was no different than being backstage at a fashion show. There were lighted mirrors where the women sat on stools, applying makeup, smoking cigarettes, and complaining about niggas and tips. Belinda, though, had a private room where she had a stylist apply her makeup and select her outfit for the night. She really took this seriously. Once she was fully dressed, if that's what you'd call it, in a leopard catsuit with so many cutouts it really wasn't a suit at all, she instructed me to sit in the audience so I could observe the show.

The club was packed. The number of women present surprised me. A DJ encouraged the patrons to pay for lap dances. Then the lights flashed, and he announced that Charlotte's very own royalty, Princess, was in the house. With that, the room exploded with excitement.

I was in a trance the minute Belinda stepped onto the stage, moving to the music of Prince singing "Sexy Motherfucker." She slithered to the end of the runway with an air of confident sexuality. Moving to the rhythm of the guitar, she tossed her long hair and ran her hands up and down her body with purpose. Like she was giving it away if you wanted it. Her hips twisted, coiled, her knees bent, and her hands sensuously touched her body. Belinda looked to be in ecstasy, lost somewhere inside herself. She bent over and gyrated her ass just enough to expose the tip of her clitoris, and that's when she began to work the pole like it was her lover. The men whistled, and the women cheered her on. I, too, found myself screaming her name. She slid onto the floor, her legs spread apart, picking up another fifty with the lips of her pussy. Belinda's dancing was wicked.

When she was finished, all that remained were her high-heeled lace-up boots. I didn't even notice when she pulled the catsuit apart. But it lay there in some man's lap, and when she went for it, he stuffed a hundred-dollar bill in her boot.

Belinda phoned early the next morning before I'd gotten out of bed, inviting Country Girl and me to lunch. On the way to her house I pummeled Country Girl with questions that she refused to answer, only telling me that Belinda would tell me anything I wanted to know.

When we arrived at her house, Belinda was lounging by the pool in a black bikini that almost matched her skin. While we ate lunch, I wasted no time trying to get answers to my questions.

"Belinda, I have to know how you mastered dancing like that."

"It didn't come natural, that's for sure. I was a klutz when I was young, then when I was about thirteen I started taking dance classes. A few years later while I was in Vegas I found out money could be made by adding a few sexy moves to what I already knew."

"But how do you get people under your spell? I mean, even the women were giving you money."

She laughed at first, and then her serious side took over. "The women are the easiest. It's the emotions of the men that you have to understand. The most important thing to do when you're dancing is to make eye contact and make each man think he's the only one you're dancing for."

"Oh, boy. Here goes. You done got her started," said Country Girl.

"It's important that you have respect for people's money. You can't forget what it represents. They work hard, so if a man gives you a hundred dollars, you have to show you appreciate it by letting him touch you just enough to make him think there's a possibility that he could have you. So what you say, you wanna try it?"

"I'd love to. But there's no way I could take my clothes off in front of strangers."

"Why not?" asked Country Girl.

Belinda continued. "You don't have to take your clothes off. Only private clubs allow you to get completely naked. And when you do, believe me, you'd forget about teaching school."

"It's not that I can't dance. I'd love to be able to dance like that, but for money in a public place, I don't think so."

"The Princess only does private shows, and that one last night netted me how much, Country Girl?"

"Three thousand. Now if you include tips and some other favors, then it'll give you a total of seven grand."

Belinda got up from the table and turned on some music. "Well, since you don't want to dance for money, then c'mon and let me see your moves. I wouldn't have heard about you if you couldn't move."

"Yeah, Maxie. Show Belinda what you can do."

"Y'all are a pain in the ass," I said as I got up to dance with Belinda, who was already moving around the floor.

Belinda had a great sound system, so as R. Kelly sang "Thoia Thong," I closed my eyes and gave it my all. When the music stopped, I was shocked to see that Belinda had gotten naked.

"Don't pay her any attention. She's always walking around in the nude," said Country Girl, laughing at my reaction.

"Damn girl, you do have skills. But you can't hardly feel sexy in them jeans. Take your clothes off and let's see how you really look."

"No way am I stripping."

"Girl, stop acting so damn citified. It's just us," Country Girl said.

"Shit, all right. I see the two of you are not going to let up."

I turned my back to them and stripped down to my panties and bra.

When I turned around, Belinda screamed out, "What the hell is that?" She pointed to the hair that poked out from my thong.

"Oh, that? That's my blanket. Lynn likes it like that. He likes burying his face it. Nothing worse than a bald pussy, he says."

"Girl, that thing looks like a throwback to the seventies," said Country Girl.

"What do you do in the summer? I mean, ain't that shit hot?" asked Belinda.

"This is our first summer together, so I'll tighten it up some when I get ready to go swimming."

"Well, it's up to you, but you won't make any money with that thing."

"I'm not trying to make any money. I just want to learn the

dance. Now, can you show me some moves, since you have me standing up here half-naked?"

We started again, and this time Country Girl put on Belinda's song, "Sexy Motherfucker," and I watched her naked body move. I looked at her perfect body. I was sure her breasts were implants, and her silky auburn hair was definitely a weave. But regardless, the control Belinda had over her body fascinated me, and I wanted what she had, every move.

So for the next week I visited Belinda. During the day we'd practice dancing for two hours, sometimes with her standing behind me, guiding my movements. She wanted to show me how to dance slow, because I preferred the fast beats of hip-hop and rap music. Afterward we'd lay naked by the pool and have lunch. I loved it because my entire body was turning a nice shade of golden brown.

Week Three

I don't know how they did it, but by Friday night Belinda and Country Girl had convinced me to go onstage. My initiation would be at Belinda's club, Fox Trap. They promised me that the bigger the crowd, the less they would notice that I was an amateur. I wasn't sure if I believed them, but I had nothing to lose. Belinda coached me on the way to the club, reassuring me that I'd enjoy myself and betting me that I'd want to do it again.

I couldn't help but feel special as they applied my makeup and fussed over what I would wear. They'd already chosen red as my signature color, even though I told them I was only doing this once. Finally, when they felt I was ready, they zipped me into a red lace corset, matching thong, and red cutout patent leather heels. However, nothing they said could settle the butterflies in my stomach as I stood on the other side of that velvet curtain. I told myself, choose your targets; whoever is looking at you the most, focus on that person and then move on to the next.

Over the music I heard them announcing the next dancer. A surge of excitement ran through me, making my body hairs stand on end—that is, the ones Belinda hadn't made me wax off.

"Remember, girl, when you see the hunger in their eyes, wind them in."

I waited until the music hit the pit of my stomach and then stepped onto the stage of another life. I wanted to close my eyes, but I had to see where I was going, so I looked over the crowd until I was at the very end of the stage. That's when I closed my eyes and let the beat of Joe Sample's "Fever" control my movements. I found my rhythm, and with my legs spread open, I leaned back until my body almost doubled over and let my hair swing. I came back up slowly, stroking my breasts and then undoing the zipper that held everything together. I spun around and straddled the pole between my legs, pretending it was a strange man I was trying to seduce. I made love to that pole until the roar of the crowd and the money at my feet overcame the music. Before I knew it, my song had ended. I took a bow and walked backward off the stage.

Behind the curtain I practically collapsed into Belinda's and Country Girl's arms.

"Shit. Girl, you were the shit! Listen to them, they loved you."

"Maxie, I love you. Look at all this money," Belinda exclaimed as I looked down at the twenty- and fifty-dollar bills that lined my thong. "We're gonna make so much money. Here, c'mon, you gotta change. I got to introduce you to some people."

Once I'd had a cigarette to calm my nerves, I walked around the club hand in hand with Belinda while she introduced me to her clients. I learned that those who didn't give you tips while you were onstage kindly offered them to you when you spent a moment talking with them.

Later that morning, when I climbed into bed, I could barely sleep from the night's excitement. I wanted to call somebody and tell them what I'd done, tell them how much money I'd made. But for now it would have to be my secret.

A few hours later Belinda's phone call woke me up. I asked her, "Didn't you tell me you had a client last night?"

"Sure did. Why, you want one?"

I ignored her comment and said, "How do you go to bed at three in the morning and get up to call me by nine o'clock?"

"Maxie, ain't you ever heard, Don't nothing come to a sleeper but a dream? Now, get your butt up and get over here. We got work to do."

"Okay, I hear you, but I have some business to handle first. How's this afternoon, around two o'clock?"

"All right, I'll see you then. And by the way, I ordered you some dancing clothes."

I did have business to take care of. My realtor was e-mailing me some photos of houses in Philly he wanted me to see, and I had to fax my preapproval application to the bank. But first I had to get at least another hour of sleep.

Sooner than I expected, it was time for my next dance. Instead of it being at another club, Belinda took me to a party at The Pointe at Lake Norman. It was being held by one of the Carolina Panthers. The only problem was, she wanted me to give a lap dance. Even though Belinda said I'd perfected it, I was still nervous about dancing that close to someone. Up until that night the only people I'd performed a lap dance on were Country Girl and Belinda. The good thing, though, was that I was gonna do it to my music,

"Shake Ya Tailfeather." Belinda thought I was crazy to attempt that on my first lap dance, but I was determined to give these rich country ballplayers something to look at.

I watched from the bedroom window where we were changing while the other dancers performed by the pool in the backyard. I watched the crowd throw money and laugh, slapping the dancers on the ass and squeezing their breasts. I was about to change my mind when Belinda told me it was my turn.

"Don't pay any attention to that shit. You got something them girls ain't got."

I wasn't sure what that was, but I was willing to give it all I had.

I stood at the doorway to the pool, and when my record came on, everyone stopped talking and looked around for who was next. I strutted into the pool area and found my mark, the quarterback who Belinda had pointed out. Once I was directly in front of him, I spread his legs with my knees and moved into him, locking my gaze with his. I dropped my robe, and I heard Belinda's and the crowd's gasp of surprise that I was completely naked with the exception of two red garter belts. I could barely hear the music because of the cheering from the men. I knew I'd made the right decision, so with the approval of the crowd I slithered my entire body onto Mr. Quarterback. I turned around, put my ass in his face, and made the cheeks of my ass clap just enough to make him scream out. I moved away just before his tongue touched me. It was all about timing.

I turned to face him, brushing my pussy against his lap and my breasts against his chest. I could feel the heat rising from his skin, which meant I could also feel his hardening dick. He ran his hands up my thighs and then wrapped them around my breasts, bringing me down onto him. I counted the beats to the song so I'd know how much time I had left before I took him where I wanted him. When I heard the beat of the next song blending in I lifted one leg up on the arm of the chair and gyrated my very bald pussy in his face, then wound myself away from him. Mr. Quarterback was toasted.

When Belinda and I left there that night, we headed to a diner with a purse full of money.

"Maxie, you had them niggas twisted. I ain't never seen no shit like that from an amateur."

"I figured I couldn't go wrong if I was naked."

"I'm so proud of you. I promise we're gonna squeeze every dollar outta this town. By the time you get back to Philly, you'll be able to buy any house you want."

"I have to admit, Belinda, this is the best break from teaching school I've ever had. It's better than Negril, the Hamptons, or the friggin' cruise I took last summer."

But as hard as I tried, one thing I couldn't deny was that dancing made me horny. When I mentioned it to Belinda, she laughed and said, "Well, it won't for long, 'cause it's all in a day's work."

I wasn't so sure.

Week Four

"Maxine, telephone. Can't you hear that thing ringing?"

I reached down to the floor and answered the house phone.

"Max, where you been? I've been calling you all night."

"Lynn, I'm sorry. My cell phone was off."

"Listen, baby. You act like you don't want to see me."

"What are you talking about?"

"I left you a message last night. I'm over at the Travel Lodge on West Trade. I wanna see you."

I sat up in bed, trying to gather my thoughts. "What are you doing here? You didn't tell me you were coming."

"Damn, baby, I wanted to surprise you. What you do, go find a big ole country boy?"

"I'm sorry. Give me an hour or so. I have to run some errands for my mother, and then I'll be over there."

"I'm gonna get some sleep. I'll see you when you get here."

Panic set in. If Lynn was planning to stay for the weekend, I was going to have to cancel my trip with Belinda to Atlanta. She'd promised me that this one trip was going to be the highlight of my vacation. However, Lynn's unexpected arrival in town could change all that. It wasn't that I didn't want to see him, but I'd been so ensconced with my new adventures that I rarely had time to think about him.

I arrived at the Travel Lodge around three o'clock and found Lynn still lying in bed.

"What time is it? I'm starved," he groaned, opening the door.

"You want to get something to eat?" I asked, trying not to act disappointed that he'd surprised me with his visit.

"Nope, just you," he said, pulling me into bed with him.

"How long are you—" I couldn't get the question out before Lynn had me stretched out on the bed, pulling down my shorts.

"Max, baby, this some sexy red shit you got on," he said, commenting on the D&G lingerie I was wearing.

"You like, huh?"

"Wait a minute," he said, moving away from me. "Where's my blanket?" He kneeled at my feet, staring at the bald spot between my legs.

I sat up against the headboard, trying to quickly think of an explanation.

"Oh, that. Lynn, it's so hot and sticky down here, that stuff was getting sweaty. Plus I wanted to go swimming, and I couldn't have that bush sticking out." I could see he was disappointed, so rather than let him continue what he'd started, I stepped out of my clothes, turned over, and spread my cheeks in his face.

"Now, doesn't that make it easier?"

"Yeah. That's what I'm talking about," he said, excitedly slapping his dick across the cheeks of my ass.

"Wait, I got something for you," I told him before he could penetrate me.

"Baby, I can't be waiting."

But he was glad he did, because I turned around and gave him the best blow job I'd ever given, and that afternoon we stayed in bed for at least two hours making love. I knew it was love because I had an orgasm, a soaking-the-sheets type of orgasm. And while I lay there in the aftershock of the best sex Lynn had ever given me, he gave me another surprise.

"Maxine," he said, his strong arms squeezing me tight.

"Huh?"

He used his hand to lift my chin. "Look up here so I can see you."

"Yes."

"I love you, Maxine."

"I love you too, Lynn."

It was the first time we'd spoken those words to each other, and it felt good. I forgot about Belinda and Atlanta and just wanted to go back home with Lynn.

As it turned out, Lynn couldn't stay for the weekend, so I went with Belinda as planned.

The red carpet was rolled out for Belinda in Atlanta. We stayed at the Swisshotel and were chauffeured to and from everywhere in a black Suburban. We ate at expensive restaurants and shopped at the Lennox Mall. She never told me who was footing the bill, nor did I really care. All I knew is that soon this would all be behind me, so I wanted to enjoy it while I could. Of course, there was dancing at gentlemen's clubs during the afternoon and private clubs in the evening. And for Belinda there were clients who came to her room late at night. But just like at home, she was up early the next morning, knocking on my door.

Saturday morning while having breakfast, Belinda revealed the real reason we'd come to Atlanta. A very rich client of hers wanted her to shoot a video, and she wanted me to join her by agreeing to dance in the background.

"Belinda, I'm sorry, but there is no way I'm getting involved in a porno. That's going a little too far."

"You're not gonna be the one fucking, you'll be dancing behind a curtain. I'm the one that's gonna be doing the real work."

"It's still a porn, and you might've forgotten that I'm a schoolteacher, but I haven't, and I damn sure don't need evidence of what I've being doing for the last month."

"Max, I swear you won't be able to see your face. Just come with me and see the setup. If there's even the remote possibility that somebody can see you, we'll just forget about it."

"I don't care what the setup is. I'm not doing it."

"No even for ten thousand dollars?"

I swallowed hard. "Don't bullshit me, Belinda."

"Have I lied yet?"

We traveled to an estate in Buckhead and entered through wrought-iron gates and a fancy security system. She never told me the name of her client, but judging from the platinum and gold records that lined the studio wall, I knew he was an entertainer—a very rich one, if he was paying me ten grand. I could only imagine what he was paying Belinda.

When we walked into the room where the video was to be shot, I was impressed by the fact that it looked like an actual movie set. There was special lighting, cameramen, and every type of camera imaginable. In the middle of it all was a king-size bed dressed in red satin sheets. A sheer red curtain was draped at the head of the bed.

Belinda excused herself to go speak with her client. She returned about thirty minutes later, and I was sure he'd become more than just the person footing this bill by the bounce in her walk.

The director made sure I was comfortable with where I'd be dancing, and he showed me on the monitor how it would be impossible for anybody to make out my identity.

We rehearsed for about an hour, me dancing alone and then with Belinda. The choreographer showed me some additional moves that she wanted me to do to stay in tune with what Belinda would be doing on the bed. By the time we were ready to actually shoot the video, I was tired and ready to get it over with.

When the music came on, I started dancing in my own shrouded red world. I'd seen Belinda naked plenty of times, and I'd seen her dance, but watching her have hard-core sex was an experience I wasn't prepared for. The sensible side of me wanted to stop dancing and tell them I couldn't be part of their porn video, but it was that untapped lust deep inside me that won out. I assumed this is what they were hoping for, because the intoxicating smell of their sex and the sounds they made caused a sensation so strong between my legs that the only way to calm it was to stroke my hardened clit. And so there I was, watching, dancing, and bringing myself to an orgasm.

I was embarrassed afterward, but the director kept telling me how pleased he was with my performance. He practically begged me to do a one-woman show. I graciously thanked him and told him I was just on break for the summer.

Back in Charlotte, I prepared myself for the trip back home. I counted up all the money I'd made, over fifteen thousand dollars in one month. I knew that the down payment on my house was going to be a breeze. The night before I left, Belinda and Country Girl took me to dinner at Fucion's on the Lake, and we made a pact that not only would I return for Labor Day, but I'd come back next summer and we'd take our show on the road.

August

Week One

Philly in August was humid as hell. Heat just seemed to rise from the noisy streets. I was back in the city, and after airing out my apartment, I was glad to be home.

At Country Girl's suggestion, the first thing I did was get a safe deposit box to store my earnings. There was no way I wanted this money in my bank account.

I contacted my Realtor and began to look at houses. For me it was all about location. What part of the city did I want to live in? I looked at a corner house in the Art Museum area, but there was no garage or off-street parking. My other option was Old City, where the streets were narrow, the houses small, and the prices ridiculous.

When Lynn came off the road that week, I wanted our night to be special, so I fixed him a candlelight dinner. For the first time he freely talked about the brief time he'd spent as a linebacker in the NFL before getting cut. He swore to me that this time he wouldn't give up, that his trucking business would be fully operational by the spring.

After dinner he wanted to watch a movie, but I told him I had a better show for him to see. I put on some music and began to dance for him. I was only halfway through my routine when I noticed him stroking himself.

"You damn sure getting better. Where'd you learn that shit?"

"Uh, just a little class I've been taking."

He didn't wait for me to come to him, he came to where I was dancing and pinned me against the wall. He kissed and sucked my breasts until they felt bruised while plunging first one, then two fingers in and out of my wetness.

"Lynn, slow down. I'm not going anywhere."

"I want you bad, baby. You looked good up there moving that ass. Now come on over here. I got something special for you."

He brought me over to the couch, where he had me kneel. When I arched my ass up to meet what I thought would be his dick, instead I was greeted by the wetness of his tongue.

Lynn licked me long and hard, from the top of my clit up through the crack of my ass. My body tensed up, knowing what he wanted. His tongue rolled in and out its entrance in an effort to relax me. I kneeled there, my face buried in the couch, and relaxed my muscles to allow him to enter me. His fingers squeezed my clit to keep my mind off his hard dick opening up the entrance to my tight ass.

"Damn, ohhh Max," he mumbled, his dick sinking deeper, until he was able to move around easily inside of me. I knew he wouldn't last long. Fucking me in the ass was more than he could take. I talked to him, asking him if he liked fucking me in the ass.

"Max, please don't make me cum. Not yet, please."

With that I pushed my ass out to him, and all I could hear him say was, "Maxine, baby, youuu . . . taking it real good. I love you."

It was the first time Lynn wasn't in a hurry to get back to work. Instead he took an extra day off and we stayed in bed, lying under the air conditioner, eating, watching movies, and making love.

"Max, I don't know what it is, but you've changed, and I like it."

I panicked somewhat before I answered. "What are you talking about, Lynn?"

"You just seem so damn sexy lately. I can't get enough of you."

"Well, I'm not going to stay in bed for the rest of the week. That's for sure."

But that's what we wound up doing. It was amazing that the dancing I'd done in Charlotte had brought out a deeper side not only of my sexuality but of Lynn's too. So much so that I was sorry to see him get back on the road.

With Lynn finally gone, I had a chance to call and catch up with Belinda.

"Maxie, girl, what's happening? We miss you down here."

"Really? Then I guess I'll have to make a guest appearance in ole Charlotte," I said jokingly, wondering what I was missing.

"From what I hear, Philly must got the money, 'cause I got a call to come up there."

"When are you coming?"

"Tomorrow night. I have a car picking me up from the airport, but I want you to meet me at my hotel."

"Where are you staying?"

"Four Seasons, girl. Where else would the Princess stay? So, you gonna work with me or what?"

"Belinda, no way. Not here in Philly. I might see somebody I know."

"I doubt it. These are some rich white boys out in the suburbs."

"Why don't I just go with you, say as part of your entourage?"

"Oh, all right, scaredy cat."

I went shopping and bought a red linen dress and red lingerie for the occasion. Just the thought of hanging out with Belinda filled me with anticipation. I found myself dancing around trying on lingerie when my phone rang.

"Country Girl? What's up? Don't tell me you're coming up with Belinda."

"No. I got some bad news. Belinda was in a car accident."

"Please tell me she's . . . I mean she's not . . ."

"No, no, she's gonna be fine. A bit beat up, and she totaled that damn car."

"I'm so sorry. Is there anything I can do?"

"As a matter of fact, that's the other reason I'm calling. Belinda needs you to do that show for her."

"Country Girl, what are you talking about? I can't dance in Philly. I can't take that kind of chance."

"Max, you got to. These are some real important people. They're some rich white boys, so nobody's gonna know you."

"I don't know, Country Girl. It's too risky."

"Max, I understand, but you're all Belinda's got."

"Well, I guess I could. I mean—"

"Please."

"All right, Country Girl. I'll do it, but let me be clear about what I won't do. I will not sleep with any of these men regardless of the money. Better yet, I don't even want to be approached about it. Make sure that's clear to these guys. You hear me."

When Saturday afternoon came, I tried taking a nap, but I was too excited to sleep. It was almost like the first time all over again. I called Lynn twice to make sure he was staying overnight in Massachusetts. The thought that I could possibly see someone I knew frightened the hell out of me, but I'd given Country Girl my word.

When I'd spoken to Belinda, she'd given me explicit instructions on how to cover my tracks. She suggested I carry my dance clothes in a small suitcase, and that I drive my car to the closest hotel to my destination and then either take a cab or have a car service drive me the rest of the way, but be sure they waited until I finished. I reserved a town car through Ali Baba limousine service and had the driver pick me up at the Adams Mark on City Avenue. To be extra careful, I reserved a room in case I needed someplace to hide out. I'd probably gone overboard with my tactics, but that is part of what excited me.

The driver took me to the address in Radnor, which was just outside Philly. Supposedly the reason I'd been hired was because one of the guests had recently acquired a major company. People in these parts of town didn't only get dancers for bachelor parties, they hired them for any occasion.

The large home sat behind a wall of trees. The driver pulled into the circular driveway and opened my door. He sensed that I wasn't an actual guest and told me, if I had any problems, to give him a call on his cell phone, that he'd be waiting in the car.

I could hear music and loud voices coming from the back of the house. I rang the bell and briefly waited until the butler answered the door.

"Good evening, Ms. Maxie. I'll get Mr. Preston for you."

"Thank you."

I sat in the sitting room—that was all it could've possibly been—until a tall, thin, forty-something man appeared in the doorway. I assumed he was Mr. Preston.

"Hello, you must be Maxie."

"Yes, how are you?" I asked, standing up to shake his outstretched hand.

"I'm glad you could make it. Belinda told me about her misfortune. However, she didn't tell me to expect you," he said, looking me over. "Can I get you anything?"

"Bottled water will do. Would you be gracious enough to provide me with the details of the person you're honoring?"

"That would be Jeff," he said, leading me to look out the dining-room window. "He's the one standing by the bar with the blond hair and khakis."

The pool held about ten women in bathing suits, and poolside there had to be at least twenty-five white men with a few black men sprinkled in between.

"How old is he?" I asked.

"Jeff is a young man, but nonetheless very wise. He just pulled off a very hostile takeover that made all of us a lot of money. But you wouldn't want to know about that."

Did this pompous asshole think I didn't want to know because I didn't understand business? If he only knew how good I really was at it! Besides being a math teacher and having a master's degree, I was a whiz at finances.

"Are you ready to get started?"

"Just show me where I can get changed."

"Maxie, don't worry about pleasing anyone else. This night is all for Jeff."

"In that case, why don't we have Jeff close to the pool in case he needs to cool off. And another thing—I'll need something to blind-fold him."

"I like your style, Max," he said, laughing.

"Excuse me, Mr. Preston, but you do know the rules."

"Everything was made clear by Belinda."

Preston motioned to the butler, who carried a tray of bottled water and sliced lemons and limes as he escorted me to my room.

I laid out the three outfits I'd brought with me, looked out to the pool, and thought about what I would wear. I chose a pair of red lace boy-cut, crotchless panties and a red bra that only held my nipples. Then I slid into a pair of ankle-strap stilettos. Yes, I had something for Jeff. I piled my hair on my head and twisted it without pins so it could easily fall to my shoulders when I was ready. Over it I wore my signature red silk robe.

I opened the door, and the butler signaled to Mr. Preston that I was ready. They dimmed the pool lights, my music came on, and I swayed out to the pool on Mr. Preston's arm as if I were an invited guest. When the music hit just the right beat, I was standing in front of Jeff, where I slid out of my robe. Poor Jeff only had a moment to look because Mr. Preston blindfolded him. I whispered in Jeff's ear what I wanted to do to him. When he tried to straighten himself up in the chair, I knew I had him.

I danced around Jeff, playing with his blond hair yet never getting close enough for his outstretched hands to touch me. I jiggled my ass in his lap then pushed my titties in his face. I watched his chest heave in and out, and I knew he would be easy.

The other men and women had now moved in closer, circling the two of us, shouting to Jeff what my body looked like. Unbuttoning his shirt, I pulled at his nipples, and when he began to slide down in the chair, I unbuckled his belt. I could see his dick piercing through his shorts, and after gripping it between the cheeks of my ass I turned and untied his blindfold.

Jeff stood up and reached out to grab me, but he lost his pants in the process, exposing his hard white dick, which stuck out through the opening in his boxers. He tried to adjust himself, and that's when Mr. Preston pushed Jeff into the water. I followed behind him. Standing against the side of the pool with only the water between us, I allowed Jeff to rub his dick against my ass. That's when the money came. It littered the pool and the ground around it. By now I could feel Jeff's dick jerking, so I slid from under him, and he ducked under the water, where I'm sure he came. Mr. Preston stood beside the pool and held a towel for me. Naked, I climbed out.

Through it all I felt someone staring at me, different from the others. Even when I was turned away from him, I could feel his stare. He'd stood at the bar almost the entire time I'd danced until I'd climbed naked out of the pool, where he'd move in as close as the others. From somewhere behind me I heard Jeff say, "Take all my money, Maxie. I love you."

I squeezed my wet hair, wrapped myself in the large towel Mr. Preston held out, and headed back to the house.

"You were superb. Please tell me you can stay for a while. Everyone wants to meet you," Mr. Preston said.

"I'm sorry, but I don't socialize with my clients."

"Max, whatever it takes, please stay for a moment to meet some of my guests. I'm sure Jeff would like to meet you."

Nothing better than a begging man. "Okay, but only for a moment."

"Thank you. I'll go gather up the money from the pool and be right back."

I took a quick shower, pulled my wet hair into a ponytail, and put my clothes on. When I walked out the room, Mr. Preston was there with an envelope.

Back at the pool I sipped on a glass of wine, surrounded by Jeff and a few of the other men. Funny thing in this business, how a woman's body is worshipped just for the mere fact that she knows how to move it. Mr. Preston's guests were full of questions, none that I answered honestly. I suggested that they call my agent if they wanted to use my services in the future. That had a nice ring to it. Made me sound professional. And then *he* came over. I was a little nervous at first because I thought he'd recognized me from somewhere. He tried not to act like he was ogling me, but it was there behind his glasses.

"I must say, Max, you're even more beautiful with clothes on."

His smile showed picture-perfect white teeth, which contrasted nicely with his brown-sugar skin. He was dressed as preppy as the others in denim shorts and a yellow polo. He obviously had good taste, judging by the expensive silver-framed glasses he wore. I figured him to be a banker or a CPA.

"Thank you. I didn't catch your name," I said, looking down at his powerful legs and well-defined calves. Probably played tennis.

"Mason. Mason Turner. And yours? Maxie? Is that your real name?"

"Now, what do you think?"

"I'd like to be able to see you again."

"Certainly, but like I told your friends, you can reach me through my agent."

"The Princess is in Charlotte, and something tells me you're not."

"I may not be, but it's the best way to reach me."

Talking with Mason Turner stirred up those feelings of untapped lust, making me want to give him my full name and home phone number. I knew that meant it was time to go.

"It was nice to meet you, Mason, but I must say good night."

"I hate to see you go. But here, this is for you," he said. I looked down at the two crisp one-hundred-dollar bills he was holding. "There wasn't any place for me to put this when you climbed out of that pool."

The driver was waiting for me with the door open. I called Belinda from the car and told her how successful I'd been. However, I didn't mention meeting Mason Turner. When we pulled up at the Adams Mark, I tipped the driver a hundred dollars, and he gave me his business card for future use.

Week Two

There was no doubt that the money in my safe deposit box was adding up. I talked myself into dancing a few more times, hoping I would earn enough money to look at one of the houses I really wanted. But if I were going to do that, then I would have to be very selective. No bars, no clubs, just private parties, referrals only. So needless to say, I was hoping Mason Turner called.

Lynn had a few days off, so he went with me to look at houses with the Realtor but was a little surprised when I suggested that we look at a house I had my eye on in Wyndmoor. It was a simple three-bedroom ranch home that sat back from the street and was surrounded by about a half acre of land. He liked the house but couldn't understand why I was looking at a property I couldn't afford.

"Baby, give me about a year. Once I get these trucks on the road, I'll get you any house you want."

"I know, but I just wanted you to see it. I really love it."

"Max, wouldn't you rather we be married and have me home every night before we get ourselves in so much debt?"

"Married? What are you saying Lynn? That you want to tie the knot? This better not be a proposal."

"Not exactly, but I do want you to know my intentions."

"That means I could be looking at an engagement ring by, let's say, Christmas?"

"You women always want to get engaged for the holidays so you can go back to work bragging."

"That's only when we have something worth bragging about. You get my point," I said, pulling him back into the house for one more look.

That night after eating pizza and drinking too many bottles of Corona, I gave Lynn the pleasure of letting him cum in my mouth. Afterward he was comatose. I wasn't tired, so I went downstairs to the kitchen, where I noticed the message light blinking on my phone. I sat on the edge of the couch and hit speaker.

"Maxie, it's me, Belinda. Girl, you must've rocked them white boys, 'cause they want you back."

Just the sound of her voice and the possibility of dancing made my belly flip. I picked up the receiver and continued to listen.

"It seems brotha Mason wants you to do a party for him and he's paying top dollar. I'm leaving you his number 'cause I'll be outta town for a few days."

Here was my chance to add to the stack of money that was growing in my safe deposit box. Regardless of what Lynn thought, I knew that with a few thousand more dollars that house would be mine, and I might even have enough left over to help him with his business.

I went upstairs to make sure Lynn was still sleeping, then back downstairs. I dialed Mason's number. We discussed my next performance just like the business deal it was, but there was so much more going on that wasn't said.

The party was scheduled for tomorrow evening, but I had to be careful this time because Lynn was still home and I had to figure out how I could get away for a few hours. I decided to tell him that my beautician was hosting a sex toy party, and that when I got home he'd be more than happy I'd gone.

I'd scheduled my driver to pick me up from where I'd checked in at the Marriott on Market Street. A half hour later I arrived at the Rittenhouse Hotel. When I walked into their lobby, Mason was waiting for me.

"It's nice to see you again, Maxie," he said, this time kissing me on the cheek.

I wasn't sure what gave him that authority, but I liked it and really liked how he smelled.

"I reserved a room where you can change, or you're welcome to stay over if you'd like."

"That won't be necessary."

"You seem a little nervous tonight," he said, unlocking my door.

"How many guests are there?"

"I would say there's about thirty-five women."

"Women? I thought this was a bachelor party."

"Does it matter?"

"Not at all, as long as they're paying."

As I walked past him to enter my room, Mason placed his hand in the center of my back, between my shoulderblades, guiding me through the doorway.

"Max, I just wanted a reason to see you dance again." With that, Mason left me alone.

I walked around the room cursing Belinda, who wasn't answering her cell phone. I couldn't figure out who'd set me up for this. This Mason must be a sick bastard, wanting me to dance for a bunch of lesbians. My cell phone rang.

"Belinda, what the hell is going on?"

"Maxie, chill the fuck out. You can do this, it's nothing but a bunch of horny bitches."

"Yeah, well, what's up with this Mason character?"

There was a knock at the door. I changed the tone of my voice. "Yes."

"Is everything okay?"

"Just give me a minute," I replied, then whispered into the phone, "Look, Belinda, I don't like this shit. We have to talk, and you better answer that damn phone when I call back."

"Aw, girl. Go shake that ass."

Since I would be dancing for women and, more importantly, Mason, I chose sheer black stockings, a strappy red garter belt, no panties, and a red see-through bra. When I stepped out of the room in my red robe, Mason was waiting for me.

The suite was filled with candles, and I could hear the women laughing as a half-naked male dancer walked past me, his fist filled with one-dollar bills. Mason already knew that nothing less than a twenty touched my skin.

I'd selected a song by Fabulous, "Into You," and as the song began to play I turned to ask Mason if he knew the rules. He never answered. I tried to look at the crowd through the candlelight, but there were no familiar faces, just black, white, and Latino, all half drunk. Even the scent of herb filtered through the room.

I could see this would be easy, so I sashayed past the women and made my way to the bride-to-be. She was a woman of average beauty, but it was obvious she had money from the diamond jewelry she sported. She was probably my age, dressed in jeans and a halter top. I whispered in her ear before I started.

"Are you sure I'm what you want?"

She obviously wasn't sure what she wanted, because her bulging eyes just stared at the brown nipples that poked out from my bra when I tossed my robe across the room in Mason's direction. I danced away from her through the crowd of women, and then I moved in close to the bride and rubbed my hands over her bare shoulders. I turned around and shook my ass in her face and then placed my legs on either side of her and began thrusting my pelvis onto hers as she squirmed in her chair. The other women were going wild. They loved me, and I had to admit I was enjoying watching the bride's nipples harden under my touch. Her friends began stuffing twenty- and fifty-dollar bills in my bra and garter belt. Who were they that they would spend this type of money to see a woman dance?

That's when I knew I could take it further. So with one leg on her shoulder I slid off my stockings, one leg at a time, and then bent over her, my pussy spread open close to her face. This position also gave the women behind me a clear view of the crack of my ass, and they made use of it by rubbing on my cheeks. That's when I undid the bride's halter top and let it fall in her lap. Her small erect titties were close enough that all I had to do was brush mine against hers. She screamed out. The women were standing so close to me that I could barely breathe. The music was almost over, so I backed away from the bride to make my exit. Instead of feeling one of the women behind me, I felt Mason's erection brush against my naked ass. The music didn't end. I heard Ashanti's sweet voice sing, "I really like what you do to me," and with that Mason unsnapped my bra.

He whispered in my ear, his lips touching its lobe. "She wants to touch you."

The women were watching, and I didn't want the moment to seem awkward, so I danced against him and what felt like a weapon between his legs. I wasn't supposed to be getting aroused, but I could feel my juices bubbling up inside me.

"That's not what I do, especially with women."

"I think you want to."

I tried to dance away from him and back into the crowd of women, but they were cheering Mason to take me.

I teased him, his glasses steaming up as I brushed my nipples across his lips.

"That's not my job."

"Why not let her taste you, Max? I have a thousand dollars that says you'll like it."

I wanted to tell him that I'd rather have him taste me, but when I looked down and saw the money gathered at my feet, I decided I'd do it for Mason. I don't know what it was about Mason, but he made me reveal a side of me I didn't know existed.

When I turned around, the drunken bride was waiting breathlessly on the edge of her chair. Before I could even get close, she pulled me into her. Her friends stood close by, encouraging her, "Suck her titties . . . Eat some pussy . . . Go 'head, I dare you."

She clumsily filled each of her hands with my breasts and stuck her tongue out to lick my nipples. I wanted to see Mason's face as I performed for him, so after I pushed my breasts into her mouth, I moved away, turned around, and clapped my ass in her face. Mason was right, this bride knew what she wanted, and she pulled me to her, opening me up and tasting a mouthful of the cream that had built up in me. Her friends were relentless. "She's eating it, she's eating it . . . What's it taste like? . . . I want some too."

But I ignored them and instead watched Mason and his hard dick that stuck to the side of his leg, and before I knew it I'd pushed down on that bride's tongue and came, right in her face.

That move created so much excitement between these women that I thought they'd all want to taste me. It was like being a rock star; they wanted whatever piece of me they could touch. So without waiting for Mason to escort me, I made my exit back to my room.

I heard Mason knocking on the door, but I ignored him and stepped into the shower. What the hell was wrong with me? This shit had gotten out of control. I'd let a woman eat me. I'd even kissed her. How far would they have gone? Would all of them have wanted to touch me? Was the money even worth it? All of a sudden I started laughing. It wasn't me, it was them. I was a professional doing a job. Fuck them horny bitches and their big diamond rings. She'd be the one standing at the altar with the taste of my juices lingering in her mouth, while my bed was littered with her money.

As expected, Mason was waiting for me, probably expecting me to be pissed that he'd set me up. He appeared nervous. I assumed it was because he'd gotten more of a show than he'd expected.

"You have my envelope?"

"Of course, including the tip for your extra service. Are you okay?" he asked, handing me a brown envelope stuffed with money. I took it and continued walking, heading for the elevator bank. He followed close behind me.

"I'm fine, but please know that's not something I do on a regular basis."

He stood close to me in the elevator, but I sensed he didn't know what to say. We both knew that my performance had been for him. When we walked into the lobby, the doorman informed me that my driver had had an emergency and had to leave. Mason took advantage of the opportunity.

"Would you like me to give you a ride?"

I knew I should've declined his offer and taken a cab, but I was drawn to him, so I answered, "I'd appreciate that."

We stood in silence until the valet pulled up in his Mercedes.

"Would you like to get something to eat?" he asked before the doorman opened my door.

I wanted him to think I had another client. "No, you can drop me off at the Marriott."

I would've loved to have gone to eat with Mason, maybe even invited him up to my room, but that would be crossing the line from business to pleasure. And then there was Lynn to think about, who was home waiting for me.

"No problem," he said, pulling into the street. "Max, would you be interested in dancing for me again?"

"I'm not so sure about your jobs."

"Trust me, it won't be like tonight. When I get the details, I'll give Belinda a call . . . unless there's a number where I can reach you."

Against my better judgment, I gave him my cell phone number.

I waited until Mason pulled off, then had my Jeep retrieved from the parking garage. When I got in that night, I crept up the stairs past Lynn's apartment. I was just halfway up the steps when I heard his door open.

"Maxine, where you been? I been waiting up for you. Why are you carrying that suitcase?"

I wasn't sure what to say. What if he wanted to look in it? He knew I hadn't spent the night out, so I quickly thought up an excuse.

"It's dry cleaning that's been in my truck since I returned from Charlotte. I'm hoping it hasn't mildewed from this weather."

"Like I said, woman, where have you been? It's three o'clock in the morning."

"Don't you remember I told you I was going to that sex toy party? We went to a club afterward."

"All right. So, lemme see what you got for us."

"It has to be ordered, silly. Let me put this stuff away, and I'll be back down."

His upturned lips let me know that I hadn't convinced him about my whereabouts, but I knew I had a way of making him forget all about it.

After seeing Lynn off in the morning, I needed to make another trip to the bank. I also had to return a call to my Realtor because I'd made up my mind to make an offer on the house in Wyndmoor. I was about two blocks from my apartment when my Jeep overheated. Another driver pulled over to help me, and once it cooled off I drove to the Infiniti dealer in Willow Grove. I'd had my Jeep Cherokee for four years and had wanted to get another car, but I'd been saving to purchase a house. But with the extra money I'd made, it was now possible to do both.

I was looking at vehicles on the showroom floor when one of the salesmen introduced me to the owner of the dealership. My face must've looked familiar to him, as his did to me. When we went into his office, I realized he was one of the men that had been at Preston's party. Once he was comfortable that I wasn't there to spill the beans on what he did for fun, he allowed me to purchase the 2004 Infiniti SUV with no money down.

I phoned Belinda and told her what had been happening. She told me she knew Mason and that he was single, rich, and some kind of currency trader. She also told me she'd danced for him in the past, but he was so stone-faced that she figured she wasn't his type.

"You taking care of yourself, right? Not sleeping with any clients, are you?"

"Of course not. I'm just going to do a few more shows, and then I'm finished."

"Good, because I have a job for you. It's at a private club called Columbus in West Fairmount, and the owner says they need a breath of fresh air."

I was glad Lynn was out of town so I wouldn't have to lie. I'd yet to hear from Mason about the job he'd wanted me to do, so this would give me something to do in the meantime. Columbus was an exclusive men's club that most people probably didn't know existed. I watched the other women who danced before me, and they were good, but they used the pole too much, and Belinda had taught me to use the crowd instead.

I waited for my turn, and when I stepped in front of the curtain, the lights came up, bringing a glow around the room. This was my stage.

"Here, all the way from Charlotte, North Carolina, is our special guest, Maxie. So bring out the big bills and put those dollars back in your pockets."

I moved onto the stage, closed my eyes, and began my dance. When I opened them, the first person I saw was Mason. Rather than give him the satisfaction of looking his way, I danced around every man except him, allowing the fantasy of watching and not touching me eat at his loins. When the dance was over, I walked through the club, giving lap dances. I could see him longing for me, but I had to make him suffer. When I saw him making his way to me, I headed out the back door where my driver was waiting.

I watched him ring my cell phone for the next two hours. When I was finally home in bed, I answered his call.

"Why'd you do that to me tonight, Max?"

"I'm sorry. Did you want a lap dance? I didn't see you waving any money in my direction."

"Belinda has already told me what you won't do. But if it's money you want, then I have plenty."

"You're right. But for the right amount you could get a private dance."

"What if I told you I like watching you dance for others even more?"

"Is that why you had me dance for those women?"

"I could care less about those women. It's you I want."

This conversation was definitely going in the wrong direction, but I liked it.

"Max, if you'd just let me have you, just once, I'd do anything to satisfy you."

"And what would you do with me, Mason? If you had me, let's say for a few hours."

He didn't say anything at first, and I knew his imagination was taking over.

"Would you just want to watch me dance?" I wanted to hear his answer, see just how bad he wanted me.

"Ohhh, Maxie. Maxie, I'd allow you to be the nasty bit—I'm sorry, I'm way out of line."

"Yeah, I think so. Why don't you call me when you have a job for me."

Two days later Mason phoned me on my cell while I was having breakfast with Lynn.

"Hello, this is Max," I said into the phone without checking the ID.

"I need you to perform for me."

I jumped off Lynn's lap and went into the kitchen. "Can you hold on a minute, please? I need to get a pen so I can take down your information."

"Borgata Hotel, Atlantic City. And the date is whenever you can make it."

Week Three

After counting my money three times, I had to talk to my mother. I needed her to agree that she'd given me the money as a gift so I wouldn't have any problems with the large down payment I wanted to put on the house. All the papers had been approved, and all I had to do was bring the deposit by the end of the week. The money I'd make in Atlantic City would be just enough for me to use as a nest egg once I moved into the house.

I arrived at the Borgata, where Mason had left a key for me at the front desk. When I got into the room, there was no sign of him. I'd almost wished he'd been waiting for me. Usually I didn't drink when I was working, but this night I fixed myself a drink from the bar and waited to hear from him. When the doorbell rang, I looked through the peephole. It was Mason.

"Are you ready for work?"

"What's the occasion?"

"A private dance for a very rich client of mine whose business I'm trying to secure. Room 1722."

If I'd had any thoughts that this dance was for Mason, his cocky attitude completely washed that away. He was all business.

After I was dressed in a red satin gown that had slits up to my waist and red rhinestone heels, I slipped on my robe and went to the room. The door was open, and smooth sounds of slow music filled the room. When I walked inside the suite, Mason was alone. I knew this was what I'd been waiting for.

He sat in a chair at the table, sipping on his drink. Before I even began to dance, I could see he was hungering for me.

"I'll let you know when I'm ready."

His hesitation made me anxious to begin, but he was paying, so I waited. As the song he wanted me to dance to began to play, he nodded that I could begin. I moved my body to the sultry voice of Kem and as he crooned out "Love Calls," I closed my eyes so I wouldn't beg Mason to take me.

"Open your eyes. I want to see what you need."

I let the straps slide off my arms, and when the gown hit my waist, he stood up and placed the straps back on my shoulders. Rather than sit back down, he allowed me to move my body against his. Then, with his arms behind his back, he placed kisses across my shoulders, then used his fingertips to remove the straps of the gown until my body was exposed. My eyes were closed. This time I was too afraid of what he might see in mine. I let the music run deep into me like I'd never done before. Kem's words took over my emotions as he sang, "nowhere to hide . . . nowhere to run . . . when love's on its way." And Mason took over my body, devouring my breasts with his eyes before he took them in his mouth. I continued to dance slow, slower than the music that continued to play.

I stepped out of my dress, and his mouth moved over my entire body, leaving no part of my skin untouched. When his mouth made its way between my legs, he opened the lips of my pussy and kissed me there, passionately, bringing with it a rush of liquids. And then he licked my sensitive clit, bringing sounds from me that neither of us understood.

A tingling sensation went up the center of my spine, and when I couldn't stand up any longer, he carried me to the bed. All the time my mind raced. Was I now a prostitute, no better than Belinda and the women that had been at her party? Would Mason pay me afterward? Did I want him to? If I let him have me, would he think I did this all the time?

I helped him undress while he talked to me like I'd never been talked to before.

"You . . . like . . . being . . . nasty . . . don't you, Max?" His fingers pushed inside me, searching for that special place. "I wanted to see you fuck that woman, Max. I wanted to see you come in her face. You wanted it, didn't you, Max?"

I told him yes, not knowing what I wanted except for him to fuck me. When he'd gotten me to the point where I was begging for him, he began pushing his wide dick deep inside me, inching it farther into my body. And when it was as far as it could go, he just lay there, letting it grow. I was afraid that if it grew too much, he would never be able to pull it out of me. But he knew what to do as he fucked me hard, slowly, passionately, fiercely.

"Tonight, Max. Tonight you're my nasty bitch. You hear me?"

"Yes, whatever you want. Just please don't stop."

"Don't talk. I'm taking the lead on this dance. You hear me, bitch? I'm fucking you tonight."

We had sex from the bed to the floor and multiple orgasms from both of us. But he still wasn't finished with me. As I lay spent from his loving, he opened my legs and lapped me, and the juices that had come from both of us.

"Mase . . . un, Mase . . . un, what . . . don't."

I tried to move away from him, but he gripped my hips and brought me into his mouth. And then he found a part of me I never knew existed. He ran his tongue along the left side of my clit unmercifully. I held onto his shoulders for support, and he continued to tantalize that spot until my body could give no more.

Who was this man, this Mason Turner, who knew my body better than I knew it myself? The dance for Mason didn't end until two days later.

Week Four

Tuesday was closing day for my new house, and things went without a hitch. When it was over, I rounded my driveway and sat there looking at my little dream house. So many things had happened to get me to this place, and now was not the time to sort them out. Lynn would be home tomorrow, and I had to leave Mason behind. Somehow I'd manage to tell Mason that I could no longer be his private dancer. He'd paid me five thousand dollars for that dance, and a part of me didn't want to accept his money. If I never danced for him again, that weekend at the Borgata would be all the memory I'd ever need.

I heard a car pulling up behind me, and when I looked in the rearview mirror, I saw that it was Lynn. Somehow he'd gotten in a day early.

"Max, I don't know how you did it, but I'm proud of you."

"Come on. I want to show you the inside. How long are you home for? Will you be able to help me move?"

"Whatever you want," he said, slapping me on my ass.

Lynn and I walked through the house, with me babbling about everything I wanted to do and buy.

"Listen, baby, I can pull together some of the brothers to help move your stuff, but it'll have to be during the week. Can you get some time off next week?"

"I can't, because school will be starting, and there are a ton of meetings before classes start. Why don't you just take the extra key, and you can handle the move."

While I prepared for work, Lynn moved most of the furniture I was taking with me into my house. I'd had several conversations with Mason, and neither of us could figure out where to go from here. Had it been business or pleasure? When he tried to make it one, I made it the other. If nothing else, he was good for phone sex on the nights when Lynn was on the road.

I had one night left in my apartment, and Lynn was on his way home. I'd picked out a one-piece red corset to wear for the occasion. I was upstairs dabbing on perfume when I heard him come through the door, shouting my name.

"Maxine, where the fuck are you?"

He didn't sound like a man who was happy to see me.

"Lynn, I'm upstairs," I answered, making my way down the steps.

I was about to give him a kiss, but his twisted-up face told me to step back.

"What the fuck is this shit?" he asked, throwing a DVD across the room.

I didn't have to ask what it was. "Where'd you get that? Lynn, I can explain. I was in Charlotte, I mean Atlanta. It's not really me. I mean, it's not what you think."

"Max, I been fucking you for almost a year, and you think I don't know your every move? Why'd you do some shit like that?"

"It was supposed to be private."

"Private my ass—this shit is sold at every truck stop up and down the road. Did you think you were that good that you could cover yourself up and I not know who you were? All this time you shaving your pussy and dancing all the fuck around the house talking about you been taking dance classes. What are you now, some damn two-dollar ho?"

"You don't understand. Just listen to me, Lynn. Please."

"Please shut the fuck up, Max, 'cause there's no understanding why my fuckin' woman is dancing in some stinking-ass porno. How many niggas did you fuck down there, Max?"

"Lynn, please just hear me out. I only did it that one time." But I was talking to his back.

"Now I know where you got the money to buy that fuckin' house and the new truck you got. And just think I wanted to marry you," he said, reaching into his pocket and throwing a black box across the kitchen floor. Then he walked out, slamming the door behind him.

I walked downstairs and picked up the black box. I didn't even want to open it. Instead, I squeezed it in my hands and sat there on the floor, crying alone in the dark.

In the distance I heard my cell phone ringing. I ran upstairs to answer it, hoping it was Lynn.

"Hello. Hello?"

"Hey, lady, what's wrong?"

"Mason, I'm sorry. I just—"

"Just thought it was someone else?"

I started crying. "Mason, I can't talk right now. It's not a good time."

"What is it, Max? What's wrong? I'm coming to get you."

I gave him my address. Twenty minutes later he was ringing the doorbell.

"Mason, I shouldn't have told you to come here . . . you're one of my clients . . . I was just going through something."

"Max, we both know I'm more than a client. Why don't you let me come inside so we can talk? Tell me what's wrong."

But I couldn't let him inside. There was so much he didn't know about me that my apartment might reveal.

"I'll be okay. I just got some bad news," I said, squeezing the black box in my hand.

"Why don't you get dressed? We can go somewhere and have some coffee, a drink maybe."

That's when I realized I was standing there talking to him in my corset. He probably thought I was a prostitute for sure. This was not working out right. Everybody was getting the wrong message.

"Wait in the car. I'll be out in a minute."

I pulled a pair of jeans and a T-shirt over my corset and went outside to his car. I noticed that the lights were out in Lynn's apartment, which meant he'd left. I was glad for that, because the last thing I wanted was for him to see me with another man.

We rode over to Broad Street to the Stenton diner, and he ordered coffee for both of us. I wasn't in the mood for talking. Instead he talked about himself, and I learned that Mason was divorced, had no children, and was an only child. He lived in a house in Villanova and had an office on City Avenue, where he was an investment banker.

By the time we'd finished, I didn't want to go back home, so he suggested we go to a hotel. He took me to the Rittenhouse, and rather than talk, I got drunk and gave myself to him.

Afterward, when he was asleep, I regretted knowing him, regretted North Carolina, and most of all regretted having lost Lynn.

September

Week One

I hadn't spoken to Lynn or Mason before I flew off to Charlotte to spend Labor Day with Belinda. There were so many things I wanted to forget, and dancing helped me do just that. We stayed in Charlotte for one night before we flew down to Miami, where Belinda had booked the two of us to dance at a few strip clubs.

By now I'd made my own contacts in Philly's stripping community. One afternoon while I was at Crate and Barrel buying some new things for the house, I ran into a woman who invited me to dance at an exclusive gentleman's club that had recently opened in Bala Cynwyd. Had I not been so disenchanted with my personal life and my big empty house, I probably would've known to say no. But after assessing my situation, I found myself anxious to do it. I craved this dancing thing now; it was like a drug. One more dance and one more dollar. I enjoyed the fantasy of being seen and touched by men and women who would never be able to take me home.

On Sunday afternoon I found myself walking through the back door of the very upscale Gestures gentleman's club. It wasn't just a strip club, it was a full-service five-star restaurant. It was luxury at its finest. Its ambience was unmatched by any club I'd ever performed at.

When it was time for me to go onstage, I realized that some of my enthusiasm was gone. All I could hear was Lynn's voice, and I imagined him being on the other side of that curtain. When they called my name, I swallowed my pride and did my thing. With my eyes closed, I was oblivious to the dark eyes that watched me from the fringes of the dance floor. As my routine ended, I turned and noticed Mason standing at the bar.

He tried to call me the rest of the day, but I kept my cell phone off. That was still the only number he had. I was sitting in the teacher's lounge the next day, listening to the boring banter of the other teachers recalling their summer vacations, when my cell phone vibrated. I saw Mason's number come up and realized that maybe my summer wasn't yet over. I moved to a corner of the room for some privacy and answered the call.

"Max, I need to see you. Let me talk to you, please."

"I'm not that girl, Mason. I'm not who you want."

"Tell me you don't miss me. That you haven't been thinking about me."

I couldn't lie. He was all I'd thought about in between my regrets at losing Lynn. When I didn't answer, he continued.

"Max, I miss you. Please, can't you at least have lunch with me?"

"I don't know. Our relationship was supposed to be business, and now you want to keep fucking me like I'm some prostitute."

"You're the one that keeps calling yourself that."

"I never should've crossed that line with you, Mason. You said so yourself."

"I don't give a damn about a line. I want you. Now. And if it makes you feel like this isn't personal, then I'll give you money. I'll do whatever you want. I have to have you, Max."

He wouldn't let up.

"I know you miss me. I could see it in the way you danced yesterday. Where are you? I'll come get you."

"No, don't do that. Mason, I can't keep letting you have your way with me. It's just not right, the way you take me like you own me."

"Listen to me, Maxie. Listen to me real close. I do own you, and when I see you, I'm going to rip your panties down to your knees and slide my mouth all over your pussy. Come to me, Maxie."

I was weakening. I looked around the teacher's lounge at the administrators opening their brown bags of leftovers and my fellow teachers trying to decide whether they would go to McDonalds or Big Georges for lunch. I wished I could tell them what I was being offered, but I couldn't concentrate as Mason continued to seduce me with his words.

"You hear me, Max? I wanna fuck you right now."

"I . . . I . . . I don't have much time. I'm on my lunch hour."

"Just let me ride you, Max. Let me ride that sweet ass."

I met Mason at his car in Fairmount Park, and we sat there talking only briefly before he reclined his front seats as far as they would go. I tried to reason with him, but he quieted me with his kisses while unbuttoning my blouse and burying his head between my breasts. There was no need to resist, so I unzipped his pants.

"I love fucking you, Max, and you love it, too. I'm the one that knows how to satisfy you. You're my bitch, remember that," he said, while dipping his fingers under my panties, stroking me.

Mason was the only man that had ever talked dirty to me, called me names. I climbed onto him, and just like he said, he ripped my panties off, allowing me to spread my legs over his wide dick. It was true, Mason did know how to satisfy me.

And there in the afternoon on Snake Hill in Fairmount Park I rode Mason, rode him behind the tinted windows of his Mercedes-Benz 500 SL.

"I love this pussy, Max. I love you."

But I learned that even though he'd exploded into me, he wasn't finished, because he had to have all of me. He somehow managed to lean me against his car door while he bent over and licked me there, in that spot, on the left side of my clit, sending my body into multiple orgasms.

I was trembling when I got back to work. Mason had a way of doing that. I went to the ladies' room in an attempt to gather myself, and that's when I realized something was missing. My panties. I'd left them in his car.

The next morning, traffic was heavy. I was going to be late for work on the first day of classes. The first day of school was always the most exciting—everyone talking about summer vacation and taking in each other's new looks.

Even though I taught math, I always started the school year off by having my students write a two-page essay on how they spent their summer break. I felt it was the best way for us to get to know one another and get things off to a good start. They agreed to do it only if I provided one, too. I couldn't imagine what I would write, but I knew it wouldn't be the truth.

One of the school rules was that you not befriend the students, but sometimes it was hard not to. Just showing an extra amount of attention would bring the students out of their shells. It was all about trust. Eleventh grade was hard, but if students passed, they could fly by the twelfth grade straight into graduation.

As the week went on, I found myself fighting off flirtatious young boys who had been honest enough to write about how they'd hustled over the summer. But I took a special interest in one young girl as she read her essay. Kareema read about how she'd worked for her uncle during the summer while her parents were going through a divorce. Her story was very moving, and it practically brought tears to my eyes.

After class Kareema asked to speak with me and told me that she was really looking forward to being in my class because she'd heard from my previous students that I had a way of making math fun. She also told me that she couldn't wait to hear me read my summer essay.

That night I agonized over what I would write. I had to read it in the morning, and nothing I wrote made sense. Frustrated, I tried to call Lynn, something I'd done about three times, but I never got any responses to my messages. I left another message asking him to come see me so that we could talk about what happened.

Mason made himself available to me, but I wouldn't let him come to the house. It was filled with things from my life, and I didn't want him to know anything about me. I was beginning to enjoy his company, and he made me believe that my being a stripper didn't make it impossible for us to have a relationship. But I knew I'd have to be careful. I hoped it wouldn't be a big deal that I was a schoolteacher and had been a stripper for the summer. Why should he care?

Early the next morning I still hadn't written my essay. I was sitting at the kitchen table with a cup of coffee and a blank piece of paper when I heard a car pull up. I went to the front door, where Lynn stood.

"I wanted to come by and bring the things you left at my apartment."

"Lynn, why didn't you answer my calls? I wanted to talk to you. Can you come in?"

"Max, I can't. Believe me, I've tried to forget about what you did, but I can't. I thought you were my woman, and I have to find out through a porno that I'm not the only one you've been fucking."

"It wasn't like that. I swear to you I didn't fuck anybody else. If you just come inside and let me explain—"

But he wouldn't step over the threshold. He set my boxes inside the door and walked back to his tractor.

"Lynn, it wasn't like what you're thinking. It was just—"

But he'd gotten into the cab of his tractor and pulled off, so I was talking to myself when I said, "—that I needed a different kind of summer break."

And so I went into class that morning with eyes red from crying. Instead of reading from an essay, I began talking.

"This was the first summer I did something different, out of the norm. I spent the summer in Charlotte, North Carolina, helping my mother care for my grandfather. And while I was down there, I was exposed to another side of life. I'd had a preconceived notion that the South hadn't grown like the rest of the world, but I was wrong. So I took a risk and tried a different way of living. . . ."

When I finished, I was sure they thought I'd been shucking corn or picking cotton. But I'd gotten through it, and I was glad to be back in the classroom.

Week Two

It was still hot by the middle of September, and school was in full swing. I'd decided to see Mason, and for the first time he invited me to his house.

When I arrived on Sunday evening, I found his house to be quite simple, simpler than I expected. He had a raw bar set up with shaved ice that held every type of oyster I'd ever eaten and some I hadn't. There were lemons to drizzle over shrimp, crab, and lobster and even sushi, which I wasn't too fond of. We sat eating on his deck and drinking a pitcher of gin and tonic. It was so different from our usual sexual escapades that I began to open up to him. I told him about my family and how I'd begun dancing in Charlotte. Then just when I was about to tell him what I really did for a living, he'd had enough of my talking. He wanted me, and I was so accustomed to him having me that I couldn't resist. Our bodies were drawn to each other.

When I got up to leave in the middle of the night, I looked around the room. The sheets were on the floor, as were my clothes and his. My red lingerie lay in the doorway where he'd finished undressing me. Glasses we'd been drinking from and a wad of money lay on his nightstand. It was everything that represented us. After I was showered and dressed, I headed down the stairs. But he stopped me before I made it out the door.

"Why do you always sneak out like you're some whore?"

"Mason, I have to get home. I have to go to work in the morning."

"I thought you worked here, for me. Isn't that what you always tell me, that I'm a client?"

"I can't believe you said that."

"You're the one who always says it's business, yet you tell me you're not a prostitute. Every time I try to get close to you, you shut down. So here, if you want money, take it," he said, and then threw a handful of money at me that scattered all over the stairs.

"Mason, please don't do this. You and I both know that I don't want your money. But you don't know me. All you know is that I'm some stripper that you've been fucking."

He briskly walked toward me and pulled me into his arms. "Max, I love you, and I'll give you whatever you want. I just don't want to lose you. I don't care what you do when you're not with me. I'm not going anywhere."

"Mason, it's not that easy."

"Max, did you hear me? I love you. And you already know I love fucking you. You can't tell me you don't love it, too. I see it in your eyes when you're coming. No man has ever made you feel like that, and I know it."

I spent the night with Mason, and in the morning I wound up going to work in the clothes I'd worn Sunday. I'd promised him that I'd give our relationship a try and invited him to my house for dinner. He told me that he had a housewarming gift being delivered to my home, so I told him where I kept the spare key.

I knew it was going to be a long day, because in addition to classes, I had open-house night with the parents. Kareema asked if she could stay and help me prepare, and I was actually glad to have her assistance. She was very mature for sixteen, and I enjoyed talking with her. She even got personal and asked me if I had a boyfriend. When I told her yes, she was disappointed because she said her uncle was coming to the open house, and she wanted me to meet him because he was single and she'd told him so much about me.

After school ended that afternoon, I was beat. I tried to reach Mason, but his secretary said he was at an offsite meeting. Around six o'clock I headed to the auditorium to meet with the parents. We'd laid out refreshments and put a school information packet on each chair. These nights went on forever because the parents never seemed to want to go home. I was also anxious to get home to see what Mason's gift had been, and I was hoping he'd be there with it. But once again it was time for me to take the stage.

I walked to the podium to introduce myself and smiled at Kareema, who was sitting in back by herself. I assumed her uncle had been unable to attend. As I told the parents my goals for the semester, I felt a familiar gaze staring at me, cutting through the crowd. I searched the room, saw Kareema, and then saw *him*. Mason was her uncle. When our eyes met, there was no wanting or lusting; last night and this morning was all forgotten. Mason grabbed Kareema's hand and walked out.

I uttered a few more words and nervously returned to my seat. I had to sit through three more teachers' speeches. When it was finished, rather than walk off the stage to greet parents, I left the auditorium in search of Mason and Kareema. I had no idea what I'd say, but I needed to explain. I went out to the parking lot, but I didn't see his car anywhere. I returned to my room, got my purse, and repeatedly called his cell phone. But he wouldn't answer.

In the middle of the night, I heard him banging on my door. Without asking who it was, I opened the door to his drunken rage.

"I just came to tell you that I'm reporting you to the school board."

"Mason, come in so I can at least explain."

He stumbled in the door, almost knocking me over. I closed the door behind him.

"So what are you, Max, the opening act for the school play?"

"Mason, I don't deserve that."

"You deserve whatever you get, or should I say, whatever I pay for."

"I see. I'm good enough to fuck but not good enough to teach school."

"You know, I can't believe I actually thought this relationship was going somewhere."

"And it's not? Why, because I'm more than just your private dancer? I'm sorry—your *bitch*. Isn't that what you always call me?"

"Let me tell you something. You're right, I thought I could help you get into something decent. You led me to believe you needed me, but the only thing you needed from me was a good fucking."

"Mason, you're drunk. Why don't we talk about this when you sober up?"

He looked around the house, swaying back and forth in one spot, then looked back at me. I didn't know if he wanted to hit me or fuck me, or maybe he wanted to do both.

"So when were you going to tell me that you were giving my niece lessons on how to take her clothes off?"

"If you weren't so busy getting me into bed last night, you would've heard what I was trying to tell you. But sex is all you ever want from me."

"You know what? Fuck you, Maxine Tate. You're nothing but a two-dollar ho, and by tomorrow you won't be teaching anybody shit."

Epilogue

Lynn

I'd planned to ask Max to marry me that night because I'd made up my mind that she was as perfect as they were gonna come. She had a stable job, and we both wanted the same things—financial security, a comfortable home, and children.

But that month in Charlotte had changed Max. Initially, I'd loved that change. She'd become sexy, more desirable than she'd ever been. But then I saw that tape. I wasn't really sure it was her, but when I rewound it, I could tell by every move she made that she was my woman, my Max.

I'd tried to forget about her, but I couldn't. I hated imagining her being with another man. But if she had, could I blame her? She never complained, but I knew I didn't always satisfy her. I tried. I tried to slow down and take my time with her, but she just got me too excited.

And anyway, who was I to talk? I hadn't always been faithful to her. There had been women on the road. Women I'd slept with, who sometimes went with me on my trips. And unbeknownst to Max, I'd been with a woman the night I saw that tape.

Maybe she too needed a change, some excitement. But why couldn't she be like other women—get a tattoo, take a trip? But not this, not selling herself for money. She'd begged me to believe that all she'd done was dance, and I had to admit she was good at it. So why wouldn't another man want her?

That was it. I'd made up my mind. If I made it home through this storm, I was taking her back.

Mason

Max loved to fuck, and I loved to fuck Max. She was a nasty girl with an innocent Goldie Hawn face that made me weak. Every time I saw her dance, I could see in each man's face that he wanted her. She had a way of making a man dig deep into his pockets just for the fantasy of having her brush her sweet ass against his dick.

She hadn't made it easy for me to get next to her. She always kept up a front. I was never sure if I was the only one that Max was fucking because it was obvious everybody wanted her. She took her job so seriously, and it was easy to see she enjoyed her profession.

In the beginning I wore a condom out of fear and good sense. It was probably the fear that fed my sex drive. I'd told myself repeatedly that I couldn't possibly love her. She was a stripper, a whore.

Then came my niece, telling me all about her teacher and how she'd be perfect for me. And she did sound perfect. I wanted to meet her because I needed somebody to pull me out of Max's grip. I needed someone to pull me back into the world where I belonged. But now for all intents and purposes Max was in that world. Hell, any man would want a woman like Max. Maybe she was perfect after all. A woman who could be both, a wife and a whore, every man's dream.

But I'd said some cruel things to her. Why the hell had I gone there so drunk? Even then she looked good to me. It was only with a little bit of sense that I didn't try to fuck her as soon as she opened the door. She was right, she was mine, my bitch, and I didn't care what she'd done. I was going to go to her and beg for her forgiveness.

Max

A storm was coming. The news had been predicting it for two days. I lay in bed, supposedly sick. That's what I'd told my principal. I didn't even care. They'd already planned to close the schools, but what did it matter? I probably wouldn't have a job soon anyway.

I had a pretty good stockpile of money, and I wasn't about to lose that. Even if I ended up being a salesperson at the local mall, I was sure I could still hold on to this empty house. The one thing I knew I could do was dance, but that too had lost its luster. Right now I didn't want anything but to be left alone.

I went into my gourmet kitchen and heated up the lasagna my mother had left. After picking at it, I went into my bathroom and ran a tub of water. I could hear the wind begin to kick up. It was 87 degrees, and I was grateful for the central air, especially in the bathroom. Lying in the tub wishing I could wash away the summer, I heard the rain start to fall, light at first, but within minutes it began to pour and thunder and lightning. I stepped out of the tub, went into my big bedroom, and the lights went out. Not just the lights but also the air conditioner, the clock radio, and the television. When I looked out on the street, it too was dark.

Great. I had no idea what to do with myself. I didn't know my way around the house well enough to go looking for anything, not that anything was there. So I said to hell with it and plopped down across the bed. I'd paid fifteen hundred dollars for my heavenly bed and had nobody to share it with. I couldn't cry again because I didn't have any more tears.

I believe it was the rain that put me to sleep. The wind beat against the trees, knocked things around on the street, caused the walls to shake. I heard something fall over. I'd forgotten to bring my chairs in off the porch. There was nothing I could do about it now but say a prayer. I picked up the phone; there was no dial tone.

The house alarm had gone off with the electricity, so quite naturally there wasn't a warning when my front door opened. My room was hot because I'd been too scared to open the windows, but he'd found me in the dark, in a bed he'd never slept in. Maybe he did love me after all. I didn't want to say anything, ask why he'd come, because if it was a dream, then I didn't want to wake up.

He never said a word, just started at my feet, kissed their soles, and worked his way up to my calves, my thighs, and buried his tongue in the beating pulse between my legs. I lay still, scared that if I said one thing, I'd scare him away. My skin, moist from the heat, burned for him. When his mouth reached the top of me, he turned me over and took in the back of me, from the nape of my neck to my spine. I refused to open my eyes because I knew he'd vanish.

He made love to me, slow and honest, not like I was his bitch, more like I was his woman, like he loved me. And afterward it was that spot on the left side of my clit that he searched for ever so gently with his tongue that brought tears from me. He felt the pain of my emotions and held me close to his chest. I loved him, and when I moved my lips to call out to Mason, the lights came on, and I found myself in the arms of Lynn.

Lynn

I assumed the storm had caused a blackout in her neighborhood. I knew that thunder and lightning frightened her, so I hoped she was okay. I wondered if she'd heard my noisy truck pull up, but I didn't see any sign of her except for her truck, which was parked close to the front door.

I'd called the school just yesterday, and they'd told me that she'd been out sick. I hoped she wasn't thinking about quitting because

I'd never really report her, even though I had to admit in my fit of anger the thought had crossed my mind. But I'm sure I was part of her sickness. Sick that I hadn't even taken the time to hear her out. Hear her side of the story. But now I didn't need to. I didn't even care about any of her indiscretions. I just didn't want to lose her.

I still had the key she'd given me, so I was able to let myself into the house. I could feel Max's loneliness in the empty house. I made my way upstairs to her bedroom.

There she was, sleeping naked, legs curled under her. I watched her turn on her back, trying to get comfortable in the hot room. I could've stood there and watched her all night, but the rigid hard-on that was growing between my legs wouldn't let me.

I crept to the foot of the bed, kneeled down, and that's where I started. At the soles of her feet I began to take back my Max.

Mason

Her neighborhood was dark, and so was the house. I hoped she was home. I thought to call her from the car before I rounded her street, but I'd decided to surprise her. I knew she thought that I thought she was beneath me, but she wasn't. Max was actually a better person than I was.

I attempted to pull into her driveway but found it partially blocked by a silver and red tractor-trailer. Maybe she had a brother or cousin who drove a truck. But then I realized she'd never talked too much about her family, so I wasn't sure if she even had siblings. But then it hit me, this probably wasn't family at all. Maybe Max really was a whore, a prostitute, and this was one of her customers in off the road.

I sat there, the car idling, trying to decide what to do. I held on to the cell phone. If I didn't go inside or didn't call, then I might never know who Max really was.

I looked up to her window, and there behind the sheer white curtains I saw her unmistakable silhouette. I hoped she didn't recognize me, but then I realized that my headlights were still on, so I shut them off but it was too late, she'd pulled back the curtain and saw me, pitying me. And that's when I knew that whoever was in there and whatever Max really wanted in life, it wasn't me.

Max

So Lynn had believed me, and he'd come to me in a way he never had before. He wouldn't let me talk or explain what had taken place during my summer break. And this time afterward I didn't mind when I heard him snoring.

As I lay there I could hear a car pulling up and then stopping. It seemed to be right in front of my house. I lay there waiting to see if it would move past, but it sat. Bright headlights shone on my darkened bedroom, and somehow I sensed it was him. I hoped he wasn't here to make trouble.

I crept out of bed so as not to disturb Lynn and went to the window. I hid myself behind the curtain and pulled it back just enough to confirm my suspicions. He was sitting there, staring up at my window, probably wondering what man I had in my house. I almost wanted to go to him and tell him that I forgave him for the things he'd said. But what would've been the point?

I stood there in the darkness watching him, and before I stepped out of view, he looked up and we made eye contact. That was my moment of truth. I looked at Lynn comfortably sleeping and looked back at Mason. And that's when I made my choice.

sex, sin & brooklyn

Crystal Lacey Winslow

Prologue

March 2004

My beauty was beguiling. So it's not a shock that I used it to get everything I ever wanted. If there was room for manipulation, I was the manipulator. If a situation called for seducing, I was the seducer. I had been raised to be unscrupulous, and I made no apologies.

When I was little, my mother once said I was so beautiful I'd break a lot of hearts. Actually, she *hoped* I'd break a lot of men's hearts—payback for all the years of grief she endured in her search for real love. For me that conversation solidified the importance of beauty and gave birth to my affinity for naughtiness.

Very early on, I was a disrespectful wild child who foolishly thought my mother was ugly. I despised her because she had a big head, large hands, and huge feet. I also considered her to be as black as tar. I would often taunt her, saying, "Your head is so big, like a St. Bernard's." That may have sounded mean coming from her daughter, but I was at a different place. Sadly, my mother would always say, "Shit! I know how I look. I keeps it real. I ain't no beauty queen."

My mother was always the first to admit she wasn't attractive. Now, when I look back, she hurt her own feelings so no one else could.

Needless to say, I grew up in a dysfunctional family. I used to listen to my grandmother say to my mother, "Chile, you sure are ugly. Why don'tcha get outta my face right now? You makin' my eyes hurt." Then she'd laugh, a hideous cackle, and say, "The only reason I fucked your ugly-ass father is 'cause I needed somethin' to eat. I was hungry—"

During our brief talks, my mother said she had a hunch that she would have a baby at a young age. She didn't want to put her child in the same position to be ridiculed for being ugly just as she was. In school she would often look at the black boys' and Spanish boys' features. Her conclusion was that the Spanish boys had softer hair and nicer complexions, so she decided to start having sex with the Spanish boys. She gave her virginity away to her first Spanish boy when she was fourteen years old. This boy wasn't her boyfriend, and she wasn't his girlfriend. They just fucked. Soon, all the neighborhood boys caught on that my mother was giving it up, and they all flocked around her. She told me all their attention made her feel loved. Her promiscuity made her the most popular girl in school.

Soon enough, my mother became pregnant with me. At the hospital, my mother said, my father never showed up, but she decided to name me Nicoli after him—his name was Nico. She knew he'd never give his last name to me, so she settled for his first.

To the surprise of no one, my grandmother doted on me from the first day I was born. She'd spend her last dollar on me, and at that time it suited my mother just fine. I had designer sneakers, shoes, and clothing. But eventually the baby my mother thought she'd love, she resented. So my grandmother took control of me and raised me, with my mother only occasionally intervening. I knew that my grandmother wasn't my mother, but I called her Momma and called my mother Gail.

When I turned fourteen my grandmother started taking me to nightclubs and local bars with her. My first drink was a Long Island iced tea. I had three drinks and handled it like a pro. My grandmother said people usually vomit on that drink, that only a "real bitch" could handle a Long Island iced tea. Even though I really didn't feel well, I didn't say anything to my grandmother. I didn't want her to be disappointed. Her praise filled my adolescent mind.

That year my grandmother died of sclerosis of the liver. I was confused and hurt, so I blamed my mother. I would lash out at her constantly, mimicking my grandmother and saying mean things—"Your head is as big as a five-pound bag of sugar. Get your ugly self outta my face!"

By the time I reached fifteen, I had my own crew to control—Joy, Stacy, and Fertashia. We all met up on our block and clicked. Fertashia and I lived next door to each other, but we all lived in the same building. At the time, we were like sisters. I was the leader of the crew and pushed my views on all of them. Soon, they were all following my flow, and we loved it.

I had been fifteen for less than a week when I lost my virginity. Ever since that moment, I've had this ferocious hunger to fuck. My hormones were continuously blazing. I was besieged with sexual fantasies, and at night I'd get so hot, I'd hump my pillow. When that didn't work, I'd stick my fingers down my panties and massage my clitoris. When that didn't satisfy my insatiable appetite, I had boy company. Soon my boyfriends were spending the whole night with me, which only made me even more popular. I foolishly thought I was grown and that these guys loved me for my inner beauty as well as my sex appeal. This went on for years, until I smartened up and realized men don't really want to know the *real* you. They like conversing with your representative. They like you pretending to be someone you're not. That way, they in return can pretend to be someone they're not. And at the end of the day, you two are merely strangers walking past each other in a crowded club.

Truthfully, if someone had had the balls to look me in my face and tell me how immature I was and how petty my antics were, I would have laughed in their face. Who am I kidding? I probably would have *spit* in their face. I was the quintessence of lust, gluttony, and vanity. And I made no apologies.

No one, least of all me, could have predicted that I'd completely change my views and values in life in just three short summer months. I went from a self-absorbed, money-hungry, promiscuous female to a young adult, channeling all her energy into being a positive role model.

Basically, I now feel like I have an old soul. I know that sounds corny, but they say you get wisdom by learning from your own mistakes. Knowledge is when you learn from other people's mistakes, and I've done enough dirt not to have to study someone else's. Often I am amazed at how I was able to transform myself from a bad person to a better person. I used to feel that when I entered a room, no other female existed but me. Now I see people—not through them. I take time out to listen objectively to my friends and then offer my support in all their endeavors. The things I once thought were minuscule are more important than I ever imagined—like talking with my mother and looking into her eyes and making a connection.

I used to exploit my body. Now I know that my body is a temple that needs to be nourished and cherished daily. I do this by abstaining from drugs, eating right, and surrounding myself with positive people and thoughts.

The summer of 2003 was a pivotal one for me. I realized that instead of progressing into a young adult who had responsibilities, goals, and aspirations, I was simply honing my skills as a whore. I didn't know it back then, but that summer fiasco taught me exactly what I needed to grow up.

Chapter 1

Summer 2003

I remember the first time Black and I fucked. It was the first day of the summer, 2003. My homegirl Joy had invited us to a BBQ out in the Hamptons where all the players were. The main attraction was the homeowner, Kevin. He had a clothing line called K-rockwear, and was the hottest record producer from coast to coast. He had had a short stint as a rapper, but when his music career flopped, he reinvented himself as an entrepreneur. I had already decided that I'd be willing to hook up with virtually anyone at this BBQ. But the challenge was Kevin.

We all decided to get dressed at my house, and Stacy brought the weed. She rolled a joint, puffed, then passed it around to everyone except me. I didn't smoke that shit. I didn't indulge in any drug that might eventually fuck with my looks. My beauty is all I got to get what I want. Why my homegirls like to indulge boggles the hell out of me. But that's them. I'm way over here when it comes to dumb shit going down.

"Joy," I said.

"Wassup, playa playaa?" she replied in her husky voice.

"You so stupid. Now, who's gonna be there?" I inquired.

"Kevin—Duffy—Jay . . . ummm, that nigga from the new flick *Hot Wire*," she said.

"Really?" Stacy exclaimed.

"Word. This is some exclusive shit. It's goin' down, ya heard," Joy continued.

"As soon as I fall up in that piece, I'm baggin' Kevin. You chicks can have any of the rest," I affirmed.

"The rest? Why settle for the rest when I can go for the best? It's fair game, Nicoli, and I'm goin' for Kevin," Joy challenged.

"Bitch, don't play wit me! I already said that I was gettin' wit that motherfucker, and here you go talkin' sideways," I exploded.

"Damn, Nicoli, calm down. He don't even know you," Stacy reasoned.

"But he's gonna *want* to know me," I retorted.

"I was just jokin', yo. You need to chill out sometimes. You always flippin' for no reason," Joy said.

They were always complaining that I had a temper because I didn't take no shit from these bitches. Joy and I had a combative relationship, but in the end she always folded. She wasn't a challenge.

"Now, I ain't one to listen to gossip, but I heard that Kevin's girl Mya is 'posed to be there. She's the half black and Asian girl in all his clothing ads. If she's there, what you gonna do, Nicoli?" Fertashia asked.

"I'ma do me. I'm a pretty bitch. No, I'm a pretty, *sexy* bitch, and I can get any man I want. If only for one night," I joked.

"Rumor is Kevin has a big dick," Stacy chimed in.

"Don't tell Fertashia that. Her sneaky ass might fuck him in the closet," Joy added.

"Then deny the whole incident," I replied dryly. Then we all burst out into laughter.

"Y'all some hatin'-ass bitches," Fertashia stated, then rolled her eyes.

"Fertashia, if you tried some sneaky shit like that, I'd whip your ass," I warned.

"Nicoli, you really need to lighten up when it comes down to these niggas. Don't nobody want Kevin," Fertashia assured me.

"Damn sure don't. In fact, I got my eyes on Duffy," Joy said.

"I can take him too," I countered.

Joy just stared at me harshly because she knew that was most likely true. I *never* lost a guy to Joy. But, truthfully, if I'm not there, Joy is runner-up over Stacy and Fertashia.

Joy has light skin, shoulder-length black hair with a Chinese-cut bang, big brown eyes, and a sexy mouth. Her greatest asset is her ass. Joy has a pear-shaped ass that could literally stop traffic, and she knows this. So her wardrobe consists of only form-fitting outfits. Tight jeans, tight shorts, tight capri pants, and cropped shirts so you can see her tight jeans, shorts, and capris.

Now Stacy is the opposite of us all. She is *really* skinny. Her body is grotesquely underweight. She has pale skin, a straight nose, ordinary brown eyes, and is taller than all of us. She stands around five foot eight, whereas we're all around five feet. Her hair is extremely thin because she's trying to keep up with J-Lo and Beyoncé with the blond highlights. But she has a cute face and fashion sense, or else she wouldn't have been down with my crew.

Last is Fertashia. Fertashia is sneaky as far as personality goes. She's the type that will go and fuck a guy, then come back and lie about it. I mean, we all girls. What's up with that? But nevertheless, Fertashia is a six out of ten beauty points. She's dark-skinned with hazel eyes. Her hair comes just underneath her ear, and she has it cut into layers. Her round face gives her a cherubic presence, but don't be fooled by the hype; Fertashia is no angel.

We all have a common thread; we were born and raised in the ghetto. So we roll together on a consistent basis. We like the same clothes, music, and men. Yet we're all different, if that makes any sense.

As the girls got dressed, I ran and jumped in the shower. I was always the last to get dressed. While in the shower, I washed my hair and left a little conditioner in it. My natural red hair curled up immediately. My mother was surprised when I came out with a caramel complexion, red hair, freckles, *and* blue eyes. How could a black girl and a Spanish boy create such a baby? It turned out that my father wasn't Spanish. His mother was white, and his father was black; thus, he came out looking Spanish. He'd later tell my mother that he'd deceived her just so he could get a piece. He said it was obvious that only the Spanish boys were able to hit it, so he pretended to be just that. He thought that his confession would make my mother angry. Instead, she reveled in the fact that she had a baby with a little white in her.

Today, I decided on wearing a pair of white vintage hip-huggers that enveloped my ass. I had a cute ass; it was round and sexy, not too large and not flat. Actually, if I may say so, it was perfect.

Then I put on a sexy halter top—also vintage. I mixed that with the latest strap Jimmy Choo heels and nylon handbag to match. I applied a pale pink MAC lip gloss and Christian Dior perfume, and I was ready. When I emerged from the bathroom, all eyes were on me.

"That's a good look," Fertashia commented.

"That's what's up," I said.

"Nicoli, you look fly, girl," Stacy remarked.

"Damn sure do," Joy cosigned.

As everyone bestowed compliments upon me, I strutted around the room, luxuriating in their praise, stopping only momentarily to assess what the others were wearing.

"Joy, I know you're not walking outside with those coochie-cuttin' shorts on," I scolded. Joy had on a wife-beater T-shirt, a pair of Jean Paul Gaultier shorts cut dangerously high with her butt cheeks slightly hanging out, a navel ring, and six-inch Prada sandals. She looked a little too sexy for my approval.

"What's wrong with my shorts?" she asked.

"They make you look cheap," I lied. "It's the wrong look for tonight."

Joy scrunched up her face in bewilderment. "What y'all think?" she asked Stacy and Fertashia.

"I think you look sexy," Stacy said.

"Me too," Fertashia chimed in.

"You chicks don't know shit. There's a difference between looking sexy and looking sluttish. We're going around an elite bunch of niggas. They not gonna wanna get wit her if they think *anybody* can get wit her," I said.

"You hatin' right now, Nicoli. I can feel that shit," Joy challenged.

"Yeah, okay," I said nonchalantly. I knew she'd never leave the house with those shorts on. She walked over to my mirror and stared at her reflection.

"Nicoli may be right," Stacy said. "Maybe they are a little too revealing for today."

"Yup, Joy. Now that I look at you closely, you look like a tramp," Fertashia joked.

"Fuck y'all," Joy said and started pulling off her shorts. "So what am I gonna wear now? Nicoli, I need to borrow something from your closet."

"No the fuck you don't," I said.

"You're a cheap bitch," Joy retorted.

Stacy came to her rescue and let her borrow a miniskirt. Soon we were all dressed and ready to go. I thought briefly about commenting on what Stacy and Fertashia were wearing, but then I remembered that they weren't keeping their clothes. Both of them had gone to Bloomingdale's and purchased outfits that they would be taking back tomorrow, even down to their shoes. They taped the bottom of their shoes so as to not scuff them up too much. I thought this was rather petty. I mean, they fuck just as much as Joy and me, so why don't they ever ask these guys for any money so they can keep the clothes?

I was wearing the latest Jimmy Choo sandals because I asked Corey, one of my beats, for the money. I call all the guys I date beats. I don't know why . . . just because. I asked Corey to give me $2,500 for college tuition. He wound up giving me $1,800. That was cool, because I'm not enrolling in college anyway, and I was really only looking to get $1,000 from him. I learned a long time ago that you always ask men for more money than you actually need. The rule is, they never give you what you ask for. Don't ask me why, but it's true. Maybe that's part of Murphy's law.

Chapter 2

We stepped out into the hot summer sun in style. On the block, kids were jumping double-dutch, playing touch football in the street and running behind ice-cream trucks. Meanwhile, the adults were riding motorcycles, getting their cars washed, and looking to get a number from a potential fuck. Yeah, it was summertime, and I loved it.

Joy had a really nice Honda Accord that one of her "beats" had purchased for her. It wasn't new, but it looked new. And, most importantly, it got us around. It was black with those Spreewell chrome rims that keep on spinning.

We piled in and put on the new 50 Cent CD and sang along to track number fourteen. *"Girl . . . you seem to love me now . . . if I were down . . . and out . . . would you still have love for me?"* That song was so hot, but the message was somewhat stupid. Why would a girl want a guy if he were down and out? But 50 was fine nevertheless. I made a promise to myself that the first time I saw him, we'd be fucking. And he better not try and front like he don't want this because when I walk in a room, I have men captivated. They get lost in my blue eyes and it's a wrap.

As we drove down the Long Island Expressway, I realized just how far the Hamptons were from Brooklyn and got annoyed. We all live in Bedford-Stuyvesant. The neighborhood is coming up now. It's alleged that the brownstones are being purchased by Jewish people, who in turn are pushing out all the black people. Don't get me wrong, neighborhood revitalization is a good thing, but why can't our own community ever bring something up and turn it good?

As we approached the Hamptons, everyone got excited. They started reapplying lip gloss and checking their hair in their mirrors. I remained cool, although, I must admit, I was a little eager to see who was there.

Joy pulled her Honda in front of an exquisite mansion. It had huge columns, manicured lawns, and a waterfall in the back. All our mouths fell open. The property was so large—it looked the same size as Brooklyn.

A valet attendant took our car and parked it for us. When he lingered around for a few seconds, Joy said, "What da fuck you lookin' at?"

I immediately interceded and pulled out a five-dollar bill and handed it to him. He graciously said, "Thank you," and left. That chick has no class. I just shook my head in disapproval.

"Oh, dip. I was buggin', yo," she retorted.

"Aren't you always," I replied.

The DJ was bumping Joe Budden while mixing it down with 50 Cent. I wondered if 50 would be here.

We were led to a motorized golf cart, where we all piled in and were driven by a chauffeur to the BBQ. We drove for what seemed like miles on this guy's property. Soon, a large crowd came into view. Everyone was dancing, eating, and mingling. We were all so happy. Not for any reason in particular, but you saw the excitement on each of our faces. The driver let us off, and of course, I had to give him the tip.

The aroma coming from the BBQ smelled delicious, but I didn't want to eat a thing. I had on all white and didn't want to risk getting something on my outfit and ruining my day. Plus, there were too many men out there to stop for a food break.

As the sun blazed across the sky, people played volleyball, tug-of-war, and tag. Everyone was laughing, flirting, and being friendly.

"Yo, this shit is off da hook," Fertashia said while grooving her body to the rap beat.

"Word. Let's go to the bar and get our drink on," I suggested.

We all sauntered over to the bar as if we were competing in a walking contest. Once there, everyone started to order Hennessy so they could get fucked up quickly. I suggested they order apple martinis instead to show we had class.

I had taken two sips when I noticed him. This guy came riding in on a golf cart real gangster style. I recognized him immediately because his face was always splashed across the *Post, Daily News,* and *Newsday,* with stories about his private life. Who's he fucking? How much money's he making? And, of course, who's he fucking? The press loved his private life. He was notorious for breaking starlets' hearts. He'd take them away from their stable relationship, use them up, and then discard them.

His cocky smile, which women loved to hate, turned me on. This guy wasn't just paid, he was rich. He owned a basketball team, restaurant chain, record label, upscale clothing line, and movie production company. He made the top-twenty list in *Forbes* last year and the year before that. I know this because I followed his life thoroughly. The press dubbed him "The Renaissance Man." This guy's name was Black King, and instantly I knew that I had to have him.

Once Black showed up, all the players came out of their respective hiding places. Kevin, the homeowner, finally came out of the house wearing a bathrobe and slippers, just like Hugh Hefner wears. He had a cigar and all. His fat stomach oozed out of his boxers, and several platinum and diamond chains adorned his neck. He looked a little funky in my opinion, but then again, I doubt he was asking my opinion. Instantly I was turned off from Kevin and redirected my efforts on getting with Black.

There were NBA players, rappers, record producers, movie stars—white and black. I mean, this was the place to be. I took a few more sips of my apple martini and observed. Girls were running up to the men, acting starstruck. Groupie-type bitches were leaving for a few minutes to go and get fucked in the bushes, in closets, the pool. You name it—it was being done.

My crew and I decided to converse, and I came up with a master plan to get someone famous to not only notice us, but want to call us the day after.

"You see these chicken heads?" Fertashia asked.

"Cluck-cluck. These silly chicks are actin' so stupid," Stacy commented, then said, "How old you think they are? Older than us, I bet."

We were all the same age. Twenty. Our birthdays spanned a few months. I'd be twenty-one first, so they all looked up to me. And I liked that.

"Okay, here's the deal. Y'all see how these chicks are runnin' up to these guys and introducin' themselves? That's not our game plan. We gonna play it cool and let these niggas come to us. We'll continue to get our drink on and dance seductively. Stay focused on each other. Laugh. Smile. Have a good time, as if we are enjoyin' each other's company so much we don't even notice that the lawn is littered with millionaires," I said.

"Fuck dat hard-to-get shit!" Joy exclaimed. "I'm goin' for mines."

"Shut up. You look just like the Garfield cartoon, with your protruding eyes. Don't she, y'all?" I said. Joy immediately looked down to the ground. It was easy to make Joy feel self-conscious about her eyes, which were unusually big and round. But truthfully they were pretty eyes. Unique. Although I'd never tell her.

"Fertashia, you wanna come wit me or stay here wit Nicoli?" Joy said, trying to divert the attention from her eyes.

"I'ma chill," Fertashia retorted.

"What about you, Stacy?"

"Well, Nicoli has a point about not chasing these men. I think it would be wiser to just stay put."

Joy always had to be difficult. She walked away, and I knew why. She wanted Kevin, which was fine with me. I already had my blue eyes set on Black.

Stacy and Fertashia stayed close to me and kept things according to plan. Soon enough, it worked. Black, Duffy, *and* Kevin came flocking over with Joy tagging behind.

Black made eye contact with me and never let his stare waver. He extended his hand and said, "You are gorgeous, sweetheart."

He licked his juicy pink lips, and my pussy started pulsating. His dark-chocolate skin was so smooth, I imagined him getting facials twice a week. He was groomed to perfection. He stood around six feet tall, with a sculptured body. He was the Adonis I'd been searching for all my young life. His pearly whites were inviting me to a sensual tongue-kissing session.

"Thank you," I said politely, but let it be known I was uninterested. Soon, everyone did salutations and so began the rhetoric. When I introduced myself and said my name was Nicoli, all the guys fell out.

"Nicoli—that's a pretty name, Shorty. What does it mean?" Kevin asked.

"It means beauty," I lied.

"Nice. Nice. I like that," Kevin said, shaking his head "Yes." Then said, "You got a man?"

"None of us got men. We're just chillin," Joy replied.

"Shorty, I'm not askin' 'bout your current status. I was askin' sexy over here," Kevin retorted, and our circle seemed to close in a little from Joy's embarrassment. But leave it to Joy. Nothing fazed her for too long, so she said, "A'iiight, player. I hear dat."

"To answer your question, I'm just datin' at the moment," I said to Kevin, but I was looking directly at Black. I think Black got pleasure from this.

"Can I date you, too?" Kevin asked, then continued, "I mean, I can certainly afford a girl like you. You know this my crib 'n shit. Out here in the Hamptons with these white mutherfuckers. I'm doin' it, Shorty. I am the American dream!" he declared.

"You can afford my wants, but you don't look like you can *meet* my needs," I said and walked away. My girls followed.

We left the guys over by the bar sipping Corona beers and walked deeper into the crowd. It was getting late, and I knew I'd better make my move. Black was irking my nerves a little with the distant eye contact. He'd better push up soon, or I'd have to opt for Kevin.

I drank my last apple martini and moved into action. I jumped onto the picnic table and started gyrating my body to "Summertime" by Beyoncé. Everyone in the crowd stopped what they were doing and stared. I was looking directly at Black and grinding my body as if I were fucking. I was going up and down on my heels in my most sexy movements. I thrust my hips forward while shaking my ass provocatively. The sultry music guided my motions as I opened my legs and squatted down to the ground. I came up slowly while moving my hips in a figure eight. I could see the fear in female eyes. They knew whoever they came with or wanted to leave with was wishing that they could leave with me.

Soon Duffy came up on the table with me. He moved in back of me and started grinding on my ass. His little dick was rock solid and poking me in my ass. I teased him for a moment, then jumped down. When I reached the grass, the guys let out a loud roar. They were clapping and screaming, "More . . . more . . . more!"

I blushed, went into "shy mode," and scurried quickly away, making sure I passed Black on my way out to nowhere. As I walked past, Black grabbed me by my arm.

"Where you rushing off to, sexy?"

"It's mad borin' up in here. I'm ready to locate my girls and go," I lied.

"Are you always this impatient?" he asked. I wondered briefly if he was talking about the party or my frustration with his actions.

"Depends on what I'm waitin' for."

"I was always told anything that's obtained easily isn't worth keeping."

"Who said that dumb shit?" I joked.

"My pops," he laughed and flashed those pearly whites again.

I looked quickly over his shoulder and could see a few groupie girls waiting for us to finish our conversation so they could get in, but I wasn't letting it go down like that. I also saw that Joy had finally gotten into a conversation with Kevin. Stacy and Fertashia were doing well themselves. They'd hooked up with a couple of rappers. My girls were doing it.

An early-evening wind blew, and my hair shifted. I took this opportunity to do my sexy Marilyn Monroe stance, licked my lips, then yawned to reflect boredom.

"Are you really that bored in here? If you don't want to stay, do you want to go into the city and have some fun? Maybe go to Mr. Chow's to get something to eat? Would you like that?"

"What about my girls? We all came together. I don't think I could just leave," I said, still playing hard to get.

"They're grown. They'll make it home all right. Come on, let's hang out and have some fun. Puh-leeze. I'm a good guy. You can trust me," he pleaded.

"Oh, I don't know," I said with reservation. "I may have to drive back home tonight."

"Oh no! You're not going to finagle your way out of this. I've been watching you all night, and I want to go somewhere so we can be alone to talk."

I hesitated a little, then said, "Okay. I will tell them I'm leavin'. *And* who I'm leavin' with. Just in case. . . ." I smiled.

He smiled back.

Chapter 3

Black drove the Long Island Expressway doing 100 mph in his midnight blue Bentley. I relaxed in his plush leather seats as the reality of my situation sank in. I was in a top-of-the-line Bentley with a multimillionaire, and it felt so-o-o-o-o good.

We pulled in back of Mr. Chow's shortly after ten o'clock. We were led through the celebrity entrance and seated behind a closed-off panel so the paparazzi couldn't get pictures of Black with his latest flame. I quickly glanced at the menu and noticed there were entrées ranging from $100 to $1,000. I allowed Black to order for me, which he enjoyed. I could tell he liked taking the initiative and being courteous because he also pulled out my chair and opened doors for me. He was really manly, and that was refreshing.

Before Black ordered dinner, he asked for a $1,500 bottle of Rémy Martin, and I thought about the latest Manolo Blahniks I could be purchasing with that money. Now, I'm accustomed to men ordering $300 bottles of champagne, and that's just about right. But spending anything more than that seemed a little excessive.

As the Rémy Martin started going to my head, I loosened up and started being coquettish with Black. I let my hands linger on top of his, while underneath the table my leg tussled with his.

"So, where you from?" he asked.

"I'm from Brooklyn," I said, real gangster-style.

"Where are you located in Brooklyn?"

"Bed-Stuy. Do or die. And you?"

"I'm from Harlem. Born and raised. I like to go back to my old neighborhood so I won't become complacent about my new wealth. The fakeness of the business I'm in can become daunting."

"Where do you live?" I inquired.

"Here and there. I have property almost everywhere in the world. I have a villa in Aruba, a flat in London, mansions on the East and West Coasts, an apartment in Midtown—the list goes on and on," he lamented.

"Real estate, that's what's up. A good investment. If I had paper, I'd purchase empty lots and build on them. Commercial, residential, that's what's really good."

Black tilted his head to one side, then asked, "How old are you?"

"Twenty," I said, then smiled.

Black nodded but didn't make a comment. So I said, "Oh, I get it. You're makin' sure I'm legal. Just in case somethin' goes down, you don't want to make the newspapers—"

Black burst out into laughter. "You can never be too sure."

"I hear that. And of course you'd make the front page of every newspaper wit the stupidest expression on your face. You have to have that dumb look on your face to be official. Talkin' 'bout 'I didn't know . . . she looked eighteen . . . God, please help me.' "

This time we both burst out into laughter. So I continued, "Then I'll come out like Laura from *Little House on the Prairie* with a maiden dress and pigtails and say, 'He hurt me. I can't take less than a hundred million. For my therapy, of course. 'Cause this isn't about money . . .' "

I put my hand over my forehead and pretended that I was going to faint. Black laughed even louder.

"You're crazy, Nicoli. You seem like a pro. Let me find out—"

"Let you find out what?"

"That you're into scheming for money."

"Who, me?" I innocently asked.

"No, seriously, what are you into?" he questioned.

"I don't have any hobbies."

"Do you work? Go to school? Both?"

"No."

"Well, did you at least graduate from high school?"

"I got my GED when I was sixteen. I'm no dummy," I said defensively.

"Baby-girl, you don't understand what I'm trying to express here. Why settle for a GED when you can have a master's degree? Do you have any aspirations in life?"

I took a moment to think, shrugged my shoulders, then said, "Not at the moment."

Black exhaled like he was disappointed in my response. Then something went awry. "If you want nothing—you get nothing. I must admit, your beauty has gotten you this far with me. Being who I am, I'm blessed with a plethora of beautiful women daily. But if you don't have a morsel of intelligence, baby-girl, I have no interest in you. I need to be stimulated *after* we fall out of bed."

I nearly choked on my drink. The Rémy had me loosening up with this guy, and I was now being perceived as dumb. I was mad as hell, but not at Black. Even though I hadn't finished high school and had no aspirations of going to college, I always had a high reading and math level.

This was all my fault. I had let my guard down with him because I had felt so comfortable. Correction—the Rémy had me feeling so comfortable. I usually give the whole "I'm going to college" spiel, but for some reason the alcohol made it easy for me to let my real character show. Big mistake.

"Well, if you think I'm dumb, what does that say about you?"

"Not much, I guess."

"What?" I asked incredulously.

"Basically, we've been here five short minutes, and I've already grown bored with you."

"Yo, fuck you. You know how many niggas would die to have

me sittin' up in their face lettin' them spend their money on me? I got on four-hundred-dollar shoes! You better recognize," I said and rolled my blue eyes. My voice had elevated to a high pitch. He just shook his head and said, "See, that's your first mistake. Don't *ever* call me a nigga. I have a name. Your second mistake is thinking your beauty could get you everything you want, or shall I say *need*."

This guy was on a fuckin' roll. Why didn't he just throw his drink in my face and call it a night? I was furious. I'd never been treated like this before.

"I guess you must be one of those college-educated, narcissistic brothers who get big kicks out of belittling people. Yeah, you're a self-made millionaire. I know your story. But you're a hypocrite just like everybody else," I said, expanding my vocabulary just to show him I could.

"Narcissistic . . . hypocrite? Those are some big words. If you could explain to me just how you came up with that analysis, I'd actually start taking you seriously."

"You say I use my beauty—well, you use your beauty as well. And then you cosign it with your money. Ordering a fifteen-hundred-dollar bottle of cognac for a girl you just met. You're showing off, flauntin' your wealth. And back at the BBQ, you were flashing that million-dollar smile of yours. And why do you work out at the gym? So that six-pack of yours can get you laid. Fuck you!" I yelled and pushed back in my chair, which crashed to the floor. I had no idea how I would be getting back to Brooklyn, but I was outta there.

Black stood up and grabbed my arm just as I was leaving. He pulled me in really close and whispered, "Could you?"

"What? Could I what?" I snapped.

"Fuck me? I'm only asking because you brought it up," he said and flashed that million-dollar smile. And yes, the pussy started pulsating. Damn him! Damn his good looks, bangin' body, and eight-figure bank account. . . .

Chapter 4

Black's penthouse apartment in Midtown had a private elevator entrance. Once inside, he pulled me in close and gave me a kiss. His lips were so soft, they felt like marshmallow. He teased me for a moment before his lips slightly parted and his tongue explored my mouth. He was the most experienced kisser I'd encountered. The kisses were passionate, as if we'd made love before.

In silence, we walked into Black's lavish apartment. It seemed bigger than Central Park. Oh, to live like a celebrity was grand. He led me into the living room, then walked to his stereo and put on Luther Vandross's greatest hits. Luther's silky voice resonated throughout the apartment. And much to my amazement Black walked about the house, lighting scented candles to help accentuate the mood.

When he walked back to me, it was as if he were walking in slow motion. His body glistened in the candlelit room as he pulled off his T-shirt. It fell to the ground.

I was ready to fuck right there in the living room, but Black picked me up over his shoulders. At first, I thought he was about to be traditional and carry me to his bedroom. But he didn't. He carried me to a sliding glass door that led outside to his terrace. It was huge—at least 2,000 square feet. He had a panoramic view of the whole city. He was truly on top of the world. The bright lights, dark sky, and tropical summer wind were so romantic, I quickly got lost in the mystique.

Black started to undress me on the terrace. He pulled my halter top over my head and stared at my ripe breasts for a moment. Then he leaned in and started to suck my nipples. I tilted my head back in pleasure, and my fingers ran through his soft hair. He fell to his knees and unbuttoned my pants. I stepped out of them instantly. I stood in front of him naked. I wasn't wearing any panties.

"You got red hair on your pussy, too?" he breathed, breaking my concentration only for a moment. When I didn't answer him, he playfully started to kiss in between my thighs. I moaned in ecstasy. Then he picked me up and brought me to his outside chaise lounge and gently put me down. There, he parted my legs and started to kiss around my pussy. My legs trembled in anticipation as he got more aggressive and began to lick, bite, and tease me with his tongue. But he didn't venture near my clitoris. So I gently guided his head back down toward my pussy, and he shook lose. Annoyed, I made one last attempt to push his head back down below. Then he said, "Stop. I don't do that."

Reluctantly, I stopped concentrating on what he didn't do and allowed myself to get swept away in what he *did* do. In a matter of moments, I was shivering from his touch. He stuck his index finger in my vagina, and warm juices seeped out. He dove right back to sucking on my nipples and dry-humping my body. I was now in a frenzy. I reached for his dick, and when I grabbed it, I thought I'd died and gone to dick heaven. His rock-solid penis was so large my hand was unable to wrap totally around it.

"Fuck me. Take me now . . . ," I pleaded.

"Not yet," he whispered. "You're not ready yet."

Then he commenced to tasting my whole body. No place was left untouched by his tongue. Slowly, he inserted each toe into his mouth and sucked until he heard me moan. Gradually, he moved to the inside of my thighs, nibbling until my body was shivering. He was so gentle and precise with his lovemaking. My body had become an inferno. I was literally drenched in sweat and he hadn't even entered me yet.

Finally he gently positioned his body upon mine and tried to enter me. My pussy resisted at first, and he tried to back out. I dug my nails deep in his back and wrapped my legs around his ass, pulling him back into me. I wasn't letting that dick go nowhere. Soon, after applying pressure, my stubborn walls caved in to his manhood, and he entered like a stallion. He moved in and out with a synchronized rhythm that came from years of experience.

Then he put me in the frogs position, so I was lying on my back with my heels raised to my ass. Black placed my knees underneath his armpits and gently entered me. As the sex got intense, he started fucking me harder. My pussy was so wet it started making melodic tunes. "Swish . . . swish . . . swish."

"It feel good?" Black crooned.

"Ummm . . . yes, Daddy. Fuck me."

We switched into numerous positions, each time trying to surpass the last. As the sun rose, so did his dick. Again. We'd made love for hours, from the terrace to the bedroom. Sometimes it was fast and frenzied, then we'd slow it down and make soft and sensual love. At times he brought me to tears as I climaxed, digging my nails deep into his muscular back.

At the dawn of morning we both fell into a peaceful sleep. I moved over to the opposite end of his king-size bed. I knew men didn't like cuddling after sex. But Black surprised me. His strong, pillarlike arm pulled me in close, and he kissed the side of my face, then quietly fell asleep.

I exhaled and smiled. I'd made it through the night with a celebrity without being sent home.

Chapter 5

Wanna go to breakfast?" Black asked. I was still asleep when he threw a pillow at my head. I yawned, stretched my body, then remembered where I was. I could feel it was early. I hardly ever got up before two o'clock in the afternoon.

I opened my eyes and focused on Black. He was fresh out the shower, body sparkling, with a monogrammed towel around his waist. I thought briefly about our lovemaking session last night and crimsoned.

"What time is it?" I responded.

"What difference does that make? Are you hungry? Or do you have to get home?"

"Naw, I'm cool. I don't have to get home, but I don't like gettin' up and puttin' back on the same shit. So, I think I better bounce."

"Women! Here, put on this," he said, tossing a brand-new Sean John sweat suit toward me. "I'm taking you shopping. Now, do you want to go to breakfast?"

Two seconds later, I was in the shower, grinning from ear to ear. He was taking me shopping! I was actually hinting for some dough, but I'd take an impromptu shopping spree any day.

I emerged from the shower feeling like a modern-day Cinderella. I put on the sweat suit, which was too big, but I put a little glamour to it. I rolled the waistline down a few times, so the pants hung below my belly, which showed off my belly ring. I took one of his

T-shirts and cut it around the neckline and waist, then I tied it on the side. I left the jacket on the bed and put on my heels. Actually, I looked rather cute. I pulled my hair back in a tight ponytail and put on my pale pink lip gloss. We headed out of his building hand in hand. I had to admit I didn't know where this relationship was going. Or if it was a relationship. All I knew was that it felt good.

Soon my girls were calling my cell phone like crazy. Each time I'd look at the number, but wouldn't answer. I was pretending they were calls that I couldn't take. I was testing Black. Soon, he fell for the bait.

"Who's that? Your man? Significant other, or boy-toy calling?" he asked. I didn't verbally respond. I just shook my head and rolled my eyes up in my head as if I was being stalked.

"Next time he call, pick up and tell that brother you're with me. Tell him who the fuck you're with," he angrily stated.

"It's not even like that," I said, then stuffed my mouth with my scrambled eggs.

Black and I were at Kato's. The prestigious restaurant was serving lunch, but Black had the chef prepare breakfast especially for us.

I decided I wanted to really get to know Black personally, so I asked, "So, Black, do you have a girlfriend?"

"I had a butter face."

"What?" I said.

"Yes. I was dating this girl, and everything was pretty but her face," he said and exploded in laughter.

I was deadpan silent.

"Bad joke."

"Indeed. But I'm glad to see you loosenin' up. Shit, the only things I like stiff are a dick and a drink."

"Are you always this honest?" he asked.

"Could you please answer my question first? Do you have a girlfriend? Someone to help you count your millions?"

"I have friends."

"Then what?"

"Then they want to live happily ever after, which isn't what I'm after. So I have no choice but to end the relationship."

"Oh," I said wondering when he would end our relationship.

"But I must admit you're the youngest person I've taken out in a long while."

"That's what's up," I cheered.

"I beg your pardon?"

"What had happened?"

"Look, I'm confused. Nothing happened. No action occurred, nor is anything up. Listen, Nicoli, either leave the slang back in Brooklyn, or we can end our friendship here and now. You seem like an intelligent young lady who gets kicks out of being facetious. I'm thirty-four years old and don't have the patience that I used to in my younger years. So if you don't want to turn me off, think before you speak," he lectured, and I almost got bored with him. He was being too uptight. But I said, "Not a problem."

And we continued our breakfast.

Next, we drove to Fifth Avenue, and just like Black promised, he took me shopping. We went from Prada to Chanel, Gucci, Christian Dior, and finally Bergdorf Goodman. Nothing was spared as he lavished his wealth on me.

Now, I was familiar with shopping in Prada, Chanel, Gucci, and Christian Dior. But I had never been inside Bergdorf Goodman. Black took me to the third floor, to a designer called John Galliano. I picked up a pair of hip-huggers, and they cost $3,000. My jaw dropped to the floor.

"You want those?" Black inquired.

I took a moment to regain my composure. I didn't want him to realize that I wasn't used to men spending such an obscene amount of money on me. So I said, "They cute. I actually just bought a similar pair last week."

"So, what does that mean?"

"Yeah . . . I guess . . . I mean yes, I want them. What do you think?"

"I think your sexy ass would look extremely attractive in those. But, truthfully, I'm really thinking about ripping them off of you," he said. He walked over to me, cupped my ass in his hands, and gave me a succulent kiss. I playfully bit his bottom lip, then sucked it. Within moments we were making out on the store room floor. His huge dick was pressing up against my pelvis, and for a brief moment, I wanted to leave this shopping shit behind and go fuck. I came to my senses, backed off slowly, and continued my shopping.

We left Midtown with numerous bags, and they were all for me. I was in an extremely jovial mood, so I decided to play a guessing game with Black, have a little fun.

"Black, you have three chances to name the movie that said, 'You don't understand, Momma . . . you don't understand. He's as big-time as you can get.' "

I was mimicking the actor in the movie. I continued, " 'I lived in Harlem all my life. I do know a *rat* when I see one.' "

Black smiled at my theatrics. He seemed tickled. He shrugged his shoulders and said, "Nicoli, I don't know."

"Guess," I pressured.

"Baby-girl, I said I don't know. Okay, *Lady Sings the Blues*."

I rolled my eyes. "*Sparkle*. How could you not know the answer?"

"It's such an innocuous phrase. I'm sorry I didn't commit it to memory."

"Well, that's my favorite movie. Maybe we could watch it some time," I hinted. I wondered if my brief time with Black would be ending soon. I had observed him looking at his watch quite a few times, so to avoid humiliation, I said, "Yo, I gotta break out. Git back to my crib . . . I mean, I should be going home soon. My mother may be worried."

"So, you just gonna take the bags and run?" he said, smiling.

"Well, I did have that in mind. Do you have a better plan?" I joked.

Black squeezed my hand and said, "You coming back with me."

For the next three days I treated Black like royalty. I'd get up every morning and cook breakfast. He fell in love with my French toast and fluffy scrambled eggs. Noticeably, Black started to loosen up. He tried really hard to crack jokes and make me laugh. One night Black brought home two large water guns. We filled them up with water and ran around his apartment completely naked, squirting each other. We laughed and giggled until our stomachs hurt. On the third day we both decided that he'd better get me home. I suggested he call me a cab, but he insisted on driving me himself. This time he drove in his Mercedes G-500 truck.

When we pulled up on Jefferson Avenue in Brooklyn with his speakers bumping Nelly's "It's Getting Hot in Herre," all heads turned. The music was so loud, I thought if he turned it up one decibel higher, my eardrums would burst. I got out the passenger's side, walked around to the driver's side, and leaned in and gave Black a succulent kiss good-bye.

"Stay put. I'll call you later," he promised.

"Okay," I sweetly replied.

Someone yelled from down the block, "Yo, Nicoli, who dat?"

Black and I ignored the question. I ran upstairs with my shopping bags to call my girls. We definitely had some juicy shit to discuss.

Chapter 6

I ran into my small bedroom and plopped on my bed. I looked around at my decor and was disgusted. The baby-pink paint on my walls and my pink carpeting seemed juvenile. I'd had the same twin-size canopy bed since I was ten years old. After Black's plush apartment, my own surroundings seemed dismal.

My girls came in.

"Omigod! What did you do to dat nigga?" Joy asked as she watched me pull my brand-new clothing out of my bags. Joy had on a blue velour J-Lo sweat suit and a pair of black Prada sneakers. Her hair was wrapped in bobby pins because she had just returned from getting a wash 'n set from the Dominican lady up the block. Her light skin was a shade darker than the last time I'd seen her.

"First off, he's not a nigga. His name is Black."

"I know his name. Did you fuck him, you slut?" Joy joked.

"Oh, did I," I lamented.

"Nicoli, could I try these on?" Fertashia asked. She and Stacy were stripping butt-naked and trying on my clothes before I could give a response. Stacy's bony body was quite embarrassing to look at, so I turned away. I couldn't figure out where she mustered the courage to prance around naked. You couldn't tell Stacy that she wasn't sexy. While she should have been wearing baggy clothing to hide the fact that she had a skeletal body, everything she owned was snug.

For some reason I felt different about *these* clothes. Usually, since we were girls, I'd let them try on my clothes and shoes. Just as long as they didn't ask to borrow them. But suddenly I felt a sharp pain in my stomach watching Fertashia and Stacy try on the new clothes that Black had just bought for me.

"Take my shit off," I exploded and the room became pin-drop silent. "You funky chicks are nice 'n nasty. Runnin' up in here tryin' on my new shit with your funky bodies. Coochies so funky I could smell it from here. I bet you too didn't even wash your ass today. Did you?" I screamed in all my ghetto fabulousness. Then I realized that that wasn't the person I wanted to be. So I said, "You can't see that I'm a fastidious woman?"

"Huh?" Stacy exclaimed.

"What da fuck is wrong wit you?" Fertashia asked.

"Just give me my garments," I retorted and started grabbing my things from off their bodies, barely allowing them to remove them themselves.

"Damn, they just clothes," Stacy sulked.

I ignored her and began putting my clothes on hangers. Just then the telephone rang. I nearly sprained my ankle trying to answer it.

"Hello," I seductively breathed into the telephone receiver.

"Where the fuck you been?" Corey said.

I had been dodging telephone calls the whole time I was with Black. Corey hadn't heard from me in days. Disappointed, I said, "I been sick. What's up?"

"What was wrong?"

"I had a stomach virus," I lied.

"Want me to come over and make you feel better?"

"I'm better. What's up for tonight?" I asked, realizing that even though Black had taken me shopping, he hadn't put any money in my hands. I hoped that I could get a few dollars from Corey tonight.

"I got some shit to take care of. I'll hit you back later. One."

We both hung up, and I continued to talk to my girls. I walked to my bed and flopped down. Something had been eating at me for days.

"You guys know I fucked Black, right?" I said.

"You told us that already. How's the dick?" Joy retorted.

"The dick is so-o-o-o-o good. We fucked all around his house. His apartment is bigger than Central Park."

"Git the fuck outta here. That's what's up. That nigga really feelin' you. Dat's my word," Joy said.

"Is he really?" I asked.

"Stop actin' stupid, Nicoli. The brother practically kidnapped you. And he took you shoppin'. He don't even know you. That's what's really good," Fertashia said.

"Well, I have to tell you girls something. But you gotta, I mean, you have to, take it to the grave."

Everyone crossed their hearts. We did this to signify that we could keep a secret. Once I felt certain that I could confide in them, I flat-out said, "He didn't eat my pussy."

"What?" Everyone screamed in unison.

I could see they were disappointed. I was the only one in the room, up until now, who had gotten my pussy eaten by every guy I ever fucked. That meant a lot to me. It signified that a guy was really feeling you. It was my rule. I would ridicule my girls if they came back home after fucking and had not gotten their clit licked. Now, my constant badgering had come back to bite me in my ass. And Joy let me have it the most.

"I thought you said, 'Nicoli, don't fuck no nigga unless he go down'?" Joy was loving this moment.

"It just happened."

"No, Nicoli. It didn't happen. Isn't that what you just said?"

"Stop being fucking facetious. You know what I mean. The first time we fucked, it happened too quickly. Plus I was drunk."

"What about every time after that?" Joy wouldn't let up, so I decided to let her have her moment and throw in the towel. No use in making excuses.

"You're right. He never ate my pussy, no matter how many times or ways we fucked. He wouldn't do it. In fact, he said he didn't eat pussy at all."

"Well, then, Nicoli, I wouldn't feel bad. Maybe he don't go down. You know not all guys do," Stacy said, coming to my defense.

"Of course all guys eat pussy, Stacy. They may not eat *every* bitch pussy. But if they feelin' you, they gonna go there," Joy challenged.

"I believe that too, Joy," I said. "So what do you girls think? Is it over between Black and me?"

"Oh, well. At least you got some fly shit outta da deal," Stacy said.

"Yeah. You right. Even if he doesn't call again, I did get something out of him," I said.

"Did you suck his dick?" Joy continued.

"No."

"Stop fuckin' lyin'. He just bought you all of that shit, and you didn't go down on him?"

"When did I start lying to my girls? I said 'No!' He didn't bless me—so I didn't bless him."

I could tell they didn't believe me.

After we sat around talking for a while, we all decided to go to DJ Red's new sports bar, Passion. It had just opened, and we had to be there. We made plans to hook up with the music industry's elite. I was hoping I'd get a shot at Red. I could care less that it was alleged that he was dating singer Brianna. Until wedding vows are exchanged, that brother has a For Sale sign taped to his dick.

My infatuation with Black had faded for the moment as the anticipation of some new prospects filled my heart.

After I finished discussing Black, Joy had her dirt to dish. She explained that she had spent the night with a new kid named Jason.

"I asked him for a thousand dollars, and he gave it to me."

"Word?"

"Word. He just reached in his pocket and tossed me a wad of cash. It was exactly what I needed for my car insurance. If I don't pay, the insurance company is going to drop me."

"That's why I'm glad I don't have a ride. Too much responsibility," I stated.

"True," Stacy agreed.

Since we were going out, everyone had to find something to wear. Fertashia ran next door, and Stacy went with her. While Joy was in my shower I thought about the money she'd gotten from Jason. I quickly went to her Gucci pocketbook and went in her wallet. I opened it, and just as Joy said, she had $1,000 in it. I quickly peeled off $700 and left her with the rest. It would take her until the next day to figure out her money was missing, and by then she wouldn't be able to blame anyone.

As I started to close her wallet and put it back in her pocketbook, Fertashia and Stacy came walking back into my room with their outfits draping over their arms, and Joy emerged from the shower. Quickly, I tossed Joy's wallet back into her pocketbook and jumped up. Joy and I locked eyes, then she looked over to her pocketbook. I walked into the bathroom with her money tightly hidden in my fist. I swiftly closed the bathroom door and hid the money underneath my sink in my tampon box. I could hear Joy flipping out. She started banging on the bathroom door, asking me to come out.

"I'm all wet. I'll be out soon," I said.

"Hurry up!" Joy demanded.

When I came out, Joy was furious.

"One of y'all mutherfuckers took my money!" she exploded.

"It wasn't me," we all said in unison.

"Well, it didn't just git up and walk away!" she challenged. She was staring directly at me.

"Well, I don't got to steal from no one. I don't have a problem with asking my men for money. You better check Fertashia and Stacy."

"What!" they both screamed.

"Y'all heard me. Why the fuck you guys left out so quickly? Y'all probably went to hide her money," I accused.

"Joy, I didn't steal your money. I swear on my mother, may she drop dead," Stacy said.

"I didn't take it either," Fertashia said.

"Well, you know I didn't take it," I said.

Joy stared at me. Then tears filled her eyes. You could tell she was trying to hold them in.

"I needed that money for my car," she cried.

"Stop crying. Just ask him again," I said. Joy just glared at me. I shrugged it off and proceeded to get dressed. We had a party to go to.

Chapter 7

It didn't take Joy long to regroup. We were all still getting dressed when my air conditioner broke. "Goddamn it!" I yelled. "G-a-i-l-l-l-l-l-l-l."

My mother came running into my room with her nightgown on and hair curlers in her hair. The hair curlers made her already large head look alien in size. She must have recently taken a shower because her dark skin was drenched in baby oil, giving her skin the look of patent leather. She looked a hot mess.

"What's da matter?"

"My AC is broken. It just stopped working."

"So, wha'cha want me ta do?" she spat. "I hope you got a coupla dollars in ya pocket. Rent due. I don't live in here by myself."

"Does it ever stop?" I asked. "All you do is beg for money. Day in, day out. I didn't get any money from dude. But he took me shopping. You wanna see my shit?"

"Nah, I don't wanna see ya shit. I'm walkin' 'round here in rags, and I bet you didn't bring me nothin'. What you got for me in those bags?" she asked with a slight hint of hope in her voice.

"Now, Gail . . . ," I said, and didn't finish my sentence because I didn't have to. Gail knew it wasn't that type of party. Everyone up in this house is fending for themselves. Gail was right about me owing rent money. I should have asked Black for some money before I left.

"Okay. Forgit you. And you ain't gettin' my AC."

"Whatever!" I snapped.

A few minutes later my mother returned, lugging her heavy air conditioner. We didn't even stay to feel the cool air. We were already heading out the front door to go to the party. It was opening night of the sports bar, and everybody plus their mothers was going to be there.

Once we reached the party, the line was at least two blocks long. Girls were begging to get in, trying to hook up with anybody that had VIP status that would let them tag along. The police had closed off the block. They weren't letting any cars drive down the street. It was a chaotic scene that got my adrenaline flowing. Security was so tight, no one was sneaking past them. I saw a has-been rapper that I had fucked a few times when I was younger and immediately ran over to him to see what was up. As he saw me approaching, he be-bopped over to me. His pimp-limp was pathetic.

"What's up?" I inquired.

"Whaddup, sexy? You lookin' right t'night. Let me git your new digits." he asked.

"No doubt," I said and began getting out a pen and paper to give him my cell phone number.

"That's what's up."

"What is?" I challenged.

"What had happened?" he asked in bewilderment.

"Nothing happened. No action occurred," I scolded. Just as Black would have scolded me. "Anyway, never mind. You rolling up in there?"

"I'm beepin' my mans 'n them right now so he can come out and get me. Too many mutherfuckers are out here t'night. Security ain't lettin' nobody up in dat piece."

"Who ya man?" I inquired, immediately falling back into my slang dialogue.

"Red."

I looked him up and down for a long moment. His clothing was worn. His sneakers were dirty, and he looked downright broke. He wasn't getting up in that piece tonight, and I seriously doubted he even knew Red. I left him standing alone and walked back to my girls. I decided to alter our plans.

"Look, we not gettin' in. We been here for two hours, and security is actin' real cocky. Let's break out while we can still get into a club," I reasoned.

"You right. Where we goin', though? I really wanted to get up in there," Fertashia sulked.

"You and me both," Joy commented.

We decided to go to the club Exit in Midtown. When we got there, we cut the long line and got right up front. Right before we were to go inside, Fertashia whispered, "Nicoli, I don't have any money. Can you pay my way in?"

"Hell, no!" I retorted.

"What did you ask her, Fertashia?" Stacy said.

"I don't have any money, and I wanted Nicoli to pay my way in," Fertashia explained.

"Why you can't pay her way in, Nicoli? I paid her way in last time," Joy challenged.

"Look, I said no. I don't have to explain. Why can't you pay her way, Joy? You still got three hundred dollars left, and that's more than what I have in my wallet."

"How do you know what I have left? I never told you," she challenged, trying to trip me up. But I'm too swift.

"Joy, the first thing you said was how much was stolen from you."

"Really?" she said trying to recollect our earlier incident.

"Yes, really."

"Well, somebody's got to pay my way in," Fertashia pleaded.

"We can't let her stand out in the cold," Stacy reasoned.

"Too bad. She knew she didn't have any money. I work hard for my shit."

"So what she gonna do?" Stacy continued.

"Take the train back home," I said.

"This late?" Joy said.

"Look, y'all bitches are all grown. I'll see what I can do. If I can get us in free, then we all roll. If not, the A train is making all local stops."

"That's cruel, Nicoli. Real fucking cruel," Stacy said.

"Shut up, Lurch. You look just like Lurch from the Addams Family," I teased and we all started to laugh. Even Stacy.

At the booth to pay, I started flirting with security and got us in free. That felt good. I knew we were going to have fun. In fact, I was dead set on having a good time.

As the DJ played cuts from Sean Paul's *Dutty Rock* album, I flew on the dance floor and started my show. Guys were fighting to dance with me. I would playfully grind up against one and then leave him to go and grind up against another. Soon, a familiar voice came up behind me. "Nicoli, why the fuck don't you return my phone calls?"

I immediately spun around to face Kevin. His overweight ass was dressed in a gray sweat suit, platinum jewelry, and the new S. Carter sneakers. He was chillin'.

"Hey, you," I flirted.

"What you drinkin' on?"

"Cristal," I said without hesitation.

We walked over to the bar and Kevin ordered five bottles of Cristal and had them sent over to VIP. I grabbed my girls, and we went with Kevin into the VIP section. We were with the one guy in the club that every girl in there wanted.

Joy was a little tight for a moment. She saw how Kevin was doting over me, but she sat back and let it flow.

Kevin snuggled up next to me. He was whispering in my ear and flirting. "You are so pretty," he crooned. "I love your hair like that. It shows your whole face. If a girl can't look pretty in a ponytail, she ain't pretty. Do you agree?"

"Yeah, not too many bitches can pull this off," I arrogantly replied.

I had my hair pulled up in a tight bun, with a pair of diamond earrings adorning my earlobes. I had actually bought the earrings myself from Gabriel the jeweler. They cost me $6,000.

"So, what's up for tonight?" Kevin asked.

"What's up? After the club? What else could be up?" I asked incredulously.

I knew what he wanted, but I wanted to make him beg for it. I thought about whether I'd go home with him after the club and decided I would. The champagne had me feeling nice, and the club was popping.

"I was thinkin' that we could go and hang out at my crib."

"My girls and me?" I teased.

"Nah, Ma. Just you."

As we were conversing, the VIP section started getting crowded. Guys were coming up to Kevin and giving him handshakes. Girls were coming by and kissing him on his cheek. All the while he never lost focus on me and our conversation.

Stacy, Fertashia, and Joy were drinking Cristal like it was water and plotting on the array of celebrities. Occasionally, Joy and I would make eye contact. She'd nod her head or wink her eye to reassure me that she was okay with me getting with Kevin that night.

I smiled at Joy and took another sip of my champagne.

Just as I was about to solidify my late-night date with Kevin, I heard someone yell, "Nicoli, what the fuck you doing up in here?"

Startled from the outburst, I swung my head around like in the movie *The Exorcist*, to face Black. I didn't respond.

"Yo, whaddup?" Kevin said to Black. Black ignored Kevin and kept glaring at me.

"What are you doing here?" Black asked again, this time a little more politely.

"What does it look like?" I sassily replied.

"It looks like I'm about to punch you in your smart mouth!" Black roared.

I sat unaffected.

Detecting an altercation, the small crowd began to grow larger. Onlookers stopped mingling to see what would transpire next. My girls scurried over to me with a look of pure terror plastered on their faces. However, I was as calm as a river at dawn.

Kevin and I stood up at the same time, but I confronted Black.

"Somethin' buggin' you, Black?" I asked, not completing my words just to infuriate him.

"Don't show off in here. Didn't I tell you to stay home, and I'd be calling you later?"

"I don't always do as I'm told. I'm a naughty girl. You should know that," I said and licked my lips seductively. We stared at each other for a long moment until the spectators became uncomfortable. I was completely amused that Black was checking for me this hard. So he's the type to leap with caution, I thought. I like that.

"Yo, Shorty, whatchu gonna do?" Kevin asked, challenging me to leave with him.

"She's leaving with her man," Black retorted. And this time I did as I was told. Black and I left the party. Together.

Chapter 8

What are you going to do to me?" I breathed. Black had just put a blindfold over my eyes. Suddenly I was in complete darkness.

Black took my hand and guided me through his apartment. I could tell that he was leading me out to his terrace because I felt the wind touch my face.

"Black, am I really your girl?" I whispered.

Black didn't say a word. Instead, his hands started to undress me. Layer by layer, my clothing fell to the floor. Once I was completely naked, Black laid me down on his chaise lounge. I breathed heavily with anticipation. Soon, I felt the slight touch of a feather lightly tracing my body, making sensuous circles around my areolas, then in between my thighs and around my belly button. Each stroke tickled me, and my body jerked involuntarily.

Black took my wrists one at a time and gently kissed them. Then I felt a cold metal object upon my skin and heard *click-clack* and knew he'd just handcuffed me to his wrought-iron fence.

The sweet taste of peach nectar slid across my lips, and I devoured the fruit juice hungrily as Black tantalized my taste buds. Next, he fed me ripe pineapple, and my mouth salivated as I bit down into the succulent fruit. When Black squeezed the juice of a sour lemon over my lips, I naughtily thought how his cum would taste in my mouth. Black kissed me with a juicy strawberry. I swallowed it, then explored the inside of his mouth with my tongue.

I heard the thunder as an unexpected storm broke out. Rain poured down hard as if to cleanse away our impurities. We continued to kiss passionately as the cold summer rain massaged our bodies. I felt like a wild beast making love in a tropical rain forest.

The blindfold prevented me from predicting Black's next movement, so it was quite a surprise when he parted my legs and beat my clit with his tongue like he was beating a drum. As he licked and sucked my clitoris, my body started shaking uncontrollably. Strong waves overcame my body, and I started screaming in pleasure. Within seconds, I climaxed.

Black continued to eat my pussy, which drove me absolutely out of my mind. He mounted me, and his hands gripped my hips. As he readied himself to enter me, I took a deep breath in preparation of what I was about to receive. My whole body was so hot, it felt like I had a high fever. Soon his huge dick entered my body, and as he rode me up and down, our bodies moved in sync. Like the hand of God his touch resurrected a passion that I didn't know existed. I laughed like a madwoman, then growled like a wild beast.

Black's silence was so damn sexy. He never uttered a word or moaned in the height of his pleasure. He kept it bottled up inside, as if he recycled his pleasure.

As Black took me to another climax, tears of pleasure escaped my eyes and streamed down my cheeks. Finally, we both exploded.

Black breathed heavy for long moments. Finally he took off my blindfold and handcuffs. Then he placed my hand on his huge dick. Much to my amazement, it was rock solid. This brother must be taking Viagra!

"Kiss it," Black had finally spoken.

I thought for a quick second, then said, "I don't know how. I've . . . never . . . did that before . . . ," I lied, perpetrating innocence.

"Are you serious?" he asked, and I could hear the yearning in his voice. He wanted to believe it was true.

"Uh-huh. Are you mad at me?" I whined, all baby-like.

Black pulled me in close, kissed my forehead, and said, "Why would I be mad? In fact, I'm glad, baby-girl. I knew you were different from the rest."

Stunned at Black's comment, I leaned over and kissed him on his lips because I didn't know what to say. Or if anything even needed to be said. The comment felt rather strange to me. How was I different from the rest? I'd fucked him on the first date. I think Black *wanted* me to be different from the rest. Yeah, that was it. No blow jobs for him. I closed my eyes and went to sleep.

Chapter 9

It was the beginning of July when Black came into our bedroom and said, "Get dressed. We're going car shopping."

"For me?" I asked hesitantly.

"Do you think I need another ride?"

I didn't answer. I jumped out of bed and ran into the bathroom to shower. Black and I had been together every day since the first day of summer. He just moved me in. No questions. No background checks. No checks for venereal diseases. Nothing. Just, "Get your shit and come on!" That's all he said. That's all I needed.

Black called out to me, "We're going to the Mercedes dealer. They have a superlative new line out."

"Thanks, Daddy," I jovially called back. I squealed and pinched myself. As I lathered my body, Black had to go and turn me off when he said, "And this fall you're registering for college." I was dead silent. Then I thought about being able to drive my new Benz to school and immediately perked up. Why not? I'd give it a shot. I'd always been good in school anyway. It shouldn't be too difficult.

Today, Black didn't feel like driving, so he had his driver take us to the Mercedes dealer on the Eastside in Midtown. As we drove up, I saw the cars on display in the showroom. My heart started palpitating. Who would have thought that Nicoli Jones from Bedford Stuyvesant in Brooklyn would be driving a Mercedes-Benz at twenty years of age?

Once inside, the salesman named John, who Black usually did his business with, came and greeted us. He was a young white guy with dark hair and eyes. I thought he was Italian because he reminded me of Robert De Niro, but he was Jewish.

"What type of Mercedes are you looking f—"

"The CL 600. Silver with midnight blue interior. Chrome rims, DVD player in the headrest, navigational system, and that alarm I heard they have that can locate my shit. Just in case someone steals it, I can get it right back," I replied. Shit! I knew what I wanted.

I looked at Black, and he had the stupidest expression on his face. He was tickled at my assertiveness.

Once I told them what I wanted, I called Joy.

"Joy, gurrrl, you ain't gonna never guess where I'm at?" Not giving her a chance to play the game, I continued, "I'm at the Mercedes-Benz dealer with Black. I'm getting the new CL 600. Bitches are gonna die!"

Joy and I chatted for a while before she called Fertashia on her three-way, who then called Stacy on her three-way line. Soon we were all chitchatting like old times. I hung up promising to come and get them just as soon as I got the keys to my new car.

While John started drawing up the paperwork, Black and I did a tour around the showroom. We walked over to the new Maybach to see what the rave was all about.

"You sure you don't want this one? This would look hot with you in it," Black said.

"Naw. I want the 600. Besides, any car would look hot with me in it," I joked.

"Get in," Black commanded, reaching for the front door.

"Let's get in the back."

Black and I got in the back, and as soon as our doors closed, I attacked him. I was so excited, I could have peed in my pants.

Instead, I decided to bless him in a way that I'd been holding out. I took my right hand and cupped his dick through his shorts. Instantly he rose to the occasion. Black pushed back in his seat because he thought I was about to ride him. I unzipped his shorts and pulled out his massive dick. When I started to lower my head, Black said, "I don't deserve this—"

"Word?" was the last thing I said before I opened my mouth and engulfed his dick. I licked and sucked his dick with a ferocious hunger. As my head moved up and down, Black made groans of pleasure. In the distance I could hear other patrons coming in and out of the dealership. I thought that at any moment we would get busted, and our photos would be splashed across every tabloid from here to London. This excited me.

When Black couldn't take the intensity anymore, his strong hands gripped my head as he climaxed. Hot juices filled my mouth as I continued to suck until I had him drained.

Slowly, I came up and kissed Black on the mouth to show him that I *had* swallowed it. I could tell he was in complete awe of my talent. His stupid grin was gratifying as he leaned in again, kissed my lips, and said, "I love you."

All I could do was return his grin. Did he mean that he truly *loved* me? Or did he just mean that he loved the blow job? Was love this easy? Because all we ever did was fuck. I scurried out the car and back over to the dealer.

That evening Black started laying down a few rules.

"Baby-girl, I'm glad you're going to enroll in college. That's a good thing."

"Uh-huh," I said and continued to polish my fingernails.

"Well, before you go, I'll have to take you shopping again. This time maybe you can get some casual clothes. A few blazers, jeans, nice dresses."

"Okay," I said and yawned. He was getting on my nerves. My cell phone rang, and it was Joy. Before I could answer it, Black asked, "Who's that?"

Ignoring his question, I picked up on the third ring. "Hello."

"Wassup, playa playaa?" she said.

"Just chillin'," I replied, but Joy couldn't hear me. We had a bad connection. So I started saying, "Can you hear me now? Can you hear me now?"

I was imitating the Verizon commercial. I hung up and started laughing. I tried to avoid eye contact with Black because I knew he was in a talking mood. But that didn't work. Black continued, "You might also want to change your cell phone number."

"Why would I want to do that? I've had this number for two years," I whined.

"That's precisely my point. I don't want some brother calling you at all hours of the night."

I raised my eyebrows. What was he talking about? My cell phone is shut off at night. But I didn't say a word.

"So, how do you feel about that?"

I shrugged my shoulders.

"Baby-girl, we need to communicate. Not expressing ourselves is a very precarious thing when in a relationship," he said.

Ignoring his last remark, I stood and went to take a shower. I needed to release some tension.

That night, I left Black to go hang out with my girlfriends. I needed some space. Black was becoming increasingly controlling. On one hand I loved it, because it meant he was falling for me. On the other hand, I wasn't used to men telling me what to do.

Chapter 10

My Michelin tires hugged the pavement as I took flight down the FDR Drive, doing nearly 90 miles per hour. I was listening to Kelis on a mix tape I had gotten from Joy. I was singing, *"My milkshake brings all the boys to the yard . . . damn right, it's better than yours."* That song was so hot! It made me feel good.

I made it to Brooklyn in no time. I pulled up on my old block and beeped my horn twice. That was my code. I knew my girls would be downstairs in seconds. It was a beautiful summer evening. The dark sky was clear, and I could make out the Little Dipper in the sky. As I was sitting there awaiting their arrival, my old "beat" from the block came up to my window. His name was Wayne. Even though it was over eighty degrees, Wayne had on a black long-sleeved shirt, black jeans, and Timberland boots.

"Yo, whaddup, Nicoli?"

"Nothing," I replied sourly. I wasn't angry, just portraying it.

"They said you down with some basketball player who got a lotta paper. Whaddup wit that?" he said and wiped his running nose on the back of his hand. He then tried to get inside my brand-new Mercedes to talk further.

"Get the fuck out my car with your dirty clothes!" I yelled.

"Fuck you, bitch!" he said and slammed my car door.

"Fuck ya momma!" I retorted.

"No, fuck you and your jughead mother!"

"Word," I said, amazed that he had the nerve to disrespect my mother. "You should be careful of the things you say. Maybe choose your battles. You have no idea *who* my man is. It would be a shame if your mother had to bury her only son," I warned.

Startled at my threat, he backed away. He didn't say anything else to me. He just stared at me strangely and then walked away, shaking his head. Rather than try and decipher his actions, I was glad to see him go.

Within seconds Joy, Stacy, and Fertashia came downstairs. Joy jumped in the front seat, while Stacy and Fertashia got in the back. Immediately, I smelled food coming from behind. My head spun around and focused on Fertashia. She was eating the remaining portion of a McDonald's Big Mac.

"I know you're not in my car eating."

"Huh?"

"If you can 'huh,' you can hear." I snapped. "Get out my car with that ghetto shit."

"Yo, you buggin'. What's ghetto about McDonald's?" Stacy interjected.

"First off, I'm not talking to you."

"Since when you somebody's momma? Speaking of mothers, when was the last time you saw yours?" Stacy snapped.

"Why you all up in her business? Today she came by to see us. She can see her mom next time," Joy said, coming to my defense.

"You ain't nothin' but a cheerleader now, Joy. All you do is cosign everythin' Nicoli do. You all on her shit."

"Bitch, please," Joy retorted.

"I'm not gonna be one more bitch!" Stacy challenged, then continued, "You and Nicoli are funny stylin'. Nicoli comin' back to da 'hood like her shit don't stink. Like she not from 'round the way. Talkin' in complete sentences now, sayin' words don't nobody know. 'Member, the people you shit on goin' up the ladder will be the same ones you'll need on your way back down."

"You still in here with that shit? I done told you to get the fuck out. Do you think I talk just to be talking?" I said to Fertashia, ignoring Stacy in her newfound philosophic wisdom.

"You serious?" Fertashia said in amazement. Her hazel eyes hooded over. I could tell she was confused.

"You're as dumb as the day is long. What the fuck did I just say? Did I stutter?" I yelled.

"But I don't wanna get out," Fertashia whined.

"Goddamn, you're an idiot," I said, shaking my head.

"Don't talk to her like that. Fertashia, don't let Nicoli speak to you like that," Stacy said.

I just sucked my teeth and rolled my eyes at her and Stacy. Reluctantly, Fertashia got out of my car. Stacy joined her and slammed the car door on her way out.

I had originally only planned to make Fertashia eat her burger outside my car. But when Stacy slammed the door on my shit, I stepped on the gas and left those two silly bitches in the 'hood.

Joy and I laughed for maybe thirty minutes. We just couldn't stop laughing at the looks on their faces.

"They are so dumb," Joy commented.

"What was so hard about not eating in my shit? This car cost more than a house."

"I know," Joy agreed.

After driving aimlessly for hours, we concluded we didn't have anything to do. My cell phone rang, and the number was blocked. I hesitated briefly on whether I should answer it.

"Hello."

"Hey, sexy," Corey said.

"Whaddup, player."

"Ain't nothing. I miss you. Come meet me, and I'll take you out to dinner."

"I'm with Joy," I replied.

"That's cool. She can come too. Hurry up and meet me at Chin-Chin on Third avenue."

"I'll be there in twenty minutes."

"Cool."

I hung up and sped from Brooklyn into Manhattan. Joy and I arrived on time, but Corey wasn't there. We waited for another thirty minutes before I called his cell phone. For a while he didn't answer. Then he picked up.

"What's up?" he replied.

"What the fuck you mean, 'What's up?'? Aren't you 'posed to be meeting me here?"

"Chill out. I'll be there shortly."

"So I'm supposed to hurry up and wait?"

"Nah, sexy. I got caught up handling some business. I'm on my way," he soothed.

"Click." I hung up the phone. He'd gotten on my last nerve. Wait? Nicoli Jones don't *wait* on no motherfuckin' body.

"Now what?" Joy asked.

"I have no idea. But I'm not ready to go home."

"Well, I met this girl named Kim the other day at a party, and she invited me to this get-together in SoHo tonight. She's cool. She dresses the mannequins for Lord & Taylor. She said she would hook me up with her discount. She could hook you up as well," Joy assured.

"You sure she'll hook me up? Did she say that?"

"Not exactly. But she did say she'll hook me up. If we go, we can ask her."

"Let's roll."

Chapter 11

An hour later we were in this fabulous apartment in Soho. The brick walls and parquet floors were divine.

The living room sofa, chair, and love seat had uppity-looking girls lounging on them. They were laughing, giggling, and almost screaming when someone said something amusing. This was a close-knit crowd. No one seemed to notice our arrival until I said, "My name is Nicoli, and this is Joy."

One girl said hello, but the rest just stared. So I challenged the crowd and said, "I know everybody heard me. I said my name is Nicoli." I put my hands on my hips and rolled my blue eyes.

"Well, happy fucking birthday," one smart-mouthed girl replied, and the crowd erupted in laughter. Before I could respond, the host started to introduce everyone. As she went around the room, a phony smile was plastered on everyone's face, including mine. We each said, "Nice to meet you."

Kim was extremely attractive. She had dark chocolate skin, high cheekbones, and jet-black hair. She seemed a bit older than us and was really nice.

"Kim, this is my friend Nicoli," Joy said, introducing us.

"It's a pleasure meeting you," she replied.

"Thank you. So Joy tells me that you have a hookup at Lord & Taylor."

"Well, it's not a *hookup*. I have an employee discount and told Joy that she is welcome to use it."

"I was hoping that my homegirl could use it, too," Joy said.

"Will you excuse me for a moment?" Kim said without responding to the question. She excused herself and rushed over to the sofa, where someone had spilled their drink.

"She's not gonna put me down," I sulked.

"Yes, she will. Watch," Joy soothed.

"I'm ready to leave. I only came for the discount," I said.

"Please, Nicoli, we can't leave yet. Besides, Gangster is gonna be comin'."

"Gangster who?" I asked.

"The rapper."

"Get out. You know how long I've wanted to meet him."

"I know. He should be comin' soon. That's Kim's cousin."

"That's hot. I'm not leavin' here without his number," I stated.

After being at the party for five minutes, I was bored. This was an all-girl affair. They started talking about how bad men were, how they were no-good bastards, and so on. I guess this was some sort of bonding get-together. The kind that I must remind Joy to never take me to.

"Come to find out that no-good motherfucker was fucking my best friend all along," someone said. I didn't catch her name, nor did I care to.

"Then you must not be doing something right in the bedroom," I said, and everyone gagged.

"How do you presume to know what goes down in my bedroom? How do his actions automatically become my fault? Why am I to blame?" the girl retorted.

"All I'm saying is that my man would never get down like that."

Everyone in the room erupted in laughter. Obviously they all belonged to the "My man is a dog" club. So I continued, "You ladies are acting immature. What the fuck is so funny?"

"No, darling, you're the one acting immature. How can you vouch for what a man will or won't do? Everyone knows to 'never say never.' Especially when it comes to a man," some chick stated.

"Let me reiterate for those who may be having difficulty understanding my point. My man will *never* fuck my best friend, associates, or any bitch. Not while we're together. In fact, my best friend is here with me now. Joy, please let them know how my situation is going down at the moment."

Joy stepped up to the plate.

"Nicoli is tellin' it like it is. Word up. First off, we don't fuck each other's men. That's a no-no. And her man is so into her right now, it's crazy, yo. He just copped her the new CL 600. Right after that he come home with a hundred-thousand-dollar Piaget watch. Last week he bought her the Presidential Rolex she's wearing now. And he cut off all his other bitches for her, and he hasn't even known her for sixty days, yo," she bragged.

The whole room stared at me in amazement. They were all jealous; I could tell such things. Women usually get jealous when materialistic things are involved in any relationship. But I saved the best news for last.

"My man, Black King, is loving me right now," I said, letting them feel my fame. I was dating a celebrity.

"Who's your man?" A petite, light-skinned sister with dyed red hair and sleepy eyes said.

"Black King, ya heard," I said, real gangster-style.

"Really? Interesting. I've been sleeping with Black for over a year now. He just bought me my Rolex as well."

The room was silent as she flashed the exact same Rolex watch I had on. Then everyone burst out in laughter. They were laughing so hard, tears were rolling down some of their faces, but through all this I heard nothing. All I did was concentrate on this bitch. I focused on her small frame and weight. I can whip her ass, I thought. How dare this ho try to play me in front of all these chicks? Briefly I wished I had time to tie up my hair and put Vaseline on my face. That's how we get down for combat in my 'hood. This was going to be an impromptu situation. We glared at each other, then, simultaneously, we both lunged at each other. Our hands locked in each other's hair, and we both began pulling and scratching at each other's faces. The crowd moved out the way to give us room to fight.

"Break it up," the homeowner said.

"No. Let them fight," someone yelled.

We were going for blood.

As we fell into the furniture, I could hear lamps crashing to the floor. Occasionally someone would try to intervene and break up the fight, but the agitated crowd would not allow it. They were watching us as intently as a man watches a Mike Tyson fight.

Though this girl was somewhat smaller than me, she was more skilled in fighting. I knew she had me beat. She was throwing accurate punches that kept catching me in my face and neck. I reached up through the headlock she had me in and dug my nails in her face. She flipped me over, and I came crashing down on the floor with a loud thud, but I managed to pull her with me. She quickly hopped up like a bunny rabbit, but before she could stomp me out, Joy jumped in. Joy whipped on her like she had stolen something. Within seconds Joy pulverized that girl. She was screaming, "Why you gotta jump? Why you gotta jump?"

"Shut the fuck up," Joy responded.

The way Joy beat that girl up, no one in the room wanted to break it up. They were too scared to touch Joy, afraid she might do them the same way.

"Fuck her up, Joy! Fuck her up!" I kept yelling. I wanted Joy to kill her, I was so mad. Finally, Joy saw the blood she was after. She punched the girl in her nose, and blood squirted everywhere. That was enough.

We left, or shall I say, were thrown out of the get-together. People were heckling us, calling us "ghetto."

The nerve of them.

As soon as I got to my Mercedes, I called Black.

"Yo, I just had a fight!"

"What did I tell you about speaking like that?"

"Oh, excuse me. I just had a fight."

"Why are you out in the street fighting and acting ghetto?" he scolded. There was that word again.

"She jumped on me," I lied.

"Who?"

"The girl you're fucking!" I exploded.

"What girl?" he calmly replied.

"I don't know her name."

"But you know that I'm fucking her? Nicoli, I got a lot of shit to do. Seventy-five percent of my day is committed to doing shit I don't want to do to make this money. I don't have time to sit here and listen to you act adolescent. I'm a grown man. And I thought that I was dealing with a lady. Not some hip-hop ghetto girl out in her 'hood fighting. I'm going to tell you this once. Anybody can fit in your shoes."

With that remark he hung up on me. I was devastated. What did it mean? I turned around to Joy, who was waiting intently for me to tell her what he'd said. Briefly, I thought about lying. But lying to my friends was not an option, so I started crying. I wanted to speak, but the words wouldn't come out.

"That shit was crazy. That stupid bitch is dumb, yo," Joy stated.

"Thanks for having my back, Joy. That little bitch was getting the best of me. I don't know how I let that happen."

"You think she was tellin' the truth about Black?"

"I don't know. I tried to ask him, but he just shut me down. He doesn't even care that I was just fighting over him."

"He cares. And he's scared right now. He thinks you gonna leave him, so he's tryin' to act all cool 'n shit."

"He said, 'Anybody can fit in your shoes.' What does that mean?" I said while tears continued to stream down my cheeks.

"I dunno. You shoulda said, 'A size six Manolo Blahnik? I don't think so.' "

Joy made me laugh, which felt good, considering I felt like shit. I was humiliated at having been beaten up. And I was devastated that Black was seeing this other woman. Plus he was buying her shit. The same shit that he bought me. What was that all about?

As if Joy had read my mind, she said, "Besides, he can buy a bitch a watch. That ain't shit compared to what he doin' for you. You the one livin' up in his crib. She not. You the one he's claimin' as his girl. She not. And you've accomplished all of that in three weeks. Puh-leeze. She's known him forever. I wouldn't even sweat that."

"You're right," I agreed. But inside I was fuming.

Then Joy said, "I'm so fuckin' mad, though. I was really waitin' around to speak to Kim about her hookin' me up with a job in Lord & Taylor."

"What?"

"Yeah, I've been thinkin' 'bout gettin' a job lately. Ever since my money mysteriously disappeared and I had to ask Jason to give it to me again, I started thinkin' that maybe I should get a job. So I don't have to keep dependin' on mutherfuckers. Only I don't have any experience, and I'm scared as hell to be interviewed, yo."

"Let me get this straight. We were there so you could beg for a job?"

"Well, not beg. But I'm tired of countin' niggas papah. I want my own shit."

"What about Gangster?"

"Don't be mad, but I just said that so you wouldn't break out."

As Joy finished her sentence, an uncontrollable rage came upon me, and I lashed out at her.

"You are the most pathetic person I've ever met. You have absolutely no pride. Here this girl was giving you an inch, and your ghetto ass wants a yard. What makes you think Lord & Taylor would hire someone like you? You can't even speak in complete sentences. Sometimes I'm embarrassed that I'm even friends with you!"

"Well, I—"

"Shut up! You're starting to irritate me."

"Yo, take me home," Joy said. I could tell that her feelings were hurt, but I didn't care. I was hurting, too. I was hurt about Black.

"Yo, take me home," I mimicked. I wanted to make her cry, but she didn't.

We sat in silence as I sped back into Brooklyn to drop Joy off. I don't know what was on her mind, but I was thinking about the confrontation I was going to have with Black. He'd never seen me lose my temper, and I was sure he wouldn't like me when I was angry.

Chapter 12

When I got home that night, Black wasn't there. It looked like he'd gone out as well. Wet towels were on the floor in the bathroom, and his clothes were thrown all over our bed. I stripped naked, went out on the terrace, and instantly fell asleep.

Shortly after one in the afternoon, I awoke. Black still wasn't home. I was furious. I called his cellular telephone, but it went straight into voice mail, which meant he had it off. Then I paged his two-way. Still no response.

As the sun set, I could hear Black's keys jiggling in the lock. Quickly, I shut off the television and lights. I was in the living room, and it was pitch black. When he clicked on the lights, I startled him.

"Hi, baby-girl. Have you eaten yet?" he casually asked.

"Motherfucker, are you stupid?" I exploded.

"What?" he asked incredulously.

"How dare you disrespect me like this?"

"First off, stop yelling in my home," he threatened.

"I'll yell all the fuck I want!" I challenged.

"Your behavior is a perfect example of why I don't date young girls like you. They can't express themselves without acting immature."

I stared at Black for a long moment. Then, nonchalantly, I said, "I don't think this is working out. I think I'll take my things and leave. Yeah, how 'bout that."

"You're leaving me?" Black laughed as if I had amused him.

"That's what I said," I called out to him. Then I let him watch as I casually strolled about his apartment, gathering my items.

When I'd grabbed my last item and was heading out his front door, Black intervened, "Baby-girl, I'm so sorry if I hurt you," he said and gently kissed me on my mouth. He continued, "Okay. Since you want to know, her name is Tracy. And I was sleeping with her off and on for a year. Even after we got together, I still continued to sleep with her."

"You don—"

"Last night, I went over her house in a rage. When you told me she put her hands on you, I lost it. You are too pretty to be out in these streets fighting. You're a lady. I told her don't she ever try and disrespect you again. She pleaded with me to stay, saying she wanted to make love. We slept together, but after that, I ended the relationship."

At this point, I really wasn't looking for an explanation. I wanted him to grovel. I was already over the whole scene. But I decided to play the wounded girlfriend, as I expect he wanted me to be.

"How could you do this to me?" I whispered, letting my voice crack in between words. Then I put my head down as if I were about to start sobbing.

Black wrapped his hands around my back and pulled me in close for a bear hug. He started rocking me back and forth, telling me how sorry he was and how he'd never cheat on me again. Then, just as I expected, he shifted the blame.

"It's just that I didn't know if you loved me or my money. You're out partying all the time. I hardly get to see you. When I want to touch you, you pull away . . ." He let his voice trail off.

I really was tickled with this whole scene. First off, when did I ever say that I loved Black? Second, all we ever do is fuck, and I've *never* pulled away. He must have me mixed up with the next chick.

You know, men do that sometimes. But I remained mute and didn't say a word. Truthfully, I rather respected his honesty. I mean, after your man comes home from staying out all night and tells you that he's been fucking, what else can you say?

"So promise me you're going to stop running the streets," Black demanded.

"Okay," I replied, less than enthusiastically.

"I'm serious, Nicoli. You out there running the street plays upon my quiet time."

"I understand. I'll slow down. I promise."

After Black finished talking just to entertain himself, he needed to get his fuck on again. He took my hand and led me into the bathroom and turned on the shower. We both got undressed and entered the steaming water.

The hot water cascaded down my back and massaged my shoulders and the nape of my neck. I let the water drench my hair and face as Black gently licked my earlobes. We started kissing passionately, as if we hadn't made love in years. Black sucked my nipples and neck, but that was the extent of our foreplay. Black sat down on the stool inside the shower, and I immediately mounted him. I rode Black aggressively as he moaned in pleasure. We were kissing, biting, and licking each other passionately.

"Yes, Daddy . . . fuck me . . . fuck me with your big dick," I moaned.

Black pulled out before either of us came. He stood me up and turned me around. Black then inserted his finger into my anus. I was curious—this was something else I wanted to try, but hadn't found a man brave enough to venture back there. As Black's fingers darted in and out, I encouraged him by moaning and sticking my ass out. I had my hands on the shower walls for support.

Black grabbed the lubricant, a bottle of which we had in every crevice of the house, and put it on my anus. Then, as gently as his big dick would allow, he entered me. The sensation was exquisite. I yelled out in pleasure mixed with pain. Our slippery bodies were one as he pumped in and out.

"You . . . like . . . this?" Black moaned. "You like this big dick?"

"Oh, yes . . . ," I breathed. "Fuck me harder!"

"Harder?" he asked as he increased his pace.

"Harder!" I commanded.

"Harder!" he said through clenched teeth as he mercilessly rammed his dick in my anus. His strong hands groped my breasts from behind as we both came in unison. It was the most exquisite feeling I'd experienced.

We both stood still for a long moment, then Black slowly removed his penis. He took the washcloth and gently tried to clean me off back there. A small amount of blood was there, and it stung a little. I took this opportunity to act like a baby. I said, "Ouch-ch-ch-ch, Daddy, it hurts . . . you're hurting me," then I pouted a little.

Black carried me to our bed and tucked me in. He kissed my cheek and snuggled in behind me.

"I love you," he said for the second time in our relationship. And for the second time, I said nothing.

Chapter 13

I decided to make up with Joy. She'd been mad at me since the night of the fight. I was long over the argument, and since things were going great in my life, I called her.

"Hey girl, do you want to go out tonight?"

"Not really," she said stubbornly.

"Okay. Fine," I said and began to hang up.

"Wait. Where did you have in mind?" she quickly said.

"Club Bue."

"That sounds cool. Come get me. I'll be ready."

Tonight I decided to look exotic. I wet my red hair and let it air-dry. My hair curled up into a curly Afro. I put on a pair of large hoop earring, red lip gloss, and blue eye shadow to accent my blue eyes. I grabbed a pair of vintage jeans, a pair of cowboy boots, and a tank top. On my wrist I put on several sterling silver bracelets, and I was ready.

When I arrived to pick up Joy, to my dismay we looked strangely similar. She had on a pair of vintage jeans, a tank top, and square-toed heels. She'd gotten her long hair set into Shirley Temple curls, and she had on a pair of the latest Chanel shades.

I contemplated on what I could say to make her go back upstairs and change her clothing, but nothing reasonable came to mind.

"Wassup, playa playaa?" she said, her husky voice sounding unusually high-pitched.

"Nada. I'm so ready to get my party on."

"You and me both."

We arrived at Club Bue shortly after one in the morning. It was packed outside as well as inside. In the nearby parking lot was a bevy of luxury cars; Mercedes, Lexus, Bentley, BMW, and Escalade. It took us thirty solid minutes to get in, but once we were inside, the place was bumping all the hottest songs. The DJ was mixing R. Kelly with Jay-Z, and I flew to the dance floor.

I was grinding my hips, spinning around, and going low to the ground when Joy came up to me with Leroy Paton. He was an NBA superstar, tall and lean with dark-brown skin and an Afro. His high cheekbones and thin lips were effeminate. The league signed him right out of high school, and he'd already gotten a $90 million endorsement deal from Nike. Joy had hit the jackpot meeting him—but I intended to leave with him.

"Nicoli, this is Leroy Paton. The NBA player," Joy said.

"Nice to meet you," I said and extended my hand.

"Likewise," he retorted.

As we all walked off the dance floor into a secluded area, we were joined by this six-foot-looking chic. I looked up. I mean, I really had to look up to see her. She ignored Joy and me and spoke to Leroy.

"I'm getting ready to leave," she announced. Briefly I wondered if she was his girlfriend, and thought how awkward she looked.

"Joy, Nicoli, this is Lisa, my sister," Leroy said as he introduced us.

"Call me Big L," she said, extending her hand. Joy and I shook it. She had a strong grip and almost squeezed the feelings out my delicate fingers. Big L had to be at least six foot five. She had her hair pulled back into a ponytail and wore a pair of oversized Karl Kani men's jean shorts and a T-shirt. She was almost as unattractive as Gail, but had the deepest dimples I had ever seen. She was so masculine from a distance, you could easily mistake her for a man.

As we all sat around our table, Leroy went on to tell us that Big L was a WNBA superstar.

"Nice. How long have you been playing?" I asked.

"I've been playing ball almost all my life. I went professional four years ago. I play a lot of games overseas, and now I'm starting to get the recognition I deserve. My agent has secured me a few endorsements."

"Good for you," I responded, totally uninterested.

"But the day my brother went pro was the most memorable day of my life."

"It feels good," Leroy said.

"I'm sure it does," I said and made eye contact.

"You ready?" Leroy asked Big L.

"Yes."

"Oh, no. You two leaving so early. The party just started," Joy said.

"I want to go back to the hotel and have a drink and relax. You're welcome to join us," Leroy said.

"That would be nice," Joy answered.

I had started looking around the club for a new prospect when Joy informed me we were leaving.

"Where to?" I asked, a little annoyed.

"We gonna go back to my hotel suite to chill," Big L said.

"Well, I wanna chill here," I said, putting up a cantankerous front. I'd seen Kevin come in and wanted to flirt with him. Leroy had lost my attention.

"Come on, Nicoli. Let's go. How often do we get to hang out with a basketball star?" she asked. Then she whispered, "We should get cool with them so we can get free tickets to all the games."

"I don't want to see no damn women playing basketball," I whispered.

"We can sell the WNBA tickets and keep the NBA tickets."

"Oh."

"Oh-h-h-h," Joy said, making fun of me. "That's what's up!"

We left Club Bue and ended up at the W Hotel. We went upstairs with Leroy and Big L and ordered room service.

The one-bedroom suite had plush cream carpeting and all the amenities anyone could ever need.

As we got comfortable, Leroy announced he had to run out for a moment. "I'll be back."

"Would you like company while you run your errand?" I asked. I didn't want to be cooped up in a hotel room with Joy and Big L. I wanted some action.

"No, thanks." He politely dismissed me.

When the champagne and strawberries came, we commenced to getting drunk. Soon, we were laughing, giggling, and acting silly like we were all old friends.

"So, Big L, what time do you think Leroy will be coming back?" I asked.

"Soon," she said and refilled my champagne glass.

"Gurrl, lemme tell you that your brother is fine. I saw his ass from way across the room and knew I had to bag him," Joy said, recounting the events of the evening. As we laughed and lamented, Big L went into her room and came back out with a baggy of drugs.

"Y'all do E?"

"Ecstasy?" I asked.

"Yeah."

"Nah, we ain't tried that shit yet," Joy replied.

"Oh, you gotta try it," Big L said.

"We don't do drugs," I said. "I'm not getting addicted or strung out on no drugs, having me singing 'Giving up' like Sister from the movie *Sparkle*."

"The only thing you will get addicted to is sex when you take E."

"That's it?" I questioned.

"Hell, yeah! This shit will have you horny as shit. Make you wanna fuck," Big L said.

"Well, what da fuck we 'posed to do after we take dat shit up in here? Ain't no men up in here," Joy asked.

Before Big L could respond, I interjected. "Let me try it. Then I'm going home to fuck my man's brains out. I must be missing something if he going elsewhere to fuck."

Big L eagerly gave us each a E capsule. Joy was reluctant to take it, but I swallowed my pill with a gulp of champagne. As the drug started to take effect, I found myself feeling exceptionally good and wanted to open up. I did a catlike stretch, then rolled around on the plush carpet.

"I've always wanted to fuck two men at the same time," I confided to Joy and Big L.

"Been there, done that," Joy said.

"I said 'at the same time,' not two men in the same day, because I've done that as well," I said.

"I heard what you said. When I went away to Fresh Air Fun Camp to be a counselor, me and two other counselors got high off some weed, and we all fucked."

"Wow," was all I could reply.

I wondered why Joy had waited until now to confide that to me. I'd known her almost all my life, and she had never told me that. Then, I realized that the E had me wanting to spill my guts as well. The only problem was, Joy knew almost everything about me.

"Joy, did you know that Kim is my idol? I really look up to that lady."

"What lady?" Joy asked.

"Kim."

"Kim who?"

"Kim Porter. Diddy's baby mama. She's really doing it. That's the kind of life I want to lead. Just be a rich man's baby mama and you're set for life."

"Oh shit, Nicoli! She's my idol too. She's pretty. She's fly. She gets with the richest guys." Joy and I were really connecting. We gave each other a high five.

Big L had the radio on, and the DJ was playing club music. For some strange reason the music sounded exceptionally good. It made me feel good. In fact, I felt great just being there with them. I felt great being alive. Suddenly, I didn't even care about fighting Black's ho. Or Black's infidelity. It all felt trivial.

I jumped up and started dancing. I tried to pull Joy up to dance with me, but she refused. I could tell Joy was resisting the drug. So I pulled up Big L. We started dancing around, acting silly. I was pulling up my shirt, flashing them my boobs, and sticking out my ass and rocking it back and forth. I may have been off beat, but it didn't feel so.

While Big L and I danced around, Joy burst out into tears, sobbing uncontrollably. Seeing her sitting there in tears looking so silly made Big L and I erupt into laughter. We started rolling around on the floor holding our stomachs. Joy had tickled my funny bone, and I couldn't explain why.

As I lay on my back laughing, Big L reached out and put her hand over my stomach. She kept it there for a moment, and I didn't remove it. Soon, her hand started to massage my stomach, then she took her index finger and started to circle my belly button. I went into a trancelike haze, still hearing the sobs of Joy in the distant background.

"This is really great," I said and looked into Big L's eyes. In my drug-induced state, Big L's tribal features now seemed beautiful to me. She was staring at me like I was some exquisite creature she'd like to get to know better. As my high started to come down, I started feeling extremely horny.

Big L's touch was stimulating, yet I felt relaxed. When she put her mouth over mine, I didn't stop her. In fact, I encouraged her to come for more. I started unbuttoning my shirt and ripping off my jeans in a frenzy. Big L followed and took off her clothing as well. As we kissed and groped each other's breasts, I got really into it and said, "Fuck me . . . fuck me."

Big L took the initiative and pushed me back on the plush carpet and spread my legs. With her two thumbs, she parted the lips of my vagina and began to eat my pussy. Her tongue darted in and out rapidly, then she slowed it down and began to suck my clit, while gently biting it. This drove me crazy. She had my knees knocking, lips quivering, and I was pulling out the hair on my head. Soon, strong waves of pleasure came rushing down, and I climaxed with such a ferocity, I yelled "Sweet Jesus!" as I came.

Without anybody inviting Joy to join us, she appeared, standing in front of us butt-naked. Big L ignored Joy at first. So Joy took the initiative to stick her index finger in Big L's pussy. And so it began.

While Big L sucked my clitoris, Joy and I started to kiss passionately. I gently inserted Joy's nipple in my mouth and sucked her soft breast. Joy moaned in pleasure. Soon we were all fondling each other and switching positions. At first I was a little hesitant about eating Big L's pussy. But she was making me feel so good, I returned the favor. When Big L put on a strap-on dildo, it only heightened our sexual escapade. Big L laid down, and I rode on top of her artificial dick while I simultaneously ate Joy's pussy. After Joy and I climaxed, I wanted to fuck Big L with the dildo, but she wouldn't let me.

We all made love for hours. It was the most memorable sex I've ever had. I kept hoping that Leroy would come back and join in our threesome, but he didn't. Once the E had totally worn off, I thought I'd feel embarrassed about fucking two women—especially since one of them was my best friend. But I didn't. I felt enlightened. But Joy, on the other-hand, had the opposite effect. She grew quiet and sullen. Her eyes were flickering from side to side and her body was twitching.

"Let's order room service," I gleefully said. "I'm hungry. And I'll have them send up a half dozen of Evian water. What do you think Big L?"

"Sounds cool. Just charge it to my room."

"Joy, what do you want?" I asked trying to get her to snap out of it.

"I'm not hungry," she said through clenched teeth. "In fact, I feel nauseous," she continued. Her whining fell on deaf ears. Neither Big L nor I really cared. We felt great. At dawn I drove Joy home. There she would remain for the next two days, fighting a deep depression. We spoke a few times, and I simply told her that E wasn't for her. And she agreed. Joy never indulged in the drug again. And that was fine by me.

Chapter 14

$\mathcal{W}$hat you doin', girl?" I asked Big L.

"I just came back from practice. Why? What's up? You coming through?"

"I guess I'll come holla at you for a moment," I said.

"Yeah, come through. I miss your crazy ass."

I had been going over to Big L's hotel suite the past few weeks on a consistent basis to fuck ever since our first encounter. However, I could only get busy if she supplied the E. I hated to think that the E pills were addictive, but I had to admit I craved them. I would love to make love to Black while on E, but Black didn't use drugs and would kill me if he knew I'd been indulging. So Big L and the E pills were my little secret.

When I hung up, I called Joy and asked her if she wanted to roll with me.

"Yo, I ain't down wit dat shit!" she snapped.

"What shit? The E? You don't have to indulge, Joy. You grown."

"Not the E! Nicoli, I'm not down with that gay shit."

"Gay?"

"Yes, gay. I know how it's goin' down, Nicoli, and I don't want to be a part of it. I don't see how you sit up in her face all day. That bitch is frightenin'."

I hung up the telephone, a little annoyed at Joy for being a killjoy. I considered not going to Big L's room, but nothing else was going down on this boring Thursday afternoon. Black had gone to his office, and it was too late to go to the beach or to any other summertime venues.

I hopped into my Mercedes and drove to Big L's hotel. She came to the door in a white terrycloth hotel robe. She'd just got out the shower.

"Hey, girl," I said.

"Come in."

I walked in and immediately made myself at home. I kicked off my Gucci sandals, then fixed a drink. The summer was almost over, and I thought about how I hadn't gotten the tan I wanted. The whole goddamn summer had been rained out. Plus, it took forever to warm up. All I knew was that it had better stay hot until at least October, or that would really be fucked up.

As Big L went to get the stash from her room, I thought about what Joy had said.

"Lisa, you gay?" I asked.

She looked at me peculiarly and said, "Hell yeah! What you think?"

"I don't know. You planned all this?"

"All what?"

"Me. Fucking. The E."

She smiled, then said, "You was down. Nobody forced you. Besides, don't you like it? The feeling I give you?"

"I do, I guess, but truthfully I just like to fuck. I like the feeling it gives me. But I don't want to be considered gay."

"Newsflash, you've been fucking a female. Now, that doesn't make you gay. But, don't you consider yourself bisexual? Bi-curious? Something is up. And are you still fucking your man?"

"Yes, I'm still fucking Black. I need dick. And not no fake dick either. I need the real thing. See, that proves I'm not gay. Besides, experimenting with the same sex is part of pop culture nowadays."

"That experimenting logic is so ridiculous. If you ask me, you're a gay female wanting to be guided by a mentor. You may be 'bi' at the moment, but hang around me a little while longer, and I'll have you detesting dick, just like I do."

"How can you detest something you've never tried? Now, *your* logic is ridiculous. Shit, I should let you fuck Black. Now that dick will bring you to your senses."

"Yo, don't talk about that nigga around me."

"First off, he's not a nigga. His name is Black. Secondly, why can't I mention him around you?"

"It bothers me. It makes me jealous. . . ." She trailed off.

"You've got issues. Serious issues, girl. Maybe a good fucking could straighten you out," I joked. I then picked up an empty champagne bottle she had in her trashcan and simulated a penis.

"All I know is that I've never liked men. Never slept with a man and never will. I'm gay and proud," she said as she swallowed her E pill.

The way she kept saying the word *gay* infuriated me. I decided this would be my last rendezvous with Big L. She was trying to turn me out. Turn me into a committed pussy licker, and it wasn't going down like that.

As the E started to come down, I got horny. Just then my cell phone rang. "Where you at?" Black said.

"I'm hanging out with my girlfriend."

"Why can't you ever keep your ass in the house? Didn't I tell you that I was tired of you running the street?"

"What the fuck am I supposed to do?"

"What?" he asked disbelievingly.

"What am I supposed to do, cooped up in the house all day? I'm young and vibrant, and I like to have a good time," I said, trying to enlighten Black on my inner being. The inner being the E had me in touch with.

Click. Black hung up the telephone in my ear.

I sat there for a moment, thinking that Big L was right. Maybe I didn't need a man. She even started to convince me of this as she went down and started eating my pussy. Ashanti was singing, *"Over and over I cried . . . and over and over you lied . . ."*

Just as I started to hum along, the stereo shut off. Next, all the lights went off. I tried to summon the strength to figure out why we didn't have any electricity in the room, but Big L had me feeling too good.

"Sit on my face," Big L breathed.

"What?"

"Sit on my face, baby."

I was lying on my back on the king-size bed in Big L's hotel suite. We were both naked. Big L and I switched positions, and I climbed on top of her and sat on her face. My pussy opened up wide, and Big L's tongue explored every crevice. I was grinding my hips in her face while her hands gripped my ass. As she ate my pussy, she would say, "How does it feel?"

"So-o-o-o-o good!" I moaned.

We made love for hours, until nightfall. When we finally decided to get up, we found out that there had been a blackout. The whole city was dark.

Chapter 15

The blackout of 2003 would prove to be the worst night of my life. First, it took me an hour to get twenty blocks. No traffic lights were working, and I couldn't get through on any telephones lines. Once I got back home, our building had adequate lighting because there was a backup generator. So I could at least see where I was going. But the elevators weren't working, so I had to take the stairs. I stuck my key in the door to Black's penthouse apartment and couldn't get in. I wiggled the key around until it sank in: Black had changed the locks. He'd threatened me for the last time about running the streets and disrespecting him.

Furious, I tried calling Black, to no avail. Desperate, I ran down to the lobby and asked if Black had left any messages.

"No, madam," the doorman replied.

I contemplated what should I do. Then I thought I'd just wait in the lobby until Black came home. I knew that he was angry with me about my behavior. As I tried to sit and wait, I was escorted out by the doorman.

"Madam, this is private property. I'm sorry. Mr. King left specific instructions that once you came back down from your initial visit upstairs, you were not allowed back into the building."

I nearly peed on myself. Was this how celebrities ended relationships? Humiliated, I left with just the clothes on my back. I went back to my car, and for a fleeting moment I was happy. I've still got my car, I thought, then realized that the majority of my jewelry was upstairs, along with all of my clothes.

When I got inside my car, I noticed that my gas tank was nearly on empty.

"Shit!" I screamed and decided to go back to Big L's room.

As I drove back to the hotel, I had an epiphany. I didn't like the way my life was headed. Black had been right to be angry. He'd given me so much, and I'd behaved like a spoiled child—the spoiled child my grandmother raised. The spoiled child I didn't want to be anymore. The thought of losing such a good thing had me frightened. I decided that if I could reconcile with Black, I'd do virtually anything he wanted.

When I walked into Big L's room, she greeted me with, "I've been worried sick. I think this may be some sort of terrorist attack."

"It is not. Shut up, stupid," I said.

I had a headache and needed to go and lay down. I needed quiet time alone so I could contemplate my next move. I walked past Big L and entered her bedroom and locked her door. Black's inconsistency had thrown me off balance. I had never suspected he was anywhere near tired of me. How foolish was I?

Chapter 16

After hours of no service, my cellular rang out of the blue. I rushed to it.

"Nicoli, where you at?" The caller's voice sounded familiar.

"Who's this?"

"This Stacy. I know you ain't speakin' to me and Fertashia, but I think I need to tell you how it's goin' down."

"What!" I was still angry at Stacy and Fertashia, but I didn't know exactly why. Then I remembered that I was supposed to be changing my evil ways.

"I just saw Black and Joy together outside. It looked like he was 'bout to go up in her house."

"What?" I said again, this time in disbelief.

"Joy is wit your man. I think they goin' up in her crib."

"Thanks," I said and hung up abruptly.

I jumped off the king-size bed, ran into the bathroom, and splashed cold water on my face. Big L had her wet towel, boxers, and dirty socks thrown on the floor. She really thinks she's a man, I thought, and became disgusted with the whole scene.

I took a moment to contemplate my next move. When I emerged from the bathroom, I was focused. Big L was butt-naked, sprawled out on the living room floor eating Twizzlers. I walked directly over to her and collapsed on the plush cream carpet, as if the life had been sucked out of me.

"Big L, does your Rent-A-Car have gas?" I said desperately.

"Yeah, why?"

"I have an emergency back home in Brooklyn, and I need to be there."

Panicking, she said, "Okay. Let me go with you."

"No. No, I have to take care of this myself."

"You got trouble?"

"No. I'm cool."

"Are you sure? Because Big L hits hard!" she said and punched her fist into her hand. She continued, "If you got a beef, I'll break a nigga or bitch face into pieces if they try to fuck with you."

"It's not even like that. I just got issues." I grabbed her car keys and jetted. She called after me, "Call me."

I left the hotel and traveled as quickly as I could to Brooklyn. Minutes felt like hours as I drove in bumper-to-bumper traffic over the Brooklyn Bridge. All I kept thinking was how we all made a vow not to fuck each other's men. Joy had snaked me. Was Black seriously thinking about hooking up with Joy? I didn't think so.

Nervously, I wondered what I'd do when I confronted them. I knew that I couldn't beat Joy. She was a little more skilled in that area. So what would I do? Just sit back and let them walk off into the sunset? The very thought upset my stomach.

I saw Black's Cadillac Escalade truck as soon as I pulled up to the block. I had barely cut the ignition off in the car before I was hopping out and running to the building. I ran up the four flights to Joy's apartment because the elevator wasn't in service. Once I got to her door, I started banging. Within seconds Joy opened it and smiled. Her smile was so inviting and warm that I took a moment to focus. When she reached out and hugged me, I exhaled and hugged her back.

"Are you all right? Gurrl, I've been callin' you all day. I kept gettin' your voice mail, so I stopped tryin'. Black came here lookin' for you. He was worried. I didn't tell him where your ass was at either."

"Is he still here?" I asked hesitantly.

"No. I sent him to your Mom's crib. I told him you'd probably go there."

I thought briefly about telling Joy what Stacy had implied about her and Black. Then I decided against it. At least, today. I'd been through enough drama for the night. I'd save that tidbit of information for a dull day.

If Black came looking for me, saying he was worried, that meant we'd be getting back together. Suddenly, my life seemed as if it might get back on track. He must have changed the locks after our earlier conversation and before the blackout. Once the blackout happened, he realized that he'd locked me out and that I didn't have anywhere to go in the mayhem. Joy accompanied me to Gail's apartment. I hadn't seen Gail all summer and felt a little guilty. When we got there, Gail said Black had already left.

"I done told him you ain't here. I said, 'I ain't seen that chile since she got wit you,' " she said.

"Did he say where he was going?"

"No, he just left."

"Thanks, Gail."

"Could you spare a few bucks fo ya momma, Nicoli? I'm broke," Gail said. I dug into my Prada knapsack and gave Gail $200. Her eyes widened, and she smiled a toothless grin.

"Thanks, baby," she said.

"You're welcome," I replied and felt strangely good about myself.

Joy agreed to come with me back into the city to see if Black had gone home. I told her that we might have to sneak inside his building. "That's cool," she said.

When we got there, the lobby was empty and dark. Something must have happened to the generator. We dashed through the lobby and ran to the staircase. Joy took out a lighter and lit the dark stairwell. As we walked up the stairs to Black's apartment, Joy kept playing around, trying to scare me. She would say silly things like, "Boo!" and we'd giggle like two schoolgirls.

As we exited the staircase, an image stopped me dead in my tracks. Joy's lighter illuminated Black and some woman, engaged in what seemed like a passionate kiss in front of his door. My hands immediately went up to my mouth, but I couldn't say a word. Neither could Joy. We were both speechless.

As the doorknob from the staircase hit the lock and made a noise, Black and the woman jumped apart.

"What the fuck is goin' on?" I yelled, and stared directly into Black's eyes.

"What?" Black mumbled and backed away from the woman.

"I know I didn't just see what the fuck I just saw."

"Yes, you did," Joy instigated.

"Black, what's going on, and who's this girl?" the woman said, waiting for an explanation from Black. She was extremely tall and thin. I could barely make out her features, but even in the dark she looked like a model.

"Girl?!?" I pounced on the woman. I grabbed her by her short hair and commenced to whipping her ass. Joy dropped her lighter and jumped in. She started kicking the woman in her stomach and face, but the woman refused to fight back. She just shielded herself from each blow as best as she could.

In the semi-lit hallway, chaos erupted. Black's neighbors started coming out of their apartments and threatening to call the cops. The woman was screaming for help while Joy and I were beating her down.

Once Black was able to get his composure back, he quickly tried his best to break it up. The woman was in a fetal position, blocking each blow and screaming for her life.

"I hate you! I hate you!" I kept screaming as Black stepped in between us.

"You ain't shit, Black!" Joy yelled.

Inwardly, I could hear my grandmother's voice say, "Nicoli, why you fightin' over a no-good man? You're better than this."

I released the woman.

The woman stood up and frantically tried to get inside Black's apartment. As I bickered with Black, Joy seized the opportunity to hit the woman in the face. The woman seemed to do the Harlem Shake as she fell headfirst to the ground. She landed with a loud thud.

"Enough!" Black said, and with one swift movement he threw Joy across the hallway, grabbed me by my arm, and squeezed. "Stop this!" he scolded.

I broke down and bawled.

"How you gonna put your hands on me?" I cried. "How you gonna hit me for that tramp?" I was screaming hysterically.

Black wrapped his arms around me and said, "Shush-sh-sh-sh, let it out."

"How could you do this to me?" I whispered, then collapsed in his arms. "Why-y-y-y-y?"

"I'm so sorry, baby-girl. It's not what you think. Let me make this up to you. Please. Let me make this up to you."

"I'm leaving you, Black. I can't live like this. It's over!" I said, and ran out of the apartment building, feeling alone and confused.

Black and Joy ran after me, but I was too quick. I jumped into Big L's car and sped off. I had had enough.

Chapter 17

I stayed in Big L's room for days in a drug-induced haze. She was barely there because of her charity basketball games. And when she was there, we were dropping E pills and fucking. Life for me had become mundane. Big L was okay, but she wasn't Black.

One night while I was watching *Making the Band* on MTV, Big L came in with a bag of Twizzlers for her and a Junior's cheese-cake for me.

"Look what I bought you," she said jovially, placing the cheese-cake on the bed next to me. I glanced at the cheesecake, then continued to watch the show.

"Don't worry, you can thank me later, if you know what I mean," she said in a suggestive tone. You would have thought she'd just purchased me ten-karat diamond earrings from the apprecia-tion she expected.

"Aren't you going to eat it?" she badgered. "I could call down to room service and have them send up some ice cream. We can toss back a few E pills and have a good time."

Big L was plucking my nerves. She was starving for attention, but I ignored her.

"What you watching?" she said, grabbing the remote control out of my hand and plopping down on the bed beside me. Her presence made me cringe. She was becoming a nuisance, and I felt like she was constantly invading my space. I wanted time to get over Black, but she refused to give me any room.

Finally I broke my silence, "What does it look like I'm watchin'?"

"This shit is weak. Let's see what they got on the pay-per-view channel. Let's rent a porno or something. Liven things up."

I snatched the remote back, and Big L went ballistic. "What the fuck is your problem!" she roared and it felt like the whole room vibrated. Not fazed by her outburst, I turned the volume up on the television until it reached its maximum.

"You my mutherfuckin' problem," I yelled. "You think somebody wanna lick pussy all day. I'm tired of you! Your ugly ass always up in my face whining like a little bitch!"

Furious at my blatant disrespect, she ripped the television from the wall and slammed it to the ground. The television broke apart instantly. In a blind fury, she ran through the hotel suite, throwing tables, breaking chairs, and yelling obscenities at me.

Soon after, hotel security came bursting into the room. It was an ugly scene. Big L was perspiring profusely, her white T-shirt was drenched in sweat, her ponytail unruly, and her breathing heavy.

I stood up, nearly nude in just a pair of black thong panties. My perky breasts greeted the security with relief.

"That bitch is crazy!" I exclaimed.

Needless to say, we were thrown out.

Chapter 18

Understandably, I needed to get my shit together. I was miserable with Big L, and yet I couldn't face going back to Gail's. Big L and I were now in the Marriot in Midtown, just blocks from Black's apartment. Every time my cell phone rang, I held my breath, hoping it was Black. It never was. He never called to see how I was doing or at least apologize. He had discarded me, as he had so many other women. But I'm not just any woman, so I mustered up the courage to confront Black. I devised a plan that I was certain would work. I'd go to Black's apartment to get my belongings. That was it. My master plan. I figured it's like they say: Outta sight, outta mind.

I arrived at Black's apartment early morning because I knew he'd be there. I banged on his door, and after a few minutes, he called out.

"Who is it?"

"Nicoli."

After a long silence, he opened the door. He had the door slightly ajar, his body blocking my entrance.

"Hey, baby-girl," he said with a smile, much to my amazement.

"I need to get my things."

"So, you leaving me?" he asked.

"Well, you left me first, didn't you?" I asked, desperately wanting to go inside his apartment and snuggle up in bed with Black holding me close. The thought made me feel like an idiot, but I didn't care. For the first time I wondered if I loved Black and his womanizing ways. Sadly I realized that if I did love him, that meant that I didn't love myself.

"Listen, why don't you come back later, and I'll take you to lunch so we can talk. I really miss you."

I knew something was up—he was acting suspicious. I raised my voice and said, "I need to get my clothes, Black! Why can't I come in now?"

"Black, who's that?" a familiar voice called out.

"My business," he replied, slightly annoyed that his guest didn't remain anonymous. "Why don't you leave—"

Just as Black was trying to dismiss me, his overnight guest came out. It was the same girl from the party—Tracy.

"What the fuck she doing here?" she yelled.

"Didn't I tell you I'm handling my business?" He turned to Tracy and said, "Get back in the room!"

"Oh, so this is why you don't have time for me. You're nothing but a liar. I thought you left her alone. Anyway, don't matter no way. I'm outta here. Keep that bitch," I said, then walked back to the elevator. Black came running after me.

"Okay, okay, okay. What do you want me to do? You want me to kick her out? She's gone."

"Excuse me?" Tracy said in bewilderment.

"Yes. I want you to kick that bitch out. That is, if you love me like you said you do," I challenged.

"It's done," Black replied and commenced to kicking Tracy out. He grabbed her by her arm and started walking her through his apartment, gathering her things. She was cursing him out the whole time.

I stood back and watched the whole fiasco with a grin on my face. It felt good to see Black disrespect this girl for me. That meant he really loved me.

Once his overnight guest had made her exit, it was time for me and Black to talk.

"You know I can't be with you? You do know this, right?"

"Come on now, Nicoli. I done got rid of that girl for you. You know how I feel about you. You my girl, and I missed you. It's time for you to come back home and to stop this madness. I've been going crazy without you."

"So crazy you up in here fucking?"

"I swear to God I didn't fuck her."

"Yeah, right!"

"I'm not lying. Look, smell my dick," he said and pulled down his boxers. I think one half of him wanted to really convince me that he didn't fuck her, and the other half wanted to convince me to fuck him.

"Well, it's not just about her now, is it, Black?"

"I know it's not about her because I just kicked her out."

"No, I mean, I can't deal with your infidelities. What about the woman from the other night?" Black had a half-witted expression on his face, as if he'd forgotten.

"Marry me."

"What?"

"You heard me. Marry me. We can go get your ring now. I told you, Nicoli, I love you."

"You've got to be joking. I don't even know you."

"We'll get to know each other on our honeymoon," he said and flashed his million-dollar smile. Instantly I fell in love.

Chapter 19

After our talk, Black jumped in the shower. I walked in the bedroom, and when I saw the messy bedsheets, my heart dropped. I walked closer to examine the bed to see if there was a wet spot. Nope. I exhaled.

Black took me to a world-renowned jeweler named Jake in the diamond district. Jake lit up as soon as he saw Black's face. They shook hands, then Black introduced me.

"Jake, this is my baby-girl, Nicoli," he said proudly.

"What a beautiful name for a beautiful girl," he complimented.

"Thank you," I said with a smile.

"What can I do for you today?" Jake asked Black.

"I'm here to get an engagement ring for my baby. We're getting married," he said grandly. I was so excited when I heard him say the word.

"Congratulations, man. I have just what you're looking for."

Jake went to a safe, pulled out a black velour box, and laid it on his display table. When he opened the box, I gasped at the lovely arrangement of clear, pink, yellow, and blue diamond rings. I was immediately drawn to an emerald-cut pink diamond.

"Omigod!" I yelled. "I have to have this one."

"You like that, baby-girl?"

"I do, Daddy. I want this one," I said in a baby voice.

"She has good taste," Jake said with a smile.

"I'll take it," Black said.

"How much is this ring?" I asked. Black didn't ask such things because he believed that if you have to ask, then you can't afford it.

"That beauty costs one-point-five million dollars."

I was smiling like an ad for Kool-Aid. This ring was making up for every unsavory thing Black had done to me.

After Black purchased my ring, he wouldn't let me put it on. He put it inside his pocket, and we left.

"Why can't I put it on?" I pouted.

"Because if we're going to do this, we're going to do it right."

"Oh. So you're calling a press conference?"

"Not like that, Nicoli. Just shut up and let me handle this."

Chapter 20

Black called Tavern on the Green and had a special table reserved for us. Once we sat down, we ordered Cristal, rock lobster tails, and Beluga caviar. I felt like Cinderella.

"Black, we could have just as easily gone to get some fast food. This is going to take too long, and I want my ring—"

"Nicoli, you're about to be Mrs. King. Baby-girl, you don't eat fast food no more. Do you understand me?"

"Yes, Black."

"Nicoli, do you know why I fell in love with you?" he asked. I honestly didn't know the answer to that question.

"You love my blow jobs?" I joked.

"That too," he laughed, then got serious. "I fell in love with your carefree spirit. When I first met you, I knew we'd sleep together on the first date. That was what I wanted, and I usually get what I want. But it was what *you* wanted as well. The women I deal with I usually fuck on the first night, then they spend the next few days trying to convince me they've done something they didn't want to. Thinking that I won't respect them. They make sure they speak correctly. Dress correctly. Show how independent they are. Make sure I know that they have their own money and that it's not about *my* money. They use every trick in the book to catch me. Now, you, on the other hand—you make me laugh. You act silly. You speak in broken sentences. You're rude. You have a temper. You don't listen to me. The list goes on and on. And overnight you have totally captivated me. You're the realest female I've ever dated, and I'm so afraid that I could lose someone as authentic as you . . ."

"Awww, baby. You're so sweet," I said, and leaned over and kissed Black.

As lunch ended, Black got down on one knee and said, "Nicoli, will you marry me?"

Much to my amazement, tears welled up in my eyes, then streamed down my cheeks. I knew I'd be entering another phase in my life with Black, and the anticipation was overwhelming.

"Yes. Yes, I will marry you."

Then Black reached in his pocket and pulled out the ring. It was like seeing it for the first time. The stone looked like pink lemonade. It was flawless.

As he slid the heavy rock on my ring finger, we both smiled.

"Let's live happily ever after. Just like they do in fairy tales," he said, and kissed my lips.

After a blissful reconciliation, things pretty much went back to normal for Black and me. Today would be my first day out on the town in weeks. Summer was coming to a close, and I wanted to get out and have more fun before it ended.

After Black went to his office, I finally had a chance to return Big L's telephone calls. She was calling me so much, I had to shut my cell phone off and keep it off for days. I was also free to go and see Joy.

I'd already told Joy about the engagement and she was dying to see my ring. I decided to wear a pair of Filthmore jeans, a wifebeater, and the new pair of Manolo Blahniks I'd just bought. I put on my $100,000 Piaget watch, luxuriating in Black's wealth. I couldn't wait to become Mrs. King.

I asked Joy to meet me at the McDonald's on Atlantic Avenue. I told her to bring Stacy and Fertashia along as well. Joy had told me that when she went back and told them that we had to beat a bitch ass over Black, Stacy and Fertashia went talking my business to the whole neighborhood.

When I pulled into McDonald's, my girls were already there. I beeped my horn twice, and they walked over.

"Whaddup, girl?" Joy said, and jumped into the front seat. I didn't respond, I just showed her my ring. As she was studying it, Stacy and Fertashia climbed into the back.

"Wassup, Nicoli?" Stacy asked.

"This," I said, and pushed my ring in her face.

"That's cute," she said, uninterested. "Now, can you move your hand from 'n front of my face."

"Stacy, a two-million-dollar ring isn't cute. It's fabulous!" I snapped.

"That cost two million dollars?" she said disbelievingly.

"It was appraised at five million," I lied. "Look at the clarity. Go on, look. Take notes and run around and tell the block that I got this because of that bitch I beat down the other night."

"Nicoli, I'm happy for you 'n shit. But I don't know what you're talking about," Stacy said in a diplomatic tone. She can be really irksome. Then she continued, "Besides, why are you fighting over a man? That's wrong. That girl didn't have anything to do with you. She can only believe what Black tells her. You should have fought Black."

"You defending that slut," I accused.

"That's what's up."

"Get the fuck out!" I exploded. Rehashing the whole incident didn't sit well with me.

"Why I gotta get out? I'm only keepin' it real. I thought we were girls? I thought we were gonna chill in the Benz," Stacy whined.

"I'm not fuckin' wit you no more. You gotta get out, yo," I said, using my street vernacular.

Stacy got out, slammed my car door, then said, "You coming, Fertashia?"

"Nah, I'm a chill wit Nicoli and Joy."

"No the fuck you not. You can get out too," I screamed.

"Fuck you, Nicoli!" Fertashia yelled as she got out. "Say, it's ten o'clock. Do you know who your man's fucking?"

"Bitches," I stated to Joy.

"You buggin,' flippin' on Stacy and Fertashia. If you stressed, go and fight Black. But Stacy or Fertashia didn't cross you."

"Oh, you on their side, too?"

"Sorry, yo. But we *all* used to be tight. Just 'cause you ain't rollin' wit them no more don't mean I have to feel the same way. I'm ya girl, no doubt. But when you ain't around, Fertashia and Stacy are what's really good."

Joy was right. I wasn't there all the time, and she was used to it being the four of us. So I smiled and treated my girl to Juniors Restaurant. We ordered jumbo shrimp and strawberry cheesecake.

As we were talking about old times, my cell phone rang.

"Hello?"

"Where have you been!" the caller screamed.

"Who's this?"

"This is Big L. I've been calling you for weeks. I thought something happened to you," she said, and I could tell she was relieved to hear my voice. Surprisingly, I actually missed the crazy broad.

"I'm cool. I had some issues."

"Well, you could have at least called," she whined.

"Well, I didn't. So what's up anyway?" I said.

"You free? Why don't you come through?"

I thought about it for a quick minute. My time with Joy was coming to an end, and I actually wanted to go to Big L's. I'm sure she'd have some E, and we could have a good time.

"I'll be there in an hour," I said, then hung up.

"Who was that?" Joy questioned.

"Big L."

"So you leaving me to go be with her?" she asked, accusingly.

"You can come, too."

"Why the fuck do I want to go over there? In how many mutherfuckin' ways do I need to tell you I ain't down wit that dumb shit?"

"Joy, I'm not down with that shit either. I'm only going for the E pills."

"Whatever."

I paid the bill and rushed Joy home. Driving on the FDR, I realized that I had become addicted to E. If I didn't curb my craving, I could lose everything.

Chapter 21

The clock is ticking," I said to Big L, who was running me a bath. She wanted to do the romantic thing, so I decided to humor her. She'd stopped at Melodrama Books & Things and purchased the Kama Sutra and a book on erotic massages. I decided I'd indulge—maybe learn some new tricks for my soon-to-be husband.

The hotel's suite had a nice-size whirlpool tub, and I told Big L to put lots of apricot bubble bath inside. While the water was still running, we both got in. She had pulled the drapes because it was still early and lit a few candles. The champagne was ice cold, and the strawberries were sweet. After I'd taken the E pill, I was ready to speed things up because I needed to be home at a decent time.

"Let's get out," I suggested, and Big L didn't object.

We both ran naked, dripping wet with soapsuds, to the bedroom. I fell onto the bed, and Big L grabbed a small bottle of scented oil and began to massage my back. Her masculine fingers kneaded into my skin and took away any stress I was harboring. As she massaged my whole body, I drifted off into a deep meditation. I thought about how wonderful it felt to be pampered. I also thought about how if I were home with Black, I'd be doing the rubbing and not getting rubbed. But before I could get angry, I thought about Black's million-dollar smile. This made the task of tending to his needs worthwhile.

Big L started to kiss the nape of my neck, and I moaned in pleasure. Then she started to make her way down my back.

"You have a really nice ass," she complimented.

"Don't stop."

And she didn't. Big L took her hands and separated my ass cheeks. Then she licked the outside of my ass, then explored the inside. I turned over and spread my legs. When my hands reached down to grab her head, she noticed my ring.

"What's that?" she said, stopping all movement.

"Don't stop," I said again, but she didn't move.

"That's a ring on your finger," she said. My eyes flew open, and I realized she was agitated.

"Oh, yeah. Black and I are engaged. Isn't this the most exquisite thing you've ever seen?"

Big L slapped my hand away, and it startled me.

"What's your problem?" I asked, jumping up. She'd blown my high.

"What do you think we're doing here, playing games?"

"We're fucking. Period. Having a little fun."

"Nicoli, I can fuck any bitch I want. I thought that you and I had something serious. I was waiting for you to realize that you loved me and not that silly nigga you keep chasing after."

"First off, he's not a nigga. His name's Black and he's my man, and I love him." That was the first time I'd said that I loved Black, and it wasn't even to Black. I had to remind myself to tell Black that later.

"You can't love him! Not the way you come in here and make love to me."

"Big L, our encounters in here, behind closed doors, are to just heighten my sexuality. I don't want to be old and saying there were things I wished I'd tried. You only have one life, and in mine I'm doing everything I possibly can. You're just an experience among many experiences. Nothing more, nothing less."

"Bitch, are you stupid! I should beat the shit outta you up in here!" she yelled, and her eyes hooded over. For a brief moment, I was intimidated. I knew that I had to end it. Today. And so I did.

"I thought you'd be grateful having someone like me sharing your bed. But instead you have to keep bitching. There can only be one bitch in my relationships, and, sweetie, that's me. Sorry to disappoint you."

"What do you mean, I should be 'grateful'?"

"Well, you should. Look at how beautiful I am. I can have any man I want. And yet, I come spend my time with you. I mean, I spend hours looking in your face. And you should be the first to admit that you're a bit hard on the eyes."

"You pompous, conceited, hateful, self-loving whore. You ain't shit!"

"So I've been told. Listen, Big L, I'm outta here. It's over. I don't need no psycho broad going ballistic on me. You got some deep, disturbing issues that need to be worked out. Too much anger built up inside of you. You need to go out and get some dick to release that shit. But your problems are your problems. I gotta go. Ciao," I said. Now dressed, I sauntered out of Big L's hotel suite, swearing never to see her again.

Chapter 22

The Labor Day weekend came and went. Black and I were supposed to fly to Hawaii and get married, but at the last minute he had to stay and handle some business. It rained the whole weekend, so I didn't come out until Tuesday morning.

In the parking garage, I clicked my alarm, and my ignition automatically started. I liked doing that. As I approached, my pace slowed down and my mouth fell open. My beautiful Mercedes-Benz CL 600 had been vandalized. Someone had scratched "lesbian bitch" on both car doors, the hood, and the trunk. Immediately, I dialed Big L, and the hotel said she'd checked out days ago. That might be so, but I knew she was behind this.

I slowly got into my car. Then I panicked. Black could not see my car like this. I drove to the dealer, dropped off my Benz, and received a loaner car. I told the dealer that I'd left it parked in Brooklyn, and it was vandalized. Still, he looked at me suspiciously, as if to say, "Who you fooling?"

I rushed home and went to the security guard on duty. It had dawned on me that the parking garage should have a video surveillance camera that might have recorded who had vandalized my car.

"Alex, last night my car was vandalized in the parking garage. Could you rewind the tape from yesterday so I could see the perpetrator and report it to the authorities?"

"What's your car location, ma'am?"

"Spot four-oh-five."

"Oh, that's too bad."

"What do you mean by that? What's so bad about it?"

"That camera has been out for weeks. I've called for repair on numerous occasions, but no one has shown up yet," he said. The whole time he never looked me in my eyes, which I took as a sign of disrespect.

"You gotta be kidding me!" I yelled. "I pay millions to live up in here, and you're telling me that my safety is in jeopardy because your lazy ass won't stay on top of your job?"

"Calm down, ma'am."

"Don't fucking patronize me. I could have been *killed*. Do you know who my husband is?"

"Ma'am, I know Mr. Black King. Is that your question?"

His smart ass was trying to be cute. So, okay, Black is not my husband. But my fiancé was going to get this piece of shit fired. Today.

"I hope you don't like your job, Alex. Because you won't have it much longer," I threatened.

"Good day, ma'am," he replied without an ounce of fear.

I stormed out of the building and called Joy.

"Joy!" I shouted.

"Nicoli, what's wrong?" she said, detecting the panic in my voice.

"I've got to meet you. I got to talk to you. Meet me at McDonald's on Atlantic in an hour. Can you do that for me?"

"I'll be there," Joy said, and we hung up.

Chapter 23

As I drove over the Brooklyn Bridge, I put on 50 Cent, *"Many men . . . wish death 'pon me . . . blood in my eyes dog and I can't see . . ."*

I let my head nod back and forth to the beat. I was frustrated that Big L was this petty and childish. Relationships end. Feelings get hurt. That's life. You don't go around tormenting someone just because they don't want to be with you.

I arrived at the McDonald's in an hour just like I said I would, but Joy wasn't there yet. I started to go through the drive-thru and get some fries but remembered that Black said we don't eat fast food. So I decided to wait in my car and chill. I had been waiting nearly an hour for Joy, when someone tapped on my window. I looked at the stranger. She was a brown-skinned girl with cornrows going all the way back, wearing a black T-shirt.

She motioned for me to roll down my window, and I complied.

"What's up?" I asked, thinking she was lost. All of a sudden she reached through my window and pulled me out. For a girl she was awfully strong. I tried to scream, but there was no time for that. Before I knew it, three other girls circled me. They were all punching and kicking me mercilessly. They dragged me in back of a Dumpster behind McDonald's. I tried to fight back as best as I could, but I was no match for this crew. I wished that Joy would come and see the commotion and help me. But she never came.

"Hold her down! Hold her down!" someone kept yelling as they tried to grab my hands and feet. But I made it hard for them by kicking my legs and flailing my arms. Finally they constrained me. I was lying flat on my back, and each girl had a limb in her hands. Everyone was breathing hard. As the tall, dark figure approached, dread crept upon me, and my heart fluttered in fear. The dark figure had on a black hooded sweatshirt, sweat pants, and a pair of huge, dark-tinted sunglasses. But even in disguise, I knew it was Big L. She looked around to make sure no one could see the chaos, then she reached in a knapsack and pulled out a pair of scissors. When I saw the scissors, I thought that they were going to pierce my heart. Just leave me for dead.

"Help-p-p—" I started to yell, but was silenced by a fist. I tasted the blood inside my mouth.

Big L leaned down with the scissors and started to cut off all my hair. Meticulously, she cut off all my locks until I was nearly bald-headed. As I listened to the scissors cut, the metal clashing together would be a sound that would haunt me for years to come.

"Take her ring," the masked Big L said. "Make it look like a robbery."

One girl wrestled with me for a moment before she was able to slide the ring from my finger.

As I lay there bald and bruised, I thought they were done. All I kept thinking about was what my girls and I would do to Big L once we caught up to her.

"Finish her off," Big L said to the girls, then disappeared. Panicking, I tried to wiggle free, but I was exhausted from struggling with the four girls. One girl pulled a razor out from her back pocket and began to slice my face as a butcher slices deli meat. My face burst open like fireworks on the Fourth of July. The sharp metal blade separated my face into parts like a math equation. Blood dripped in my eyes, ran down my cheeks, and dripped into my ears. 50 Cent's song kept going through my head, *"Many men . . . wish death 'pon me . . . blood in my eyes dog and I can't see . . ."*

My face started to sting. I prayed, maybe for the first time in my life. Overwhelming feelings of helplessness tormented me as I lay on the ground. I couldn't understand how I got to this place in my life where someone would seriously want me disfigured. I cried for sympathy.

"Please, please stop. *Please* stop cutting my face. It's all I got . . . It's all I got . . . ," I moaned in anguish.

"Shut up, bitch!" one girl replied.

The girls dispersed into the night. I lay there, too stunned to move. I think one of the workers in McDonald's found me and called an ambulance.

"What's your name?" the attendant asked. When I tried to respond, a great pain went through my body and I realized that my lips were sliced open as well. I went into shock and passed out.

Chapter 24

I awoke in the emergency room's recovery unit. My face felt tight, and my body was aching. I wished it were all a dream, but it wasn't. I burst into tears, and the nurse ran over to comfort me.

"No-o-o-o-o!" I screamed as the reality of my circumstances hit me.

"Dear child, who did this to you? Do you know? We've notified the authorities. They will be here shortly. We were able to get in touch with your mother, and she's waiting in the other room. I'll go and get her—"

"No," I managed to whisper. I didn't want to see her. I didn't want to see anyone. I didn't even want to see me.

The thought of going through the rest of my life with facial scars didn't seem promising. For the first time in my young life, I thought about killing myself. I wanted to die rather than live my life as a disfigured freak. I didn't think I could handle people staring at me in pity.

Inside I felt empty. I lay there staring up at the ceiling. A small commotion erupted outside my room, and immediately I became frightened. Had the girls come back? When my curtain was pulled open, I saw Black, Joy, Gail, Stacy, Fertashia, *and* Big L, all arguing with the nurse, who had told them I didn't want any visitors. They all pushed past her and entered my room.

Big L and I locked eyes. I knew she had come to see the end

result of her madness. This infuriated me, and I flipped out. I tried to get up, but I was weak. I lunged forward at her but collapsed, and Black caught me. He laid me back down, and as the nurse called hospital security. Anger combined with grief started to rise from my stomach to my throat, and I found it hard to breathe. The feeling was stifling, as if someone had put a pillow over my face and applied pressure.

Even though I had yet to see my face, everyone's facial expression explained to me just how badly I was hurt. They all had a look of pity, except Big L. She looked satisfied.

Black embraced me. "Baby-girl, don't worry. I'll take care of you. You just need to convalesce at the house," he soothed. The pity in his voice made me start screaming like a madwoman. I simply lost it. I started off with a low moan and then hit my crescendo. I was kicking and screaming, "Why, God? Why me? I wanna die . . . I wanna die . . . I hate my life."

Two nurses came running in and pushed Black to the side while they tried to give me a sedative. However, I wouldn't let them. "Okay, okay, I'm fine."

"Security is on the way to escort you guys out!" the nurse shouted.

"Baby-girl, who did this to you?" Black said, ignoring the nurses.

Tears streamed down my cheeks as I managed to say, "She did." He turned around slowly to see just who "she" was, but couldn't figure out who I was referring to.

"Your friends?" he asked in amazement.

"No. No. Lisa. Big L did this. That girl right there."

Black got up off his knees to confront Big L, and she punched him in his face. His head went back like a weeble-wobble toy, but he didn't fall down. Stunned, Black swung back but missed. Big L met Black's right cheek with a left hook, then followed up with an uppercut to his gut. Instead of Black regrouping, he almost doubled over. Big L hit him with an uppercut right in his jaw that threw Black off balance. He stumbled a little, and when he tried to regain his composure, Big L hit him again. Then again. And again. She pulverized Black within seconds.

Soon hospital security and the police came running. After the mayhem Big L was arrested, and Black was treated and then arrested as well for assault in the third degree.

To say I was devastated would be like saying it's hot in the summer. There's just no point.

Chapter 25

My name is Officer Davis, and this is Officer Pollock. Ma'am, could you please tell us what happened to you today."

The two officers were standing beside my hospital bed with their pens and pads out, ready to take notes.

"I was going to Brooklyn to meet my girlfriend Joy. I waited for nearly an hour, and she never showed up. Suddenly, a lady tapped on my window—"

"Could you describe her?"

"She was ordinary looking. Five feet two. Brown-skinned, tan lips. That's all I can remember."

"Okay. Please finish."

"As I said, she tapped on my window. I rolled it down, and she attacked me. She pulled me through the driver's-side window, and then three other girls came."

"Could you give a description of these other assailants?"

"No, sir. I can't. I'm sorry. Too much was going on . . . and I was scared."

"I understand. Please continue."

"Once I was dragged to the back of McDonald's, a fifth girl appeared. It was Big L. Lisa. The girl that was arrested in here today."

"Did you see her face?" the officer said, suddenly excited that they could make an arrest.

"No, sir. I didn't. But it was her. I could tell from her body frame."

"What was she wearing? Any identifiable jewelry?"

"She was wearing all black. Her face was covered with dark glasses. But I knew it was her!"

"Ma'am we can't make an arrest unless you actually saw her. It's the law. What about this Joy? Do you think she had anything to do with this?" My eyes quickly went over to where Joy was standing with Gail. That thought had never occurred to me. Why hadn't Joy ever shown up?

"Joy," I said, and both officers turned around to face her. "Where were you?"

"I didn't have anythin' to do wit this. Nicoli and I are best friends," she said.

"Answer the question. Where were you?" Officer Davis pursued.

"I was gonna meet Nicoli when I met up wit this dude I used to fuck wit. Darren. He came through, and I hopped in his ride. He was 'posed to take me right to Nicoli, but he kept actin' stupid. By the time I got there, it was already too late. The ambulance was drivin' her away."

"Dat don't sound right," Gail said, finally breaking her silence.

"Oh, shut up!" Joy retorted.

"No, you shut up. Don't disrespect my mother, Joy," I snapped.

"Quiet! Everyone!" Officer Pollock yelled. "Give me this Darren's telephone number. I need to check your story."

"Even if I wasn't with him, that don't mean I had anythin' to do wit this shit. I know my rights!" Joy said, suddenly flipping out. "Nicoli know why the fuck she got cut up. Don't try and pin this shit on me!"

"What does she mean by that, Nicoli? If you know something, you gotta tell us."

"I told you everything I know."

"Except a motive. Why would someone want to leave you in stitches?"

"I don't know. Jealousy, perhaps."

"Okay. I think we've got enough. We'll look into the matter. If we find out anything, we'll give you a call," Officer Davis said.

"That's always your excuse!" Joy blurted out. "Everybody's always jealous of you. Why don't you tell them the truth!"

"Why don't you tell us?" Officer Davis said, clearly agitated.

"The reason Nicoli suspects Big L of gettin' her face cut up is because they were havin' a fling. Some gay shit was goin' down. All the while Nicoli was cheatin' on her fiancé. Somethin' went down earlier today—that's why Nicoli called me to meet her. She said she would tell me what happened once we met up. But that time would never come."

Both police officers turned around now to face me. I was embarrassed, but I decided to come clean if it meant that Big L would get arrested for what she did to me.

"That's true. We were sleeping together. I couldn't tell you in front of my fiancé. Besides, it was just for kicks, or so I thought. I ended it weeks ago. Today, I came out, and my car was vandalized. Someone scratched 'lesbian bitch' on my car, and I suspected Big L. So I called Joy to meet me. That's all I know."

"How many people, other than you and Big L, know about this fling?" Officer Pollock questioned.

"Just Joy. She's the only other person." And once again the speculation focused on Joy.

"So Joy could have easily scratched 'lesbian bitch' on your car?" Davis interjected.

"Not likely. Why would she do that?" I asked.

"Joy, we may be calling you in for questioning. Just to hear what you may know. Don't take any sudden trips, okay?" Officer Pollock said, and with that they left.

After the police officers left, I stared at Joy and asked, "Joy, did you have anything to do with this?" My voice cracked as the reality of the possible truth came to light.

"Turnabout is a fair game, and karma is a mutherfucker!" she gloated.

"Joy, answer me. Did you have anything to do with this? Give me a direct yes or no, Joy. Come on, you owe me that."

"You trifling, *ugly* bitch! I don't owe you a mutherfuckin' thang." Joy stormed out. That left me speechless.

Chapter 26

After Joy stormed out of the hospital in a fury, I wanted to cry, but nothing came out. I just lay there stunned—stunned at today's events, stunned at how rapidly my life was spinning out of control. And most importantly, stunned at being called "ugly."

My mind couldn't get past the fact that Joy could have set me up. I kept searching for a motive and coming up empty. It was painful for me to go over my past actions toward Joy. I used to make her feel low about her looks. I would berate her with snide remarks. I even stole money out of her purse. I was a real lowlife. And I pretended to be her friend. Was all this animosity building up over time until Joy ultimately hated me?

My mother stayed behind and helped discharge me out of the hospital. I wanted to go and see about Black at the precinct. He'd gotten arrested and beat up defending his fiancé. When we made it to the precinct, we were told that Black and Big L would be given DATs, which meant they would have to appear in court later to answer charges of assault and disorderly conduct. They told me I could sit and wait for Black.

Gail and I sat patiently for hours while they processed their paperwork. My mother had given me her baseball cap to cover my unsightly head, but there was no camouflaging my stitched-up face.

Finally Black came walking out, escorted by a police officer. His lips were busted, and his left eye was swollen. Other than that, I can say he looked a helluva lot better than I did. When I stood up so Black could see me, his eyes hooded over. He pursed his lips tightly together in a thin line.

"He must be embarrassed at being beaten up by Big L," I whispered to my mother.

"I don't think that's it," my mother replied.

I walked over to Black and extended my arms, expecting him to hug me. He pushed past me and kept on walking.

"Black," I called after him. "What's wrong? What did I do? I need you now!" I screamed out in frustration.

Black continued walking, so I ran after him and pulled his arm.

"Am I ugly? Is that it, because if it is, just say so. Don't torture me like this."

"Your face has nothing to do with it, Nicoli. It's your heart I'm concerned about."

When he saw the perplexed look on my face, he continued, "The police told me. They told me you fucked her. You were fucking her while you were with me. They laughed at me, Nicoli. . . ." He paused, then continued, "That's what this is all about. While you had my ring on your finger, you were fucking that bitch!" He screamed with such passion, tiny tears of frustration escaped his eyes. I had truly hurt him.

"Black, I love you." I finally said it to him. "I love you, Black."

Black stared at me for a long moment. Then he said, "It's over, Nicoli."

"Over? What about me? What am I supposed to do now? Where do I go from here? Black, please don't go. I forgave you! How many times did I forgive you for cheating?"

"That was your choice. My choice is to leave—you chose to stay."

His logic silenced me.

Epilogue

March 2004

After Black and I broke up, I found out I was pregnant. At first I was really sad. I didn't want to bring a baby into a broken home. But then, as the baby grew inside me, I grew to love it. For a while Black and I weren't on speaking terms, but through his lawyer he had promised to take care of our child. Gradually, Black started calling the house and speaking with my mother, asking how I was doing. He was so proud when my mother told him I'd enrolled in college. Still, he didn't want to speak to me.

I was six months pregnant when Black came over with four deliverymen. They had a beautiful crib, high chair, and car seat. Black had picked out an array of beautiful baby clothing—more clothing than an infant could ever need. He'd bought a host of sleepers and T-shirts in pastel colors, since we didn't know the sex of the baby.

That was the first time I'd seen him or spoken to him since the incident. We were both cordial. I told him how I was progressing in college and that I attended a Baptist church around the corner. He said he was proud of me, and I could tell he was genuine. My heart hurt just staring in his eyes.

"I miss you. . . . I miss you, Black," I said, my voice barely a whisper.

His eyes welled up with tears, and he quickly left.

After that encounter Black would occasionally call me on the telephone. We'd have short conversations, and I desperately wanted to tell him how I dreamed about him every night. I wanted to tell him how much I messed up. I wanted to tell him how much I needed him. But I said nothing. I let days turn into weeks. Weeks turn into months. Hope turn into hopelessness.

No one was ever arrested for cutting my face. And although the wounds healed, the scars remained. And I never got down to the bottom of whether Joy had anything to do with it. She and I aren't speaking. And that's her choice. Going to the Baptist church taught me how to forgive.

My mother and I now have a wonderful relationship. She's excited about the baby. We're now concentrating on having a mother-daughter relationship as opposed to a sister-sister relationship. I realized that I was a lot like my mother—always in search of someone to love me. Now, we love each other, and it feels wonderful.

"Ouch," I said. The baby was kicking. "Mommy, the baby's kicking again."

"Babies do that, Nicoli. Just sit still. Do you want somethin' to eat? I'll fix you somethin' to eat," she said. She was always feeding me.

"I guess I could eat a little something. Maybe a sandwich with a pickle," I said, then continued, "Mommy, don't forget my pickle."

Faintly, I thought I heard the doorbell ringing.

"Mommy, is the doorbell ringing?"

My mother walked back from out of the kitchen and said, "I didn't hear it, but I'll check. Nicoli, you expectin' comp'ny?"

"No," I said and watched my mother look at her reflection in the living room mirror.

"What are you doing, Mother?" I inquired.

"I'm just seein' how I look. That could be my future husband knockin' at my door." She chuckled.

"You look fine," I said. "In fact, you look beautiful."

My mother smiled, "Thanks, baby. I'll get the door."

Stacy and Fertashia came bouncing in with cheer. They came

back sporadically to chat and see how I was doing. I could tell that they felt sorry for me. That's why they came by. All they saw was a girl with her face ripped apart. They didn't notice that I was happier now because even before my face was ripped apart, my soul was ripped apart.

"Hey, girl," Fertashia said. "You look like shit. You all big 'n shit," she teased.

"Nicoli, don't even worry about it, 'cause you gonna be paid, just as soon as the baby drops. I read that Kim Porter gets fourteen thousand dollars a month in child support from Diddy. I know you can get more money than that."

"Stacy, don't believe everything you read. And I don't need fourteen thousand dollars a month to take care of a baby. That's just ridiculous."

"Nicoli, I wish you'd snap out of it! We need your guidance. Girls are upping the bounty out here. They screaming rape with athletes, poking holes in condoms to get pregnant, resorting to blackmail. It's a jungle out here. If we keep playing by the rules, all the rich guys are going to put their penises on lockdown. We need you to tell us all your secrets. How do we get knocked up by a celebrity?"

"Stacy and Fertashia, if you two don't get out of here talking such nonsense—I'm a changed woman. You're talking Greek to me. Now give me a kiss, and you guys can stop by once the baby is born," I said, dismissing them.

"Wait, Nicoli, we came for a reason. There's this new hot spot up in Harlem that we need to be in. Could we please, please, please borrow somethin' to wear from out your closet? We promise to keep it neat and return it as soon as possible," Stacy begged.

"You two can take whatever you want from out of my closet. Help yourselves. Just promise me you'll be safe."

"We promise," they both said in unison.

Eventually they gave me hugs and left.

I can truly say that the summer of 2003 was 'the best of times and the worst of times.' But it was an enlightening time that taught me a valuable lesson. I used to believe that outside appearance was everything. And that you could find true love at the bottom of someone's wallet. Now I know that just because you've known someone all your life, that doesn't mean that you really know that person. Joy's betrayal has taught me that I should value and cherish my friends and treat them with love and respect, if I want that in return. In my immature phase, all I really wanted to do was have a good time, at anyone's expense. When I think about the person I used to be, I become so sad. I disrespected my mother, humiliated my friends, and didn't respect my own body. I think about that chapter of my life as a haunting dream that I needed to open my eyes from.

Big L's bitterness used to haunt me like the kindred spirit of my grandmother. My grandmother was a mean-spirited person, and I fight every day not to end up like her. If it were not for the devotion my mother showed me in my time of need, I don't know where I'd be. This whole situation has been cathartic. And now I feel cleansed and optimistic about my future. I have a beautiful baby on the way. And maybe there's a chance that Black and I will get back together. Or maybe we won't. That's life. It's consistently inconsistent. But I'll never stop loving my beautiful Black King. And I know he still loves me.

summer madness

Rochelle Alers

Chapter 1

The weather was perfect for a June wedding.

Afternoon temperatures had peaked in the low eighties, the sun was a brilliant sphere in a cloudless azure sky, and the low humidity made the warm, gentle breeze even more delicious.

A DJ, caterer, and bartenders were waiting for the wedding party guests as they filed into the backyard of the restored brownstone belonging to newlyweds Dr. Wayne and Mrs. Carmen Medina-Nelson in Harlem's Mt. Morris Park Historic District. A canopy draped in hundreds of yards of creamy white silk organza had transformed the expansive outdoor space into a fairy-tale setting.

Nina Watkins stiffened before relaxing her back as her partner's fingers tightened on her waist. This is the last time I'm going to be a bridesmaid, she swore silently, affecting a winning smile for the photographer.

It was the third time she had become a bridesmaid, and she was the last in a quartet of best friends who was still single. She also held the distinction of being the only one who had never been engaged. At thirty-four, she had become a professional bridesmaid.

Tilting her head to the left, she raised her chin and stared directly into the camera lens. The photographer snapped two more frames. "That's it for now," he announced, nodding and smiling his approval.

Nina let out an audible sigh and curbed the urge to massage her jaw. Her face ached from smiling. She had expected her feet to hurt. When she'd slipped into the silk-covered stilettos, she anticipated limping after being on her feet for more than two hours. As a high school librarian, she was used to wearing comfortable, functional footwear. However, there was something positive to be said for the pricey flower-embroidered Manolo Blahnik sandals.

Richard Nelson, the groom's brother, reached for her hand. "Come, let's sit down."

She smiled at him for the umpteenth time that day. She wasn't about to argue with him. He led her over to a damask-covered table set aside for the wedding party and pulled out a tufted chair swathed in the same diaphanous silk organza that billowed around the canopy.

Lifting the skirt of her magenta, floor-length satin gown, Nina sat down. Richard took a chair to her left and draped an arm over her bared shoulders. "Could you please get me something cold to drink?" she said quietly, as two other groomsmen and bridesmaids joined them at the table.

She did not need a drink as much as she wanted him to remove his arm. They'd met for the first time earlier that week at the wedding rehearsal, and Richard had zeroed in on her like a heat-seeking missile bearing down on its target. He'd draped himself over her until she began to think of him as a permanent tattoo. Tall, handsome, and considered a good catch, the urban planner just happened not to be her type; she'd found him too needy and clingy. Over the years she had believed she had a type, but recently she'd come to the conclusion that she would not know her type if he sat on her lap.

Richard stared at Nina, his dark brown eyes moving slowly over her face, finding himself entranced by her delicate beauty. Her shoes added several inches to her diminutive frame, while the slinky

halter-styled gown showed her curvy figure to its best advantage—
especially the revealing décolletage. Her stylishly cut short hair flat-
tered a round face with high cheekbones, dark brown slanting eyes,
a button nose, and a full, lush mouth. The result was an enchanting feminine package.

"What would you like?"

"Club soda." She never drank anything alcoholic before eating.

Leaning over, Richard kissed her cheek. "I'll be right back."

"Don't rush," Nina mumbled under her breath to his departing
back.

"You're next to walk down the aisle, Nina," crooned a sultry
feminine voice next to her.

Turning to her right, she stared at Michelle Sims. She'd been
Michelle's maid of honor three years before. "Dream on, girlfriend."

Michelle smiled. "You and Richard look nice together."

"Forget it," she drawled.

"What's wrong with him?"

"Nothing. He happens not to be my type."

A frown appeared between Michelle's light brown eyes. "Do you
really have a type, Nina?"

She rolled her eyes at her best friend. "Of course I do."

Undaunted, Michelle sucked her teeth. "I showed my cousin
who lives in Denver your photograph, and he told me that when he
comes to New York in the fall, he'd like to meet you."

Nina shook her head. "Please, Michelle. I don't want to meet
any more folks in your family. Your Miami cousin needs a dentist
big-time, while your uncle from New Orleans looks like the quin-
tessential pimp with an outdated wet-look curl. And I'll reserve
comment on his cologne." She couldn't tell Michelle that the scent
reminded her of cat urine.

"Thanks for looking out for me," she continued, "but I'm tired
of going out with men who are habitual liars, who refuse to commit,

and who have baby-mama drama that rivals the plots of daytime soaps. The only thing worse than finding my own loser is dating the ones recommended by well-meaning friends."

Michelle frowned again, vertical lines marring her smooth forehead. "There's nothing wrong with Joseph's mouth. He has a slight overbite most women find sexy."

"It wasn't the overbite. He has at least half a dozen missing teeth in the back of his mouth," Nina countered softly. She hadn't noticed the absence of teeth until he laughed.

Michelle's retort was preempted as a round of applause greeted Dr. and Mrs. Wayne Nelson as they took their seats at the bridal table.

The opening verse of Kool and the Gang's "Celebration" came through speakers concealed behind trees and flowering rosebushes. Heads bobbed, feet tapped, fingers snapped, and several couples gyrated over to the portable stage set aside for dancing. The celebrating had begun in earnest.

Richard returned with Nina's club soda. He set it on the table and extended his right hand. "May I have this dance?" Before she could refuse, he grasped her hand, pulled her gently to her feet, and steered her toward the dance floor.

As soon as Nina raised her arms, swaying to the catchy tune, she decided she was going to enjoy herself. So what, she was a three-time bridesmaid, so what she didn't have a steady boyfriend, so what she hadn't had a date in more than six months, and so freaking what she had been celibate for more than a year. The upbeat tempo segued into a slow love song, and Richard wound his arm around her waist, pulling her close to his body.

"A group of my friends are going down to Virginia Beach next weekend," he whispered close to her ear. "I'd like you to come with me." Easing back, he flashed a Cheshire cat grin.

Nina closed her eyes. Oh, no, he didn't go there! They hadn't gone out on one date, and he expected her to go away with him. And do what together? she asked, continuing her mental monologue.

She forced a smile she did not feel. "Thanks, but I can't."

His grin vanished. "You can't or you won't?"

"I have other plans."

"Can't you change them?"

"No. Will you change yours?"

He shook his head. "I can't, because my boys and I planned this trip a couple of months ago."

Nina affected a facetious smile. "And I can't change my plans because I made them a year ago."

Every year for the past six summers she had loaded the trunk of a rental car with what she would need for her vacation and driven to Sag Harbor, Long Island, for the season; and this year was no exception.

"What do you say we get together after I come back?"

"I don't say," she said, deciding to be honest with him. "I'm going to be out of the city for the summer. I won't be back until after Labor Day."

Spinning her around, Richard dipped Nina, his mouth hovering over hers. "You can't blame a brother for trying."

She smiled up at the face looming inches from her own. "No, I can't."

He eased her up, and they finished the dance number. They hadn't taken more than three steps when Richard stopped abruptly. Nina bumped into him, losing her balance in the three-inch heels. A hand reached out to steady her, strong masculine fingers curving around her upper arm.

"Oh!"

"Careful."

Nina and her rescuer had spoken in unison.

"Well, I'll be damned!" Richard said, grinning at the tall, impeccably dressed man. "How the hell are you, D.L.?"

"Just getting by, cousin." Even though he had spoken to Richard, his gaze was fixed on Nina's upturned face.

"I didn't expect you to come."

"I don't see why not, Richard. After all, I did send back my response card indicating I planned to attend."

"I'll give you that, but how many family functions have you missed over the past three years?"

The man Richard had called D.L. shifted his gaze to his cousin. "You're forgetting your manners, Richard. Aren't you going to introduce me to the lady?" He'd deftly shifted the topic away from himself.

Nina had watched the interaction between the two men, transfixed. D.L. was tall, dark, and handsome. And there was no doubt that his suit had not come off the rack. A blended silk and wool navy blue double-breasted jacket with a subtle pinstripe was literally draped over his broad shoulders. The platinum silk tie knotted under the spread collar of a crisp white shirt was the perfect complement to the suit. She noted a pair of conservative silver cufflinks in French cuffs.

Her rapt gaze lingered on his lean, sable-brown face. The brown eyes, with flecks of gold, missed nothing. His catlike slanting eyes and refined features called to mind a sleek black panther.

Richard stared at Nina, frowning when he saw the direction of her entranced stare. "Nina, this is my cousin, Andrew Lancaster. Drew, Nina Watkins."

Nina extended a manicured hand, smiling. "My pleasure, Mr. Lancaster."

Drew angled his head, an eyebrow lifting as he registered the low, dulcet voice of the petite bridesmaid. He cradled her smaller hand in his, noting that the color on her nails matched her dress.

Raising her hand, he lowered his head and pressed a kiss to her knuckles.

"No, it's *my* pleasure to make your acquaintance, Miss Watkins." Their gazes met and fused, the corners of their mouths inching up in a knowing smile. Reluctantly, Drew released Nina's soft hand. "Please excuse me, but I want to congratulate Wayne and his beautiful bride."

Nina nodded numbly, watching as Drew walked away. He might have been Richard's cousin, but he projected an aura that was different from her wedding partner's.

Waiters and waitresses, carrying trays perched on fingertips, were offering hot and cold canapés, and Nina accepted a napkin, a chilled jumbo shrimp dipped into a piquant cocktail sauce, and two overstuffed mushrooms. Richard had returned to the bar to get a drink, and she rejoined Michelle and Kim Stewart, the third member of their quartet.

A mysterious smile touched Michelle's mouth when she saw the direction of Nina's gaze. "Is that your type?"

"So, you noticed?"

"Oh, yeah. Only a blind person would miss the silent fireworks between the two of you."

"Was I that obvious?"

Michelle waved a hand. "Don't sweat it, Nina. He was staring at you as if you were dessert. Don't look now, but he's looking this way."

"His name is Andrew Lancaster, but Richard called him D.L."

Michelle stared at Andrew as he reached into the breast pocket of his jacket and handed Wayne an envelope. "I take it he's a friend of Wayne." She, Nina, Carmen, and Kim had grown up together, and over the years they'd come to know one another's relatives.

"He's a cousin."

Kim whistled softly. "Damn! The Nelsons have a helluva gene

pool. There's no doubt there will be another generation of beautiful babies."

"I hear you," Michelle whispered conspiratorially. "Speaking of babies—"

"You're pregnant?" Kim asked, interrupting her.

Michelle lowered her gaze. "I'm only a few days late."

"Take the test," Nina said, grinning.

"It's too soon," Michelle insisted. "I don't want a false positive."

Kim rolled her hazel eyes. "I'm with Nina. I say take the test."

Michelle shook her head. "I'm going to wait until Thursday. The school year will be over, and Lloyd and I can stay in bed all day celebrating *if* I am pregnant." Michelle, Lloyd, and Nina worked in the same Brooklyn high school.

"Oh, *no!*" Michelle gasped. "Look at Carmen's fast-ass cousin cheesing at your man, Nina. Uh-uh! There ain't no excuse for that nasty hoochie mama to bend over that far. Someone should've milked her before she put on that scandalous dress."

"Have you been holding out on us, Nina?" Kim asked.

Nina stared at Kim. "Holding out what?"

"Do you have something going on with D.L.?"

"Of course not. I just met him," she said, but she wanted to say yes. There was something about the way Drew had looked at her that stoked a fire that had been banked for far too long. Pushing back her chair, she stood up. "I need a drink."

Kim rose with her. "I'm right behind you, girlfriend." She turned and looked at Michelle. "Are you coming?"

"I'm not drinking anything alcoholic until I find out one way or the other."

"Take the test," Nina and Kim chorused, laughing.

Chapter 2

Drew sat at the table with his mother, aunts, and uncles, his gaze following the gentle sway of Nina Watkins's hips as she got up with the women who crowded together in an attempt to catch Carmen's bridal bouquet.

Nice. That was the only word he could come up with to describe her. There was something about Nina that intrigued him, but he had managed to quell his curiosity and not ask Wayne about her because he wanted to be pleasantly surprised. Now that she had gotten up with the other single women, he could cross one query off his list as to her marital status.

"Are you behaving yourself, Drew?" his mother's twin sister asked him for what was now the tenth time. Although she was only in her mid-sixties, she had been diagnosed with the early stages of Alzheimer's.

He smiled. "Yes, Aunt Bettina."

"You're not still running with those criminals that used to give everyone on the block grief."

"No, Aunt Bettina."

"You got a job, Drew?"

"Yes, Auntie, I have a job."

"What is it you do?"

He sobered, his expression stoic. "I'd rather not say."

Bettina slapped the table with the plastic fan she always carried with her. Her eyes narrowed to slits. "You'd rather not say because you're still doing stuff on the down-low. They don't call you D.L. for nothing, boy."

Drew wanted to tell his aunt that he wasn't a boy, hadn't been one in a long time. At thirty-eight, he was approaching middle age, but he knew it was useless to argue with Bettina. His maiden aunt had earned a reputation for being mean-spirited and opinionated even before her illness.

"Audrey told me you paid for her to take a cruise to the Panama Canal later on in the year. She claims it was your retirement gift to her," Wilbur Nelson said in a deep, authoritative voice.

Drew gave his uncle a direct stare. "I told her to take an around-the-world cruise on the *QE2,* but she wanted to see the Panama Canal."

The older man shook his head. "Your daddy must be praying for you from heaven to keep your butt out of jail. And I'll have you know no Nelson has ever served time in prison. That's because we're God-fearing people who always try to do the right thing. What you're doing isn't right, Andrew. You know it, and I know it. And if you're arrested, don't call me, because I'm not going to lift a finger to help you."

He dismissed his attorney uncle's tirade and turned his attention back to the women in front of the bridal table. This was the reason he did not frequent many family gatherings. He'd grown tired of the interrogation, insinuations, and accusations. His family had never forgiven him for dropping out of college; it was a Nelson tradition to graduate from college and become a professional. What they did not know was that he *was* a professional—without a college degree.

"One thing you did right was not make any babies, even though my sister wants grandbabies in the worse way," Bettina continued, mumbling angrily.

Drew stared at Carmen, who'd turned her back. Then, without warning, she turned and handed her bouquet of white flowers with streamers of pink ribbons to Nina. A loud groan mingled with laughter as Nina dropped the bouquet as if it were a venomous reptile. Carmen bent down, picked it up, and handed it to her again. Throwing back his head, Drew laughed loudly with the others.

Wayne joined his wife and curved an arm around her waist. The best man brought over a seat, and Carmen sat down. Kneeling, Wayne lifted the skirt of the white sheath gown dotted with seeded pearls and slid a lacy garter down her thigh and off her leg.

He twirled the garter around his forefinger, grinning broadly. "Come on, brothers, it's your turn." Twice as many men stood up, ranging in age from late teens to over seventy. "Sit down, Grandpa, before Grandma puts a hurting on you." Grinning sheepishly, the elderly man made his way back to his table, where his wife awaited him. She swiped at him with a cloth napkin, eliciting another round of laughter.

Pushing back his chair, Drew rose to his feet and joined the others. He'd thought about not getting up, but then changed his mind.

Bettina smiled across the table at her sister. "There's hope for your boy yet."

Drew's mother rolled her eyes at her twin sister before sucking her teeth. "At least I have a *boy*, Bettina Nelson." What she did not add was that at least she'd had a husband, even though she had been widowed for the past eight years. "But in case you haven't looked lately—he *is* a man."

"There's no need to take that tone with me, Audrey. Just because he put on a suit and tie, that still don't make up for his thuggish lifestyle."

Audrey decided it was useless to argue with her sister and watched Drew as he waited for her nephew to throw the garter. A bright smile lit up her face when he reached over a shorter man's head to snag the lacy garment.

Amid a chorus of groans, Drew held tightly to the garter. Turning, he stared at Nina, who had retreated to her table. Crossing his arms over his chest, he angled his head. He raised a forefinger and beckoned her.

Kim placed a hand on Nina's back. "Get up there, girl."

Nina shook her head. "No. Let him come to me." Raising her left hand, she repeated his gesture.

There was a stunned silence as Drew walked toward her like a stalking cat. Nina hadn't realized she was holding her breath until he stood over her. Everything that was Andrew Lancaster swept over her in an instant: his height, the breadth of his wide shoulders, the golden eyes that burned with a mysterious fire, and the hauntingly sensual scent of his cologne.

A wave of heat swept up her chest and settled in her face. Her gaze met Drew's as he went to one knee in front of her. The lacy garter trimmed in a pale blue ribbon hung around his wrist like a bracelet.

His gaze never wavered as he stared at her. She jumped slightly when his fingers feathered up the generous front slit in the dress and parted it to reveal a pair of shapely legs encased in sheer nylon.

"Hurry up," she hissed between her teeth.

Drew shook his head slowly. "It would've been quick if you'd come to me. But since you didn't, then I'm calling the shots." Nina closed her eyes against his grin once he eased her dress up over her knees.

"Very nice," he crooned once the tops of her thighs were exposed. He hesitated, visually feasting on her legs before he took the garter from his wrist. Lifting her foot, he slid it up her leg and over her thigh. He straightened and offered her his hand. She placed her hand in his, and he led her out to the dance floor as everyone applauded.

The DJ played the Temptations' oldie, "Just My Imagination," as Drew eased Nina to his chest. The top of her head came to his shoulder.

"How long have you known Carmen?"

Nina raised her head. "All my life. We grew up together."

"So you're a Harlem girl." She nodded. "Do you still live here?"

"No. I live in Brooklyn."

"Where in Brooklyn?"

"Park Slope."

He lifted his eyebrows. "That's a nice neighborhood."

"I like it."

"What do you do?"

"I'm a high school librarian. What's so funny?" she asked when he chuckled deep in his throat.

"You don't look like any librarian I've ever seen. At least not like the ones with buns, orthopedic shoes, and half glasses perched on the end of their noses."

"I wear reading glasses whenever my eyes get tired."

Drew wanted to tell Nina that even with glasses she still would look sexy. "What do you do for relaxation? Other than read," he added quickly.

"I listen to music, swim, and occasionally write poetry. How about yourself? Where do you live? What do you do for a living?"

"I live uptown from here."

"How far uptown?"

"I have a place in Riverdale."

Nina affected an attractive moue. "That's not uptown. That's the Bronx."

He smiled, flashing a set of perfect white teeth. "Okay. I live in the Bronx. Would you mind if I call you sometime?"

"I'm leaving the city for the summer."

"Where do you go?"

"Out east to Sag Harbor."

Drew stared down into her sparkling brown eyes. "I go out there occasionally. Let's exchange phone numbers, and I'll call you before I come out. Perhaps we can have dinner together."

Her mouth curved into an unconscious smile. She couldn't remember the last time a man had asked for her telephone number. "I'd like that."

"So would I."

Drew led Nina over to a secluded portion of the backyard and wrote down his name and cell phone number on a napkin, handing it to her. He gave Nina his pen, and she wrote the telephone number to the house where she would spend the summer on another napkin.

He put the napkin with her number in the pocket of his trousers. Leaning down, he kissed her cheek. "I'll call you."

Nina wasn't given the opportunity to reply when he turned on his heel and walked away. She waited a full minute before returning to her table. She ignored Richard's scowl as she sat down. He got up and walked away. It was obvious he had seen her with his cousin.

Michelle inched closer. "What were you doing over there with that chocolate licorice stick?"

Nina's jaw dropped. "Who are you talking about?

"Drew, Nina. Now, you have to admit that he's long, dark, and sweet-looking."

She smiled. "I'd say he's more like a Tootsie Pop. I wonder how many licks it would take to get to the chocolate center."

"Stop it, girlfriend!"

Nina showed Michelle the napkin she cradled in her hand. "I got his number."

"Does he have yours?" Nina nodded. "All right! I want you to call me with all of the details."

"We've only committed to having dinner together."

"That's a start, Nina."

She nodded, smiling. "Yes, it is."

It was a start, but she'd never had much success with summer romances. Perhaps this summer she would have a fling, enjoy whatever came out of it, then come fall she would settle back into a predictable routine that was guaranteed to be angst- *and* stress-free.

Chapter 3

Nina sat on a chintz-covered chaise on the screened-in front porch. She had turned the radio to a station that featured love songs. A smile softened her mouth when she saw the intermittent glow from a firefly. It was twilight, her favorite time of the day.

The beachfront bungalow had been in her family since the mid-1840s, and although it had been updated, the original structure had remained virtually the same. The only exception was a backyard patio.

It had taken only two days for her to settle in and reconnect with her childhood friend, Deborah Simpson. Deborah had grown up on Sag Harbor and taught math at the local high school.

The tangy smell of salt water lingered in the air. The wind that swept lingering clouds across a darkening sky had subsided. Two hours before dark, angry thunderclouds had rolled in, while sea oats swayed with an increasing wind, and before the whitecaps broke with the incoming surf, thunder and lightning sent bathers and boaters scurrying from the beach and water to escape nature's fury. Nina had retrieved her blanket and book and retreated to the porch to wait out the downpour. The rain had stopped, but she hadn't returned to the beach.

The soft chiming of a telephone on the table on the other side of the screen door caught her attention. She sat up, swung her legs over the chaise, and went into the house. It was either her brother or her parents.

"Hello."

"Hello, Nina."

A bright smile spread across her face when she heard the velvety baritone voice. Why, she thought, did Drew make her name sound like a caress?

"Hello, Drew."

"Have you settled in?"

"Yes."

"What are you doing?"

"Relaxing."

"Are you reading?"

Nina laughed softly. "Yes. How did you know?"

Drew's chuckle came through the earpiece. "Perhaps I'm a psychic."

"Psychic, my foot. You don't have to be a clairvoyant to know that a librarian and books are matched sets."

"And for a librarian you have beautiful feet."

"You've never seen my feet," she said after a moment of silence.

"I saw more than I'd ever hoped to see once I put Carmen's garter on your leg. I told you that I'd call when I was coming out east," Drew continued, deftly changing the topic.

Nina could not stop the heat that swept over her face and moved lower to settle in her chest. There was no doubt Drew had eased her dress high enough up her legs to catch a glimpse of her pink bikini panties.

"When are you coming?" she asked.

"Tomorrow. I have an afternoon meeting with a friend, and then I'm free for the evening. I'd like to take you out to dinner— that is, if you are available."

Nina smiled. "I just so happen to be available."

"Good."

"What time do you want to meet?" she asked.

"How about seven?"

"Seven is good."

"Where should I pick you up?"

"Do you need directions?" she asked after she'd given him her address.

A soft chuckle came through the earpiece. "No. I believe I know where you live."

"That settles it. I'll see you tomorrow."

There was a slight pause before Drew spoke again. "Thank you, Nina."

Her brow furrowed in confusion. "For what?"

"For agreeing to go out with me."

She held the phone to her ear, unable to form a comeback. A man had never thanked her for dating him; they usually thought they were doing her a favor.

"You're welcome," she said softly, smiling. "Good night, Drew."

There was another pulse beat of silence. "Good night, Nina."

She hung up, her smile still in place. Despite what Richard had deigned to tell her about his cousin, she looked forward to seeing him. After she had danced with Drew at Carmen's reception, Richard felt it was his responsibility to tell her that his cousin had a less than admirable reputation. Some family members referred to Drew as D.L., standing not for Drew Lancaster but for "Down Low." None of the Nelsons knew what he did for a living, and a few suspected he was involved in something illegal.

Her smile faded once she realized she had agreed to go out with someone whose life was shrouded in secrecy. What if what Richard had told her about Drew was true? Was he involved in illegal activities, were law enforcement officers monitoring his whereabouts? When had she become so reckless that she would date a criminal?

There was only one way to find out. She would ask him when she saw him the following day.

*   *   *

Drew slowed to less than ten miles an hour along the sand-littered street and maneuvered the sleek sports car into a driveway behind a late-model Mitsubishi sedan. He had taken a helicopter from midtown Manhattan to Southampton, met with his client, then borrowed a car for the drive to Sag Harbor.

He turned off the engine to the racy Porsche, reaching for the package on the passenger-side seat wrapped in silver foil and tied with narrow black velvet ribbon.

Sand grated under his shoes as he stepped out of the car and approached the house. The one-story, white-shingled house, trimmed in gray with matching shutters, looked homey. Its screened-in porch had a chaise, a glider, and a rocker covered with a rose-patterned fabric. A white wicker table between the chaise and glider held a portable stereo system and several books. A knowing smile lifted the corner of his mouth when he remembered Nina telling him that she was a librarian. The door to the house stood open.

He rang the bell and waited. Less than a minute later, Nina appeared from the rear of the house. Drew hadn't realized he was gawking until he was forced to swallow to moisten his dry throat. His gaze was fixed on the length of her smooth, bare legs showing beneath the hem of her slim knee-length black skirt. A white shell in a stretch fabric clung to her upper body, outlining the roundness of her full breasts. She'd thrown a black jacket over her arm.

Her smile was as brilliant as the sparkle in her dark eyes. "Hello. Please come in."

Drew stepped into the living room, and everything that he'd tried remembering about Nina came rushing back in vivid clarity. Her flawless face, her fragrant perfume, the sound of her beautifully modulated voice, and the sensuality that was inherent without her attempting to flaunt it.

He handed her the package. "I bought a little something for you."

Nina blinked once. She shook it gently. "You didn't have to bring me anything."

Angling his head, Drew stared down at her. "I know. But when I saw it, I thought you would like it."

"What is it?"

"You'll have to open it and find out." He held up a hand. "I'd prefer if you'd open it later."

She gave him a sidelong glance, smiling, and wondered if he had given her something he'd obtained illegally. "Now, that sounds ominous."

His smile matched hers. "Mysterious maybe, but definitely not ominous. Are you ready?"

"Yes." She placed the package on the table, slipped into her jacket, picked up a small handbag, and closed the door behind her, which locked automatically.

She'd told Drew she was ready. But now, after seeing him again, she wasn't certain whether she was ready for him. He wore a pair of black linen slacks with an off-white silk T-shirt. A narrow black ostrich-skin belt circled his slim waist. His exposed arms were corded with lean natural muscle. He appeared taller, imposing, and a little intimidating.

Drew reached for her hand and led her off the porch to his car. She felt a shiver of awareness snake up her arm as his strong fingers closed over hers. The palm of his hand was smooth. It was apparent he did not use his hands to earn money—except perhaps to count it. But then again, perhaps he used a machine to count his money, the way banks did.

After his call, Nina had tried to convince herself that what Drew did for a living was not her concern. However, common sense prevailed once her overactive imagination conjured up images of rival criminals putting out a hit on him, or federal agents arresting him while they were together.

Drew opened the Porsche's passenger-side door for Nina and waited until she was seated and belted in before he came around and took his seat behind the wheel. The smell of new leather filled the car's interior. He turned the key, and the engine roared to life in a soft purr.

His right hand covered the gearshift, but before he could shift into reverse, Nina's fingers curved around his wrist. Turning his head, he stared at her. "Did you forget something?"

"No. But I need to ask you something."

His expression was impassive. "Ask."

She removed her hand and laced her fingers together in her lap. "Are you involved in anything illegal?"

His left eyebrow flickered. It was obvious some people in his family were spreading rumors again because he refused to tell them what he did for a living. At first he'd told them that it was none of their business, but after a while even that got tired, so he stopped saying anything. Only his mother knew how he earned his money.

"No, Nina. I'm not involved in anything illegal."

She let out an audible sigh and nodded. "Thank you."

"You believe me?"

Nina gave him a direct stare. "I have no reason not to believe you—unless you show me otherwise."

Drew curbed the urge to run his fingertips over her silken face. Her skin was flawless, giving the appearance of whipped chocolate mousse. "That will never happen."

"Thank you," she said again.

Drew shifted into reverse and backed out of her driveway. "I thought we'd eat at B. Smith's."

"Good choice." She had eaten there twice—the week it opened for business, and last year when she'd invited Carmen, Kim, and

Michelle out to Sag Harbor for a female bonding weekend. They'd practically lived on the beach, only retreating to the house to shower, change clothes, and sleep.

Drew drove to the restaurant and pulled into a parking space at the Long Wharf Marina. He cradled Nina's hand in the curve of his elbow as they walked the short distance to the restaurant. The maître d' asked whether they preferred dining inside or on the deck, and Drew looked at Nina.

"Which do you prefer?"

"Outside." The night was warm and the sky clear.

Drew nodded to the maître d'. "Outside." His left arm curved around Nina's waist as they were shown to a table with a view of luxurious yachts and other pleasure craft moored in the marina.

He sat down opposite her, smiling. "This is nice."

"Very, very nice," she said, referring to her dining partner. His strangely colored gold-flecked eyes bore into her, and she felt a flame of awareness flare to life between her thighs.

There was something so different, so foreign, about Drew that she found herself a little off balance. His manners were impeccable, his bearing different from any man she had ever met before—and in thirty-four years she had met a lot of men. But she hadn't slept with a lot of them—that just wasn't her style.

Could she sleep with Drew and not ask for something more? *Oh hell, yeah!* the naughty voice shouted in her head. She would sleep with him just to find out how many licks it would take to get to his dark chocolate center. Lowering her gaze, she stared at the menu on the table in front of her, not seeing any of the selections.

"Would you like to share a bottle of wine?" Drew asked. Her head came up with the query.

"Yes, I would."

"White or red?"

"White or blush."

"Pinot Blanc, Riesling, Rhine, white Zinfandel, or champagne."

Drew was quite versed in wines. "I'll take the Zinfandel."

A sly smile crinkled the corners of his slanting eyes. "That happens to be a favorite of mine."

"You seem to know a lot about wines."

"That comes from dining with clients."

"Who are?" she asked, lifting her eyebrows.

Drew's smile vanished quickly. "I'm afraid I can't disclose their identity."

"Are you telling me to mind my business, Drew?"

"No," he said smoothly. "It's like doctor privilege. I'm bound by an agreement not to reveal who they are."

Nina gave him a long, penetrating look. He *had* told her it was none of her business, but in the most gracious way possible.

"This is the last time I'll ask you about your business."

"I didn't mean to insult you, " he said quickly.

"I'm not insulted."

Reaching across the table, he covered her hands with his. "Are you sure?"

"Very sure." There was a hint of laughter in her voice.

He nodded. "I'd hate for us to be at odds before we get to know each other."

"I hardly think we'd get to know each other after one date."

"Who said anything about one date, Nina?" Drew tightened his grip on her fingers when she tried pulling away.

"But I'm spending the summer here."

"So?"

"You live in the city."

"So?" he repeated.

"If you want to see me, then you're going to have to come out here."

"So?" he repeated for the third time. "It's only a few miles."

"It's more than a few miles from Sag Harbor to the Bronx."

He gave her a narrowed look. "You don't think you're worth the distance?"

Her breath quickened, heat warmed her face. "Whether I'm worth it has nothing to do with you coming out here just to see me."

He released her hands and leaned against the back of his chair. "Now I am going to tell you to mind your business, Nina." He ignored her audible gasp. "If I want to come here to see you, then that should be my concern and not yours. The time it takes and the number of miles is also my concern, not yours. Is there anything about what I've just said you don't understand?"

Mixed feelings surged through her. She had finally met a man who'd shown an interest in *her,* and she was pushing him away—a man who was not only intriguing, but also candid. Hadn't she complained to her girlfriends that she was tired of lies, alibis, and those who couldn't commit or spell it correctly?

And she was more than aware that Drew did not have to drive more than eighty miles to get a woman to sleep with him.

"I read you loud and clear."

He smiled the sensual smile she'd come to look for. "Good. Now that we've settled that issue, what would you like to eat?"

Chapter 4

After her second glass of wine Nina placed her hand over the top of the glass when Drew attempted to refill it. "No more, please." They'd finished their entrées, but lingered at their table to enjoy the balmy summer breeze.

"But you're not the designated driver."

She gave him a lopsided smile. "That's okay. You don't need me to fall asleep on you."

The flickering light from a candle in the middle of the table threw long and short shadows across his face. "That wouldn't be such a terrible thing. I'll just sit up and watch you sleep."

"I've been told that I snore."

"Who told you that?"

"My mother."

He nodded and stared at her under lowered lids. He was certain Nina had no idea how desirable she was.

"Your mother told you?" She nodded. "How about a boyfriend?"

"What about a boyfriend?" she asked, answering his question with one of her own.

"Are you seeing someone?"

"Not at the present time."

"How long has it been?"

"A little more than a year."

"What happened?"

She averted her gaze. "I couldn't trust him."

Drew let out an audible sigh. "That will do it every time."

Nina stared at him. "Are you seeing someone?"

Drew shook his head. "No one I would consider special. Present company excluded," he added quickly.

"What makes me special, Drew?"

There was a pulse beat of silence before he said, "I don't know." And he didn't know, but he intended to uncover what it was. "Would you like dessert?" He had once again segued smoothly from one topic into another.

Smiling, she shook her head. "No, thank you."

Motioning for their server, Drew settled the bill and left a generous tip. Nina noticed he'd paid with cash, not a credit card. She wondered if he had any plastic, then reminded herself to stay out of his business.

Many of the shops near the marina were closed as they left the restaurant and made their way to the parking lot. The exceptions were eating establishments and the movie theater.

Nina stared out the windshield and into the blackness of the night as Drew drove back to her house. An occasional light shone from a window in the homes set back off the narrow, winding road.

"How long have you summered here?" Drew asked as he maneuvered into the driveway behind her rental.

"All of my life. My family has owned this property since the mid-1840s." She smiled when he whistled softly. "My parents are retired schoolteachers who now live in a D.C. suburb, and my brother and his wife, who are also teachers, live in New Haven, Connecticut. Sometimes they take the ferry across the Sound and stay a week with me, or vice versa."

He draped his right arm over the back of her seat. "You have a lot of teachers in your family."

"Becoming an educator is a family tradition."

"It's a very noble profession that doesn't get the respect it deserves." His mother and grandmother were teachers.

Nina waited for Drew to come around and help her out. The instant he placed his arm around her waist to escort her up the porch steps, she knew she did not want the evening to end. "The next time you come, I'll cook," she said quickly.

He gave her a skeptical look. "You cook?"

"Don't make it sound as if I have a contagious disease. Of course I cook."

"I just thought today's modern woman was too busy to do any more than heat up something in the microwave."

"I'm a librarian, not an emergency room doctor. I work an average of one hundred eighty days a year, so I'm not *that* busy."

Spanning her waist with both hands, he eased her to his chest. "If that's the case, then I'm looking forward to our next date." He lowered his head and brushed his mouth over hers. "Good night, and thanks for the company."

Nina inhaled his masculine scent. "Good night, Drew."

He released her, stepped back, and made his way off the porch to his car. Then he was gone, the sound of the car's engine fading into the night.

Nina unlocked the front door and walked into the house. She dropped her keys on the table beside the gaily wrapped box. She removed the velvet ribbon and the shiny silver foil paper. A bright smile crinkled the skin around her eyes.

He had given her the first volume of *The Diary of Anaïs Nin*. She opened the fragile cover and went completely still. It was a first edition, signed by the author, dated 1966. He had given her a collector's copy.

Holding the book to her chest, she smiled. The alleged bad boy had a sensitive side. She reached into her purse and took out her cell phone. Scrolling down the directory, she stopped at Drew's name and punched a button.

He answered the call after the second ring. "Yes, Nina?"

"I'm calling to thank you for the book."

His rich laugh came through the tiny earpiece. "Save your thanks for when I see you again."

"When will that be?"

"Next week."

"Which day?"

"Thursday. I'll come out early, and we can spend the day together."

She smiled even though he couldn't see her. "Okay. I'll look for you on Thursday. Bye."

"Bye back to you."

She ended the call as she walked across the living room to turn off the lamp. The wine had made her sleepy, but she was not too sleepy to begin reading the work of a woman who definitely was ahead of her time.

Chapter 5

Drew experienced a sense of urgency that was alien and utterly foreign to him as he maneuvered his rental car along the winding road leading to Nina's home. He wasn't certain what it was about the petite librarian that had him thinking about her when he least expected it, but this weekend he intended to find out.

His early-morning meeting had gone better than he'd expected, and there was nothing to clutter his mind as he prepared to spend more than a few hours with Nina.

Nina rose from the chaise as she heard the slam of a car door. Glancing up from the James Baldwin classic, *Go Tell It on the Mountain,* she saw Drew striding up the path. This time he'd driven a BMW SUV instead of the Porsche.

Drew had surprised her when he called the night before and told her that he planned to stay on Long Island through the weekend. He hadn't said whether it was for business, so she assumed it was a pleasure outing. The little smile that played at the corners of her mouth became a full grin as she opened the screen door to greet him.

"Welcome back."

Drew entered the screened-in space and smiled. "Thank you," he said before lowering his head and pressing a kiss to her cheek. "It's good to be back."

"Come inside and rest yourself."

Drew followed her into the living room, his gaze taking in everything in one sweeping glance. The space was spotless, inviting, and the fact that it was uncluttered made it appear larger than it actually was.

He passed a dining room and walked into the kitchen. Hanging copper pots, wood countertops, and exposed beams imbued the space with warmth.

"We'll sit out on the patio," Nina said over her shoulder as she opened a set of French doors.

"Now I see why you spend the summer here." He moved closer, his breath feathering over Nina's ear.

She smiled. "It's beautiful, and so peaceful."

He nodded. "Yes, it is."

"I'd planned for us to eat dinner out here, but now I'm not so sure. Looks like rain is coming."

"There's always tomorrow, Saturday, or even Sunday," Drew said in a quiet voice. "Unless you're expecting company."

Nina stared up at him, meeting his amused stare. "I'm not expecting company."

"I noticed there are a lot of new homes around here."

"Are you considering building one?"

"Yes, I am," he said slowly.

"Would you like to see a few homes up close? We can see them if we walk the beach."

Sitting down on a cushioned rattan chair, Drew took off his sandals and rolled the hem of his khakis up to his knees. Glancing up at Nina, he smiled. "Now I feel like a clam digger." Rising to his feet, he reached for her hand, and they headed for the beach.

"If you build in Ninevah, then you'll have B. Smith, owner of B. Smith's restaurant, and her husband Dan Gatsby as neighbors. Earl Graves, publisher of *Black Enterprise,* and Susan Taylor have also built here."

"Do they live here year-round?"

"Some do."

Drew took a quick glance at Nina's profile. "How do you feel about all the building?"

"I think it's spectacular because it indicates black success. A few longtime residents weren't pleased with the palatial homes that look as if they should be in Malibu. They claim the ostentation robs the area of its folksy charm."

They walked together, holding hands until the darkening skies and a rising wind forced them to turn back. Large fat raindrops dotted the sand as they sprinted to escape the imminent downpour.

Nina couldn't keep pace with Drew. He was running too fast. She pitched forward, nearly losing her balance when he tightened his hold on her hand. Seconds later, she found herself in his arms as he sprinted up the path to her house. They were only a few feet from the patio when the rain came down in torrents. They stood under the protective cover of the patio, breathing heavily, their clothes pasted to their bodies like a second skin.

Drew's gaze was fixed below her neck, prompting Nina to glance down at her chest. The outline of her distended nipples was clearly visible through her silk bra. As casually as she could, she crossed her arms over her breasts.

"You should get out of those wet clothes."

"You should, too," she countered, hardly lifting her voice above a whisper. The golden eyes staring at her lit a fire that flared throughout her body, threatening to incinerate her into tiny pieces, pieces that would disappear with the slightest breath.

Nina walked toward the French doors leading into the kitchen but was thwarted when Drew reached out and curved an arm around her waist. His hands slipped down her hips and pulled her up close to his body. There was no mistaking the solid bulge in the front of his soaked khakis.

She rested her hands in the middle of his chest, feeling the heat emanating from his body.

"Drew?" His name was a whisper.

His fingers tightened on her buttocks. "I want you."

Nina closed her eyes. He wanted her and she wanted him, had wanted him from the first time their gazes met, it was just that she hadn't known it at that time.

Tilting her chin, she stared up at him. "Let's go inside."

The moment Drew curved his arm under Nina's knees, sweeping her off her feet, her world blurred, becoming surreal.

"Go that way." She directed him down a hallway to where the bedrooms were located. He stopped at the first one, and she nodded.

Drew knew he and Nina had to get out of their wet clothes, but he did not want to rush what was to come. He wanted her so badly that he feared he was going to come out of his skin. Everything that was Nina seeped into him: her scent, the fullness of her breasts pressed to his chest.

His gaze locked with hers, he lowered her to the bare wooden floor, reached down, and pulled the T-shirt over her head. Nina was tiny, her shoulders and waist narrow, but her breasts were full, the nipples showing through the sheer fabric of her bra dark and prominent.

Reaching around her back, Drew released the clasp on her bra and slowly slipped the silken garment down her arms.

"You are so beautiful, Nina."

Nina closed her eyes against his intense stare. "Don't talk, Drew. Please."

His hands circled her waist. "What do you want, honey?"

Her fingers tightened in the fabric of his wet golf shirt. "I want you inside me," she breathed through compressed lips.

Smiling, he dipped his head, pressing a series of kisses along the column of her neck as he undid the button and zipper on her slacks.

One hand slid down her silken bikini panties, tightening over the firm flesh on her behind while the other moved around to her belly, slipping under the elastic and covering her mound. Nina gasped, arching as his fingers searched the folds, finding her wet, hot, throbbing, and ready for his possession. He removed his hand long enough to ease her slacks and panties down her legs in one continuous motion. She stepped out of them, standing before him naked.

He put his hand to his mouth and licked the tips of the fingers that had explored her body, a smile curving his lips. "You taste as good as you look."

Nina dug her fingernails into Drew's shoulders, shuddering as his hand slipped up her thighs to continue to work its magic. Moaning and writhing, she found that she couldn't get close enough. She gathered his shirt and pulled it from the waistband of his khakis. He was forced to release her as she attempted to ease the shirt over his broad shoulders. He gently brushed her hands away, unbuckling his belt and unzipping his pants.

It was her turn to stare in awe as he bared his body to her. The blood-engorged flesh jutting between his muscled thighs was mesmerizing. She thought about Michelle's assessment of him: a chocolate licorice stick, while she'd called him a chocolate Tootsie Pop.

She smiled. He was both.

Drew reached for the condoms in his pocket and placed them on the bed. Curving an arm around her waist, he lifted Nina and placed her on the bed, his body following. Cradling her smooth legs between his, he lowered his head and pressed a kiss to her parted lips, their breaths mingling. His tongue slipped into her mouth, and he tasted her for the second time.

Nina drank in the sweetness of Drew's soft kisses; he nibbled at the corners of her mouth, leaving her wanting more as his hardened sex pressed against her belly and ignited a burning desire, an aching need for him to penetrate her. Passion pounded the blood rushing through her heart, chest, and head. First she was hot and then cold.

She could not stop her moans when his mouth moved lower, exploring every inch of her body. Her legs trembled of their volition as Drew buried his face between her thighs and drank deeply from her pool of feminine nectar.

Suddenly she was falling, slipping away from reality as waves of pleasure stiffened her body. Drew moved up her body, mapping her belly and breasts with his tongue. The lull in pleasure lasted seconds; he'd slipped on a condom. Nina gasped in sweet agony and welcomed Drew into her body, his tumescence easing into her with a slowness that set her teeth on edge.

"Easy, darling," Drew crooned softly.

The texture of her satiny skin and sampling the flesh between her silken thighs threatened to make him climax before he had the opportunity to claim all of her. He wanted to bring her more pleasure before taking his own. He moved his hips, pushing into her body. Her flesh closed around his like a glove that was a size too small.

Nina trailed her fingertips up and down the length of Drew's back, intertwined her legs with his. He increased his thrusts, and she followed, matching him stroke for stroke, thrust for thrust. Her body melted against his, and her world tilted crazily on its axis as pleasure, pure and explosive, hurtled her to a place she'd never been.

She screamed his name over and over until her voice faded to a whisper. Contentment and peace washed over her before she closed her eyes and succumbed to the numbed sleep of a sated lover.

Drew buried his face between her neck and shoulder and shuddered violently, his passions erupting and the strong sensations milking him until he felt as weak and vulnerable as a newborn.

Collapsing heavily on her slight frame, he waited for his heart to settle back to a normal rate. Somehow he found the strength to roll off Nina, she moaning softly as he pulled her hips to his groin. They lay together, his fingers splayed over her belly, and slept.

Chapter 6

Nina turned over and found the space next to her empty. Glancing at the clock on the bedside table, she realized she'd been asleep for almost three hours. She rarely napped in the middle of the day, but this time she had a wonderful excuse. Sleeping with Drew was an incredible experience, one well worth waiting for.

She sat up and picked up the slip of paper on the pillow that bore the imprint of Drew's head. She read the note, a smile softening her mouth: "I'll be back. Hugs, D.L. P.S.—You do snore, but I like it—big-time!" Her smile became a full grin. A warm glow swept over her as she recalled what she had shared with a man who was more than her sexual counterpart. She was certain that once this summer ended, she would have no regrets.

She slipped out of bed and padded on bare feet over to the window. It was still raining. A song from her parents' music collection came to mind: the Carpenters' "Rainy Days and Mondays." It may have been raining, but it wasn't Monday, and she wasn't down. In fact, she hadn't felt this good in a long time, and for her that was a very good thing.

Turning away from the window, she returned to the bed and removed the linen, then walked into the bathroom.

As soon as Nina reentered her bedroom, she felt the chill. She had planned for her and Drew to eat on the patio, but now those plans had to be scrapped. She would offer him a choice: the dining room or the kitchen.

Mentally going over what she intended to cook for dinner, she made her way to the kitchen. She'd just opened the refrigerator when the doorbell rang. Glancing up at the clock over the stove, she noted the time. It was two-twenty.

She went to the front door, opened it and stared at Drew. He was wearing a beige baseball cap with WRIGHT GROUP stitched across the front, a matching waterproof slicker with the same logo, jeans, and running shoes. He cradled a large wooden crate against his chest.

"Please come in."

Drew put down the crate on the floor of the porch and took off the poncho and his cap, hanging them on a nearby wicker coatrack as Nina peered into the crate.

"What on earth did you buy?"

He smiled at her shocked expression. "Just a little something from a farm stand that I saw on the way over."

Her gaze met his. "A little something?"

Drew picked up the crate and walked into the living room. "Corn, watermelon, potatoes, some Granny Smith apples, snow peas, and salad fixings," he said over his shoulder as he headed toward the kitchen. "I also picked up a few bottles of wine, cheese, and ingredients to make our own bread. I hate store-bought bread."

Nina followed him. "I don't know who's going to bake bread, because yeast, dough, and I don't get along."

Drew placed the crate on the floor in front of the sink and began emptying it. "I'll bake the bread."

Crossing her arms under her breasts, she gave him an incredulous stare. "You bake bread?"

He stared at her under lowered lids. "You got jokes, Nina?"

"No, Drew," she countered quickly, attempting to hold back the laughter bubbling up in the back of her throat. "I never would've imagined you as Betty Crocker."

Before the name was out of her mouth, Nina found her body molded to Drew's from chest to knees. Not only did he look good, he also smelled wonderful.

"You smell so nice," she whispered softly.

"So do you, honey." His voice was low, sensual. "You also taste good."

Her cheeks burned in remembrance. "Will I like your taste?" she asked.

He chuckled. "I don't know. But you can always find out."

"When?"

"Later. But only if you'll allow me to spend the night."

"Yes, Drew. You may spend the night. I'd like for you to—" Her words trailed off when the telephone rang. "Excuse me." His arms fell away as she went over to pick up the receiver on the wall phone.

"Hello."

"Hey, girlfriend."

Nina bit down on her lower lip. "Michelle?"

"Hey-y-y-y!" She'd drawn out the word.

"You are?"

"Yes!"

Nina screamed, then placed her hand over the mouthpiece as Drew shot her a questioning look. He went back to emptying the crate, placing foodstuffs on the countertop.

"When, Michelle?"

"The doctor gave me a date of March twenty-third."

"You won't finish the school year." Most teachers planned their pregnancies to coincide with the end of the school year so they could spend the summer months with their babies.

"I don't care. Lloyd and I have been trying for over a year for a baby. I'd given up, then bam!"

"Congratulations to you and Lloyd." She made a mental note to send them flowers. "How's Lloyd taking the news that he's going to become a daddy?"

"He's acting real stupid. Just because my obstetrician said the first three months are the most critical ones, he's not permitting me to lift anything, or do housework. The fool hired a maid."

"Enjoy it, Michelle—once the baby comes, you'll appreciate it."

"I know you're right, but I'm not used to doing absolutely nothing."

"I'm going to give you your words back nine months from now."

"You're probably right, girlfriend. I'm going to hang up on you and call Kim. She's been calling me every day since Carmen's wedding."

"That's because she's nosy as hell," Nina said, smiling. "You can't mention anything to her without her either haunting or interrogating you."

"That's why we love her."

"You're right," Nina said. "If you and Lloyd want to come out and spend some time away from the city, just let me know."

"Thanks for the invitation, but Lloyd has made plans to go to Memphis to see his folks."

"Have a safe trip."

"We will. Love you, Nina."

"Love you back, Michelle."

She ended the call, feeling her friend's joy. Michelle would be the first of the quartet to become a mother. Carmen had confided that she and Wayne were going to try for a baby as soon as they were married. Now that left Kim Stewart, who said she and her husband would begin planning a family next year.

Turning back to Drew, she stared at the countertops. He had purchased two whole chickens and filet mignon.

Leaning against the counter, Drew angled his head. "What if I cook for you tonight, and you return the favor tomorrow?"

Nina nodded. "What about breakfast?"

A slow smile spread over his handsome face. "We'll eat out."

She lifted an eyebrow. "You have everything planned, don't you?"

His smile faded quickly. "That's how I run my life, Nina. I plan out everything in advance."

He had plans, and so did she.

Nina sighed softly. Her legs were sandwiched between Drew's as they lay on a blanket on the living room floor. She had placed a dozen votive candles in the fireplace before turning off the floor lamp, and the flickering flames reflected off the wall and floor like twinkling stars.

Drew shifted and rested an arm over her hips. "Are you ready for dessert?"

She rolled her eyes at him, knowing he probably couldn't see her face clearly in the diffused light. "I ate too much to even think about dessert."

He chuckled softly. "I told you to save room for dessert."

"Yeah, I know," she drawled. Nina knew Drew was right, but she hadn't been able to help herself when she had two helpings of salad. "Who taught you to cook?"

"No one. I taught myself."

"You're kidding, aren't you?"

"No, I'm not."

"Did you ever think about becoming a chef?"

Drew smiled. "No. I'd planned to become an accountant like my father, but I dropped out of college in my junior year."

"You never got your degree?"

"No."

"Have you thought about going back to college?"

"No," he repeated.

"Why not?"

Shifting, Drew moved over her body and dipped his head. "I think I need dessert," he crooned against the side of her neck. He did not want to talk about himself.

"Don't, Drew. I'm too full."

His right hand moved slowly along her ribs before resting over her belly. "It is a little bigger than it was this morning."

"You're going to make me into a porker."

His fingers stilled. "You could use a little more weight. I can pick you up with one arm."

"I weigh enough."

"You're a tiny little thing," he countered.

She giggled. "I'm hardly anorexic. Give me a few years, and I'll probably be battling the bulge once I hit the big four-oh."

Drew's forefinger made tiny circles around her belly button. "You have a long time to go before you're forty."

"Six years."

"I've got you beat by four years."

She went completely still. "I'd never take you for thirty-eight."

"How old did you think I was?"

"No more than thirty-three, thirty-five tops."

He kissed the end of her nose. "Thank you, sweetheart."

Nina decided to ignore the endearment. "Are you looking forward to turning forty?"

"Yes, I am. The day my father turned forty, he announced he was quitting his accounting job and going to Chicago with his band. He'd put together a small band after graduating high school, and he and his friends became quite popular once they played a summer season at the Catskills."

"Was he good?"

Shifting his head, he stared directly at her. "He was an incredible sax player. He loved music, but he went into accounting because he knew he couldn't support his family with the money he earned playing weekend gigs. I was sixteen when he quit his job and took his band on the road. They played every major city in the country, including some of the Caribbean resorts. They finally settled in California, becoming a studio band for a record company."

"How did your mother take his leaving home?"

"She wasn't surprised. She said he'd stayed longer than she expected him to."

"Not many women would support a man who decides to leave her and their children to live out his dream."

Drew registered the wistfulness in Nina's voice. "My mother loved my father and had always told him that she never wanted him to use her as an excuse not to follow his dream. Whenever he returned to New York we celebrated big-time, eating out at our favorite restaurants and going to Broadway plays. It ended eight years ago when my father came back to New York, complaining of chest pains. He thought it was indigestion. By the time my mother convinced him to go to the doctor, it was too late. He died in the doctor's office from a heart attack."

Nina buried her face between Drew's neck and shoulder. "I'm sorry."

Cradling the back of her head in his hand, Drew pressed his mouth to her hair. "Don't be, Nina. He died in my mother's arms, content with the way he'd lived his life."

There was a moment of silence. "Are you content with your life, Drew?"

"Very. How about you?" he asked after another pause. "Are you content?"

"Yes."

"Don't you want more than your career?"

"What more is there?" she asked.

"Marriage. Motherhood."

"There was a time when I wanted both, but now it doesn't matter. I have a lot of school holidays, and I use that time to travel," she continued. "I usually get together with my family in Alexandria at Thanksgiving, go to the Caribbean during the Christmas recess, hibernate at home during the winter recess, and go abroad during spring break. And for the past six years I've spent my summers here."

"There's no doubt that you keep busy. What's your favorite European city?"

"I'd have to say Venice, then Paris. But there's also Istanbul and Mykonos."

Nuzzling her scented neck, Drew caught her earlobe between his teeth. "I think Venice is the most romantic city in the world. I like Venice, Paris, and Nina Watkins, but not necessarily in that order." He angled his head and kissed her, increasing the pressure until she parted her lips.

Nina moaned softly and returned his kiss with reckless abandon. The touch of his lips on hers sent a shock wave through her entire body. Drew gathered her off the floor and carried her to the bedroom. Her breathing was labored as Drew stripped off her clothes. A minute later he stood before her naked. They moved over to the bed and offered each other the most sensual dessert either had had the pleasure of partaking.

Chapter 7

Nina and Drew shared a smile as they sat in Spinnakers sipping lattes. They had spent the past five weekends together in what had become an uncomplicated, easygoing relationship.

Reaching across the table, Drew placed a hand over Nina's. "A friend of mine is hosting a party in Southampton next weekend, and I'd like for you to come with me."

Nina stared at Drew in astonishment. It was the first time he had offered to take her to meet any of his friends. All of their encounters took place either on Sag Harbor or in a surrounding community.

"A friend or a business acquaintance?"

Drew stiffened as if Nina had struck him, and his mouth tightened into a thin hard line. Although she had not asked him about his business dealings since their first date at B. Smith's, there was no doubt she continued to believe he was involved in something illegitimate.

"A *friend*," he said, stressing the word.

Nina heard the censure in Drew's voice and flashed a tentative smile. She thought he sounded a little defensive. "Okay. I'll go with you."

Drew smiled, his expression softening. "Thank you."

The two words were barely out of his mouth when a shadow fell over the table. He glanced up to find a casually dressed African-American man grinning at Nina.

Seeing the direction of his gaze, she looked up, her jaw dropping. One second she was seated, then she was on her feet, her arms going around the neck of a man she hadn't seen in fourteen years.

"When did you get back to the States?" she asked him before he kissed her flush on the mouth.

"A couple of days ago."

Dropping her arms, she turned to face Drew, who had risen from his chair. "Drew, this is James Sparks. James, my friend Andrew Lancaster." The two men shook hands. "James, his brother, and my brother were inseparable whenever we summered here."

James's dark eyes lingered on Nina's upturned face. "Are you going to be here through the summer?"

"Yes, I am."

Leaning over, he kissed her cheek. "I'll drop by early next week, and we can catch up on old times."

"I'd like that, James."

Nina waited until James walked to the rear of the restaurant, where tables were set up under a faux pergola, then retook her seat, Drew following suit.

"How long has it been since you've seen James?"

Picking up her cup, Nina took a sip of her latte. "Fourteen years." She smiled at Drew over the rim. "James is a doctor with the World Health Organization. He's currently practicing in Namibia."

"Do you keep in touch with one another?"

"We always exchange birthday and Christmas cards." She took another sip of her drink. "James was my first boyfriend. He took me to my high school prom."

"How does his wife like living in Africa?"

Nina shook her head. "James isn't married. He's always joked that if he didn't marry me, then he'd never get married."

Oh, it's like that, Drew mused. "Maybe it's not a joke, Nina. It's apparent he's still carrying a torch for you."

"I doubt that."

Drew wanted to tell Nina she was being naive. He'd seen the way James looked at her. He had to admit it was no different from the way he looked at her himself.

He studied the timepiece on his wrist, then reached into a pocket of his slacks, took out several bills, and left them on the table. "I think I'd better start back before the traffic starts building up."

Nina stared at her own watch. It wasn't quite two o'clock. Drew usually did not leave Sag Harbor until midnight. That way he avoided the exodus of thousands returning to New York City.

She waited for him to come around the table to pull back her chair. She walked out of the restaurant, he following. It was the first time since he had come to Sag Harbor to visit with her that he hadn't curved an arm around her waist or held her hand.

She was puzzled by his abrupt change in mood, and it did not take a genius to know that it had something to do with the appearance of James Sparks.

Was Drew jealous of James? She dismissed the notion as soon as it entered her head. She and Drew were having a summer fling, and that was that.

Keith took the cigar from between his clenched teeth, blowing out a smoke ring, then glanced over at Drew as he puffed on his. "Do you like this one?"

Drew shook his head, snuffing out the burning embers in a cup half filled with beer. "No."

Keith sat up, scowling. "Hey, man. You just ruined a perfectly good cigar."

Drew lifted a thick black eyebrow. "I told you I don't like smoking cigars, yet you keep saying this one is milder than the last one you offered me."

"These babies were specially ordered. I had to wait two months to get them."

Swinging his legs over the lounge chair, Drew gave his best friend a Kool-Aid grin. "The money you spend on cigars could finance some kid's preschool education."

"The last time you looked at my portfolio, you gave it the seal of approval," Keith retorted.

"True. In fact you're doing very well with your investments."

"How are you doing with your latest squeeze?"

"She's not a squeeze."

"Oh, excuse me, my friend." Keith removed his sunglasses and stared at his childhood friend. "You're serious about this woman, aren't you?"

Drew stared out to where Keith's wife splashed in the in-ground pool with their children. The Jackmans were living the American dream: a house in the suburbs, two cars, two children, a menagerie of birds, fish, dogs, and a cat.

"More serious about her than she is about me."

"Why would you say that?"

Drew met Keith's direct stare. "We've been seeing each other for the past six weeks, and she's never even said that she likes me."

"The fact that she's still going out with you should be enough. Some women aren't that demonstrative."

Drew wanted to tell him that Nina was more than demonstrative in bed. There was never a time when they came together that she did not leave him gasping for his next breath. Their last night together had been so passionate that he'd almost blurted out that he loved her.

"How long did it take for Lisa to tell you that she loved you?"

A sly smile deepened the lines around Keith's eyes. "Hell, the first time I finally convinced her to go all the way with me. You have to remember that we had dated two years before that. Going out with a minister's daughter can have its drawbacks. She was indoctrinated with all of that fire-and-brimstone business at an early age. What does your lady do for a living?"

"She's a librarian."

Keith's jaw dropped. "Don't tell me she has a bun, them funny orthopedic shoes that make swishing sounds on the floor when she walks, and a pair of half glasses perched on the end of her nose?"

Drew shook his head slowly. "Oh, hell no, brotherman. She's the complete opposite of that."

Leaning forward, Keith said, "So, she's hot?"

Drew merely nodded, not wanting to reveal just how hot Nina actually was. She was beautiful, sensual, smart, and good in the kitchen *and* the bedroom.

"What are you going to do?"

"Continue to see her until she says it's over."

"Until she says it's over?" he repeated. "You're going to give her up, just like that?" Keith snapped his fingers.

"I can't stay in a lopsided relationship. I think she's reluctant to commit or even ask for a commitment because of the rumors she's heard about me. I think my cousin Richard told her why he calls me D.L."

"Did she ask if you were shady?" Drew nodded. "What did you tell her?"

"I told her I wasn't a criminal. "

"I hate to say it, Drew, but your boogie-ass family ought to lighten up on you. They act like not having a college degree is akin to becoming a crackhead."

"They are who they are," Drew said in defense of his family. "I suppose I'm more like my father—marching to the beat of my own drum."

"Now, your dad was cool."

"That's because he was a Lancaster, not a Nelson." Drew pushed to his feet. "I'm going to say good-bye to Lisa and the kids, then I'm going to push off." He extended his hand.

Keith stood up and grasped the proffered hand before he hugged his friend. "Good luck with everything, especially your lady. By the way, does she have a name?"

"Nina Watkins."

Keith pushed out his lower lip. "Nina Lancaster. That flows nicely together."

It flowed nicely, but Drew doubted it would ever become a reality.

Chapter 8

Nina rushed out of the bathroom when she heard the phone ring, a towel wrapped around her damp body.

She picked up the receiver. "Hello."

"Hey, girlfriend."

She smiled. "Hi, Michelle. What's up?"

"I was just calling to check up on you. How are you doing with your Tootsie Pop?"

Sitting down on a chair in front of a vanity, Nina cradled the phone between her chin and shoulder and blotted the moisture on her upper body. "We're good."

"Just good, Nina?"

"Okay, Miss Know-It-All, we're doing very good."

"Did you get to the chocolate center?" Michelle whispered conspiratorially.

Nina laughed. "Child, baby please! Yes—I—did."

It was Michelle's turn to howl. "Do you like him, Nina?" she asked, sobering.

"Of course I like him."

"How much?"

"A lot."

"A lot, a lot, or love a lot?"

Nina's motions stilled. Michelle's query elicited a gamut of emotions she did not want to feel or acknowledge, because she had lied to herself and denied her feelings for Drew. He made her feel things she did not want to feel, made her wish for something that would never be.

"Nina?"

"I'm here, Michelle."

There came a pregnant silence. "Are you in love with D.L.?"

"I think so."

A snort came through the earpiece. "Don't make me get in my car and drive all the way out there to slap you!" Michelle snapped angrily. "You're thirty-four years old, yet you sound as unsure as a fourteen-year-old. Do you love the man?"

Nina sat up straighter and pulled back her shoulders. "Yes, I do."

"Hot damn! That's more like it. Now, what are you going to do about it?"

"Nothing."

"Sheee-it," Michelle groaned. "What am I going to do with you, girlfriend?

"You're going to let me hang up so I can get dressed for a party."

"Where are you going?"

"Southampton."

"Ooo-oo girl! Don't forget to give P. Diddy and Russell Simmons a shout out for me."

Nina couldn't help smiling. "I will, if I run into them."

"Have fun, Nina."

"Thanks, Michelle. And don't forget to take it easy."

"That's all I'm doing. Right now I'm lying here looking like a trussed-up Thanksgiving turkey. I'm eating so much that Lloyd's threatening to put a padlock on the refrigerator."

"Good-bye. I'll call you in a few days." She hung up and returned to the bathroom to complete her toilette before Drew arrived.

*   *   *

Nina showed Drew her back. "Please zip me up."

His gaze was fixed on the expanse of her back and shoulders. They were going to the house of a record producer he'd met several months before to celebrate the label's signing a new rap artist.

Holding the bodice over her breasts, Nina waited for Drew to zip up the strapless black silk chiffon dress. He zipped the dress, then lowered his head, and placed a series of kisses over her shoulders. "I think we should stay here tonight."

Nina glanced over her shoulder at him. "You don't want to go out?"

"We're going, but we're out of there as soon as some man forgets who he is and steps out of line with you." He had been to enough parties where people had too much money and no social boundaries to last him a lifetime.

"Don't tell me you're the jealous type?"

"No." And he wasn't. Not until he'd met her.

Taking his hand, Nina laced her fingers through his. Drew was breathtakingly handsome in white. The cream against his sable-brown skin enhanced the rich, deep color of his face, which was darkened further by the rays of the hot summer sun.

"I think we'll do okay as long as I don't have to go Harlem on a hoochie who steps too close to my man," she teased.

He stared at her under lowered lids. "Am I your man, Nina?"

"Tonight you are."

He affected a smile that did not meet his eyes. "If I'm your man tonight, then you have to be my woman."

Pressing her chest to his, she smiled sweetly. "You've got yourself a deal."

A rising wind off the ocean molded the delicate fabric of Nina's dress to her body before lifting and settling around her exposed legs. Each time she took a step, the silk ties around her ankles were visible, and Drew found it hard to concentrate on what his host was saying as he stared at her talking to a young man several feet away.

The crowd was three deep at the bar, and the music loud enough to be heard across the Atlantic Ocean. Drew had to shout to be heard. He went completely still when a man with a shaved head touched Nina's arm, and she shook her head at him.

"Excuse me," Drew shouted to Glenn.

Weaving his way through the throng, he came up behind Nina. "I think it's time we get back to the kids. After all, we did promise the babysitter we'd be back by one."

The rapper stared up at Drew, his eyes widening in shock before he glanced at Drew's and Nina's bare fingers. He released her arm. "She yo wife?"

Drew shrugged a broad shoulder. "Baby mama."

"Yo, man. You better marry yo baby mama before someone snaps her up, 'cause she's fine as hell!"

Drew, deciding to play along, looked Nina up and down. "Hey, you right." He and the rapper gave each other a pound. Curving an arm around Nina's waist, he smiled so wide she could see most of his teeth. "Let's go home, baby. We need to talk about hookin' up—permanently. I mean, with the piece of paper and all."

Nina waited until the valet had brought Drew's car around and she was sitting beside him before she said, "Thank you for rescuing me, but there was no need for you to ad lib about me being your baby mama."

He shifted into gear and drove away from the glass and steel house perched on a dune overlooking the ocean. "It got us out of there without drama. I've seen guys pull guns on one another over a woman."

She rolled her eyes at him. "That wouldn't have happened."

"What shouldn't have happened is his putting his hand on you,

Nina. ABC, or whatever the hell his name is, may be the latest rap genius since Tupac, but if he hadn't let you go, then either he or I would've been in the morgue or the hospital."

"Stop being so dramatic."

"Get real, Nina. You work at a high school. Haven't you seen two guys go at one another over a girl?"

"Too many times," she admitted reluctantly.

"Exactly," Drew countered. "Your admirer is all of twenty years old, which makes him a boy, not a man. You really don't want to see this boogie-down Bronx brother beat the crap out of that kid."

The rest of the drive from Southampton to Sag Harbor was accomplished in complete silence.

Nina did not wait for Drew to come around and help her out of his SUV. She opened the door as soon as he cut off the ignition. She had made it up the porch to the front door when fingers curled around her wrist.

"Don't, baby. Please don't shut me out."

Turning around, she stared up at him. The lights flanking the door illuminated his face, but there wasn't enough light to see his eyes.

"I don't want to fight with you, Drew."

He moved closer, cradling her face between his hands. "Then don't." Lowering one hand, he took the keys from her clenched fist and opened the door.

They walked into the living room, kissed, arms around each other. Drew shrugged out of his jacket, leaving it where it lay on the floor. His shirt followed as he alternated between undressing himself and Nina.

Both naked, their open mouths devouring each other, he picked her up and headed toward her bedroom. Her legs wrapped around his waist, and he was lost.

They fell across the bed, and for the first time since they'd shared a bed, there was no foreplay. Nina's mouth mapped every inch of his body. He rose off the mattress, swallowing back the groans threatening to erupt deep in his throat. Her tongue took him to the moon and back as his blood boiled in his veins.

Nina was relentless in her assault on Drew's body. She couldn't tell him verbally what lay in her heart, so she let her body speak for her. She lost count of the number of licks it would take to get to Drew's center after she had taken him into her mouth.

Up.

Down.

Around.

In.

Out.

Deeper.

Her tongue had become a magic wand, bending him to her will. They had one more weekend together, and she did not want him to ever forget her, just as she knew she would never forget him. Maybe, just maybe, they could repeat what they'd shared this summer the following year.

Drew's body shuddered, trembled, and shook uncontrollably. Just when he thought he was going to lose his mind, he reached down and pulled her up. Seconds later she lay on her back, and he pushed into her feminine heat. A fire, hotter than any before, swept over them as they struggled to get closer, become one.

His hips moved faster and faster, like a piston hitting its mark. Reaching down, he lifted Nina's legs over his shoulders. He held her gaze until she closed her eyes and surrendered to the ecstasy sweeping her out to sea. He joined her, their moans mingling in erotic pleasure.

Once his pulse slowed, he lowered himself to the mattress beside her. "I love you," he whispered against her ear.

Nina went completely still. "No, Drew," she cried, her voice filled with panic.

He went up on an elbow. A frown creased his forehead. "No, what?"

She closed her eyes against his intense stare. "You don't have to say it."

"I love you?"

She placed her fingertips over his mouth. "I don't want or need any promises or declarations of love. We're not kids, Drew. There's nothing wrong with us enjoying what the other is willing to offer without a commitment."

His eyes glittered dangerously as he pulled her hand down. "What the hell are you talking about?"

"A summer fling, Drew. That's what you've been for me. I've enjoyed you and everything we've shared this summer. I'm not asking for more."

Drew scrambled off the bed. "If I'm just a piece of meat to you, then put a fork in me, Nina, because I'm done."

Turning on his heel, he walked out of the bedroom. She lay in bed, unable to go after him. It wasn't until she heard the slam of the front door and the roar of the engine of his BMW that she was released from her stupor.

She hadn't planned for it to end this way. He had aborted her rehearsed speech with his declaration of love. Of all of the men she had known, none had ever admitted to loving her before she gave her own admission.

Pulling her knees to her chest, she rested her head on them and closed her eyes. "Good-bye, Drew," she whispered to the silent room. "I love you."

Chapter 9

Nina sat on the tall stool in her utility kitchen, holding the cordless phone between her chin and shoulder. "I just got back. I decided to come back early this year. Of course I won't miss Wayne and Carmen's cookout. I'll see you Saturday."

She hung up. She had called Michelle, Carmen, and now Kim to let them know she was back in the city. It had taken her three days to close up the little house on Sag Harbor, but it would take a lifetime to close her heart to the love she had shared with Drew.

Her plan to reject him before he could reject her had backfired. She had unfairly lumped Drew in with the other men she had known who had dealt her a losing hand.

Sighing heavily, she moved off the stool. Her love life was where it had been at the beginning of the summer—nowhere. But there was one thing she was certain of, and that was she would never be a bridesmaid again. All of her friends were married.

Nina stepped out of the taxi, cradling a shopping bag against her chest. Like Carmen's wedding day, the weather was perfect for a backyard cookout. The mouthwatering aroma of grilling meats lingered in the warm air.

A small crowd had already gathered. Some sat on folding chairs, while others stood around in groups, holding cups. She spied Michelle and Kim sitting together under the shade of a maple tree.

"The summer looks good on you."

Nina turned when she heard a familiar male voice behind her. "Hello, Richard."

Leaning down, he kissed her cheek. "Hi, Nina. You look great."

She wanted to tell him that if she looked great, then his cousin had something to do with her transformation. "Thank you." She handed him the bag. She had purchased a three-piece set of sterling silver frames in different sizes as a housewarming gift for the Nelsons. She'd also brought two bottles of their favorite champagne. "Please give it to Wayne."

Grinning, he took the bag from her grasp. "Of course. I'll be right back." It was almost an instant rerun of the wedding reception, when Richard had gone to get her a drink.

Nina walked over to her friends. Kim was rubbing Michelle's back as she took furtive sips of a pale carbonated beverage. Bending down, Nina kissed Michelle's cheek.

"How are you feeling, girlfriend?"

Michelle shook her head and rolled her eyes. "She's kicking my butt."

Nina stared at Kim over Michelle's head. "It's too soon to know if it's a girl."

"Oh, I know it's a girl. A boy would be a lot nicer to his mama."

"Now, you know that's sexist," Kim chided in a soft tone.

Nina held Michelle's hand. "Why don't you go inside and lie down?"

Michelle stared up at her. "I just got up."

Lloyd appeared with a damp cloth. "Wayne said you should lie down with a cool cloth on your head."

Forcing a weak smile, Michelle extended her hand to her husband. "Help me up, baby."

Nina and Kim stood back as Lloyd gathered his wife off the chair and carried her into the brownstone. The two friends stared at each other, slowly shaking their heads.

Kim sucked her teeth. "Watch homegirl milk this for all it's worth."

"I'll give you your words back when you're in the family way."

"You've got that right. Ever since Billy put a ring on my finger, he's gotten a little slack. Every once in a while I have to remind him that he married an African . . ." Her words trailed off as she stared at something over Nina's shoulder.

Nina felt his presence even before she was given the opportunity to turn around. She schooled her expression not to reveal what she was feeling at that moment—fear and uneasiness. Fear, because she did not want him to know how much she loved him, and uneasiness, because she did not know what to say to him.

Turning slowly, she stared at Drew. He was casually dressed, like most of the other guests. He wore a beige linen shirt, matching shorts, and a pair of brown woven sandals. She forced herself not to stare at his legs.

"Hello, Drew." Her voice was steady, calm.

He inclined his head. "Hello, Nina." He lifted an eyebrow behind his sunglasses. "It's good seeing you again."

"Same here."

He nodded to Kim. "Hello. I hope you don't mind if I borrow your friend for a few minutes?"

Kim waved a hand. "Of course not. I was just going in to ask Carmen if she needed any help."

Drew extended his hand. "Nina?" She placed her hand in his, and minutes later she found herself standing on the sidewalk along the tree-lined street.

"What do you want, Drew?"

He tightened his grip on her fingers. "Come, walk with me while we talk."

Why, she asked herself, hadn't she noticed how soft his voice was? It was always evenly pitched, controlled. "What do you want to talk about?"

Drew led Nina down the block, his hand covering hers in the crook of his elbow. They'd been apart a week, and in a week he'd tried remembering everything about her and failed. All he remembered was the hypnotic scent of her perfume and the feel of her silken skin. And now that he had seen her again, everything else came rushing back: the sultry timbre of her beautifully modulated voice, the dark slanting eyes that challenged him not to look away, and her quick mind.

He'd spent a rewarding eight weeks with her, discussing their favorite writers, reading poems to each other, watching classic movies, and listening to music from a prior generation.

"What happened between us at your summer place on Sag Harbor, Nina?"

Stopping, she stared at him. "We slept together."

He shook his head slowly. "Wrong, Nina. You may have slept with me, but I fell in love with you. "

Nina's eyes filled with tears, and her lids fluttered as she tried blinking them back. "I fell in love with you, too."

Cradling her face between his hands, Drew brushed a kiss over her trembling mouth. "Marry me, darling."

Smiling through her tears, she nodded. "Yes."

He released her long enough to glance at his watch. "Come, Nina. I want to get there before it closes."

"Where are we going?" she asked, quickening her pace to keep up with his longer legs.

He smiled at her. "You'll find out soon."

Nina sat in the back of a taxi, wrapped in the protective warmth of Drew's arms. She hadn't registered his "Fifty-seventh and Fifth" to the driver until the cabbie stopped across the street from Tiffany & Co.

He gave the taxi driver a fifty-dollar bill. "Keep the change."

Not waiting for the light to change, he scooped her up in his arms, skirting cars, taxis, and a lumbering bus, and sprinted into the store.

"Put me down, Drew," Nina hissed in his ear. "People are looking at us."

There was a stunned silence as shoppers and clerks turned and looked in their direction. Sheepishly, Drew lowered her feet to the floor. "We're in love," he announced in a loud voice. There was a smattering of applause before everyone went back to their buying and selling.

Nina held back as Drew went over to an older woman with short coiffed hair. They shook hands, then put their heads together. He pointed to several trays of diamond rings under the glass.

Holding out a hand, he said, "Come, darling, and pick out what you want."

Heart pounding, knees shaking, Nina closed the distance between them. When she'd gotten up that morning, she hadn't thought she would ever see Drew again, and now she was picking out an engagement ring.

Someone brought over a chair for her to sit on, and less than an hour later she wore a two-carat brilliant-cut diamond with a platinum paved band on her left hand. Her heart had slowed to a normal rate as she and Drew selected matching bands.

She hid a smile when Drew placed an American Express credit card on the counter. He curved an arm around her waist and pressed his mouth to her ear. "On the way back uptown I'll tell you about my business."

"Why didn't you tell me before?"

"Because you were only my girlfriend, not my wife or fiancée."

"I was never your girlfriend," she said softly.

"What were you?"

"Your lover."

Smiling, he shook his head. "You were my girlfriend when I took you to B. Smith's."

"Okay, I'll concede that. And because I was your girlfriend for about a week, I expect you to court me properly, Andrew Lancaster, before I become your wife."

"Are you saying we won't sleep together?"

"How long can you hold out?" she teased.

He angled his head. "Probably a month."

"Are you sure?"

"No. But I'll try."

Curving her arms around his neck, Nina rested her head on his shoulder. "When do you want to get married?"

"How about Christmas? We can honeymoon in the Caribbean, or would you prefer Tahiti?"

"I've never been to Tahiti."

He kissed her. "Then Tahiti it is."

The salesclerk gave Drew his receipt and a blue shopping bag with their bands. "Congratulations, Mr. Lancaster. Miss."

"Thank you," they chorused in unison.

They stood on the corner, arms around each other. Drew whistled through his teeth for a taxi for the return trip uptown. A streak of yellow screeched to a halt in front of them. They were barely seated when the driver took off. Drew gave him the address to his cousin's brownstone, then held Nina close to his heart.

Chapter 10

Nina and Drew returned to the cookout, her left hand hidden behind her back.

Kim met them carrying a plate overflowing with food. "Where were you two?"

Nina gave her a mysterious smile. "We were celebrating."

"Celebrating what?" Wayne asked. He wore a bibbed apron with KISS THE COOK printed on the front in big red letters.

Pulling her hand from behind her back, Nina held out her splayed fingers. "This."

"*Damn!*" roared several people standing close enough to see the brilliant stone on her finger.

Wayne caught Drew's shoulders and pounded his back. "Yo, Slick, you finally did it. When are you getting married?"

Drew smiled at Nina. "Christmas." He gave Wayne the shopping bag with their wedding bands. "Put this in the house for me."

Carmen came over to join the people gathering around Drew and Nina. "Who's getting married?" She saw the diamond on Nina's hand and screamed, dropped her oven mitt, and hugged Nina.

Nina barely had time to react when she found herself sandwiched between her three best friends. Michelle burst into tears, and within minutes all of them were crying.

Michelle sniffled. "Even though I'm pregnant, I still want to be a bridesmaid."

Nina kissed her damp cheek. "And you will be."

Richard strolled over and dropped an arm over Drew's shoulder. "Congratulations, cuz. You've got yourself quite a prize."

Drew nodded. "Thank you."

"Tell me something, D.L. How do you plan to support your wife? You know hustling ain't easy."

Resting an arm on Richard's shoulder, Drew angled his head close to his cousin's. "Have you ever heard of the Wright Group?"

"Sure. They rent private jets and limos to captains of industry, entertainers, and athletes." Richard noted the smug expression on Drew's face. "You're one of the partners?"

Drew nodded. "Bingo, cuz."

Richard shook his head in dismay. "Dammit, Drew. Why didn't you say something before they started calling you D.L.?"

"D.L.'s all right. It's a lot easier to say than Drew Lancaster."

There was a popping sound, and everyone turned to see Wayne uncorking a bottle of champagne, while Carmen handed out flutes.

Drew released Richard and walked over to Nina. Crossing his arms over his chest, he crooked a finger at her.

Smiling, she shook her head and repeated his gesture. He closed the distance between them and gathered her close to his chest. Smiling, he stared down at her smiling up at him.

"I love you, Nina."

"Love you back, Drew."

He lowered his head and kissed her to rousing applause. He stopped to accept a flute of champagne as Wayne waxed eloquently about married life.

Carmen interrupted him. "Enough, Wayne." She lifted her glass. "To Nina and Drew. May love and happiness be with you always."

"Hear, hear," everyone chorused.

Drew pressed his mouth to Nina's ear. "How long do you want to hang out here?"

She smiled. "Long enough to be sociably polite."

"Your place or mine?"

"Which is closer?"

"Mine."

Nina nodded as her gaze fused with his. She was astonished at the sense of fulfillment she felt.

Drew emptied his glass, set it down on a table and curved an arm around his fiancée's waist. "I'd say it's been quite a summer."

That is has, Nina thought. In fact, what they'd experienced was summer madness.

rebound

ReShonda Tate Billingsley

Chapter 1

Victoria stared at her reflection in the full-length mirror. She looked as she always imagined she'd look on this day—absolutely radiant. Her makeup was flawless across her caramel-colored skin. Her sandy brown shoulder-length hair was swept up into a bun, with several strands hanging loosely around her face. The intricately beaded Victoria Wang gown hung from her body like it was created especially for her. Her voluptuous breasts protruded from the A-lined front of her dress. Yes, she was indeed a beautiful bride.

Victoria forced a smile as she gazed at herself. As her mother and friends banged on the door outside the bride's room in the church, Victoria wiped away the single tear that had found its way down her cheek.

Mary J. Blige's "I'm Not Goin' Cry" echoed in her head.

"Come on, Victoria, open the door, baby!" her mother yelled.

Victoria ignored her mother, just as she had been doing for the last hour—since the love of her life, the man who she thought she would grow old with, had sent a note saying he couldn't go through with it. He couldn't marry her.

A fucking note.

Had she not given that man her heart and soul? Had she not devoted ninety-nine-point-nine percent of her time to making him happy? Yet he couldn't even be man enough to dump her to her face. He sent a fucking note. By a stranger, at that. Some homeless man he paid $20 to bring it to the church.

Victoria sighed as she thought of how she had just had a long talk with Kendrick three days ago. He could've told her then. Hell, he could've told her last night, when they said their respective good-byes before heading off to their bachelor and bachelorette parties. She had noticed that Kendrick had seemed withdrawn and aloof the last couple of weeks. But every time she asked him what was wrong, he'd said nothing. Even the night of their extensive talk, he acted nervous and scared, but he kept saying he was fine, so Victoria struck it up as prewedding jitters.

Victoria reflected on their fairy-tale romance. Kendrick had spotted her buying coffee at Starbucks—her regular morning routine. He asked for her number, but she blew him off. He pursued her relentlessly, showing up at Starbucks every morning until she finally gave in and agreed to a date.

They'd dated exclusively for two years, and while Victoria knew she was ready to get married, she had never pressured him. In fact, getting married was his idea. He had gone through this whole elaborate proposal, renting a billboard and everything. Why would he go through all that just to leave her at the altar?

Victoria looked down at the note still crumpled in her hand. She gently unfolded it, hoping she could find answers she hadn't previously seen. But the note still read the same: "Victoria, I'm sorry, please forgive me. I'm just not ready. K."

That was it. No real explanation, no nothing.

"Victoria, sweetie, it's Iman. Please open the door and let me in."

Victoria glanced toward the door. She could just see Iman in tears on the other side of the door. Iman was her best friend since elementary school, a true sisterfriend. Iman would kick your ass, then cry with you about it. She was an unusual mix of sensitivity and sassiness. Her histrionics could also work some nerves, which was why Victoria didn't want to let her in either.

Iman had been with Victoria styling her hair when that dirty-looking, dreadlocked man had walked in and handed Victoria the note. Iman had immediately started crying as a stunned Victoria called Kendrick on his cell phone. At first, Victoria thought it had been a cruel joke. But when she got Kendrick's voice mail and it said, "Victoria, I hope you can one day forgive me," she knew this was for real.

Through her tears, Iman had tried to hug Victoria, comfort her, and tell her everything would be all right. Victoria couldn't take the pity, so she had sent Iman to tell everyone at the church the wedding was off. As soon as Iman left, Victoria had locked the door and tried to deal with what was happening. As of yet, she hadn't really cried. Although her heart hurt like hell, Victoria was the strong one of her friends and family. She was the one who set and accomplished all her goals, not letting anything deter her. Everyone called her "the rock" because she was so together. She couldn't let that change now. She refused to let them see some jilted, driveling bride.

"Fuck him," Victoria numbly muttered as she stared at her reflection. "It's his loss. I don't need him."

Now, if only she could really make herself believe that.

"Victoria, honey, if you don't open this door, I'm going to call the fire department and have them break this door down," her mother called out.

Victoria closed her eyes and inhaled. Her mother, Rhonda, would definitely call the fire department, the cavalry, and anyone else she could think of. Victoria reached down and swooped her train up in her arms as she walked over to the door. She took a deep breath before opening it.

"Oh, baby!" her mother cried as she rushed in. "I'm so sorry." Victoria managed to pull herself from her mother's grasp. There had to be fifteen people, mostly bridesmaids, along with a couple of relatives, standing just outside the door. All of them looked like their best friend had just died.

"Are you okay?" Iman asked, clutching a handkerchief in her hand.

Victoria gulped, making sure her voice didn't crack. "I'm fine. Dang. What's the big deal?" She turned, walked back toward the dressing table, and began removing her jewelry.

"Baby, you can't be fine," Rhonda softly said. "Don't act like this isn't affecting you."

Victoria dropped her pearl necklace into her jewelry bag. "Can one of you help me out of this stupid dress?" She reached back, trying to unzip the dress. "Um . . . Hello, can somebody help me here?" Victoria repeated when no one moved. "Why are you all standing there staring at me with those pitiful looks?"

"Baby,"—Rhonda stepped toward her daughter and started unzipping the dress—"I think we should talk about it. I know this has to hurt."

"Mother, please." Victoria sighed. "It's probably for the best." She stepped out of the dress. "Iman, hand me my bag over there, please."

Iman fought back tears as she handed Victoria her overnight bag.

Victoria forced a laugh. "Girl, you act like you're the one that got left at the altar."

Iman gently stuck out her bottom lip. "I just can't understand why he would do this to you."

Victoria started pulling stuff out of her overnight bag. "Better now than later, don't you think?"

"But you're acting like it's not even bothering you," Iman replied.

Victoria slipped a sundress over her head. "What do you want me to do—fall to the ground, sobbing? Cut my wrists? Track Kendrick down, drag him to the church, and make him marry me? Give me a break."

"But I know how much you love him. How much you were looking forward to your life together," Iman said.

Victoria shrugged as she started gathering up her things. "Oh, well. Cry two tears in a bucket and fuck it." She turned toward her mother. "Sorry, mom."

Rhonda blew off her daughter's profanity. "I told everyone in the church. Do you want to hang back here until everyone is gone?"

"Why? So I won't have to face them? Please, I didn't do anything wrong."

"Well, do you want to come stay with me for a few days? We can rest, relax, and I can help you get over this. You always try to act so strong. But I'm your mother. I know you. And I know this is hurting you. So let me help, come stay with me a few days," Rhonda said.

Victoria was getting sick and tired of the pity. It was starting already. She could only imagine that it would just get worse. Everywhere she went, people would be looking at her with sad eyes, telling her how she didn't deserve this, waiting to see the infallible powerhouse of a woman crumble. True, she had some really good friends, but she had always been the glue that held everyone together. In fact, she took pride in always being the strong one, the self-assured real estate attorney who took all of life's blows and used them as stepping-stones to something bigger and better. That was how she wanted to approach this situation. She wanted to go back to work and tackle the mounds of cases that she had resolved to let sit on her desk while she was enjoying her honeymoon in Belize.

Belize. Victoria had forgotten all about that. She and Kendrick were set to leave for Belize at nine-thirty in the morning. Not only had they wasted all that money on the wedding, but their $2,000 wedding package at one of the finest resorts in Belize was now down the tubes as well. Victoria wanted to cry as she thought how much she had been looking forward to her honeymoon.

Hell, how much she had been looking forward to being married. At thirty-three, Victoria hated the idea of starting over. Dating trifling man after man, in hopes of finding Mr. Right. That was part of why she had wanted to get married; she hated dating. And she thought her prayers had been answered with Kendrick.

"So, it's settled," Rhonda announced, interrupting Victoria's thoughts. "You're coming home to spend a few days with me. Iman can run by your house and pick up some of your things, won't you, sweetheart?" Iman nodded. Rhonda clapped her hands together. "Good. Now, don't worry about the church. I've already spoken with the coordinator, and she will make sure both here and the reception hall get cleaned up."

Victoria looked at her mother, trying to get control of the situation. Maybe that's where she had gotten her need to control from. It was one of the things Kendrick hated about her. They were always arguing about what he called her "independent and controlling nature." He wanted her to be submissive, something she had extreme difficulty doing. Victoria wondered if that's why he'd decided not to marry her. She shook her head, refusing to let negative thoughts overcast her self-worth. Kendrick was a flaky, commitment-phobic man, and she was not going to let him make her doubt herself. She had to regain control—or at least some semblance of control—no matter how much she was hurting.

Victoria turned to one of her bridesmaids. "Rachel, can you go see if there's anyone left out in the church? I'm sure there is, as people always love some good drama. Anyway, can you tell them to please go on over to the reception and eat that three thousand dollars' worth of food. Otherwise it will all go to waste." Rachel nodded and scurried out of the room. Victoria turned back to her mother. "Mother, I appreciate your concern. But I will be fine. Haven't I always?"

"But—"

"No buts. I am not coming to your house so you can treat me like a broken-hearted baby." Victoria's mind suddenly flashed to Belize. They had a full-expense-paid week at that resort. She and Kendrick had pooled their money to pay for the wedding, but the honeymoon had been entirely his treat. He had footed that whole bill, saying it was his gift to her. They were already wasting tons of food at the reception. Why waste any more money just because Kendrick's ass decided to bail out?

"I'm going on my honeymoon," Victoria announced.

"What?" several people said in unison. They were all looking at Victoria like she had lost her mind.

"I said, I'm going on my honeymoon," Victoria repeated.

"The girl is losing it," Victoria's aunt Ella muttered.

Victoria laughed as the idea started to make more and more sense. Kendrick had truly hurt her, and at some point, Victoria knew she would break down and have a good cry. The way it was looking, if she stayed here, she wouldn't get a moment's peace for weeks. "No, Auntie Ella. All of my facilities are fully operational. I have a beautiful week planned in a beautiful city. So, although the plans have been slightly altered, I'm still going."

"By yourself?" Her mother asked.

"Not unless you think Denzel Washington would be willing to join me." Victoria laughed. No one laughed with her.

"Look," Victoria said, turning to face everyone. "I need this. I just want to get away, relax, and try to forget about this disastrous day."

"But by yourself? You want to go to another country by yourself?" Rhonda acted like it was the most absurd thing she had ever heard.

"Yes, Mother. I just want to get away, is that okay?"

"Let me come with you," Iman interjected. "We can make it a girls' week out."

Victoria smiled gently at her friend. "You just had a baby, and your husband would not even be trying to hear how you plan to leave a one-month-old child to go hang out in Belize."

Iman contemplated Victoria's response. "Yeah, but—"

"Well, I'll go then," Aunt Ella interjected. "You know your mama won't set foot on an airplane, and hell, I could use a free trip to a whole other country."

Victoria moaned as she thought of spending a week with her chain-smoking country aunt. Aunt Ella would probably fry up some chicken and carry it on the plane in a brown, grease-stained paper bag. No thanks.

"Umm, Auntie Ella, no offense, but I not only *want* to go by myself, I *need* to go by myself. Everyone, please understand, I just want to be alone."

"Victoria . . ." Her mother sighed. "Can't you just stay here and let me help you through this?"

"If I stay here, I'm just going to go to work, and I don't need that stress right now. I don't want to deal with the incessant questions, the pitiful stares, and the 'Are you sure you're all right?' questions twenty-four/seven."

"I won't let you work, and I'll keep everyone away from you," Rhonda tried to assure her.

"Please, don't fight me on this," Victoria pleaded.

Her mother took a deep breath. "Fine. You have to promise to call me every day. And at least let me take you to the airport."

Victoria smiled for the first time since she had gotten Kendrick's note. She actually was getting excited about the prospect of going to Belize. She had never been on a vacation by herself, let alone halfway across the world. But she wanted to get away, get all of her crying out, relax, relieve some stress, and forget about that asshole Kendrick. Hell, maybe she could even break from her prim and proper nature and find her a Latino island hunk for some good nights of sex.

"Thank you all for understanding, and I promise, I'll be fine."

All eyes remained on Victoria. They were all still full of pity. Iman was fighting back tears again. Victoria shook her head, more confident than ever that going on this trip was the right thing to do.

Chapter 2

Victoria removed her sunglasses and took in the rays of sunshine beating down on her face. She was really here. It was not the way she had planned it, but she was here nonetheless, and determined to make the best of a bad situation.

After getting checked into the Sea Lago resort, Victoria settled in to her room and poured herself a glass of wine to soothe her nerves. She then walked out onto the balcony and inhaled the fresh air. This was truly a beautiful place. She had asked to be moved from the honeymoon suite, but this room was just as nice, especially the ocean view from the balcony. Victoria leaned against the railing, took a long gulp of the wine, and closed her eyes as it slid down her throat.

"What's missing from this picture?" she mumbled. Victoria opened her eyes and looked down at the oceanfront. There were several couples down on the beach. Some walked hand in hand, some cuddled together, most were kissing and hugging all over each other.

"That should be me," Victoria whispered as she felt a lump form in her throat. She plopped down in a patio chair. Why would Kendrick do this to her? *How* could he do this to her?

Victoria could no longer hold it in. She let her glass slip out of her hands. As it crashed to the floor, she buried her face in her hands and sobbed for a good two hours.

* * *

"Now what?" Victoria muttered as she stared at her puffy-eyed reflection in the bathroom mirror. How was she supposed to find a Latin lover with swollen eyes?

Maybe she didn't need to be getting involved with a man anyway. Hell, after Kendrick, a man, even if it was just for sex, was the last thing she probably needed. Then again, she and Kendrick had abstained for the last two months. Ironically, it was his idea to "make the wedding night more special." What a load of bullshit. Regardless, Victoria's hormones were in overdrive. She laughed to herself. "I came here to have a good time, and I'm going to have a good time. Fuck Kendrick."

Victoria walked over and grabbed her suitcase out of the closet. She unzipped it, then sifted through her clothes, angrily tossing aside the white teddy and G-string she had planned to wear on her wedding night. She found a strapless black dress and held it up. "Not too casual, not too dressy," she said, nodding her approval.

Twenty minutes later Victoria was standing on the resort patio. It looked like the party was in full force. Several people were dancing to the sexy salsa tunes. Many others were cuddling at various tables. The very sight of these lovesick couples was turning Victoria's stomach.

"I need another drink," she mumbled as she made her way over to the bar. After that glass of wine she'd had earlier, she figured she probably shouldn't drink anything else, but she shrugged it off. "I deserve to get drunk," she said to herself.

"Hey, handsome." Victoria leaned on the bar and flirtatiously played with her spiral-curled hair. "Hello, Hector," she said, eyeing his nametag. "Can I have a Sex on the Beach?"

The dark-haired bartender flashed a smile. "You want *a* Sex on the Beach, or you want *some* sex on the beach?" He laughed.

Victoria scooted onto a barstool. "Either one is fine with me. Which one can you provide?"

The bartender smiled and laid a napkin in front of her. "One Sex on the Beach drink coming right up."

Victoria surveyed Hector's backside as he walked off. Nice butt, she thought. A little too small for my taste, but nice nonetheless.

Victoria swung around toward the band as she waited for Hector to return with her drink. The band was playing salsa, and they had the crowd on its feet. Everyone looked like they were having such a good time. Victoria scanned the patio. There was an elderly man sitting at the end of the bar by himself, but other than that, it seemed Victoria was the only person there solo.

"Maybe this wasn't such a good idea," she muttered.

"Here's your drink, ma'am. Do you want me to start a tab?" Hector asked.

Victoria hesitated, then reached in her small purse, pulled out her credit card, and laid it on the bar. Hector noticed her mood change.

"Hey, pretty lady, what happened to that beautiful smile?"

Victoria turned back toward the bar, then forced a smile. "Maybe I'll be better after another drink."

Hector playfully poked out his bottom lip. "Let me know if I can do anything to bring back that smile."

Victoria thought about telling him to meet her in her room when he got off; that would brighten her smile—but she decided against it. As horny as she was, she didn't want to screw a little-butt Latino just for the sake of it.

"Thank you, Hector. I'll keep that in mind." Victoria sipped her drink as Hector turned to help another customer.

Two Sex on the Beaches and one Amaretto Sour later, Victoria felt her head spinning. She had been sitting at the bar for almost two hours. No one had asked her to dance. Probably because everyone here is with someone else, she thought. The elderly man had paid for the Amaretto Sour, then gave her a flirtatious, toothless grin, but she held up her wedding finger—the one still sporting her three-carat platinum engagement ring—and waved him off. He shrugged, then hobbled on to flirt with someone else.

Victoria fingered the engagement ring. She contemplated walking down to the beach and flinging the ring into the ocean. "Yeah, right," she mumbled. "I may be drunk, but I sure ain't stupid." Nope, the ring was staying. Even if it didn't mean shit, it was still a bad-ass rock.

Victoria waved to Hector. "Hey, Hector!" she called. "One more for the road!" She tried to stand up and fell off the stool. She caught herself before she fell to the floor. Laughing, she pulled herself up. Hector looked at her with concern.

"Ah, *mi amiga,* maybe you've had enough for the evening," he said.

"Enough?" Victoria rolled her eyes. "I'm on vacation. I can drink all I want!"

"I'm just concerned, that's all. You're here by yourself, and it's not safe for a young lady to be alone in your . . . um, condition."

Suddenly, not only was Hector not cute, but he was getting on her damn nerves. "I know I'm alone! You think I don't fucking know I'm alone?" Victoria was getting loud, and people were starting to stare, but she could've cared less. The liquor was flowing through her body, and all her inhibitions were out the window. "You hear that, everybody? This smart-ass, little-butt bartender wants to remind me that I'm all alone in Belize. Like I can't see that! Like everybody can't see that!" Victoria held on to the bar as she felt her knees get weak. She felt the tears forming again. "It was supposed to be my honeymoon," she sobbed. "That bastard left me at the altar. I'm supposed to be enjoying Belize with my husband, but I'm all alone sitting at a damn bar for the last two hours while Hector tells me I can't have another drink!"

Several people had stopped and were staring. Normally, Victoria would have died from embarrassment, but right about now she didn't care. "I'm pretty. I'm smart. I would've made a good wife," Victoria sobbed to no one in particular. "But nooooo, that asshole had to dump me—*on my fucking wedding day!*"

Victoria was so busy yelling, she didn't see the two men in muscle shirts that were now standing in front of her.

"Ma'am, how 'bout we help you out of here?" one of them said as he reached for her arm.

Victoria jerked her arm back. "How 'bout you let go of me and tell this Nacho, Taco, whatever his name is, to fix me another drink."

"I think you've had a little too much to drink."

Victoria leaned in toward the guard. "Did you not hear me? I've been dumped. At the altar. Don't you think I'm entitled to get drunk?"

"Are you a guest here at the hotel?" the other muscle-bound guy asked.

"Yes I am. In room . . . ummm . . . room . . . Well, I can't remember the room, but I'm a guest!" Victoria slurred.

"We're going to have to ask you to leave," the first man said.

"Leave? All the damn money I paid—well, actually I didn't pay it." Victoria laughed. "But all the money that asshole, no-good, sorry son-of-a-bitch fiancé of mine paid? Hell, naw, I ain't goin' nowhere."

The two men looked at each other, then started moving in toward Victoria.

"Lisa! There you are, girl. I've been looking all over for you."

Everyone turned toward the deep baritone voice. The tall, handsome man stepped in. "I'm sorry, guys. It appears my friend has had a little bit too much to drink. As you just heard, her fiancé left her at the altar, so she's a little bit despondent. I'll take care of her from here."

Victoria squinted her eyes. Her vision was a little blurred, her head was pounding, and she felt ready to throw up, but she was sure she didn't know this man. She looked him up and down. "Do I know you?"

"Girl, stop playing," he said as he reached in and took her by the arm. "I'll take her on back to our room and put her to bed," he told the two men.

"Just do something with her, man. We can't have her messing up everybody else's good time," one of them replied.

The man nodded, then began leading Victoria back in toward the lobby. She could barely walk and probably would've tumbled over had he not had one hand gripped firmly around her waist.

"Where are you taking me?"

He ignored her question. "What room are you in?" he asked as he punched the up arrow at the elevator.

Victoria thought about it for a minute. "I don't know."

The man sighed. "I really don't need this."

"You don't need what?" Victoria spat. Her speech was slurred, and she could feel a string of saliva dribbling down her chin. She wiped it away, then tried unsuccessfully to pull herself away from his grasp. "Did I ask you to come to my rescue, Mr. Prince Charming, Mr. Knight in Shining Armor, Sir . . . Sir Mix-a-Lot?" Victoria cracked up at her feeble attempt at humor.

The man guided her onto the elevator without saying a word. He pushed button fifteen, then stood back silently. He kept one arm holding Victoria up.

"Why your panties all in a knot?" Victoria cackled. She suddenly stopped laughing and grabbed her stomach. "I'm gonna be sick."

"Shit. Can you at least hold on until we get to my room?"

Victoria tried to look at the little light to see what floor they were on, but she couldn't make out the numbers. She slid down onto the floor of the elevator. "I feel like I'm dying."

The man pulled her up just as the elevator doors opened. "Come on. I'm the first room off the elevator."

Victoria reluctantly got up. "I'm gonna be sick," she said again just as the man got his door open.

"Come on, the bathroom is right here—"

Too late. Victoria threw up all over the floor, much of it splattering onto the man's shoes.

"Damn it! These are Bruno Magli."

Victoria hurled some more, then stumbled over to the sofa and collapsed. She felt her dress rise up over her behind, but she didn't have the effort to pull it down. The last thing she remembered was hearing the man pick up the phone and call for room service.

Chapter 3

It felt like somebody was playing that Smash the Gopher game from Chuck E. Cheese's restaurant on Victoria's head. She groaned and rolled over. She had never in her life had a hangover like this. Her mouth felt dry, and her head was pounding.

Victoria managed to pull herself up. She didn't even remember how she had got back to her room. She tried to focus on her surroundings. This wasn't her room. She rubbed her temples in confusion.

"I see you finally decided to get up."

Victoria jumped. "What the—? Who are you?" she asked, clutching the covers to her chest. Her eyes bulged, not so much out of surprise but rather at the sight of the sexy, muscular man standing in the doorway. A tan T-shirt and Polo jeans hugged his perfectly sculpted body. His hazel eyes, chiseled chin, and deep dimples were just the icing on the cake.

The man leaned against the door frame. He was holding a cup in his hands. "I'm Damon. This is my room. And those"—he pointed to her body—"those are my clothes."

Victoria looked down at the Morehouse College T-shirt she was wearing. She glanced around the room. Things started slowly coming back to her.

"Oh, my God," she whispered.

"No need to be calling on God now." Damon walked over and

handed her the cup. "Here, drink this. It's coffee. It may be a little cold, as it's been waiting on you to get up for more than an hour."

"What time is it?" Victoria took the coffee and sipped it. It was lukewarm and straight black. She hated black coffee, but at this point, she needed whatever she could get.

Damon sat in the chair across from the bed. "It's one o'clock."

"In the afternoon?" Victoria asked with astonishment.

"In the afternoon," Damon repeated.

"Oh, snap."

"Do you always go to foreign places by yourself and get sloppy drunk?"

Victoria tried to recall as much as she could from last night. "Oh, my God, I am so totally embarrassed." She set the coffee cup on the nightstand and buried her face in her hands.

Damon laughed. "You should be. I had to intervene before the bouncers threw you out. They had no sympathy for you being stood up at the altar."

Victoria looked up, confused. "How do you know that?"

Damon laughed again. "Everybody knows that. You made sure everyone in the restaurant knew. You were getting a little out of hand, so I stepped in."

Victoria glanced around the room. "And you brought me to your room?"

"Yeah, you couldn't remember your room number. And after you threw up on me, I just thought you should get to bed."

Victoria didn't remember any of that. She was always so together, but her tolerance for liquor was really low. What was she thinking, having all those drinks? "Did we, um . . . oh, I can't believe I'm even asking this. Did we—"

"Did we what? Have sex?" Damon chuckled. "No, I hate to burst your bubble. I changed your clothes, but that's it. I don't take advantage of sloppy-drunk women. Besides, I've got too much going on to try to seduce someone who doesn't know she's being seduced."

Victoria was getting tired of him calling her sloppy drunk. *But you were*, that nagging little voice in her head said.

"Well . . . I . . . um . . ." Victoria didn't know what to say. She was so ashamed she had let this man see her like this. She could barely look him in the eye. Good thing she never had to see him again. Victoria threw back the covers and tried to ease out of the bed. Damon stood up and extended his hand to help her out. She took it as she pulled herself up. His hands were smooth, and she could've sworn she felt an electric charge shoot up her arm. She let her grip linger before stepping out of the bed. He smiled at her again. It was an enchanting, sexy smile that lifted up on only one end of his mouth. There was an awkward silence. Then finally he spoke.

"Don't worry about the shirt. As a Morehouse man, I have plenty more."

Victoria nodded. "My dress?"

Damon stepped aside and pointed to the chaise longue. "Right there."

Victoria stepped around Damon and reached for her clothes. "Well, thank you. For everything."

Damon nodded. "No problem." Victoria looked at him again. He had a sadness in his eyes. She noticed the wedding ring on his finger. So maybe that was why he hadn't tried anything with her last night.

"Well, enjoy your vacation." Victoria wondered what he was doing here alone. He had to be alone, if she had spent the night in his room. He must be on business.

"Trust me. This isn't a vacation."

Victoria debated asking more questions. But she was so ready to get out of this man's room, since she could barely look at him. "Oh, well, thanks again."

"Hey," Damon stopped her just as she reached the door. "I never did catch your name."

This strange handsome man with the sad eyes had seen her at her worst. He probably thought she was a pitiful lush. "It's Cassandra. Cassandra Casady," Victoria said as she stepped out the door.

"Have a good day, Cassandra," Damon called out as the door closed.

Chapter 4

Victoria debated calling home. She had briefly checked in with her mother when she arrived, leaving a message letting her know everything was fine. She made it a point to call when she knew her mom had gone on her weekly trip to the horse track. The last thing she needed was her mom telling her how she shouldn't have come by herself. Now, with a headache that wouldn't go away, Victoria again didn't feel like hearing her mother's mouth.

The message light was blinking on the hotel phone, but Victoria didn't even bother checking it. She was lying across her bed, trying to recall all that happened last night. She knew she was hurting, and she knew she had had a few drinks too many, but she never thought she would get drunk and throw up on a stranger. A fine stranger at that.

Victoria couldn't get Damon out of her mind. He might have been good for a romp in the hay while she was in Belize. But throwing up all over him probably ruined any chance of that happening. Besides, he looked like sex was the last thing on his mind. It had to be. Most red-blooded men would've tried to make some type of move. Victoria had had enough men tell her how pretty she was, so it wasn't like she was some butt-ugly woman. And if her looks didn't turn them on, her 36 double D's usually did.

The ringing of the telephone startled Victoria out of her thoughts.

"Hello." Victoria hoped it wasn't her mother, because she wasn't in the mood.

"Uggh, girl, you sound like crap. You're supposed to be relaxing and enjoying yourself."

"Hey, Iman. I'm just nursing a hangover."

"Oooooh, you down there getting drunk. Go on, girl."

"It's not like that at all. I had a little too much to drink last night, met a gorgeous-ass man, threw up all over him, then ended up in his bed."

"You're shitting me!" Iman screamed. "In all the years I've known you, I've never known you to get drunk."

"I know." Victoria shook her head, replaying what she could remember about last night. "It just kind of snuck up on me. Then this guy helped me out and took me back to his room and put me to bed."

"You went to a stranger's room?"

"I know. I know. I was out of it."

"Did you sleep with him?"

"I don't think so."

"What the hell you mean, you don't think so? "

Victoria sat up and pulled the covers over her. "He said we didn't."

"You don't know?"

"No! I told you I was wasted. Besides, he had on a wedding ring."

"And? That don't mean shit."

"Well, no, I didn't sleep with him. But I was still embarrassed." She could just picture Iman sitting there with her eyes bugged and her mouth wide open. Victoria was about as straitlaced as they came. She'd only been drunk one other time in her life, and that was at their college graduation and at Iman's urging. She'd never had a one-night stand and usually dated a guy for two to three months before she would even consider sleeping with him. So Victoria could only imagine how this was just flooring Iman.

"Girl, I cannot believe this. I knew your ass could get buck wild. Trying to play that role," Iman joked.

"Yeah, yeah, yeah. I'm paying for it today."

"At least you only have a few more days, and hopefully you won't bump into him anymore."

"You're right."

"Well, I just wanted to check in with you. Let me get off this phone because I know this call is costing me a grip."

"All right, girl. I'm going to go downstairs and grab me something to eat and try to relax the rest of the week."

"Cool, but lay off the drinks," Iman called out.

"You don't have to worry about that." Victoria tried to laugh, but the simple act made her head pound.

The women said their good-byes, and Victoria dragged herself out of bed. She jumped in the shower and let the cold water penetrate her skin for twenty minutes. When she finished, she dried off, lathered herself down with Victoria's Secret Pear Glaze lotion, slipped on a silk sundress, and pulled her hair into a ponytail. She checked herself out in the mirror, determined she now looked halfway decent, and headed down to the hotel's patio restaurant. She debated going to one of the restaurants down the street for fear that someone would recognize her from last night, but decided against that after feeling the rumbling in her stomach.

Victoria found a table nestled back in the corner and asked the waitress if she could sit there. The waitress nodded, and Victoria eased into the chair, grabbed a menu, and started peering over it, trying to decide what would ease the pang in her stomach.

"Hello, Cassandra."

Damon tapped Victoria on the shoulder after she didn't look up. Victoria jumped as she looked up at him. "Hello, Cassandra," he repeated.

It took Victoria a minute to register what he was talking about. "Oh, hi. You startled me." She really had hoped not to bump into him, but of course, luck wasn't on her side.

"You know, I called the front desk and asked for Cassandra Casady's room because I wanted to check on you. Funny, they said they don't have a Cassandra Casady."

Victoria hesitated before speaking. She didn't even feel like trying to come up with a lie. "That's not my real name."

"I know that, Victoria."

Victoria's mouth dropped. "How—"

Damon reached into the bag he was carrying and handed Victoria her small clutch purse. "You left this in my room. I had to look at your license to see how to return this to you."

Victoria gently took her purse. "I'm sorry. I . . . I was just a little embarrassed."

"No need to be. If I hadn't come to your rescue, I probably would have been sloppy drunk before the night was over myself."

"You like that word, don't you?"

"What word?"

"Sloppy drunk."

"Actually, that's two words." Damon laughed. "Don't get me wrong, Victoria, I'm not trying to judge you. I couldn't judge you even if I wanted to."

Victoria realized she liked this guy. "Let me repay you for your generosity. Would you like to join me for lunch, or do you have a meeting or something to get to?"

"Meeting?"

"Yeah, I just assumed you were here on business."

Damon shook his head. "I wish it were that simple. But yes, I would love to join you for lunch. I need a distraction before I do something I regret."

Damon eased into the chair across from Victoria. He summoned the waitress, who had yet to return since seating Victoria. "You want something to drink?"

"No way. I don't want to even see a drink for a long time."

He smiled that pretty, crooked smile, and Victoria felt that charge again. This man was so fine, it was unbelievable. He must be a model or something; he definitely looked like he belonged on somebody's magazine cover, Victoria thought.

They ordered iced tea and club salads. After the waitress left, Damon leaned in. "So, Victoria, what do you do? Where are you from, truthfully?"

Victoria smiled. "I'm a real estate attorney. And I'm from Houston—truthfully."

"No kidding? I'm from Dallas. It's a small world. We come halfway across the country, meet, and find that we live less than four hours from each other back in the States." Damon laughed. They caught each other's gaze and held it. "You have beautiful eyes," Damon said.

Victoria felt herself blushing. "Thank you." She averted her eyes so he wouldn't see how nervous she was. Damon squeezed her hand and leaned back. They enjoyed the light salsa playing on the sound system until the waitress brought their food. Over lunch, they talked like they were old friends. Victoria was amazed at how well they clicked.

"You know, I joked about saving you last night, but I think you might have actually saved me," Damon said as he finished up his salad.

"What do you mean?" Victoria dabbed the corners of her mouth with her napkin before setting the napkin down on the table.

"Well, when I spotted you, I had been sitting down at the bar, trying to come up with a plan."

"A plan for what?"

Damon took his gaze off Victoria and got that forlorn look again. "A plan that probably would've gotten me in a lot of trouble."

Victoria surveyed Damon as he toyed with his napkin. That sweet, sexy look was gone, replaced by the same hollow look she had seen this morning in his room. He looked like he had a lot he wanted to get off his chest. "What's wrong? I'm a good listener."

Damon hesitated before saying, "My wife."

So he did have a wife. Victoria had been hoping maybe he was divorced and just hadn't gotten around to taking off his ring.

"Yeah, my wife *and* her lover."

Victoria was stunned.

Damon laughed. It was a maniacal, disheartening laugh. "I found an e-mail on an e-mail account I didn't even know about. It was from somebody named Felix Cambridge—what the hell kind of name is that, anyway? Anyhow, it was talking about how he was looking forward to their vacation in Belize. I didn't confront her with it because part of me was hoping it was all some big misunderstanding. I followed her down here. She told me she was going on a trip with her girlfriends." Damon shrugged.

Damn, Victoria had thought her situation was bad. "Have you seen her here?"

"Yeah, I saw them yesterday. I was on my way to their room to wait so I could murder them in their sleep when I saw you. So that's what I mean when I say you saved me."

"So what do you do now?"

"Oh, I haven't ruled out murder." Damon snickered.

"You have a good attitude about this."

"Really I don't. I'm trying to stay sane. I'm an assistant district attorney, and I'm in line for the actual district attorney spot. Murder could throw a monkey wrench in my career goals."

"Yeah, I don't think you can prosecute yourself."

"When I saw them together, it took everything in my power not to wring both of their necks right then."

"Why didn't you?"

"I've prosecuted enough crimes of passion to know that they still result in some jail time. And I can't do jail. Hell, I put too many of those fools in jail myself. I'd be a marked man."

Victoria didn't know how to respond. Looks could truly be deceiving. Damon didn't look like he would even think vengeful thoughts, let alone seriously contemplate carrying them out.

"So, what now?" Victoria asked again.

Damon shrugged casually. "I play it by ear, I guess. I think if I stay here, I'm going to end up hurting someone. But I need her to know I know, so at some point today, I will be confronting her."

Victoria didn't know what to say. Most men would've pounced on their wife and the other man right then and there. She admired Damon for trying to think the situation through. She found herself taking his hand and gently caressing it.

"I can't believe I'm spilling my guts to a complete stranger," Damon said.

"Maybe because you know I know your pain."

"I guess so." His expression softened. "How are *you* doing?"

Victoria released her hand and leaned back. "Better than last night. I need to apologize to you again."

"Don't worry about it. I understand. Since I spilled my guts, it's your turn."

Victoria sighed. "You know what happened to me." They were cut off when the waitress returned to see if they needed anything else. Victoria couldn't help but notice how attentive she was to

Damon, while all but ignoring her. Victoria smiled when Damon asked for the check without ever taking his eyes off her. The waitress, obviously irritated that her flirting was getting nowhere, spun off to go get their check.

"So your fiancé didn't show up on your wedding day?" Damon asked after she left.

"Nope, and the bastard sent a note by a homeless man." Victoria tried to laugh, but there was nothing funny about the pain that rippled through her heart.

"Damn."

"You can say that again."

"Damn."

Victoria laughed. This time it was genuine.

"You have a beautiful smile. Must be to go with those eyes."

Victoria's grin widened. "I haven't smiled much in the last few days."

"So, what are *you* going to do?"

Victoria thought about it for a moment as her smile diminished. "I'm going to enjoy my time here, then just try to return to normal when I get back home. We were supposed to come here for our honeymoon. Since everything was paid for, I came on. I just wanted to take a little time to myself, get away from everybody fussing over me and constantly asking me, 'Are you okay?'"

"Well, I won't ask you that anymore, deal?"

"Deal."

"Besides," Damon continued, "I think we both deserve to—" Damon suddenly stopped talking, and the smile faded from his face. His brow furrowed, and the veins in his forehead popped out. Victoria turned to see what had him speechless. Damon's eyes were planted firmly on a tall, cocoa-brown woman with long, jet-black hair. She was wearing a hot-pink bikini top and a matching wrap around her waist. She had her head back and her eyes closed as the man she was with nibbled on her neck. Her laughter sounded like it came from a woman in love.

Victoria turned back to Damon to say something, but it was too late. He had pushed away from the table and was storming toward the couple, his strides were long and determined. Victoria jumped up to follow him, but Damon reached them before she could even get away from the table.

Victoria watched in horror as Damon grabbed the man, swung him around, then planted his fist firmly in the man's jaw.

"Oh my God! Damon!" the woman screamed.

"Yeah, Damon. Your fucking husband, Damon! Or did you forget you had a husband?"

By this time, the music had stopped playing, and several people had turned their attention to the ruckus. The man lay on the ground, moaning and rubbing his jaw. Damon turned toward the man. "Get up!" He kicked the man in the stomach, and the man slumped back to the ground. "You want to fuck around with other men's wives, then get up and take this ass-beating for it." Damon swung his foot back and kicked the man in the side.

Damon's wife grabbed his arm. "I'm sorry, baby. It's not what it looks like. Don't do this!" She was crying as she tried to pull Damon off the man. But he was like a madman. He just kept kicking and hurling obscenities. The man's nose and mouth was bleeding. Victoria didn't know if she should try and jump in or what. She didn't have to make a decision, though. Security was now on Damon, pulling him off the man. It took three of them to bring Damon under control. Two of them were the same men who had tried to throw Victoria out yesterday.

Damon's wife was still sobbing as she knelt next to the man, who lay on the ground like he was unconscious. "Felix, wake up," she said, patting his face. The guards managed to pull Damon away and slam him against the wall.

"Don't hurt him," Damon's wife muttered as she lifted the man's head into her lap.

"Bitch, don't act like you're concerned about me now!" Damon yelled, trying to break free.

"Sir! You need to calm down!" one of the guards yelled.

Damon took a deep breath as the realization of what was happening began to set in. "I'm straight. I'm straight," he kept repeating, trying to calm himself down.

Victoria decided she needed to do something. She stepped toward the guards. "Please don't call the police. Just let me take him out of here. He just caught his wife with another man. Show some compassion," she pleaded.

Damon's wife cocked her head to the side and studied Victoria. She let Felix's head drop as she stood up and walked toward the guards. She stepped in front of Victoria and placed a hand on one of the guard's shoulders. "Sir, this is all my fault. There's been a big misunderstanding. Neither myself nor my friend wish to press any charges. Please, can't we just let this go? We won't be causing you any more trouble."

One guard shook his head. "Naw, man, we can't be dealing with this."

The other guard looked more compassionate. He turned to Damon. "Dude, I feel you about catching your wife." He scowled at Damon's wife. She placed her hand on her hip and gave him a disgusted look. "But this isn't the time or place. The last thing you want is to be thrown in a foreign jail."

All it took was the word "jail" for Damon to come back to his senses. He nodded. "Look, I'm sorry. I just lost it. I'll leave so I don't cause any more problems." He held his hands up to show he was sincere.

The third guard turned to Victoria. He looked as if he recognized her, but decided against saying anything. "Can you make sure he gets somewhere and calms down?"

Victoria didn't hesitate. "Absolutely."

"What the fu—?" Damon's wife said as she glared at Victoria.

The first guard stopped her just as she moved to step toward Victoria. "Ma'am, you need to see about your boyfriend here," he said, pointing to Felix.

"He's not my boyfriend!"

"Whatever he is, you need to see about him." He turned to Damon and Victoria. "And you two need to leave."

Victoria slipped her hand into Damon's and gently tried to pull him away. He still had some anger in his eyes, so she wanted to get while the getting was good.

"Damon! Who the hell is that?" his wife yelled as they headed out.

Damon stopped like he wanted to say something.

"Don't," Victoria whispered. "She's not worth it."

Damon bit down on his lip as he inhaled deeply. "Enjoy your little vacation, Trina. Your shit will be on the front lawn when you get back."

"Damon, let me explain," Trina pleaded. Damon ignored her. He reached in his wallet, pulled out a twenty-dollar bill, and handed it to the waitress, who was standing by watching the ruckus. Damon wrapped his arm around Victoria and walked out the door.

Trina's tone changed. "How the hell you goin' try and bust me and you down here with another bitch?" she screamed.

Victoria knew the arm around her was just for effect, but after what they had just been through, she let it slide. Damon was trying to walk out of there like he wasn't fazed, but Victoria could tell he was hurting, deeply hurting. And Lord knows, she knew exactly how that felt.

Chapter 5

The moon was casting an eerie glow on the soft ocean waters. It was almost as if it wanted to guide the two lost souls drifting along the beach. And that's exactly what Victoria and Damon had been doing for the last few hours, drifting. They were walking barefoot along the beach, each lost in his or her own thoughts.

Victoria glanced over at Damon, who seemed to be fighting back tears. "You really love her, don't you?"

"Loved," Damon replied. "As in past tense."

"Too bad it doesn't work that way. You know, somebody does us wrong, and we just wipe them from our lives," Victoria responded, kicking the sand around with her feet.

"Yeah, too bad."

They walked in silence for a few more minutes. "Do you know I never, ever cheated on my wife?" Damon asked out of the blue. "My friends run women like pimps, but not me. I've always been the good guy. My boys would always tell me, 'Damon, when you goin' learn, nice guys finish last?' "

"You know, none of them liked Trina. We grew up in the same neighborhood. I've been knowing her a long time. But they said she was a gold digger who saw me as her ticket out of the ghetto."

"She didn't seem, well, she didn't . . ." Victoria didn't know how to tactfully sum up Trina's behavior.

"Like the type of woman I'd be attracted to?" Damon interjected.

Victoria nodded.

"Believe it or not, I grew up in the 'hood. But my mother was determined that her kids would live better than she did. So she scraped up money for me to go to private school, then I got a scholarship to college and a grant to law school. So I made it out and have been living the nice, respectable middle-class life my mama always dreamed of. But Trina has a way of bringing out that other side of me, that rough side I'm not proud of. I guess you can take the man out the ghetto, but you can't take the ghetto out of the man, because I had to go and hook up with someone like Trina. She always talked about how boring I was, about how boring our life was. But I never paid it much attention. I was always too wrapped up in work. So maybe it's my fault I drove her to another man."

"Damon, I don't know you very well, but I know you can't blame yourself for your wife's actions. She did what she wanted to do. Now you have to do what you have to do. If that means forgive her and take her back, then so be it."

Damon looked at her like she had lost her mind. "Forgive her? Hell, no, that ain't happening. Like I said, I still have some street in me, and next time I might not be able to calm myself down, and everything my mama worked so hard for would be gone."

Damon looked over at Victoria, who was walking with her head hung low, her arms wrapped around her body, trying to shield off the crisp night air.

"I'm sorry. I'm just rambling. I know you're dealing with your own problems, and the last thing you need is to be burdened with mine."

Victoria tried to force a smile. But images of her botched wedding day wouldn't allow it. "I'm okay, I guess. Or rather, I will be okay. I guess I would just like to know why." Victoria bit down on her bottom lip to fight back the tears she felt. "Why couldn't he tell me beforehand? He had so many opportunities. Why would he wait until our wedding day?" she asked, more to herself than anyone else. It's not like she expected Damon to provide her with any answers. He didn't even know Kendrick. Hell, he didn't even know her, for that matter.

Damon stopped and turned Victoria toward him. "He's a coward. That's why he left you at the altar." Damon gently lifted Victoria's chin. "He wasn't ready to get married, and he was afraid if he looked into those beautiful brown eyes of yours, he'd realize what a fool he was being."

Victoria stared at Damon. She felt so safe with him. It was strange. Standing here with him in this place, at this moment, she felt like she had known him forever. She looked deep in his eyes. The pain was evident in both of their faces. They were so close now, Victoria could feel the heat from his breath. Her heart began beating faster as he leaned closer to her. She closed her eyes in anticipation of his kiss. But instead, he just pulled her to him in a tight embrace. "You're going to be fine. We're both going to be just fine. I just know it."

Victoria was glad he couldn't see the disappointment in her face. But then, she thought it probably was best he didn't kiss her. The last thing she needed was to be getting involved with another man. Especially a man with issues of his own.

"It's getting late," Damon finally said, breaking the awkward silence between them. "I'd better be getting you back to your room."

Victoria simply nodded, and Damon took her hand and started leading her back down the beach.

They walked back to the hotel in silence. Once they were in front of her hotel room, Damon reached in and hugged her again. "Thank you for saving me from doing something stupid—again." The feelings running through Victoria's body were undeniable.

It has to be because I'm hurting, and he's a good-looking man, she thought. *That's all it is.* "What was it you said? We're saving each other," Victoria whispered as they released each other's embrace. Both of them just stood there for a few seconds, like they didn't want the other to go.

"So . . . um . . . how long are you here?" Damon finally asked.

Victoria slightly shrugged. "The room is paid for for a week. So I guess a week. What about you? Now that you've gotten what you came here for, when are you leaving?"

Damon looked off. "I guess I'll head back tomorrow. I have some divorce paperwork to begin."

Tomorrow? Victoria thought. She didn't know what it was, but she was hoping to spend a little more time with him. If anything, just for the company. She enjoyed talking to him, and the thought of spending the rest of the week by herself was no longer appealing.

"Oh . . . tomorrow, huh? Well . . ." Victoria struggled to find something to say. "Well, maybe we can have breakfast or something before you head out."

Damon smiled for the first time since his fight with his wife. "Breakfast sounds great. So, um, I guess I'll call you in the morning?"

"Yeah, that sounds like a plan." Again, they just awkwardly stood there. Victoria felt like a nervous teenager.

"Well, good night," Victoria finally said as she slipped her key into the door. Damon watched as she walked into the room. He waved softly just before she shut the door. Victoria leaned against the door and closed her eyes. What the hell was going on with her body? Even though Kendrick had done her wrong, she still loved him. She had always been a one-man woman. It had been years since she had been even remotely turned on by anyone other than Kendrick. So why was moisture building up between her legs over this man she barely knew?

Victoria softly banged her head up against the door, wishing she had made a move to at least kiss Damon. She wanted to kiss him. She needed to kiss him. Just to see what it felt like, feel his tongue intertwine with hers. That's it. A little kiss.

"Too late now," Victoria mumbled as she made her way to the bedroom. The oversize king bed was beckoning her, it looked so inviting. But it also looked like it was definitely made for two. Victoria shook off thoughts of Damon as she changed into her nightgown. The thoughts wouldn't go away, and as she slipped underneath the covers, she rubbed herself between her legs and mumbled, "It's going to be a long night."

Chapter 6

What the—?" Victoria groggily pulled herself out of the bed. Was that banging on her door? It took her a minute to compose herself and focus. She had tossed and turned since Damon dropped her off at her room. She finally got to sleep around two. Victoria glanced at the clock on the nightstand: 4:09. Who the hell would be banging on her door at four in the morning?

Victoria dragged herself over to the door and looked out the peephole. What was going on? She ran her fingers through her hair, made sure to wipe the sleep out of her eyes, then opened the door. "Damon? What's up?"

Damon was standing there, nervously twisting his hands. "Hi, I'm . . . I'm sorry to wake you up, but it's just, um . . ."

"It's just what?" Victoria asked. As much as she enjoyed talking with him, it was four in the morning.

Damon didn't say anything else. He just pulled Victoria toward him and planted a firm kiss on her lips. It caught her off guard at first, but then she relaxed, and her body seemed to melt in his embrace. He eased into the room, his tongue now making its way down her neck. Victoria felt on fire. She wanted to stop and ask him why he was doing this. She knew his passion was coming from pain. *So is yours,* a voice in her head answered. He planted gentle, moist kisses on her neck.

As Damon began gently lowering the strap on her gown, Victoria briefly considered stopping him. Was she really about to sleep with a man she had just met? What the hell? He wanted her, and she wanted him. Who cared what had driven them to each other's arms? She led him to her bed and eased onto it, never taking her eyes off his muscular physique. Damon stood at the edge of the bed and slowly began removing his shirt. After throwing it on the floor, he unbuckled his pants, then stepped out of those. Victoria smiled as she gazed at the huge, rock-solid lump in his briefs.

"Are you okay with this?" Damon asked as he leaned over her.

Victoria nodded. "I know we're both going through some things, but this just feels so right," she said.

Damon nuzzled her neck as he massaged her breasts. "Let's forget about them. Tonight is about us."

Victoria was glad she had decided to go ahead and put on her sexy negligee, although she could've probably been wearing a burlap sack and Damon wouldn't have cared. Damon took his time with her, teasing her in all the right places, working his tongue like a pro. He kissed her breasts like they were treasure mounds, gentle and slowly. He ran his tongue around her nipple before biting it just enough to send sensations fluttering through Victoria's body. While he continued to suck and caress her breasts, he moved his hand slowly down her stomach. When he reached her pubic hair, he massaged her gently before inserting two fingers into her moistness. He worked those fingers so good, Victoria felt like she wanted to cry. By the time Damon was ready to enter her, she had already climaxed twice.

Victoria felt him guide his penis toward her, and some semblance of common sense prevailed. She forced herself to stop and mutter, "Condom?"

Damon didn't stop kissing her as he took her hand and guided it down so she could feel the condom firmly in place.

Victoria smiled, wondering how he had got it on without her knowing. "Damn, you're good," Victoria muttered.

Damon pushed himself inside Victoria and moaned, "Baby, you ain't seen nothing yet."

Victoria lay staring at the ceiling. Part of her felt like she should feel guilty or something. Here she was in a foreign country, in bed with a strange man. This was so out of character for her. But damn, it had felt so good. They had made love the rest of the night. It was unbridled passion. And something Victoria definitely needed.

Damon stretched his arms out. "Hey, how long have you been up?"

"Just a little while. Just lying here, thinking."

Damon was silent for a few minutes. "Any regrets?"

Victoria thought about it briefly. "None. You?"

"The only thing I regret is that I didn't meet you sooner."

They lay there in silence for a few more minutes. Victoria wondered what was going through his mind.

"You're a very beautiful and sweet woman."

"Thank you. You're not so bad yourself." Victoria paused, then decided to say what was on her mind. "Do you always sleep with strangers?"

"I could ask you the same question. But no. I told you, I have not been with another woman in four years, since I married Trina."

Victoria propped herself up next to Damon. She couldn't believe how comfortable she felt after sleeping with Damon. If someone had told her she would actually have a one-night stand and not feel bad about it, she would've told them they were crazy.

"So tell me, did you talk to Trina any more?"

Damon grimaced, like the mere mention of the name was painful. "She actually came to my room last night. She had the audacity to be crying, telling me how sorry she was and how we could work through this. She said this Felix made her feel vibrant and alive and all I cared about was work. That was her justification for having an affair."

"Did you buy that?"

"Hell, no. I work so hard because Trina wants the finer things in life. She doesn't work, doesn't want to work, yet loves to spend money. I'm not taking the blame on this. For a second, just a second, I felt my resolve weakening, then I noticed a hickey on her neck. What the hell is a thirty-two-year-old woman doing with a hickey? I finally just had to put her out because I swear to God, I would've ended up strangling her and trying to dispose of the body."

Victoria leaned over and kissed his chest. He closed his eyes and rubbed her hair. "Thank you for making me forget how bad things were . . . if only for a little while."

Victoria loved his compliments. They were so genuine. "No—thank *you*—you just don't know how good it felt being with you," she responded. They enjoyed the silence between them for a few minutes before she asked, "Are you still leaving today?"

Damon looked like he was contemplating his answer. "You know what, I think I'll stay, now that I have a reason to stay."

"What's your reason?"

"I'm just getting to know you. I can't very well leave now, can I?"

"If you stay, you have to stay the rest of the week. You can't just tease me a day, then bail out."

"That's no problem. I'm on personal leave because I thought I was going to have to cover up a murder."

"I was just kidding. I'd love for you to stay, but I understand if you have to get back." Victoria really did want to spend some time with him, but she didn't want him to feel pressured.

"I want to stay. I like you, Victoria. You make me smile, and it's been a long time since I've had a smile on my face." He massaged her breast as a devilish look crossed his face. "Can you make me smile again by giving me some more of what you gave me last night?"

Victoria climbed on top of Damon and straddled him. She was surprised at her behavior. Maybe she was releasing her inhibitions because she never thought she'd see Damon after they left Belize. Maybe she just wanted to make herself feel good for a change and not worry about what anyone else thought. Whatever the case, she was determined to make the most of the rest of the week. "Do you think I'm a bad girl?" she asked.

Damon glanced down at her naked breasts, looked back up into her eyes, and while palming her naked behind, responded, "You're so damn good, it should be against the law."

"Good answer," Victoria said as she leaned down and gently bit Damon's ear. "Very good answer."

Chapter 7

So this was what they meant when they said time flies when you're having fun. Victoria couldn't believe that five days had gone by since she'd met Damon. They had spent every waking (and sleeping) moment together. They discovered that they had so much in common, from their love of college basketball to their interest in movies. Their conversations were lively, and they had spirited debates. She really enjoyed talking to him. They had gone snorkeling, Jet Skiing, dancing, and parachuting. She even tried to get him to go bungee jumping, but he had told her there were some things he just wouldn't do. "Not even for a pretty lady like you," he had said.

Victoria didn't know why she was gravitating to him; why they were so drawn to each other. Yes, they both were on the rebound, but you wouldn't know it from the good time they had when they were together.

"Ummmm, right there."

Victoria held her breath and tried to talk out of her nose. "You want, I massage you without de towel."

"Umm, yeah, that would be nice." Damon was lying facedown on the massage table. He thought she was next door getting a facial, but she had actually convinced the masseuse to let Victoria take her place. Now she was standing over Damon, rubbing oil up and down his back.

"So," Victoria said, her voice still disguised, "de lady you with, she be your girlfriend?"

"Naw, she's just some girl I met here in Belize, a piece of ass to tide me over." Damon kept his face buried. Victoria's smile faded, and a look of confusion crossed her face.

"Yep," Damon continued, "she's just a chick I met here. She is good in bed, though, so I think I'll keep her around until I leave."

"Huh?" Victoria was dumbfounded. She could not believe what she was hearing.

"Did you get a load of those breasts? I know you're a woman and all, but I think even a woman can appreciate how a man would want to have sex with a woman with tits like that. She's all right, a little slow in the brains department, but those breasts. Lord, have mercy. Can you believe she threw up on me the first night I met her?" Victoria couldn't hold it in any longer. She was straight pissed. How could she have been so stupid? Although she wasn't looking for anything special, she at least thought she was more than just a "piece of ass."

Victoria threw the towel and hit Damon across the head. "She should've thrown up on you." She stormed toward the door.

Damon's laughter stopped her. "Good thing you don't claim to be an actress."

Victoria turned around, planting her hands firmly on her hips. "Excuse me?"

Damon flipped himself over. "You're in Belize, so what's up with the Jamaican accent?"

Victoria pursed her lips and tried not to smile. "So you knew it was me all along?"

Damon draped the towel around his waist and eased off the table. He walked over to Victoria and pulled her to him. "Sorry, but your accent stinks." He leaned in to kiss her.

Victoria playfully tried to pull herself away. "Don't kiss me. I'm just a piece of ass with big boobs."

"Okay, I'm sorry. But you do have big boobs."

Victoria swung at him. He jumped back, causing her to barely miss him. "You know I'm just messing with you, girl." He grabbed her arm and pulled her in toward him. "Let me make it up to you."

"How?"

Damon gently ran his fingers across her chest. "Let me show you."

There went that moisture again. "Let's go back to the room," she muttered. Victoria couldn't believe how absolutely horny she got around him.

"No."

"No?"

"I want you right now."

Victoria looked around the room. "Here?"

Damon backed up to the massage table and patted it. "Right here. Right now."

"You've got to be kidding me," Victoria said incredulously.

Damon extended his hand, and Victoria could tell he wasn't kidding. "But the masseuse will be back any minute."

"Let her watch." Damon dropped the towel from around his waist. Victoria's eyes made their way down to his full erection. Her hormones went into overdrive. She gently stepped back.

"Baby, let's go back to the room."

"Baby, let's get our freak on right here."

Victoria started to protest. She was usually pretty conservative when it came to having sex. But, hell, nothing about this week had been usual for her. Why start now?

"Okay."

Damon grabbed the sash on her wraparound skirt and pulled her into him. She closed her eyes and leaned her head back as he started kissing her neck. He kissed her earlobe, her chest, her breasts. Victoria felt on fire just from his kisses.

Damon didn't stop kissing her as he backed up toward the massage table. He swung her around, lifted her up, and sat her on the table. She lay back and began unfastening the buttons on her tank top. Damon pulled the sash on her skirt, loosening it until it dropped to the side, revealing a hot pink thong—another out-of-the-ordinary thing for Victoria.

He sighed when he looked at her lying on the table. Her firm breasts were beckoning, and he happily obliged, taking as much into his mouth as he could. After several minutes of kissing and caressing her breasts, he moved his tongue down her stomach, over her belly button, and down to her vagina. He gently teased the outside before pushing his tongue deep inside. He worked his tongue for all of two minutes before Victoria exploded all over him.

"Ummmm," he said, savoring her juices. Damon climbed on top of her. "Can I get you to do that again?"

"It would be my pleasure," Victoria moaned.

Victoria arched her back as Damon entered her. It took everything in her power not to have another orgasm too fast. She tried to wait so they could come together. Finally, just when she thought she wouldn't be able to take any more, he started moaning, "Come with me! Come with me!"

Victoria released the hold she was trying to have on her body and relaxed. All her frustrations about Kendrick, all her inhibitions about being with Damon, everything, went out the window as Damon took her to a plateau she hadn't experienced in a very long time.

Damon had just slumped over on Victoria when they heard a noise.

"Ahem."

Both of them turned their attention to the door, where the massage therapist stood with her arms crossed. "Oh, shit!" Damon jumped up and fumbled for his robe. Victoria slid off the table and shrank down on the side of it as she reached for her clothes.

"I . . . I'm sorry," Victoria fumbled.

"Did you have to do that on my table?"

Damon grabbed his robe and pulled it around him. "Look, I apologize. We didn't mean . . . I mean—"

The masseuse held her hand up. "Don't. Don't even try to explain. Could you all just take that back to your room? You getting me all hot and bothered, and my girlfriend is out of town." She broke out in a huge smile. Victoria could have died from embarrassment. She couldn't even look at the woman as she scurried out of the room. Damon reached in his wallet and handed the masseuse a twenty-dollar bill. "Thanks." He quickly followed Victoria out.

Victoria was around the corner, her hands massaging her head. "I just do not believe this."

Damon smiled. "She seemed cool about it. She probably was getting off watching you."

"Me?"

"Yeah, you. Didn't you hear her say her "girlfriend" was out of town?"

"Oh, dang, she did say that." Victoria laughed. "Seriously, how long do you think she was standing there watching?"

"Who cares?" Damon started unbuttoning Victoria's top again.

Victoria slapped his hand away. "Would you stop? You already got me busted by the masseuse."

Damon held his hands up. "Fine, if you want to walk around with your top on backward, so be it."

Victoria looked down. Her tank top was turned inside out, and her wrap skirt was draped askew around her waist. She couldn't help but laugh. Damon joined in.

"Let me go throw on my clothes," Damon said after their laughter died down. "Then I'm taking you shopping."

"Shopping? It's been a long time since a man took me shopping," Victoria kidded.

"Don't get too excited, we're just going to the flea market down the street," Damon snickered. He quickly jumped out of the way as Victoria playfully tried to punch him again. "Damn, you're a violent woman, aren't you?" he said as he darted into the dressing room to get his clothes.

Victoria relaxed in a chair in the lounge as she replayed the past few days in her mind. She absolutely, positively could not remember the last time she'd felt so happy.

After Damon changed, they walked two blocks over to a nearby shopping strip, where Victoria almost lost her mind at all the good deals.

"Oh, my God! Would you look at this necklace?" Victoria shrieked. She held up a green crystal beaded necklace. "It's beautiful." She had already spent over a hundred dollars on jewelry, so she gasped when she looked at the price on the necklace. It was a hundred dollars by itself.

"That's real crystal. I make a good deal for you," the clerk said.

"We'll take it," Damon responded.

Victoria looked shocked. "Damon, you don't have to. I can buy this myself."

"I'm sure you can." He took the necklace and handed it to the clerk. "Can you box this up, please?"

The clerk was grinning like a Cheshire cat. She took the necklace and Damon's money.

"Damon—" Victoria protested.

"How can I take you shopping if you give me a hard time?"

Victoria could just hear Iman. *Girl, if the man wants to buy you a necklace, let him buy you a necklace, and whatever the hell else he wants to buy.*

"Okay, fine," she finally said, a huge smile across her face. "Thank you."

They had just left the shop when they heard someone yell. "You bastard!"

Victoria and Damon turned toward the voice. Both of them exhaled in frustration when they saw who was behind it.

"How the fuck you goin' try and follow me down here to bust me and you gallivanting around with this ho?" Trina was wagging her neck from side to side.

"Ho?" Victoria stepped toward her. She wasn't a fighter, but she definitely was about to kick this bitch's ass.

Damon put his arm in front of Victoria to keep her back. "Trina, you would want to get out of my face. Go find Felix or something," Damon calmly said.

"Why are you so concerned about Felix when you're cheating your damn self?"

Victoria surveyed Damon's wife. How could he end up with someone like that? Trina wore a bright red sleeveless catsuit and a huge straw hat with a scarf tied around it. She looked like a ghetto queen who had hit the lottery.

Damon's lips tensed, and he stepped toward Trina. She backed up as he leaned toward her and stuck his finger in her face. "I *never,* do you hear me, *never* cheated on you! I gave you the world, my heart included, and how do you repay me? By running off to Belize with another man. Don't fucking talk to me about cheating!" He took a deep breath, like he was trying to calm himself down.

"Why are you still here?" Trina whimpered.

"No, the question is why are *you* still here? You'd think after I caught you with your lover, you'd want to get home and try to explain things, but it's obvious you don't give a damn about explaining anything."

"I . . . I was coming home. I'm leaving today, as a matter of fact. I . . . I just stayed because Felix is in the hospital. You broke his jaw and his rib," she stuttered.

"He's lucky I didn't kill him. But you know what? Stay here as long as you like. Move here for all I care. We're through."

Trina tried to hug him. He pushed her away.

"You don't mean that, baby. You're upset. I know you're messing with this tramp just to get back at me. I forgive you." Trina never looked Victoria's way.

Damon stared at her like she'd lost her mind. "You forgive me? If that isn't the funniest thing I've heard today. I'm glad I have your forgiveness. But you damn sure don't have mine." Damon turned toward Victoria. "Come on, baby, let's go."

"Baby?" The ghetto started coming out in Trina. She spun toward Victoria. "Don't your trick ass know he just using you?" she snarled.

Victoria contemplated cussing this woman out. But she decided the best payback would be to walk off with Damon. She draped her arm through Damon's. "Come on. Let's go so you can use me up." They both laughed as they walked off to the sound of Trina's cursing and screaming.

Chapter 8

Victoria spotted her mother standing just outside the baggage claim area. Who couldn't spot her mom standing there in a big-brimmed leopard-skin hat, a strapless tank top, and some skintight jeans? One of these days her mother was going to realize she was fifty-five years old and start dressing her age.

"Oh, baby, welcome back. Are you okay?" Rhonda asked as she ran over to her daughter. Iman was right behind her.

"I'm fine, Mama," Victoria responded, hugging her mother. "Hey, girl." She hugged Iman as well.

Rhonda finally noticed the man lingering behind her daughter, and her eyebrows rose.

"Oh, ummm, Mom, this is, ummm, this is my friend, Damon. Damon, this is my mom, and my best friend, Iman."

Both Rhonda and Iman tried to mask the shock on their faces. "Hi, Damon." Rhonda extended her hand, which Damon gently shook before doing the same with Iman.

"Do you want me to take your bags out?" Damon asked.

Victoria smiled. "No, I'll let the skycap do it."

Damon stood there as if he didn't want to leave. Rhonda and Iman stared intensely at both of them.

Victoria ignored them, figuring she'd deal with them in a few minutes. "Well, ummm, I really enjoyed this past week." She caught herself feeling like a giddy teenager again. She actually felt sad about seeing him leave. "How long before your flight?"

"I only have to wait about thirty minutes."

"Oh, okay." Victoria turned toward her mother and friend, who hadn't taken their eyes off the couple. "Excuse me. You can go on to the car. I'll be out in just a minute."

"But you don't know where the car is," Rhonda protested as her eyes made their way up and down Damon's body.

Victoria gave Iman a pleading look. Iman smiled. "Come on, Miss Rhonda. We'll just pull back around and pick her up. We don't want to keep the skycap waiting." She motioned toward the skycap, who was waiting patiently nearby with Victoria's bags.

Rhonda looked like she wanted to protest some more but decided against it. "Fine then. Good-bye, Damon. It's nice to meet you."

"Nice to meet you, too." Damon waved as Iman dragged Rhonda toward the door. Rhonda broke free and ran back over to the couple. "Excuse me, I just have to ask. What's going on? Are you interested in my daughter?"

"Mother!" Victoria snapped.

Rhonda ignored her. "I see it in your eyes. I'm good at reading people. You like her, don't you?"

"Iman, will you get her?" Victoria's voice was laced with frustration.

Iman smiled apologetically and grabbed Rhonda again.

Rhonda snatched her arm back. "Girl, you better stop grabbing my arm like you done lost your damn mind." She turned back to Damon. "As I was saying, I know you like her. Just be careful. She's already had her heart broken once. That's all I had to say." Rhonda strutted off toward the car.

Victoria lowered her head in embarrassment. "Oh, my God, I cannot believe my mother."

Damon laughed. "She's cute."

"She's crazy. You have to excuse her. I'm an only child, and she's a tad bit protective."

Damon's gaze turned serious. "Well, tell her yes."

"Yes, what?"

"Tell her yes, I like her daughter. A lot. A whole lot."

If she didn't know any better, Victoria could've sworn those were butterflies she felt fluttering around in her stomach.

"Tell me I can see you again," Damon said.

Victoria was grateful he said what she was thinking. *Is it really smart for you to be getting involved with someone right now?* There went that nagging little voice again. Probably not, she wanted to yell. *But I don't care.* Victoria pushed the thoughts out of her head.

"So you want to see me again?"

"You know the answer to that question." Damon's gaze seemed to be penetrating her soul. She felt herself getting moist just standing here talking to him.

"Well, I would love to see you again. When are you free?"

"I have an appointment in New Orleans in two weeks. Trying to set up an extradition hearing on a double-murder suspect. How about I come back through Houston and see you then?"

"Sounds like a plan to me." Victoria smiled, shifting her weight to try and squelch the burning desire that seemed to be seeping through her body.

"My mother used to always say everything happens for a reason," Damon said as he leaned in closer to Victoria. Her heart was beating fast. "I couldn't understand why my soon-to-be ex-wife would do what she did. I couldn't understand why I was in Belize to catch her cheating. But I'm really starting to believe it was because of you. Fate brought us together. I was meant to meet you."

Either this man was the ultimate player or a dream come true. Victoria didn't know what to think, and right now, she didn't care. All she knew was she felt better than she had in a long time. And she had Damon to thank for that.

"I'm glad we met, too. I really—"

Damon pulled Victoria to him and kissed her passionately, a long, intense kiss, one that made Victoria feel like every inch of her body was about to explode.

"You have my numbers," he said after releasing her from his embrace. "Call me. And I look forward to seeing you again."

Damon let his hand linger in hers before dashing off to catch his connecting flight.

Victoria stood in the middle of baggage claim, watching him, until he was out of sight.

"Okay, I want all the details." Iman was standing there with her arms crossed.

Victoria smiled. "I thought you were going to get the car."

"It's outside. Your mother's in it. Now what the hell is going on?"

"Nothing to tell." Victoria gently pushed past Iman and headed outside, the huge grin still plastered across her face.

"Bullshit. Stella done got her groove back. Spill it. I want all the details from A to Z. Tell me the good stuff you don't want your mom to know," Iman said as she followed Victoria out.

"He's a nice guy. I enjoyed him." Victoria opened the car door. "Did you all tip the skycap?"

"Yes—now how did you meet him? From the looks of it, it definitely wasn't on the airplane. So what is going on?" Iman asked as she climbed into the driver's side of her Infiniti.

Victoria hadn't even fastened her seat belt when her mother started in.

"I'd like to know the answer to that question as well," Rhonda said.

"So did you all miss me?" Victoria responded.

"Don't change the subject. Who is this guy, and did you have sex with him?" Rhonda put her hand to her head. "Oh, Lord, tell me you did not have sex with him. He'll think you're a slut."

Victoria rolled her eyes while Iman stifled a laugh.

"Don't tell me, I don't even want to know," Rhonda continued. "You know you're vulnerable. And Lord knows that man was fine. But I raised you better than to be sleeping with perfect strangers."

"Mother, please." Victoria groaned.

"Please, my ass. Now, you went there because that trifling-ass Kendrick broke your heart. You were supposed to have some 'me' time. Not hooking up with some man."

"I did have a nice time. And most of that was thanks to Damon."

Rhonda looked skeptical. "What was he doing there? Nobody goes places like that by themselves."

"It's a long story."

Rhonda unhooked her seat belt, shifted so she could face Victoria in the back seat, then refastened her seat belt. "I got time."

"Mother, look, I don't feel like hearing a lecture. I'm grown. I know what I am and what I'm not getting into, okay?"

"No, it's not okay."

Iman stepped into the conversation. "Kendrick called me." She didn't take her eyes off the road.

Both Victoria and Rhonda's mouths dropped in surprise.

"I hope you hung up on him," Rhonda finally said.

"Actually, I didn't." Iman peered out the window like she was giving her full attention to navigating onto the freeway.

"Hmph. I wouldn't have given the bastard the time of day. I guess he knew better than to call me, because I woulda cussed his ass out." Rhonda crossed her arms and angrily glared at Iman.

Victoria didn't know if she wanted to hear the answer to her next question, but she decided to ask it anyway. "What did he say?"

"That he was sorry."

"Yeah, he said that in the note."

"Don't get me wrong, I'm not cutting him any slack," Iman said. "But I'm glad he didn't marry you. He said he knew he wasn't ready to be faithful for life, and he knew you deserved better than that."

"He didn't know that shit before he asked her to marry him?" Rhonda shouted.

"Mother, would you calm down, please?" Victoria turned her attention back to Iman. "But I would like to know the answer to that question."

"He said he thought he could do it, and the day of the wedding, he just knew he couldn't. He sounded really despondent."

"Iman, I don't believe you're sitting here sounding like you feel sorry for that asshole," Rhonda said.

Iman shook her head. "I don't feel sorry for him. My loyalty is to my best friend, but I just wanted Victoria to know he sounded like he was in a lot of pain."

"Pain! You want to know pain! Try being stood up on the most important day of your life. Try not even being given a rational reason why. That's pain!" Rhonda yelled.

Victoria sighed. "Mother, I swear you act like you were the one left at the altar."

Rhonda leaned back in her seat. "I'm just saying, I don't know why he wants to talk to someone now."

Victoria tried to ignore her mother's ranting. She had learned to deal with her mother's overprotectiveness years ago. Once someone had wronged Victoria, they moved to the top of Rhonda's shit list, and there was nothing anyone could do or say to change that. "Iman, did he say if he ever plans trying to talk to me?"

"I think he's scared right now. He asked me where you were. I wouldn't tell him. I only told him you were fine."

"Good." Victoria sighed. "I don't want him to think someone is somewhere wallowing in despair over him."

"From the glow on your skin, you don't seem to have done any wallowing at all." Rhonda smirked.

Victoria leaned back against the seat and replayed the past week in her mind. Yeah, Damon had been just what she needed to get her mind off Kendrick. And even if they never saw each other again, the memory of this past week would forever be etched in her mind.

Chapter 9

I want to see you."

Victoria couldn't believe she was lying across her bed, feeling like a young girl with her first boyfriend. She twisted the phone cord around her finger. "I want to see you, too." She had talked to Damon almost every day since she returned home. Their conversations ranged across everything from politics to entertainment. He was so easy to talk to. And as much as she tried to fight it, Victoria felt herself getting wrapped up in him. Something she knew was a big mistake, but it's like her heart took over whenever her mind tried to get rational.

She decided to try and steer the conversation in a different direction. "So what happened with your wife? Did you get all that worked out?"

"I filed the paperwork for the divorce the day after I got back. I let her have the house because I didn't want the drama. I'm staying with my brother until I get my own place. But that's not what I want to talk about. I want to talk about seeing you."

Victoria sighed. She knew she needed to get this under control, or she was going to fall head over heels for this man, and that just didn't seem like a good idea. "Damon, I had such a wonderful time with you. I enjoy talking to you. I enjoyed being with you, but we both know we each have some issues to deal with before we move on to another relationship."

"Stop analyzing everything. Just let nature take its course."

"But we've both been hurt, and we're on the rebound." Victoria was wrestling with the emotions running rampant throughout her body.

"So what if we are? I'm feeling you, and you're feeling me. Who cares what brought us together? Let's just enjoy each other now."

"But—"

"But nothing. Are you planning on getting back with Kendrick?"

"Hell, no."

"Well, there's no way in hell I'm going back to Trina, so we're good to go. Now, back to what I was saying. I want to see you."

Victoria relaxed. Damon was right. Yeah, it was too soon. But who cared? She had felt free in Belize. Why not keep that feeling going? He made her happy, and even if it was only for a short time, so be it. "You'll see me next week, right?"

"I want to see you now." Damon's voice had deepened, like he was trying to sound sexy. It was working, because he sounded damn good.

"I would love to see you now, too," Victoria sang.

"Good, my flight gets in at nine-fifty-five. Tonight."

Victoria sat straight up and looked at the clock. It was just after six. "What are you talking about?"

"That's what time my flight gets in. Call me presumptuous, but I was hoping you would say yes. So I booked a flight on Southwest. I leave at nine."

"Oh, so you just knew I was going to agree to this." Victoria jumped up and started pulling the pink sponge rollers out of her hair. She had been lounging around the house today and needed to get not only herself together, but her house as well.

"No, I knew I was *hoping* you'd agree to it. I was hoping you wanted to recapture Belize as much as I did."

Victoria stopped and smiled as she recalled Belize. "I'll see you at nine-fifty-five. Outside Southwest baggage claim."

"I'll be waiting."

"I'll be driving a pearl Lexus GS 300."

"Ohhhh, big baller."

"It's a 1995. I'm not balling too much."

Damon laughed. "I'll see you tonight."

"I can't wait."

Victoria hung the phone up and sat back down on her bed. She was really about to see Damon again. She was just about to go into analyzing mode when she decided against it. Just let nature take its course. That's what she would do. She would enjoy Damon, and whatever happened, happened.

Chapter 10

I can't believe you're going to cheat!" Victoria threw a pillow at Damon. He ducked and smiled mischievously.

"I'm not cheating. That is a word."

Victoria turned her lip up. "Yeah, right. Wowser?"

"Does that mean you're challenging me?" They were lying on the floor in her living room. This was his third visit in three weeks. She'd met him at the airport two weeks ago, and they'd spent the weekend closed up in her house. They had considered going to the movies, but decided they would much rather rent one so they didn't have to share their time together with anyone else. They had ended up renting four movies, only two of which they ever got around to watching because they spent the whole weekend making love.

They had sex so much, Victoria was starting to wonder if that was all their relationship was. Even though they both obviously enjoyed each other's company, she couldn't help but wonder. Then, Damon had come through last Saturday after his meeting in New Orleans. He told her as much as he enjoyed her, that weekend, he only wanted to make love to her mind. He almost blew her mind when he said that shit. And true to his word; they didn't have sex. They just talked and cuddled. That in itself was orgasmic. He had left that weekend promising he would be back the following Friday. And here he was, lying on her living room floor, trying to cheat her in a game of Scrabble.

"I said, are you challenging me?" Damon asked.

Victoria snapped out of her thoughts. "Of course. That's not a word."

"You wanna bet?"

"I told you I'm challenging you."

"No, I mean do you want to bet for real?"

"Bet what?"

"Hmmmm, fifty dollars, a backrub, a roll in the hay, your heart."

Victoria stopped laughing. Damon pushed the game aside and scooted closer to her.

"We both know that getting together is probably the last thing we need, but you, me, us, this—it just feels so right." Damon leaned in and kissed Victoria. She was so into it, she didn't hear her doorbell ringing.

"Umm—" Damon gently pulled himself away. "Are you going to get that?"

"No." Victoria didn't know who it was and didn't really care. It was probably her nosy mother coming to see what was going on.

Damon stood up and helped Victoria up. "You get that. I'll put the game up. I'm tired of playing. With the game, that is."

Victoria pinched his chin. "You are so naughty." She made sure she put a little twist in her walk as she made her way to the door. She was floating so high that she just swung the door open. All the good feeling drained from her body after she had opened it.

"You have a lot of nerve," Victoria snarled.

"Hello to you, too."

"Kendrick, why are you standing outside my door?"

"I wanted to see you."

"Well, now you've seen me." Victoria started closing the door. Kendrick stuck his foot in the door and stopped her.

"Come on, V, I need to see you. We need to talk."

"Need to see me?" Victoria laughed hysterically. "You didn't need to see me on August thirty-first. You remember, our wedding day. You didn't need to see me then, now you come talking about you need to see me now? You want to talk? Go to hell."

"Can you at least hear me out? Just because I couldn't go through with the wedding doesn't mean I don't still love you." Kendrick was dressed nice as usual, with his signature Polo cologne emanating from his body. Usually the sight of him could make her melt. Not anymore; it only made her stomach turn.

"Kendrick, get the fuck out of my face, out of my doorway, and out of my life." Victoria tried to close the door again, but Kendrick still refused to move.

"You can't tell me you don't still love me," he said.

Victoria was just about to start spewing obscenities when she heard Damon call her.

"Babe, is everything okay?"

Kendrick's mouth dropped open as his eyebrows furrowed together. "Who the hell is that?"

Victoria found herself wanting to smile. Damon's timing couldn't have been better. She stood firm blocking Kendrick's view at the door. He was standing on his toes, trying desperately to peer inside. Victoria turned her head and called out. "I'm okay. I'll be there in just a minute."

"What the fuck? I said who is that?"

Victoria relished the anger she saw building in Kendrick's face. He always had been jealous. Even now, after standing her up at the altar, he had the audacity to try and act pissed that she had another man in her home.

"If I were Mrs. Kendrick Kelly, like I thought I would be, then I would gladly answer that question. But since I'm not, I won't. So beat it." Victoria tried to push the door closed again. This time, though, Kendrick's anger must have empowered him, because he pushed the door in, almost knocking Victoria over in the process. He stormed into the living room only to see Damon standing near the bedroom door in nothing but his boxer shorts.

Victoria surveyed his glistening chest as she pulled herself up off the floor. She was too pleased at how good Damon looked. His rippled chest and abs were nice and firm. She knew Kendrick would take note because he was always lamenting about how he wanted a six-pack.

Kendrick glared at Damon, who glared right back. "Victoria, you want to tell me what the hell is going on?"

Victoria walked over to Damon's side. "I'm not telling you anything, except get out of my house before I call the cops."

"I see you ain't too broken up about our wedding," Kendrick said, never taking his eyes off Damon.

"News flash! We didn't have a wedding. Your ass didn't show up. Now you have the nerve to show up here, demanding to know who is in *my* house. You must be on crack!"

Kendrick finally broke his gaze on Damon, who hadn't flinched, and spun on Victoria. "So were you fucking him while we were together?"

"You know what, Kendrick? I don't have time for this. Get out." Victoria pointed toward the door.

Kendrick ignored her and turned to Damon. "Yo, bro, she tell you she got a man?"

"As a matter of fact, she did. She told me she had one, but she figured they had broken up, since the chicken-shit brother didn't show up for her wedding and only sent a note by a homeless man." Damon stepped toward Kendrick, his fists balled at his sides.

"So you just thought you'd step right in and console her?"

"Somebody needed to."

Kendrick looked like he wanted to lunge for Damon's throat right then, but the three inches and about thirty pounds in size difference seemed to have made him think twice.

Kendrick took a deep breath like he was contemplating his next move. "Look, man, my beef ain't with you. I'm goin' need you to leave so I can work things out with my woman."

"I am not your fucking woman!" Victoria screamed. Damon grabbed her arm and pulled her back, trying to calm her down.

"I think she asked you to leave," Damon said forcefully.

"This is between me and her."

"If you don't leave now, it's gonna be between me and you."

Kendrick paused. "So, Victoria, it's like that?"

"Kendrick, get out of my house. Please."

Kendrick looked like he wanted to cry. He swallowed. "Fine. I knew there was a reason I didn't want to marry your skank ass."

Victoria was about to light into him again, but Damon stepped in. "Trust me my man, her ass is anything but skank." Damon reached down and palmed it. "In fact, it's quite luscious."

Kendrick stepped toward Damon, ready to pounce. Damon moved toward him as well.

"Motherfucker, if you even think about jumping, your ass is good as dead."

Kendrick thought about it, then flipped his hand. "Fuck it. You can have her. That's why I left her controlling ass at the altar. You'll see." Kendrick forced a laugh as he headed toward the front door. "Yep, you'll see."

Victoria almost picked up the vase sitting on her sofa table and hurled it at Kendrick's head. Instead she just let him leave and shook her head at his nerve.

"You okay?" Damon asked, rubbing her back.

"I'm cool." She smiled as she pictured Damon playing the tough guy with Kendrick. "Wow, the D.A. getting tough."

"I told you I'm from the streets." Damon ran his hand gently up and down Victoria's arm. "Seriously, though, are you okay?"

Victoria looked away. Her heart was aching. How could she feel anything but utter contempt for Kendrick? "I hate him," she whispered.

Damon draped his arms around her waist. "But unfortunately, you love him, too." He gently kissed her neck. "Trust me, I understand." Damon spun Victoria around to face him. "If only our hearts would follow our heads. You can't choose who you fall in love with. Because common sense is telling me, 'Man, you're not even divorced yet. This woman is going through some things herself. You don't need to jump from one relationship to another.' Common sense is telling me all that."

Victoria slyly smiled. "And what are you telling common sense?"

"To go to hell. I love how I am with you. I love how you make me feel." Damon took Victoria's hand and placed it on his chest. "So between the head and the heart, the heart wins every time." Damon leaned in and kissed Victoria passionately. "Let me make you forget Kendrick," he whispered as he kissed her breasts.

"Kendrick who?" Victoria moaned as she closed her eyes and savored his touch.

Chapter 11

Victoria glanced out the peephole. It had been a couple of months and she'd only seen her once, but no doubt about it, that was Trina standing on her front porch. What was she doing here? Damon had only been gone a few minutes. He'd gone to visit one of his fraternity brothers who lived nearby. Trina must've been watching the house and came as soon as she saw him leave.

"May I help you?" Victoria asked after she opened the door.

"I came to talk to you. Woman to woman." Trina stood there with her arms crossed and attitude written across her face.

"You know, I don't think that's a good idea. I don't think you have anything to talk to me about." Victoria moved to close the door.

"Oh, I think I do." Victoria hesitated before looking outside. Her neighbor across the street, old nosey Mrs. LaReau was peering at her. Victoria decided she didn't need a scene in her front yard so she took a deep breath, then stepped to the side allowing Trina to enter.

"You have five minutes," Victoria said. She didn't know why she was giving this woman the time of day, but Trina seemed determined, so she might as well get it over with.

Trina glared at her. "I only need four." She adjusted her Kate Spade bag on her shoulder. "Look, I don't know what you call yourself doing with my husband—"

Victoria cut her off. "He's about to be your ex-husband."

"But he's not yet." Trina's stare was piercing. "As I was saying, I don't know what you call yourself doing with *my* husband, but you need to leave him alone."

Hit the bitch in the eye. Victoria shook off the evil thoughts creeping into her head. "I think that should be left up to Damon. I'm not making him do anything he doesn't want to do."

"Damon is acting out right now. He's like a little boy scorned, and for your own sake, you need to back off."

Victoria snickered. "Oh, so it's my feelings you're concerned about?"

"I'm just trying to tell you."

Victoria sighed. She didn't know why she was even indulging this woman. "How did you find out where I live?"

"I am very resourceful. I felt obliged to tell you, Damon and I have a bond that you will never be able to break."

"Well, you weren't too concerned about that bond when you were gallivanting around with Felix Cambridge." Victoria crossed her arms and glared back. *If this heifer thinks she can come here and intimidate me, she is out of her mind.*

"My relationship with Felix was a mistake. I felt neglected, and I made a mistake. I've told Damon that. He's a little bitter right now, but he'll come around. You, however, all up in his face are clouding his judgment."

Count to ten. She wants you to act a fool so she can play the helpless wife. "I'm not in his face. I live three hundred miles away. Damon is in my face because he wants to be."

"Well, he talks to you daily."

"How do you know how often he talks to me? Are you spying on him?"

"I will do whatever I have to do to save my marriage."

"So now you're interested in your marriage?"

"I will save my marriage," Trina stressed. Her voice softened, like she was genuinely concerned about Victoria. "You have to realize that this relationship is headed nowhere. Damon is impulsive and stubborn. When common sense prevails, he'll want to honor his vows of for better or for worse. But you, you should be able to see that you don't mean anything to him. Think about it. Have you met his family? Has he even talked to you about meeting his family? Have you even been to Dallas to see him, or does he just come here, fuck you, and go back home?"

Victoria shook her head. This was getting ridiculous, and she'd had enough. "Your five minutes are up." Victoria headed toward her front door. Trina might be ghetto, but she was not. So she refused to let this woman reduce her to the point of acting a fool, and that's just what would happen if she spent one more minute with this bitch. And she damn sure wasn't about to get to fighting over a man.

Trina defiantly plopped down on the couch. She crossed her long, sultry legs and tossed back her hair. "I just felt if I came and talked to you woman to woman, we could get this straight. But it's obvious you're not getting it, so let me break it down. You're something to do. A rebound. Payback. I hope you realize, messing with my husband, you'll only end up hurt."

Victoria took a deep breath. No, she wouldn't fight this woman over a man, but she would fight her for her blatant disrespect. *Just keep your cool.* "Thank you for your analysis, but I'm a grown woman; I can take care of myself. I think the only reason you have any interest in salvaging your marriage is because Damon doesn't want you anymore."

"Oh, that is so funny. Doesn't want me?" She laughed before suddenly stopping and turning serious. "Sweetheart, he will always want me. I'm in his blood. Have been since he hit puberty. He's just a little hurt right now. But when he gets over that, he'll come begging me to come back like he always does." Trina looked at her fingernails, then extended her hand like she was examining it. Victoria figured she was trying to make sure Victoria noticed the huge wedding ring on her finger. "I'll admit it," Trina continued, brushing off imaginary lint on her sleeve, "I was a bad girl. But I know that in time, Damon will get over it. He loves me that much. You can never compete with me."

"Get out of my house."

"I'll leave, but consider yourself warned." Trina grabbed her purse, stood up, and strutted to the door without so much as a glance Victoria's way. Victoria slammed the door as hard as she could.

"Uggghhhh! I can't believe that bitch!" Victoria stood in the middle of the living room, seething. Slowly, she started to think about Trina's words. The woman was right. He was still married, and no doubt about it, he got involved with her because he was hurting over Trina. Maybe she was setting herself up. Maybe she had fooled herself into thinking their relationship was more than it really was. She was a rebound, plain and simple. How could she compete with the woman who had been in Damon's life since he was a little boy?

Victoria's anger was now mixed with doubt. She walked over to her cordless phone, picked it up, and punched in Damon's cell phone number. She got his answering service and left a message asking him to call her back.

When the phone rang a few minutes later, Victoria snatched it up on the first ring.

"Damon?"

"Uh, no. It's Iman."

"Hey, girl." Victoria sank into her love seat.

"Well, damn. Don't sound so thrilled to hear from me."

"I'm sorry. It's not that. I'm just waiting on Damon to call me back."

"What's wrong?"

"His wife."

"His what? You didn't tell me he was married. You're messing with a married man?"

"It's complicated. The only reason I gave Damon the time of day was because I knew they were divorcing."

Victoria heard Iman clicking her lips with skepticism. "That's what they all say."

Victoria had debated telling Iman how she and Damon actually met. But at this point, she needed someone to talk to. "Let's just say the whole reason Damon was in Belize in the first place was to catch his wife with her lover."

"Oooooh."

"Yeah, but you wouldn't know she was the one caught cheating. All she wanted to know was who I was. Forget the man she had come there with. Damon said he had her served with divorce papers as soon as he got back. Despite what she did, she seems to think there's still hope."

"Is there?" Iman's words made Victoria think. She had been proceeding full speed ahead with Damon without any real thought to his situation. How do you just throw away four years of marriage to someone you really love?

"I thought it was over, but now I don't know." Victoria sighed.

"What does that mean?"

"Trina showed up at my door today, demanding I leave Damon alone."

"I hope you cut that bitch."

Victoria laughed. As sensitive as Iman was, she could be extremely volatile—she probably *would've* cut Trina. "I came close," Victoria responded. Just then her other line clicked. "Hold on, that may be Damon."

"Hello," Victoria said once she clicked over.

"Hey, baby, what's up? I got your page." It was Damon. "I'm still here chilling with Bruce."

"Hold on." Victoria clicked back over, told Iman she'd call her back, then clicked back to Damon. "I had a visitor right after you left."

"Don't tell me Kendrick had the nerve to come back?'

"No, not my ex, yours."

"My Trina?"

Victoria didn't like the sound of that. "Yeah, *your* Trina."

Damon must've detected the sarcasm in her voice. "I didn't mean it like that. I'm just dumbfounded. What the hell is she doing here? Why would she come to your house?"

"Why else? To warn me to stay away from you."

"How does she know where you live?" Damon sounded like a frantic, cheating husband whose wife had discovered his mistress. Victoria got a sinking feeling in her stomach.

"She made it clear that I'm keeping you two from reconciling."

Damon was silent for a minute, and the sick feeling in Victoria's stomach deepened. "I'm sorry, Victoria. Trina can get quite ignorant. I hope she didn't show her ass."

"She did. But it wasn't anything I couldn't handle." Victoria felt herself ready to cry. How could she be so stupid? She knew better than to get involved with a married man. Until he was actually divorced, no man was really free. "Damon, what's going on? Am I standing in the way of you trying to work things out with Trina?"

"What are you talking about?"

Victoria fiddled with the cord on the phone. Her heart had barely healed from Kendrick, and now she'd allowed it to be broken again. She'd only known Damon a short time. Why in the world would she let herself get so wrapped up in him? Do not cry. Do not cry? The old Victoria would've done whatever possible to keep herself strong, not let a man see her cry. But after Kendrick, this had just become too much to bear. "Damon," Victoria sniffled as the tears began trickling down her cheeks, "I don't blame you. It's my fault. I should've known better than to get involved with you. You're still married."

Damon sighed. "This is crazy. I'm still married only because there's a waiting period."

"But if I wasn't around—" Victoria had to stop talking to keep her voice from cracking.

"Victoria, are you crying?"

Victoria didn't respond.

"I'm on my way back over there." Victoria was about to protest, but Damon had already hung up the phone.

Victoria placed the phone back on the cradle and leaned back against the sofa. She knew they were together on the rebound, but she thought they'd progressed so much further than that. Victoria rubbed her temple. Her head was throbbing. This was supposed to be a nice, relaxing weekend; now one visit from Trina, and everything had changed.

Victoria hadn't even realized she had dozed off when she heard the doorbell ring. She jumped up, raced to the door, and swung it open.

Damon came storming in. Victoria was poised, ready to break things off right then and there.

"Look," Damon said, "I know we came together through less-than-desirable circumstances. But I need you to understand." He grabbed Victoria and pulled her to him. "I don't want Trina. I want you. Only you."

Victoria didn't know what to say. He was so convincing, but so was Trina.

"But if I weren't around—"

"If you weren't around, I'd simply be by myself. Trina lost my heart in Belize. You found it there." Victoria looked off as she felt herself tearing up again.

"But I haven't even been to visit you in Dallas."

"Is that what this is about? You want to come see me in Dallas? You have my home number, my cell number, my pager number, and my work number. I talk to you every night into the wee hours. So I can't possibly be still living with Trina, if that's what you think, now can I? I've been coming here because you know I'm staying with my brother for now, and I thought we'd have privacy. But if coming to Dallas will make you feel secure with what we have, by all means come on. We can get a hotel. I don't care, I just want to be with you."

Victoria thought about that. He had a point. There was never a time she couldn't get in touch with him. And their conversations went to three and four in the morning. But she'd seen her share of men who knew how to play the game. Or maybe he was devoting his time to her now—but all that could change once he got over being mad at Trina.

"I think you know me well enough by now to know, I'm honest. I don't play games. If I thought there was even a glimmer of hope for Trina and me, I would not be here with you. Look at me." Damon pulled Victoria's chin toward him. "I want you. I love only you."

Victoria gazed into Damon's eyes. If she had any doubt about their relationship, it was gone that very moment. She wanted to trust again. She wanted to love again. And Damon was just the man for the job. She knew it wouldn't be easy, but it was worth a try. With Kendrick, all the signs were there that he wasn't ready to fully commit to her. But Victoria realized she had overlooked them because *she* was ready. Before Kendrick, she had never had her heart broken. After Kendrick, she had sworn no one would get that close again. Maybe she'd grown. Maybe she'd realized true love was worth some risks. Whatever the case, Victoria knew Damon was her destiny. This time, as the tears came forward, Victoria didn't even consider holding them back. She let them flow freely as she hugged Damon tightly and muttered, "I love you back."

Chapter 12

Victoria stood out on the balcony overlooking the ocean. It was the same view she had before. Only this time, she wouldn't be drowning her sorrows in liquor.

"Ummm, breathtaking view, isn't it?" Damon stepped up behind her and wrapped his arms around her. He buried his nose in her hair.

Victoria closed her eyes and leaned back into his embrace. "It's beautiful." They stood in silence for a minute, before Victoria finally spoke. "I still don't understand why you wanted to come back here."

Damon pulled her hand and sat her down in the patio chair. He sat down next to her, never releasing her grip. "Because Belize is where my life changed forever. I came here one year ago with only one hope, that I was mistaken about Trina. When I found out I wasn't, I felt like my life was over. You brought me out of my despair. And honestly, we were both so messed up emotionally; I never thought we'd make it. But we did. We not only survived, we flourished. Ours may have started as a rebound romance, but it definitely ended as the real thing."

Victoria felt her eyes watering. He had said everything she felt. When she was little, her grandmother always used to say, "Baby, we may not understand why God does some of the things He does, the way that He does them. But give it time, and the picture will become clear."

Now, her picture was crystal-clear. Because of Damon, not only had she gotten over what Kendrick did to her, she had found the true love that she always felt like she deserved. If she had married Kendrick, she would never have known the love she felt right now.

"We got over your drama—" Damon said.

"And your drama," Victoria interjected. They both laughed.

"My divorce is final, and I think Trina has finally realized that it's over."

"Not for lack of trying." Victoria recalled the numerous phone calls, hang-ups, and threats she had received for about a month after Trina's visit. Victoria had ended up changing her phone number, and Trina had even gotten a friend at the phone company to get her that number. She stalked Damon twenty-four/seven, pleading for another chance. Damon had her served with a restraining order, and that seemed to be the wake-up call she needed. She cursed him out, then called Victoria and cursed her out. The last message she'd ever gotten from Trina said, "Hey, home-wrecking bitch. You can have Damon's sorry ass. I'm moving on." They'd had no more problems since.

They did have a problem or two with Kendrick, who couldn't handle the thought of Victoria with another man. He'd had his family and friends beg her for another chance, and he'd shown up at her house a couple of times. But after getting nowhere, his communication had suddenly stopped. Victoria had heard he hooked up with a hairdresser on the North Side, and that was just fine.

Damon caressed Victoria's face. "I just wanted us to end up where we started."

"So are we ending?" Victoria joked.

"Quite the contrary." Damon lifted Victoria up and turned around and straddled the chair in front of her. He took her hand. "This is not a proposal, yet. But it is a promise. That I will love you unconditionally. I can't lie and tell you I'm ready for marriage again—yet—but I am ready for love. The rest, the rest will come with time."

"I couldn't have said it better myself." Victoria leaned in and kissed Damon intensely while the Belize sunset cast a warm glow all around them. If she had ever had any doubt that blissful happiness really existed, it was gone. What she felt right now, what she'd felt the last year with Damon, that was the happiness she deserved. And the happiness she finally felt like she had gotten.